6/22

SOUTHERN
CROSS

AN ERIN SOLOMON MYSTERY

SOUTHERN CROSS

AN ERIN SOLOMON MYSTERY

JEN BLOOD

Adian Press
Maine

Adian Press
934 River Rd #1
Cushing, Maine 04563
www.adianpress.com

Publisher: Adian Press
Cover Design: damonza.com
Author's Photograph: Amy Wilton Photography

For Ruth and Mariah
Who taught me to celebrate my independent spirit,
embrace my creative side, and, above all, never forget
the healing power of a good belly laugh. Every girl
should be blessed with the gift of such sassy, classy,
wonderfully weird aunts.

PART I
JUSTICE FIRST

PROLOGUE

"REPENT," A VOICE WHISPERED IN THE DARKNESS. Wyatt Durham was on his hands and knees. Pebbles from the dusty ground dug into his palms. He lowered his head like a bull just hit with a cattle prod, trying to get his wits back. Someone stood beside him, a heavy hand between his shoulder blades to keep him down. Wyatt tried to speak, but his voice didn't work.

Nothing worked.

"Repent," the voice said again, lower this time.

There was dried blood under Wyatt's fingernails. The smell of something sweet and cloying in the air, like a jar of wet pennies: more blood.

"The goat," he whispered. He'd come for the goat. Mae was home waiting for him. The kids were gone for the night. *Put the poor thing down and come on home, darlin'*, she'd said to him before he left.

The man beside him knelt, his mouth close to Wyatt's ear. "One more chance, Doc. The end's already nigh. Make your peace."

Wyatt closed his eyes, his body getting heavier. His elbows buckled. A hand came at him from behind, pushing him gently to the ground, tender as Mae on those sweet nights when they lay together. It was all familiar—nearly forgotten but still there, somewhere at the back of his mind, from days gone by and a life best left behind.

Repent.

1
DIGGS

EVERY SUMMER FROM TWELVE ON UP, I abandoned the ocean breezes and cool nights of coastal Maine for the wet swelter of western Kentucky, where the Durham family provided refuge from my stormy New England home. When I was fifteen, Wyatt Durham and I were playing baseball one overcooked July day when I said something he saw as over the line about his little sister. He didn't waste his breath explaining his views on the subject, though. Instead, he belted me in the stomach with a Louisville Slugger. It brought me to my knees, tears in my eyes, and for two days afterward every lungful of air burned going down.

That's the closest I can come to an analogy for what I felt when Wyatt's wife Mae called me twenty-five years later, and told me my oldest friend was dead.

I landed in Louisville at eight a.m. on a Tuesday in March, after sixteen hours traveling by boat, bike, bus, and plane to get there. Mae had tracked me down in the middle of a two-month trek in Costa Rica, where I was doing an in-depth piece on the surf scene at Guiones. I still wasn't sure how she'd found me since I'd left no forwarding address and told no one where I was headed, but I had a feeling Erin Solomon had something to do with it.

I've known Solomon since I mentored her at a Maine rag called the *Downeast Daily Tribune* when she was fifteen. Despite the fact that I was in my mid-twenties at the time, we struck up a close and possibly ill-advised friendship. In the seventeen years since, that friendship has morphed into something far more difficult to define. If anyone could find me, it was Solomon.

Mae would neither confirm nor deny; she just asked me to come to Kentucky.

I came.

There was no one waiting for me when I landed—I'd already told Mae I'd rent a car, so she didn't have something else to worry about while she prepared to bury the man she'd loved since grade school. Still in board shorts and sandals, I watched the natives while I waited for baggage claim to regurgitate my duffel.

A gray-haired man in Dockers and a sweater vest embraced a pretty, fair-skinned woman a head shorter and maybe a decade younger than him. They kissed, his hand at the soft slope of her neck as he pulled her closer. It wasn't like some teenage tonsil-hockey kiss, with too much tongue and that self-conscious need the very young have to prove their virility as publicly as possible. It was more intimate than that; more electrified. The man's arm settled naturally around her shoulders when they parted. Their heads were tipped close as they walked away, hip to hip, and I could hear her laughter and see the light in his eyes as they left the airport.

I retrieved my duffel. Despite three marriages, one of them to the very same little sister I'd taken a baseball bat to the gut for as a teenager, there was only one person I could imagine greeting me in the airport like that.

Not for the first time—or even the hundredth—I thought of Solomon. And not for the first time, or the hundredth, I pushed that thought out of my head.

As I made for the door, I felt the now-familiar weight of someone's eyes on my back. I turned and scanned the crowd. A slow crawl of fear ran up my spine when a thin man with a receding hairline and angular features caught my eye and then ducked into the crowd before I could get a clear picture of him. He wore a black trench coat and carried an expensive leather briefcase. For a full thirty seconds of blind panic, I watched his progress in the crowd. The latest incoming flight was broadcast over the PA system. The man paused, listening. He turned once more, giving me an unobstructed view of his face.

I didn't recognize him.

The slow crawl of fear faded, but it hardly disappeared.

Six months before, a nameless ghoul had threatened me at gunpoint while Solomon sat tied twenty feet away, a belt looped around her throat, a monster touching her in ways I was helpless to stop. That moment had changed something about my world, and the way I viewed it. More troubling, it had changed something fundamental about the way I viewed myself. Since then, I'd spent a lot of time looking over my shoulder.

True, the traveler with the trench coat and the briefcase wasn't that nameless ghoul. That didn't change what I knew to be true, though: He was out there somewhere. And he was watching us.

From baggage claim, I went straight to the rental place to pick up the car I'd reserved, still trying to re-acclimate to civilization. A spit-shined, fresh-faced kid of no more than twenty greeted me at the counter. His hair was cut short.

His tie was perfectly centered. I hadn't bathed in two days, hadn't shaved for considerably longer, and it turned out that my forty-year-old bones didn't recover from wipeouts nearly as well as they had a decade ago.

My shiny young friend didn't look fazed, though.

"I reserved a rental," I said. "The name's Daniel Diggins." I pulled out my wallet to retrieve the confirmation code I'd scrawled on a napkin.

The kid blinked at me, his smile faltering. "Uh—I'm sorry, sir…"

I frowned and pushed the napkin toward him. "They've already charged my card—I've got the confirmation number right there. I don't care what you give me. It doesn't have to be what I reserved."

"Well, no, sir—we have cars. But you already picked up yours."

I stared at him, eyebrows raised. "Then why am I here?"

"Not you," he amended. "But your girlf—" He stopped, sensing that I didn't know what the hell he was talking about. "She said you were meeting at the airport," he insisted. "Red hair? Little thing… real pretty?" He sighed in relief, pointing toward the door. "There."

I turned around. Erin Solomon herself pushed the door open and crossed the threshold. Her hair was cropped shorter than I'd seen it since she was in high school, her fair skin a shade paler than I remembered thanks to the long Maine winter. She wore boot-cut jeans and a striped jersey, oversized sunglasses pushed back on her head. All the air left the room.

"Hey, ace," she said after a moment. "Need a lift?"

•

"No," I said the moment we were outside.

"What do you mean, 'no'?" she asked. "I just thought you could use some moral support."

"Nope. I'm fine, thanks." The rental—my rental, a white Ford Focus—was idling in front of the rental office. Solomon's second-in-command, Einstein, had his fuzzy white head out the window, his whole body wagging.

"Look, I know we haven't talked in a while—"

"Six months, actually," I said. "We haven't talked in six months, except for one panicked phone call in the middle of the night in September, when you'd had a bad dream and needed to hear my voice. You can't just show up like this—"

"I wasn't trying to piss you off," she said, more quietly than I'd expected. "You're right: I have no right to be here. I was trying to help. If I'd just lost someone important, you'd be there. You always have been. I was just trying to do the same."

I didn't say anything. She shrugged, looking awkward and miserable. "I'll go if you really don't want me here."

I should have told her to do exactly that—as much for her sake as mine. It wasn't like she didn't deserve it. But the fact was, the idea of returning to my old Kentucky home and all the Kentucky folk I'd left behind—including an ex-wife who, last time I checked, hated my guts—in order to bury my childhood friend, was only slightly more appealing than being run down by a freight train. Twice.

And it really was good to see her.

Solomon chewed her lip. I was caught suddenly by the memory of luminescent green eyes and the feel of her body pressed to mine over the course of forty-eight hours last summer, when we were running for our lives and sleeping in one another's arms and the only thing that mattered was survival. And her.

"You're a pain in the ass," I said.

"I know that. Do you want me to leave?"

I scratched my neck, digging in hard enough to feel it. Breathed deep. And took a step toward her. "You're here. I guess you might as well stay."

"Okay," she said. Something sad and quiet that hadn't been there before last summer flickered in her eyes. "I guess I might as well."

It was cool and clear when we left the airport. The grass was green. The sky was blue. According to a local with whom I'd flown, it had been a mild winter and now, in March, spring had taken hold of Kentucky and showed no signs of letting go. I took the wheel of the rental without the aid of GPS or Rand-McNally and kept my foot heavy on the accelerator, rediscovering the Bluegrass State like the half-forgotten lyric of a once-favorite song.

Once we hit I-64, I glanced at Solomon when she wasn't paying attention, searching for signs that she'd fallen apart without me. There were none. There was, however, a thin scar running along the side of her right wrist, another remnant from our forty-eight hours of hell in August. She caught me looking and covered the scar with her left hand uncomfortably.

"How's the wrist?" I asked.

"Better," she said. "More or less. I just had another surgery about a month ago."

"And that makes…?"

"Three."

Three surgeries. Six months since we'd seen each other last. Another memory flashed through my mind: Solomon ripping off the splint I'd made and pulling herself out of our cave prison to safety; shouting down to me as I bled on the ground below. *I'm not leaving you.*

I sighed. It sounded wearier than it should have,

considering I'd just gotten back from two months of hanging out on the beach. We fell back into silence.

"So, what did Mae tell you?" she finally asked.

I frowned. I still hadn't wrapped my head around the information I'd gotten so far on that count. "It's a little bizarre," I said.

"There's an understatement. Did she give you details?"

"Wyatt disappeared on March second—a Saturday night," I said, reciting the scant facts I'd been given. "His truck was still at the site of his last appointment, but there was no sign of him. He was found on the side of the highway late Wednesday night with an injection mark in his neck and no other sign of physical trauma, wearing a suit Mae had never seen before. And no shoes."

"That's what I got, too," she said. "It's weird. And someone like Wyatt… I mean, who didn't like the guy? He was a country vet. James Herriot in a cowboy hat. Who murders James Herriot?"

"Apparently, someone."

We fell silent again. I realized after a few minutes that I wasn't the only one sneaking sideways glances. I caught her eventually and quirked an eyebrow.

"What?" I asked.

"You look good."

"The last time you saw me, we'd just spent two days running for our lives with a madman on our heels. It's not hard to look good when that's your yardstick." I paused. "You sound surprised."

"No… not exactly." I waited patiently, eyes on the road, while she sorted through what she wanted to say. "Actually, I wasn't sure what I'd find when your plane landed," she conceded.

Between the ages of ten and eighteen, Solomon spent most of her free time cleaning up after her mother—who was a stellar surgeon by day, and the town drunk by night. Then she followed that up with a nice little stint looking after me in her twenties, before I got clean four years ago. Old habits die hard.

"Ah," I said. "So there's the real reason you showed up today: still playing designated driver after all these years."

"You quit your day job, dumped your girlfriend, and took off for Costa Rica with a bunch of extras from *The Endless Summer*. Is it really so crazy for me to think you'd be doing lines off some beach bunny's backside?"

I laughed out loud. "Jesus, Solomon. It was a surf trip, not spring break. I was with a bunch of forty-year-old guys—hell, half of them had their wives and kids with them. Someday, I'm taking you on one of these trips. Your perception of the lifestyle is just bizarre."

She didn't say anything to that. Translation: Solomon wasn't free to think about surf trips with me anymore.

"How's Juarez?" I asked, taking the silence as sufficient segue. Juarez was Jack Juarez, God's gift to the FBI. Tall and lean and vaguely Cuban. And nice, actually. The bastard.

"He's good," she said.

"He knows you're here with me?"

"It was his idea." Of course it was. "I mean—not totally his idea," she amended. "I mentioned it. He said I should come without him."

I looked out the window at the landscape passing by. "He's a bigger man than I am," I said. She turned to face me, her green eyes darkening with her mood. "Not that I'd be dumb enough to try and stop you. But if we were together, there's no way in hell I'd suggest you head off on a road trip with some other guy."

"He trusts me."

I turned to look at her. Her jaw was hard, her anger plain. I smiled. "How evolved of him."

●

About an hour and a half from our destination, Solomon pointed out a road sign for Smithfield U. that featured two penguins in sunglasses and baseball hats.

"Why are penguins the mascot for a Kentucky college?" she asked.

"It's Kentucky. Logic doesn't always play a big role in things. It's part of the charm."

"Good to know."

We'd just passed the campus when Solomon caught me looking in the rearview mirror. She turned around in her seat.

"Did you see someone back there?" The edge of panic in her voice was new. I knew it wasn't unwarranted given our recent experiences, but that didn't mean I had to like it.

"No," I lied. A dark blue sedan had been keeping pace with us since we'd left the airport. I wasn't really concerned until I realized the car was still behind us after we hit I-69 and the Purchase Parkway. It could still be coincidence, I reasoned. Plenty of people could be making the trek from Louisville to the westernmost corner of the state on an overcast Tuesday in March.

"I'm sure it's nothing," I said.

"Yeah, right," she said. "Me, too. I mean—seriously. What are the chances we get knocked off the road and hunted down by a crazed serial killer twice in one year?"

"Not great," I said.

"Exactly," she agreed. She didn't sound convinced.

Outside, new leaves were just budding on a wall of trees that lined the road on either side: oaks and ash, maple and poplar and sycamore. I turned on the radio and tuned it to 89.9, smiling at the voice that scraped through our speakers.

"Weather today in Justice looks gray with a healthy side of rain, so stay on in and keep those toes by the fire. Crazy Jake Dooley's here till nightfall—we got records to spin and memories to make. Now y'all turn up the noise and stay close."

Crazy Jake faded out and Lightnin' Hopkins faded in. Jake sounded like scorched gravel, but he had a mind for music and an endless supply of classic records that kept me entertained through three long years married to Ashley Durham.

"What was that?" Solomon asked.

"That," I said, "was Crazy Jake Dooley. He broadcasts out of Justice, but he's kind of a cult figure in Kentucky. If you're going to Justice, I want to make sure you get the full experience. Jake's part of the immersion."

I turned up the music and refrained from checking the rearview mirror again. Solomon settled in, her feet tapping, for the rest of the journey.

It was just past one in the afternoon when we got where we were going. The sun had vanished behind a blanket of thick, menacing gray clouds, and the temperature had dropped a good fifteen degrees since Louisville. I tried not to view that as a sign of impending doom, but considering Solomon and my luck in the past, it was hard to write it off completely.

Justice is a one-streetlight town on the Mississippi that was booming up until the 1970s, when levees rerouted the river. Since then, the population has held steady at about fifteen hundred, with the bulk of those people working in neighboring towns. Visitors are greeted by a sign that reads simply JUSTICE FIRST as they cross the town line. Just beyond that was a sign that hadn't been there when I'd left five years before, however.

" 'Hell is real.' " Solomon read the flaming orange letters aloud. "Or at least it is according to Reverend Jesup T. Barnel. Well, there you go. One theological debate ended."

Ten feet later, a second sign appeared. " 'Repent all ye sinners. The fire awaits,' " Solomon read. Her voice was light enough, but she was doing the knee-bouncing thing that usually means she's either nervous or she has to pee. When it's the former, the knee-bouncing is accompanied by an endless, one-sided, rambling dialogue, which is how I knew this was anxiety and not just an overactive bladder.

After another ten feet, the largest sign of all appeared— ten feet high, maybe twelve across. On it was a picture of an overweight, elderly white man with a white beard and a cowboy hat.

"There's a tent meeting tomorrow night," Solomon said. "In which Reverend Barnel will purportedly 'Set the clock ticking: forty-eight hours 'til the End is Come.' " She looked at me speculatively. "Look at that—we made it just in time for Armageddon."

"Of course we did," I said. "This is you and me we're talking about."

"Good point." She shook her head as we approached the center of town. "So, this is Justice. I can't believe you lived here for three years. It's not really how I imagined it."

"What were you thinking?"

She had to think about that for a minute. "Kind of a cross between Dodge and that town in *Footloose*."

"Actually, you're not that far off."

The town of Justice consists of a main stretch of boarded-up storefronts and a few diehards still managing to hang on, despite Walmart's chokehold on the local economy: the

Justice Qwik E Mart, True Value Hardware, and Martin Feed & Grain. Across the way, you'll find the historic Justice City Hall, built in 1862, flanked on one side by the local police station, and on the other by WKRO Radio and the old Twin Cinemas movie theater.

It took five minutes to leave Justice proper behind. From there, I took River Road past churches and shacks, For Sale signs posted at every third house or so, and then turned onto a pitted dirt road shrouded by old oak trees. We trekked through a mile of mud and deep ruts until Wyatt's house came into view. The sky darkened further as I pulled in behind a twin-cab 4x4 parked in the driveway.

Dogs barked. Einstein barked back at them. Roosters crowed. Three goats and a donkey eyed us curiously from behind wire fencing off to our right. I stopped the car, but made no move to get out.

"You all right?" Solomon asked.

It was an excellent question. I only wished I had a good answer. "Not at all. But what are you gonna do, right?"

She took my hand in hers—carefully, like she was taking hold of a live wire. Her hand was cool and dry, soft and strong. Her eyes met mine, a frown tipping the corners of her mouth. "Whatever you need, I'm here. It's what we do, right?"

We stayed that way for a minute or more before she let go. It had gotten too warm in the car. Too close. I thought again of her body against mine. The way her lips had tasted, the words she'd whispered. *Don't let go, okay? Not until you have to.*

"We should go in," she said.

We did.

2
DANNY

THE HOUSE WAS BUSTING at the seams with every relative they'd ever had, and then some. Danny had never been much for family anyway, and now to have everyone here carrying on about how much they loved his daddy and what a good man Wyatt Durham had been and how he was probably setting at Jesus's right hand right then… It just got to be too much, is all.

He went back out, careful to wait till Rick—his twin brother, the good son—and Ida, the baby of the family, were out of the way. He cruised past the grove of birches and the horse barn and the creek, ignoring the howl of the dogs and the threat of rain. *Just keep moving*, he kept saying to himself. He was seventeen now. Too old to cry; too young to go off and get blisterin' drunk like his college buddies. At least, not right now, with his family around. Maybe later.

Instead, he kept going till he reached the old treehouse his daddy built him and Rick when they was just kids. He climbed the rickety wooden rungs nailed into the trunk of a solid old oak, pushed open the trapdoor, and went on in.

You hadn't oughta leave your mama alone on a day like

today, he imagined his daddy saying. Danny pulled a joint from his back pocket and fetched a lighter from a cubby hole built into the treehouse. He sat back, knees just about to his chin to make room in the cramped space, and leaned his back up against the rough bark. *You got a lot of nerve, boy, smokin' dope today.*

"Quiet, old man," Danny growled. He closed his eyes and leaned his head back. His throat hurt, a lump in there he hadn't been able to get rid of since his mama broke the news.

A branch snapped somewhere below. Danny opened his eyes. The weed was already taking hold, taking the edge off just enough.

"That you, Ida?" he hollered down. "I thought you was off somewhere."

"Don't get your panties in a bunch," a girl's voice called up to him. He smiled, relief washing over him like warm summer rain. "It's just me."

Half a minute later, Casey Clinton poked her head up through the hatch. Casey played bass in Danny's band. She was a couple years younger than him, about a head shorter, and she was about the only person he could talk to these days about…well, anything, really. Music, family, life, school… He could say anything to Casey. It didn't hurt that she was the prettiest girl in the sophomore class—not that there was anything going on between them, of course.

She pulled herself up through the hatch and settled across from him. He passed her the joint.

"They lookin' for me over at the house?" he asked.

"Nah. I had to scoot, though, in case your mama saw me."

Danny's mother hated Casey—said she come from trash and was all about devil music. They'd fought about it too much over the years. Now, Casey just kept her head down whenever his mama was around.

"What about Rick?" he asked.

"He saw me, but he won't say anything."

"You sure about that? If he thinks it'll earn him more points with Mama…"

Casey took a good long drag and held the smoke in before she passed the joint back to him, shaking her head. "You oughta go easy on him—he ain't so bad as you make him out to be. What's he ever done to you?"

"Nothin'," he said. "The kid just bothers me is all."

It came out sulky. It felt like most of his life he'd been standing off on the sidelines doing his own thing while his brother couldn't take a leak without their mama wanting to throw a parade. Rick was the highest-ranked high school tennis player in the state. He got the lead in all the school plays and only dated girls their folks liked and already knew where he was headed to college, when Danny wasn't even sure he'd graduate.

Casey bumped her leg against his and he jolted back to the here and now. "How're you doin', anyway?" she asked.

He shrugged.

"After Mama died, I didn't feel much like talking for a couple months," she said. "Everybody was always on me, though: 'You gotta talk about your feelings.' Thought I'd go crazy, everybody hounding me so much."

Danny nodded. "They want me to go see Ms. Guilford. Like talking to the guidance counselor's gonna help anything. I been dodging her so far, but I don't know how much longer I can do it."

"Just get it over with. Make up some shit about dealin' with your feelings, maybe talk about a dream, and she'll get off your back. Otherwise, you'll just spend the rest of the year on the run."

"Okay," he agreed. Casey's mother died in a car accident

a couple years back. This whole thing was old hat for her.

Another branch cracked down below—this one right under the treehouse.

"Dangit, Ida, leave me be for two seconds, would you?" Danny hollered down.

Casey poked her head down the hatch. "There ain't a soul down there. Weed's makin' you paranoid."

Danny shook his head, his shaggy hair flopping in his eyes. For the first time, he felt a little clutch of fear. Casey kept her leg against his, jostling it a little like she knew he needed the reminder: they were okay.

"Your uncle comin' in today?" she asked.

"Yeah. That's what I hear, anyway. Should be around anytime now. You'll like Diggs—he knows music like you wouldn't believe. And he's been everywhere. Done just about everything."

"He's a looker, too," Casey said. She blushed when he looked at her. "You showed me them pictures, remember? You've talked about him enough—I reckon it'll be good, meetin' the man behind the myth."

They got quiet for a little bit after that, the outside of her leg warm against the outside of his. Danny pocketed the roach when they were done smoking, but he wasn't ready to go yet. He felt that fear come at him again.

"You think they're gonna find who did it?" he asked Casey. He didn't have to explain what he meant.

She shrugged, looking sad. Casey always liked her daddy—Danny used to be a little jealous of the two of them, the way she took to talking to him whenever she had troubles.

"I still don't know why anybody'd want to go after a man like Dr. Durham," she said. "He was just about the nicest man I ever met."

But you know why, don't you, boy? Danny imagined

his daddy saying. Clear as you please, he pictured Wyatt Durham sitting across from him in the treehouse. A wrinkle in his forehead, eyes sadder'n a hound dog on his worst day. *You know there's only one reason anybody ever would'a wanted me dead,* his daddy said evenly. *And that's you.*

3
SOLOMON

THE DURHAMS LIVED in a little white farmhouse in the middle of nowhere. Like, literally. I left Einstein in the car until I could be sure he wouldn't be devoured by the family dogs, of which there seemed to be half a dozen. Diggs and I went in without knocking, and were immediately besieged by well-meaning relations. I stayed on the outskirts of the action, watching as Diggs was welcomed back into the fold.

It took a while before we were able to wade through the first wave of greeters to get to the inner sanctum, an overcrowded parlor filled with family photos: Wyatt on a sunny summer day, swimming with his twin boys; studio portraits of the kids from toddler-hood on up; a candid of those same twin boys, now teenagers, at what I assumed had been their high school prom. In the prom picture, one of the boys looked like he was straight out of a Mormon recruitment flyer: short hair and a standard-issue tux, bright white smile, a bland blonde girl with braces laughing beside him. The other brother was more my speed, in a suit jacket over an anarchy t-shirt, the girl on his arm every good mother's nightmare: pierced eyebrow, dyed black hair, plaid miniskirt and combat boots.

The Mormon poster boy sat on the couch now beside his sister, a blonde-haired girl of six or seven missing her front teeth. I saw no sign of the shaggy-haired rebel. There was a playpen in the corner of the room, from which a pudgy blond toddler of indeterminate gender peered out at us. Wyatt's wife, Mae, sat on an overstuffed sofa at the center of it all.

She got up as soon as she spotted Diggs, and he gathered her in his arms and held on tight, swaying gently, while Mae cried. Wyatt's son looked down, his shoulders tense, while the girl watched with that fifty-yard stare you see on kids sometimes when the world's shifted in incomprehensible ways and they're still trying to regain their footing.

Diggs whispered something in Mae's ear and they finally parted, Mae laughing, wiping at her tears. She was short and plump, country pretty, with healthy pink cheeks and that rural efficiency that suggested she could handle anything from pickling preserves to breach births. Since the only thing I know how to pickle is my own liver, I always feel a little out of my element in the presence of such competence.

All the same, Mae beamed when she saw me. She pulled me close and held on tight. "Thank you for finding him," she said in my ear.

I felt a wash of sadness of my own, and managed a mute nod. The kids descended from there, but before hellos could be exchanged or regrets conveyed, a tall, lean brunette appeared in the doorway. The toddler gurgled with what I assumed was pleasure. Diggs looked up, forced a smile, and walked up to the woman.

Ashley Durham—my least favorite of Diggs' three ex-wives. And that's saying something.

"I'm so sorry, Ash," he said.

The whole room looked on curiously. Ashley's not high strung, necessarily, but she's not exactly sunshine and puppies, either. The last time I'd seen her in the flesh, she was threatening Diggs' manhood with a grilling fork for an all-nighter he pulled with me while he was supposed to be vacationing with his lovely wife. In other words: a beat-down wasn't out of the question. After a tense minute or two, she gave a sigh of concession and they hugged it out.

I noticed she didn't extend any such gesture my way, though.

●

That night, after the rest of the family had retired to their respective corners, Diggs snagged me and announced there was someone I had to meet. It was cool and gray outside, a refreshing change of pace from the stuffy homestead. Einstein ran on ahead, peeing on trees and digging up toadstools as he went. It was ten o'clock. I'd promised Juarez I would call as soon as I could, but so far the opportunity hadn't presented itself. I was surprised how much I was looking forward to hearing his voice again, though. No games, no pretenses, no torment; just a stable, interesting guy I liked, who seemed to like me back. Nice. Simple.

Diggs and I walked about half a mile, until we reached a log cabin in a wooded glade far from the road. There was a handmade wooden chair on the front porch beside a pen with three floppy-eared rabbits inside. Stein nosed at them curiously through the mesh as Diggs knocked on the door.

"Are you sure I should be here?" I asked. "I mean, maybe you should have this reunion in private. I could hang with Stein and the bunnies out here."

"Relax," he said. "I want you to meet this guy." He pushed the door open without waiting for someone to answer. "George? You in here?"

Somehow, I'd been expecting a withered old man with a ZZ Top beard and no teeth. Instead, a tall, very bald, very broad-shouldered man in his sixties with a cigar between his teeth emerged from a door in back. Think Mr. Clean meets Hannibal from the *A-Team*. He paused, taking us both in as we stepped into the cabin. I thought we were in for a good old-fashioned southern lynching for a second there, but the hostility vanished once he realized who it was.

"Daniel?" he asked.

"In the flesh," Diggs said.

The man broke into a wide grin, though a vestige of sadness remained as he limped across the cabin and enveloped Diggs in a bear hug.

"You cost me ten big 'uns, boy," he said, patting Diggs heartily on the back. "Mae said you'd be here. I told her between Ashley, Harvey Jennings, and Jesup Barnel, there wasn't enough tail in Hef's mansion to bring you back to this part of the world once you was out."

"If anyone could do it, it'd be Wyatt," Diggs said. "I'm sorry for your loss, George."

The man's eyes misted over. He brushed at his tears roughly. "World's a twisted place, son. Sometimes I don't know which side's up anymore, there's so much wrong with it."

"Wyatt was one of the good ones, though," Diggs said.

George looked at him thoughtfully. "That he was," he agreed. It looked like he meant to say more on the subject, but he turned his attention to me instead. "And who's your pretty friend here?"

"This is Erin Solomon," Diggs said. "An old friend from Maine. Sol, this is George Durham. Wyatt's old man."

George took a step closer, looking me up and down and up again. He had an undeniable magnetism about him, beyond the shining blue eyes and the square jaw—a man who had wielded a lot of power in his day, and still wore that power like a badge. He smiled.

"So, you're the reason Daniel here married my Ashley, huh? You been quite the mystery to me all these years."

"Excuse me?" I asked.

Diggs glared at him. "Don't listen to him," he said to me. "He's obviously gone senile since I saw him last."

"Senile my behind, boy," George said. He returned his attention to me. "He come 'round here back in… what, '05? Nursing a broken heart—'course being Diggs he wasn't much for sharing till you got a few sips in him. But as I recall, he did mention you that first night. Next thing I know, he's up and asked Ashley to marry him. Lord only knows why she said yes—those two never could stand each other. I love my little girl, but she's got about as much personality as an old toothpick. But here's Diggs, sayin' he's ready to settle down. Be part of the family."

Diggs eyed me with just a hint of desperation. "Seriously—it was a long time ago. Memories get twisted with time. I don't know what he's talking about."

I couldn't even imagine an appropriate response—particularly since I remembered 2005 pretty damned well, and none of what George said fit into those memories in any way, shape, or form. The old man finally took pity on both of us and recanted.

"He's right," he said. "Don't listen to me. It's just the ramblings of an old man's just lost his only son. Come on in here. Have a drink with me."

"We'll visit awhile, but I'm gonna take a pass on the drink," Diggs said. "I'm trying to keep my nose clean these days."

George actually pouted. "Well, that's a damn shame. How 'bout you, darlin'?" he asked me. "I got some rotgut back there with your name on it."

"That sounds great," I said, "but—"

"No buts!" He hot-footed it to the back of the cabin. I looked at Diggs. His cheeks were still burning.

"Sorry about that. I don't know what he's talking about—I don't even remember mentioning your name around him."

I nodded, still trying to figure out how to react. Thankfully, there was a knock on the front door before we had any more time to dwell on it, and Mae let herself in. A man I hadn't seen at the house followed her.

"You find him all right?" Mae asked Diggs.

"Yeah," he said. "He's getting the whiskey."

"Good," she said. "God forgive me, but I could use a belt myself about now."

Einstein had been relegated to the front porch with the bunnies, but he let himself in with the others and settled at my feet. George came out, saw everyone, swore, and went back to haul out another jug. Introductions were made.

"This is Deputy Holloway," Mae told me of the man beside her. He was about Diggs' age, smaller and leaner, with dark hair and the kind of wide, genuine smile that makes the bearer about three times more attractive than they might seem otherwise.

"Everybody calls me Buddy, ma'am," he said.

We shook hands. George returned and set us up with glasses all around while Diggs grabbed a soda from the fridge.

As soon as we were seated around the table in George's kitchen, Mae slammed back a mug of what, as far as I could tell, was pure lighter fluid. She gasped, coughed, and then looked Diggs in the eye.

"I need to ask a favor," she said to him. I got the feeling she'd been waiting for this moment to present itself.

"Mae," he began.

She held up her hand. "Don't you 'Mae' me—you owe Wyatt this much, and you know it. I just want you to ask around—"

"We're working with KSP, Mae," Buddy said.

I looked at Diggs. "Kentucky State Police," he whispered. I nodded.

"None of them are gonna want some Yankee reporter poking around in this," the deputy continued. "Never mind what Sheriff Jennings has to say about it once he knows Diggs is back in town."

"There's no reason Harvey Jennings needs to know anything about this," Mae said. "And no offense to you or him or the Kentucky Police, but I want somebody I trust askin' questions. Somebody I know won't stop till he figures out the whole story."

George frowned. "She's right, you know," he said. "Nothin' about this makes a lick of sense. And you know it."

"What the hell happened?" Diggs asked—the question I knew had been plaguing him since he first got the news.

Buddy looked at Mae unhappily. "You shouldn't be goin' over this right now."

Mae shook her head with stark determination. "I'm all right, sugar. If I owe Wyatt anything, it's at least this. I mean to find out who did this, and see that they answer for it." She sat down, her eyes never leaving Diggs'. "That last night, Wyatt went out to Roger Burkett's farm—Roger used to live 'round here, but he packed up and left for San Francisco back about ten years ago.

"Then he shows up a couple years back with some skinny city girl plucked right out of a fashion magazine. Roger took over the farm after his daddy passed. Bought a herd of Alpines—milking goats," she explained to me. "Half Wyatt's calls this past year've been over there, taking care of one damn fool problem after the other. Wy says all Jenny

Burkett does is fuss over them goats and lounge around in her skivvies watching reality TV. She teaches a couple classes over to Smithfield—political science. Thinks she's better than anybody here in Justice."

"You think they did this? The Burketts?" I asked, trying to get her back on track.

"I don't know. Roger's nothin' to write home about, I'll tell you that much—a snake oil salesman's got more scruples. And I never much cared for the way his wife looked at Wyatt. Wouldn't surprise me if they had something to do with it." She looked at Buddy. "You think maybe you can take Diggs through some of the pictures and some of your notes tomorrow, while the sheriff's outta the office?"

"If he catches me, it's my job," Buddy said. "And probably my hide to boot."

Mae didn't say anything to that, her gaze fixed on her mug. "You know, I don't remember a time I wasn't in love with Wy," she said. "I remember the first day I set eyes on him; I remember our first kiss, our first…everything. All the space before that, though, just seems like one long, colorless blur."

Diggs draped his arm over her shoulders and kissed her temple. She closed her eyes, but she held it together. "I'll stop by the office tomorrow morning," Diggs said, directing the statement at Buddy. "I've got plenty of experience dodging Sheriff Jennings. No reason I can't do it one more time."

Mae took a deep, steadying breath, and stood with a shaky smile. "Thank you. That's all I'm askin'. Now, if you'll excuse me, I'm gonna round up the kids and head to bed myself." She looked at me. "I made up the guest room for you and that pup of yours, Erin. Diggs, you mind bunking with the boys? Wyatt never did like folks sharing a room without a ring—you understand. I hope that'll be all right."

We both nodded. "That'll be fine," Diggs said.

"Rick snores," Mae continued. "And Danny—well, I don't think that boy goes to bed before three most nights, and we're lucky if we can haul him up by noon."

"Takes after his uncle," George said, eyeing Diggs. "Wouldn't know he had any Durham blood in him at all."

Mae laughed. "He's right. Rick's already got everything figured out—he did a project last year over to Smithfield, ended up gettin' in early. He starts this summer. And he did a project over to city hall for their plannin' office, mapping out the Underground Railroad here in Kentucky. Folks said he found stuff under Justice that nobody even knew was there.

"But Danny," she continued. "Wy says it all the time: 'If I didn't know any better, Maisie, I'd think Diggs slipped it to you one day while I was out of town.' " She stopped. Realization dawned in that cruel, cutting way it does in the days after you lose someone. "He said, I mean," she finished. "Wyatt said it all the time."

"I know what you meant," Diggs said. "Go get some sleep. And let Uncle Diggs here take care of Danny for you—I'll get him straightened out in no time."

She looked doubtful, but she didn't argue.

After she left, George poured drinks all around and raised a toast to Wyatt.

The night's kind of a blur after that.

4
DIGGS

"SO, NEXT THING I HEAR on the scanner," George said, in fine form between half a jug of his best moonshine and the captive audience of me, Buddy Holloway, and especially Solomon, "Sheriff Jennings has Diggs' motel room surrounded, and the police are ordering him out of there with his hands up…"

"Which he does." Buddy picked up the story while Solomon followed along, rapt. I grimaced, knowing all too well what came next. "But when he comes out, it's without so much as a stitch on—naked as the day he come into this world. And of course we all know the sheriff's wife's in there, too, but there ain't no way old Harvey Jennings is gonna be humiliated by risking Mrs. Jennings comin' out in her altogethers, too."

We'd been through a few of these stories by now. Bringing Solomon along for this trip down amnesia alley didn't seem nearly as good an idea as it had when it first occurred to me.

"And here I thought Harvey Jennings was the bad guy in all this," Solomon said. "You're such a tool."

"In my defense," I said, "my marriage had just broken

up, I'd finished off two pints of Jameson's on my own that morning, and—while I don't have a clear picture of exactly what happened in that motel room—I'm pretty sure it didn't involve much sleeping."

"Besides that," George interrupted, "if anybody deserved it, it was the sheriff. Harvey Jennings is a bully, and an ass to boot."

"You got a point there," Buddy said. "If I remember right, Sarah Jennings paid through the nose for that night."

"The sheriff went after her?" Solomon said.

"'Bout near killed her," George said. I remained quiet, my gaze on the floor, thinking back to days I'd been trying to put behind me for a while now.

"'Course, that meant Diggs here went after Harvey the next day," George continued. "Put him in the hospital for a good spell. Likely would'a killed him, if Wyatt hadn't gotten there."

"He deserved it," I said. "Sarah was a good woman. He treated her like shit."

"Was?" Solomon asked. "What happened to her?"

"She left town after that," Buddy said. "Not more'n a week after Diggs, if I recall correctly. Took her little girl, and nobody never heard from either of 'em again. 'Course, you walk out on a man like Harvey Jennings, you don't exactly leave a forwarding address." He looked at me. "I'd bet tomorrow's lunch ol' Diggs knows where she is, though."

Solomon took another slug of whiskey and set it down, eyes on me. "I wouldn't take that bet," she said.

Our gazes locked. Her eyes had the kind of feverish intensity Solomon only gets when she's drinking—which is rare. The air between us caught fire. She cleared her throat.

"Well, I hope you at least showed her a good time," she said to me.

I held her eye. "I've never gotten any complaints, sweetheart."

I never tire of making Solomon blush. She looked away first, cheeks burning, and rolled her eyes. I waited for a comeback that never came.

Another few seconds of charged silence ensued before Buddy spoke up. "Well, believe it or not, the sheriff's a changed man these days. He just might surprise you, if you two do cross paths."

"Yeah," I said. "I'll believe that when I see it. Nothing short of a lobotomy changes a man like Harvey Jennings."

"Buddy's right," George said, though his tone belied his skepticism. "He's gotten pretty deep into the word, goin' on about a year now. Follows Jesup Barnel's church."

"There's a terrifying combination if I ever heard one," I said.

"Nothing worse I can think of," George agreed.

"Okay, that's the third time that name's come up today," Solomon interrupted. "This is the preacher with the big billboard in town, right? What's his story?"

"Diggs and Wyatt never would've met if it weren't for Reverend Barnel," George said before I could field the question myself. Or deflect it. "You was, what...? Twelve years old at the time?" he asked me.

"Yeah," I said.

"Here we go—this is the story you and Wyatt would never tell me," Solomon said. "Let's hear it."

"Diggs and Wyatt met at Jesup Barnel's church camp," George began. He'd never been a fan of Barnel's. It was clear from his tone that that hadn't changed in my absence. " 'Course, Wyatt never would'a been there in the first place, but Retta—my late wife—took it into her head that the boy needed straightenin' out. The reverend runs this camp for boys havin' more than your usual problems in the world—you know what I mean?"

"I think I get the idea," she said.

"Reverend Barnel has some odd ideas about the ways of the Lord," Buddy said. "He does a big ol' ceremony, legendary round these parts, to cast out demons makin' youngsters act out."

"And that's how you and Wyatt met?" Solomon asked me.

I nodded.

"After that, they was thick as thieves," George said. "Diggs would come for summers, vacations—anytime he could convince his daddy to send him down, this is where he'd be. I got pictures of the two of them out here on the farm, back when Diggs had his hair like that fella—" He looked at me. "Who was it, now?"

There was no way this could end well. "Sorry, I don't remember," I said.

"Vanilla Ice," Buddy said, nodding. "Thought he was God's gift, this one."

"Listen, we really should be going," I said to Solomon. "It's been a long day."

"Are you nuts?" she asked. "I've barely seen a single picture of you besides class photos at Littlehope Middle School. If there are candids of you as the Ice Man, you can bet your sweet ass I'm gonna see them."

"They're in the shed out back," George said. "Hang on, let me get 'em." He started to haul himself out of his chair, but I shook my head.

"Stay where you are, George. I'll get them. Just tell me where."

Two minutes later, I was outside in the fresh air again, grateful for the reprieve. It was almost midnight, the woods an eerie cobalt blue under a clouded sky. When I was with Ashley, I used to sit on the front porch out here with George, drinking until we were blurry with the booze, talking life, philosophy, music, women… Anything I could come up with to avoid going home. Whatever George might have to say about his daughter, she sure as hell had deserved better than I'd ever given her.

I hoped she had that now.

I could hear them laughing inside the cabin. Solomon wasn't much of a drinker usually, and George's homemade whiskey wasn't the best time to make an exception to that rule. She'd stood by and watched me get blackout drunk enough times that I wasn't about to tell her when to quit, though. She—

I stopped, caught by a sound I couldn't identify behind me. The ground was too soft for footsteps, but there was… something. Movement. Or I thought there was. I flashed back to the summer before with Solomon and fought the urge to run back inside. There were a whole host of night creatures that could be moving out here about now. I wasn't being hunted anymore.

Probably.

George's shed was behind the cabin, sheltered by a grove of trees and all but invisible to the outside world. I slipped the latch and opened the door, shining a flashlight George had given me. The shed was maybe 12x18, barely big enough to walk around in, with tools hung neatly on pegboard on one wall and shelving built along the others. A single, rectangular window was positioned on the opposite wall, about six feet up—too high to see anything, but adequate if you needed a little light. When there was light to be had, of course.

I spotted a dozen photo albums lined up on one of the shelves, and stepped inside. It smelled of sawdust and cigar smoke, two of George's favorite things. I grabbed a couple of the photo albums without checking the dates on the spines and strode back across the shed toward freedom. Since the caves and tunnels of the previous summer, enclosed spaces weren't a favorite of mine. Something clattered against the outside wall. I whirled toward the sound, heart racing.

"Solomon? Is that you?"

I turned back around just in time to watch the door swing shut.

"Buddy? All right… Good one, guys. You're friggin' hilarious." I reached for the door and tried to push it open. It didn't budge.

Something scratched against the outside of the shed, just below the window—like someone was scaling the wall. The clattering could have been a ladder, I realized. And this was George's idea of a practical joke: his way of welcoming me back to the fold. I wet my lips and reminded myself that panicking at this point was exactly the kind of story that would follow me to my grave, once the lights came on and the idiots pulling the prank were revealed.

Better to play it cool. Ride it out.

"All right, you got me," I said. "I'm trapped in the shed. In the dark. You guys are comic geniuses."

Something scratched against the windowpane. I trained my flashlight beam in that direction, but all that did was reflect the light back at me.

I realized then that there was no way Solomon was behind this—she knew too well what we'd gone through six months ago. And she wouldn't let the others do anything like it, either. Sweat beaded on my forehead and the back of my neck. Just outside the window, I heard a faint rattling sound.

"Harvey?" I said. If Sheriff Jennings had found out I was back in town, this might be the kind of thing he'd pull to welcome me back. "Is that you?"

The rattling got louder.

I pulled my cell phone from my jacket pocket and hit number one on speed dial. It went straight to Solomon's voicemail. Perfect.

My pulse was racing.

The window opened, the sound of metal against wood like a scream in the stillness. I grabbed the closest thing I could find—a hammer hanging on the pegboard—and held it aloft, my back pressed to the far wall, waiting to see what would happen next.

Whoever was out there dropped something through the window, followed in quick succession by two more somethings. They fell too quickly for me to see what they were, but it was painfully obvious when I heard the wet thud and ensuing hiss as they hit the floor.

The rattling was deafening now.

The window slammed shut.

I stood very, very still.

●

There are non-poisonous gopher snakes that mimic the movement and sound of the common rattler. A once-over with the flashlight was all it took to tell me these were not gopher snakes. These were rattlers—three large ones, maybe six feet long, and they were pissed. The best move when encountering a pissed-off snake is a backward one: stay calm, back the hell up, and keep walking the other way.

Trapped in a locked shed, however, that wasn't an option. I dialed 911. The dispatcher picked up after three rings and asked me my emergency. I told her I was trapped in a shed with three rattlesnakes.

There was a very long pause.

"Three live rattlesnakes, sir?" she asked.

"Yeah. Pretty live."

"Maybe you should get on outta there," she said. "Have you been bit?"

"Not yet, but I'm not loving my chances here. Listen, all I need you to do is call Buddy Holloway—he's a deputy at the Justice Police Department. Tell him Diggs called."

From the shed.

Because rattlesnakes were after him.

Yeah, this was gonna go well.

There was another long pause. The snakes slithered closer, the rattling like the sound of fat frying in a pan. The largest of the three hissed, head up. Preparing to strike.

"Sir, it's a crime to prank an emergency line."

"Please… I'm telling you, this isn't a prank. Just call the deputy, all right?"

She assured me that she would, and I hung up. The rattlers weren't looking any happier about our situation.

"Easy, guys," I said. "We can talk this over, right? You go your way, I'll go mine."

The other two advanced, all three hissing now. Shit.

I stepped backward and tried the door again: still jammed. I still held George's hammer in one hand, but going on the defensive was out of the question unless I was feeling especially suicidal.

I wasn't.

Tired of waiting me out, the largest rattler advanced again, focused on my pant leg. I had jeans and thin hiking boots on—not enough to keep me protected should he strike. The same noise I'd heard before clattered against the side of the shed again, making me jump. Unfortunately, it had the same effect on the snakes; already on edge, the sudden noise was all it took to push them over. A breadth of a second later, the first rattler struck.

He caught me in the calf and dug in deep. If I shouted, thrashed, or tried to fight the bastard, the others would come at me and I'd be done. All the same, the time to wait passively for someone to come to my rescue was clearly behind me. The snake snapped back after striking, still watching me anxiously. I started to creep along the wall toward the window. My leg was on fire, the pain searing. I fought to stay calm while the snakes slithered back and forth across the floor in a rhythmic dance.

I reached the window. There were shelves beneath it—I had no idea if they were sturdy enough to hold my weight, but I didn't have a lot of choices. My leg was already swelling, pain radiating down my foot and up past my knee. Sweat ran down my back, the air stifling as I managed to find a foothold and pull myself up. I used my hammer to knock the glass from the window, dimly aware that the rattling was getting louder below me once again.

The second strike only caught the heel of my boot, but I was moving too fast for the fangs to penetrate. I pushed myself through the narrow window and somehow managed to avoid breaking my neck when I fell headfirst to the ground below.

Apparently the dispatcher had followed through and called Buddy, because the others were on their way to my rescue before I hit the ground. I opened my eyes to find Solomon looking down at me, the damn dog licking my face.

"What the hell are you doing down there?" she asked.

George was already headed around to the front of the shed to open the door. I shouted after him. "Keep it shut—snakes!"

A little melodramatic, maybe, but effective. Solomon's eyes widened. She'd sobered up in record time. "So the call Buddy just got was real?"

"Someone locked me in. There are rattlers in there—three of them. I got tagged in the leg."

She went pale. George returned to my side as soon as the words were out.

"All right, son—let's have a look, and Buddy here," he nodded calmly to the deputy standing on the sidelines. "He's gonna run and get the car. I got a first aid kit in the kitchen," he said to Solomon. "Go on and get that, and we're gonna keep him nice and still."

Solomon and Buddy took off at a run. George rolled my pant leg up and carefully removed my boot and sock. Solomon returned a minute later with the first aid kit. She followed George's gaze to my calf, but there was no revulsion or panic when she saw the bite. So, that was a good sign. Of course, Solomon spent her formative years helping her mother stitch up fishermen all along the Maine coast. Medically speaking, there's not a lot that makes her panic.

She laid her hand on my head and brushed the hair back from my forehead. "Just relax," she said easily. "And count your blessings the medical community decided sucker-fishing the poison out of people is a bad idea."

"I think *you* should count your blessings on that one, actually," I said weakly.

Buddy tore back into the yard shortly thereafter, and he and George helped me to the car. I sat in the back with Solomon, leaning back against her with my leg stretched out on the seat.

"Shouldn't someone who's not drunk be driving?" I asked.

"Don't you worry about that," Buddy said, calling back over his shoulder. "I switched out to water 'bout two hours ago, just didn't tell y'all. I was too ashamed being outdrunk by your girlfriend there."

Solomon checked the swelling on my leg for the twelfth time, then lay her hand against my forehead. "Still no nausea? Dizziness? Chills? Inexplicable craving for live rodents?"

I closed my eyes. "No, on all of the above. I just want to know who did this."

"And you're sure it was a rattlesnake?" Solomon pressed. "Because gopher snakes—"

"It wasn't a gopher snake," I bit out. "I may not have the symptoms you listed, but it feels like my goddamn leg's being eaten by fire ants. Gopher snakes don't do that."

"It was rattlers all right," Buddy confirmed. "I got a look at 'em before we left, just to make sure. What in hell are they doin' out this time of year, anyway? They're not common in these parts anytime, but this early I don't know why they'd be hangin' around at all."

"They weren't hanging around, Buddy," I said. "Someone dropped them through the damn window and locked me in. Why they're out this time of year really isn't the thing to be obsessing over."

"No, I s'pose not," he said.

"You guys didn't hear anyone?" I asked. George had gone uncharacteristically silent. I shivered, a wave of nausea running through me. Solomon wrapped a blanket around both of us, her body cradling mine.

"No more questions," she said, loudly enough to include the others up front. "No more talking. Just be still," she whispered to me. I could feel her heart, beating too hard; maybe Solomon wasn't so calm after all. The thought was oddly comforting. She continued stroking the hair back from my forehead.

"You would've been a good doctor," I mumbled.

"Well, you would've been a terrible patient," she returned. Her lips brushed against my temple—or I may have imagined it. I closed my eyes, Solomon's arms around me, her body cushioning mine, and focused on being still.

I was in the hospital overnight, waiting for symptoms beyond excruciating pain to develop.

None did. No swelling, no fever, no vomiting, no chills.

It wasn't until Buddy came in at nine the next morning that I found out why.

"What do you mean, the snakes belong to Jesup Barnel?" I demanded. It had been a long night of needle jabs and strange nurses and—since I refused the morphine drip they recommended—pain.

Buddy shifted uncomfortably. "I guess the sheriff got a call from Reverend Barnel last night," he said. "Sayin' somebody got into his snakes. He's got a license to milk them—for the anti-venom, you know? But he told the sheriff somebody stole a few just after they'd been milked last night. That's probably why you didn't show no symptoms. You got a dry bite."

"Bullshit," I said. "He's behind this—you know him. It would be just like him to take three of his neutered rattlers and lock me in with them to teach me a lesson. Test my faith."

"I'm not saying you're wrong," Buddy said. "I'm just saying, he's got a story, too. An alibi. His butt is covered."

"His butt's always covered," I muttered.

"Who the hell is this guy?" Solomon said. George had gotten a ride back to Justice with Buddy, but Sol had been camped out by my bedside for the better part of the night. Her good humor wasn't faring well as a result. "I know you and Wyatt met at his extreme church camp or whatever—but clearly there's more to the story than that."

"It doesn't matter," I said shortly. "It wasn't the most sane week of my life. Let's just leave it at that."

She narrowed her eyes at my tone, her lips pressed into a tight, pissy little line. "Don't bite my head off. It's a valid question."

"And it brings up something I wanted to talk to you about last night," Buddy interrupted. "But I didn't want to talk about it with George there. I thought we'd do it down to the station today, but maybe this is better. Less chance of the sheriff walking in on us."

"Wyatt's case?" I asked.

He handed me a short stack of manila folders. "That's the files," he said. Solomon came over and sat on the edge of my hospital bed. I opened the top file and tried to remain impassive. Half a dozen 8x10 crime scene photos of Wyatt's dead body didn't make that easy.

"Mae called in about two a.m. Saturday night, weekend before last," Buddy began. "She said Wyatt wasn't home yet, and he wasn't answering his cell phone. I got a bad feeling right then—I've seen newborns can stay away from their mama longer than that boy could stand being away from Mae."

"And after that?" I asked. "What happened after you got the call from Mae?"

"I took Floyd—our other deputy—and we headed out to the Burkett farm straightaway. That was Wyatt's last call. He was out tending a goat he had to put down. When we got there, Wyatt's truck was still there. Jenny Burkett told me he'd been around long enough to take care of the goat… and then he just up and disappeared."

"And they didn't see a sign of anyone?" I asked. "The Burketts?"

"Their place is set up so you gotta travel about an acre and a half between the barn and the main drive. Jenny was back in the barn with the kids. From what I can tell, Roger was sleeping one off just then."

Solomon furrowed her brow, but she didn't say anything. I knew what she was thinking: an emergency trip from the vet seemed like a prime opportunity for some spousal support. Or at least a brief cameo from the husband. Chances were good there was a story as to why Roger Burkett hadn't shown his face.

"Okay," I said. "What happened then?"

"Well, we scoured the countryside for a few days, with no sightings and no sign of Wyatt. Then along about eleven Wednesday night, we got a call."

"They found him," Solomon said.

"Laid out at the junction of I-69 and Route 45 in a new suit a size too small, hands on his chest like he was just taking a Sunday nap."

"The junction of 69 and 45," Diggs repeated. "That's, what, an hour from here? How is this even your case?"

"It's not," Buddy said. "Not technically, anyhow. We got the KSP on it. Since Wyatt's from here in Justice and he went missin' from here, they promised to keep us in the loop."

"And what's the official cause of death?"

"Overdose of ketamine," Buddy said. "It's that club drug, you know the one."

"Special K," I said. "Not exactly a drug running rampant on the streets of Justice."

"Never had one case of it that I know of around here," Buddy agreed. "But it's also used as a sedative by vets. Looks like they might've stolen it from Wyatt's practice. Some went missin' about a month ago. Anyway, the coroner says Wyatt'd been gone maybe twenty-four hours by the time we got to him."

Which meant that for seventy-two hours while Wyatt had been missing, he'd been alive. I scratched my chin. Buddy eyed the photos nervously, as twitchy as a virgin bride. Solomon caught my eye. She'd noticed it, too.

"So, what aren't you telling us, exactly?" she asked.

Buddy shifted uneasily and looked from Solomon to me. "She's got the eye, huh?"

"Nobody better," I said. "Short of me, of course. She's right. There's something you're not telling us."

Buddy nodded toward the photos. "Wyatt wasn't in bad

shape when we found him—I mean, so far as the body goes. Neat and clean…peaceful-like, strange as that sounds."

"Except…" I prompted.

He frowned. "He had a mark on his chest—a cross that'd been there since he was a boy."

"Like a tattoo?" Solomon asked. I didn't have to probe any further, though. I knew just what he was talking about.

"Not exactly," Buddy said uncomfortably. "More of a… brand, I guess you'd call it. You seen it before?" he asked me.

I nodded silently.

"Well," Buddy said. "Somebody cut all the way around that cross. Then they took off the skin on his chest like it was just some patch, turned it one hundred and eighty degrees, and sewed it back on like that."

My stomach rolled. Buddy looked at me.

"You all right?"

"Yeah," I said. Solomon watched me like she knew better. I took a breath and kept going. "So, they turned the thing into an inverted cross?"

Buddy nodded. "Coroner says it was done postmortem, thank the good Lord."

I went through the photos with Solomon. Pale flesh; rough, uneven stitches; a raised cross turned upside down, branded into the skin just below Wyatt's collarbone. I looked at Solomon, trying to determine whether she'd made the connection. My cross isn't really recognizable as a cross anymore, but the scar is in the same place as Wyatt's. The same size. Solomon kept her gaze fixed on the photos, giving me no clue whether she'd figured it out or not.

"This whole thing's got me worried," Buddy said. "Fact is, this isn't the first time I've seen this done."

"You mean the cross excised and turned upside down?" I asked. "Where else have you seen it?"

"Years ago now," Buddy said. "I pulled the file after I

saw it on Wyatt. It was back in '02. Marty Reynolds. He was forty-two at the time. Two kids, and a rundown farm out toward the outskirts of town. There was a rumor he killed his first wife—he said she walked out on the family, though, and there was never an official investigation. Rumor was he done it, though. There weren't too many people cryin' at his funeral, if you know what I mean."

"Cause of death was the same?" I asked.

"No, sir," Buddy said with a shake of his head. "They found him with his throat cut. But he was dressed in some nice clothes his kids never saw before. Left on the side of the road just outside Paducah."

"But there hasn't been anyone since then," I said. "Those are the only two?"

"So far as I know," Buddy said. "I went through our records looking for anything. Seems as though it would've made an impression if somebody had seen it before." He looked at me. "You know where that mark come from? The original cross, I mean?"

Solomon was all ears.

"Yeah," I said. I put the photos back and closed the file.

"Where did it come from?" Solomon pressed.

"Reverend Jesup Barnel," the deputy said. "We told you, he's got some odd ideas about the Christian way."

"So, is Barnel still working the same circuit?" I asked before Solomon could pursue the next logical line of questioning.

"Not so much no more," Buddy said. "His health's gone south, but he still does tent meetin's when he can. There's one out in Miller's Field tonight. It's a hike, but worth the gas if you ask me. He puts on quite a show."

"And the rattlers," I said. "Are they part of that show?"

"Not officially," Buddy said. "Snake handlin' is illegal in Kentucky now, 'course. But everybody knows he skirts around it, brings 'em out for those middle of the night, invitation-only services out to his place, like he used to run."

I'd heard enough. I sat up, nodding across the room. "All right. Since I'm apparently not about to drop dead of rattlesnake fever, somebody toss me my pants."

Buddy looked to Solomon, no doubt hoping she'd talk some sense into me. But Solomon's never really been that girl.

"He's been here eight hours," she said with a shrug. "There's not much chance the venom will hit his bloodstream unexpectedly at this point. I'll be watching if it does, and I'll just bring him back." She fetched my clothes and tossed them on the foot of the bed. "I'll grab us some coffee while you get dressed." Her gaze slid back to the files, now in Buddy's hand. She shook her head. "Leave it to you to piss off someone crazier than Will Rainier."

5
SOLOMON

AFTER HIS HARROWING MISADVENTURES with the neutered rattlesnakes, Diggs and I got back to the Durhams at ten o'clock the next morning. Wyatt's funeral wasn't until two, and we'd passed the window in which Diggs was most likely to swell up and die from his snake bite. Since I hadn't gotten any sleep to speak of since leaving Maine, I apologized to anyone who may have been expecting sparkling conversation, grabbed my dog, and retired to the Durhams' attic guest room.

I lay on the bed beside Einstein and idly scratched his fuzzy belly. He groaned, stretching out his front paws while one of his hind legs kicked into gear when I hit a choice spot. It would be so much easier to be a dog. I thought of Diggs cradled in my arms last night, his heart racing. My heart racing. Unlike the nightmares I'd been having for the past six months, though, at least with the snake bite I could do something when he was in danger, instead of just standing there, frozen, like I always did in those freaking dreams.

Einstein turned his head and lapped lazily at my jaw.

Yeah... Definitely easier to be a dog.

I retrieved my cell phone and dialed Juarez. He answered on the second ring, though it was the middle of the work day.

"Hey, baby," he answered. He always answered that way—or he had since we'd started dating, anyway. Terms of endearment aren't usually my thing, but I was getting used to it. It didn't hurt that Juarez made 'baby' sound just a little dirty when he said it.

"Hey," I said. "Is this an okay time?"

"Just catching up on paperwork," he said. "Perfect timing."

"Sorry I didn't call last night. Things got a little...crazy."

"I figured they would. Don't worry about it. How's Diggs?"

I hadn't lied when I told Diggs me coming to Kentucky had been Juarez's idea. In fact, he'd kind of insisted on it.

"He's all right," I said. "You know Diggs. He's solid as a rock, right up until he's not." I tried to figure out how to broach the subject of the rattlesnake attack. *Funny story: how much do you know about pit vipers?*

"And you're doing okay?" he asked.

"Yeah, I am. I'm actually getting ready to take a nap." I hesitated. Open, honest communication isn't usually my thing, either. "I just wanted to hear your voice." I rolled onto my back, still holding the phone to my ear. "Tell me about your day."

We did this a lot. Juarez isn't a phone sex kind of guy, but with the smooth voice and the subtle Cuban accent, he really missed his calling. Since we were still working out the whole long-distance thing between Maine and DC, most weekday evenings for the past three months had been spent on the phone. Lately, I found myself craving the sound of his voice at bedtime. Jack Juarez: Human Xanax. May be addictive, but no groggy drug hangover in the morning.

"Erin?" Juarez said after a few minutes. I forced myself back to some state of coherence.

"Yeah," I said.

"Were you sleeping?"

"No…not yet. Almost."

"I should go, then." He paused. "You think you'll be back in Maine by the weekend?"

It was Wednesday. The funeral was today, but I wasn't sure how much investigating we'd be doing into Wyatt's death after that.

"I think so," I said. "I'll let you know as soon as I have a better idea. Why? You miss me already?"

He laughed. Juarez has a great laugh. "I always miss you, baby. Be safe. I'll talk to you soon."

We hung up. I slept.

When I emerged, the house was unexpectedly quiet. Eventually, I found Danny—the miscreant son Wyatt and Mae had named after Diggs—sitting on the front porch alone. For a kid with no actual Diggins blood in him, he really did have an uncannily Diggs-like vibe. Not that he actually looked like Diggs, mind you. But clearly there was some hero worship going on there, his shaggy blond hair heavily gelled, his rumpled suit a size too small. The kicker was the joint he held in his left hand. Just like Uncle Diggs. He looked up, startled, when I opened the front door.

"Uh—sorry," I said. "I was just looking for Diggs."

He made no effort to hide the weed, though he did have the decency not to keep smoking it while I was standing right there.

"He's just gettin' dressed. He said I could ride with y'all. Hope you don't mind."

"No, of course not."

"Good," he said, nodding. He patted the seat next to

him. "Come on out. Diggs'll be along. It's too dang stuffy in there."

He was right about that, anyway. I'd already changed into my funeral clothes, so there wasn't a whole lot else I could do with the next ten minutes until Diggs wandered down to join us.

Einstein loped out into the yard with one of the resident hound dogs. They sniffed butts, he graced the hound with one of his best play bows, and they raced off together. There were clouds on the horizon, and rain was in the air. I took the seat Danny had indicated. He offered me his joint.

"Just to take the edge off," he said.

It was tempting, but I've never been much of an enthusiast myself. Diggs smoked enough for both of us back in the day.

"No, thanks. You sure you should be out here in the open with that?"

"Everybody's already headed on out to the church," he said. "Except you and Diggs, I mean. And I knew you guys'd be cool with it."

I wasn't sure how accurate that was as far as Diggs was concerned anymore, but who was I to burst the kid's bubble?

"So," he continued. "Is it true what happened last night? Somebody really locked Diggs in with them rattlers?" He looked more curious than horrified. That could have been the pot, though.

"Yeah," I said with a nod. "It was nuts. You have any idea who would have done something like that?"

He took a long hit from his joint, held the smoke in his lungs, and then put it out and pocketed the roach before he responded. His eyes were glassy, splintered with red veins.

"Diggs made some enemies when he was here before," Danny said. "I was just a kid then, so I didn't pay too much attention. He was just ol' Uncle Diggs, you know? But the stories are still around—Mama doesn't even know we've heard half of 'em. How he knocked boots with the sheriff's wife and then was out on the front lawn of the Motel Six butt naked. Plus everything that happened with Reverend Barnel..."

"What did happen with Reverend Barnel?" I asked.

Danny considered that for a minute, clearly torn between loyalty to Diggs and the high of being the one in the know.

"Forget it," I said. "I don't want you to betray any confidences, kid."

"I ain't no kid," he said. "I got a truck. I got plenty of girls for any night I choose. I got a band, even—and we're good, too. Play out down to Nashville and Memphis, Louisville and Lexington." He looked at me knowingly. "But good job makin' me feel like a loser just so I'd spill Diggs' secrets to feel like a big man."

"I thought the weed might slow you down," I said with a rueful smile. "Maybe you wouldn't figure my angle."

He shook his head with exaggerated disappointment. When he looked at me, there was a predatory gleam in his eye. He was a good looking kid, and he knew it: the kind cougars the world over would stand in line for. I've never been much for younger men, though.

"Don't give me that look, Dimples," I said. "I've got enough problems with your uncle. Now, what do you know? Let's have it."

"Yes, ma'am. Well, when he lived here before, with Aunt Ashley, I know him and the reverend got into it a couple times. Diggs was always writing articles about Barnel's church, you know? And he went to a couple of his services, rip roarin' drunk, and Sheriff Jennings had to haul him off."

"Why does he hate Barnel so much, though?"

"Same reason my mama loves the guy so much, I reckon," Danny said. For the first time, he looked uncomfortable.

"Anyway, that seems more like a story Diggs should tell you himself. What happens at Barnel's camp... that changes a body. It's not so much a story you want other people tellin'."

"You sound like you speak from experience."

I might as well have suggested he was secretly into wearing his mom's lingerie. He looked at the ground.

"Just telling you what I've heard," he said. "That's all."

Diggs came out a minute later, freshly scrubbed and sporting jacket and tie. Being a manly man, he'd of course scorned the hospital's recommendation of crutches—though he'd bizarrely been fine with George Durham's old man cane.

"You moving in on my girl?" Diggs asked when he came out, eyeing Danny.

"First off, I'm not your girl," I said. "And secondly... He was just giving me a little dirt on you, as a matter of fact."

"Dirt? On me?" Diggs asked, wide eyed. "Pfft. None to be found."

"Well, except for that summer you and Daddy—" Danny began with a spark in his eye.

"All right, you proved your point. I think we best be on our way." Diggs sniffed the air knowingly. "But first, what's that I smell? It's vaguely familiar. Smells like..."

"Teen spirit?" Danny said. Wiseacre.

"Smells like weed, shithead," Diggs said. "And if I catch you smoking it on your Mama's front porch again, I'll kick your ass six ways to Sunday."

Danny sobered. Clearly, it wasn't the reaction he'd expected. So much for Uncle Diggs, frat brother in arms. "Yes, sir. Won't happen again."

"Good," Diggs said. He held out his hand. Danny took it, letting Diggs pull him up. "Now, come on. Put some eye drops in, and let's do this thing." He draped his arm across Danny's shoulders and looked at me. "You ready, Sol?"

"Go on ahead—I just have to grab something, I'll be right there."

I went in, settled Einstein and the other dogs inside, and grabbed my purse. When I came out, Diggs and Danny were walking together, heads tilted toward one another. I had one of those brief, not-at-all-advisable flashes of What Might Have Been between the two of us, if things had gone differently over the years. Of course, given his background he probably still would have become an addict...and a drinker...and the kind of man who slept with anything that moved. Our friendship was strong, but I doubted it could have withstood the two of us dating in his heyday.

He was four years' sober now. A changed man in any number of ways, from the one I'd known back then.

"Get the lead out, kid," Diggs called back to me. "We're not getting any younger here. You coming or what?"

Okay, not totally changed. I set my tumbling thoughts aside and made for the car. Danny got in the back despite my protests, and Diggs gave me a cryptic smile as he put the car in gear.

The sky was getting grayer, though it hadn't started raining yet. We'd been driving maybe ten minutes when I noticed Diggs checking the rearview again. We were on a rural road, only a few cars in any direction. It made it very easy to spot the dark blue sedan with tinted windows keeping pace a couple of cars back.

I fisted my hands in my lap. Idle thoughts about Diggs and me and our storied past faded, muscled aside by the bone-deep fear that had become a constant since Black Falls.

"We're being followed," I said.

He nodded, not even bothering to deny it. "I know," he said.

6
DIGGS

JUSTICE BAPTIST WAS A LITTLE WHITE CHURCH at the end of a short dirt drive on the outskirts of town. I knew as soon as we rounded the corner and the church was in sight that something was wrong. The parking lot was packed, the road lined with cars, and people had started parking in the field out back. I wasn't looking at them, though, my attention caught by a crowd gathered in a clearing across the road.

A cluster of a dozen men, women, and children stood at the church property line holding signs and chanting nonsense. Danny leaned toward the front seat, straining to see through the windshield.

"What's going on over there?" he asked.

"Go on in the church and get settled," I told Danny and Solomon. "I'll be right there."

The kid wouldn't be so easily dissuaded, his attention still fixed on the demonstrators. "Is that Reverend Barnel?" he demanded. He got out of the car before I could answer. Solomon and I tore after him as he strode toward the crowd. I caught up to him and grabbed his arm.

"Get in the church—you hear me? Now. I'll handle this."

"I don't need you to handle it." Danny tore his arm away. "I got it."

I could hear the chanting the closer we got. At the center of it all was Reverend Jesup T. Barnel. Even now, I felt the cold, bowel-clenching fear I'd known as a boy around him.

"The Lord is gathering his flock," he preached. "The end is upon us—judgment time is here, brothers and sisters. Wyatt Durham was found wantin'. How many more will the Lord smite before the fires consume this land of ours?"

Danny pushed through the onlookers. "What the hell are you doing here, old man?" he demanded. "You ain't got no right being within a hundred miles of this place. My daddy was a good man."

"Your daddy strayed," Barnel said. He was a barrel-chested old man who hadn't aged well, his face slack and his coloring a deep, unhealthy red. "And you know it full well, son. We're just here to warn anybody who comes near, just what we're facin' right now. Somebody put your daddy in the ground for the sins he done against the Almighty."

"Somebody oughta put you in the ground, you old bast—"

I grabbed Danny before all hell broke loose, and physically dragged him back to the church while Barnel shouted after us.

For the first time since I'd set down in Louisville, I felt myself slipping.

Between the two of us, Solomon and I managed to wrangle Danny into the church. Once he was inside, I walked away for a minute—away from Barnel and his flock, away from the church, up the road toward freedom. Solomon walked alongside, eyeing me with concern.

"I could beat that guy up for you if you'd like," she said. "The crazy old preacher, I mean. Juarez taught me some moves. I'm not saying I'd come out on top ultimately, but I'd probably give him a run for his money."

"Maybe later." I walked another few feet. A cold drizzle started, but I couldn't bring myself to go back. Solomon laid her hand on my arm. She gave me a solid smile. Rock steady when it really counts—that's my Solomon.

"You can do this, Diggs."

I nodded. My palms were damp, my suit too warm despite the chill in the air. "I know. No sweat, right?"

We turned around and headed back. The air smelled like damp earth and fresh rain. I thought of Wyatt and me, leaping streams and crashing parties as kids. Our freshman year, rooming together at Columbia, Wyatt left every party early to call Mae. I bitched him out all year long for passing up opportunities to sleep with the hot coeds throwing themselves at him.

I don't want whatever those girls are sellin'. I pictured him, always a head taller than anyone else in the room. Broad shouldered and powerful, with a sense of empathy that ran deeper than anyone I'd ever met. Women loved Wyatt. *They're too skinny. Anybody's that skinny, it's bound to make 'em mean. I don't want my girls mean. That's the difference between you and me.*

That's the only difference? I'd asked, grinning.

Well, that and I dress better. Other than that, we might as well be livin' in the same skin.

The pressure increased in my chest. Solomon bumped up against me as we walked. She wore a deep blue sundress that fell above her knees and made her green eyes shine. The cut showed off the new definition in her arms and calves, the physical manifestation of whatever transformation she'd been through in the six months since I'd seen her last. A transformation Juarez had been witness to; maybe was even partially responsible for.

She stumbled on the uneven terrain, and I held onto her elbow.

"Just a second," she said. She took off her heels and held them in one hand. "I never did get the hang of walking in these things."

"I don't think Wyatt would mind."

She glanced at me sadly. "No. I don't expect he would."

●

I sat in the front row beside Mae and the kids during the funeral. Wyatt's father never showed—not a surprise, really. I remembered him at his wife's funeral and in the days that followed: not a pretty sight. George was the kind of man who preferred to grieve in privacy. Solomon told me she'd find a seat on her own, insisting that I should be with the family. When I scanned the crowd, I spotted her sitting alone in the back. There's always been something solitary about Solomon, something strong and isolated and a little sad about her, as though she was set adrift at some point and has never quite found her way back to the world. I got that cold, unfurling pain in my chest again—like something was trying to break free, trapped by blood and muscle and bone. Ida, Wyatt's youngest, whispered to me. I leaned down to hear her. She took my hand in hers. It was warm and damp, her freckled face blotchy from crying.

"What's that, sweetheart?" I whispered.

"Daddy's glad you're here," she whispered back. "I know he's watchin'. He's glad you come back home to us."

"I'm glad I'm here, too," I lied. In a church. To a seven-year-old kid. If I believed in hell, I would have felt the flames licking at my feet.

The service wasn't long. There was a lot of praying, and a lot of singing, and a lot of crying. People snuck glances out the windows toward Barnel's demonstrators and there was plenty of angry whispering from those in the congregation, but otherwise the service was wrinkle-free. Toward the end, I stood, adjusted my tie, and smoothed out the eulogy Mae had asked me to write. I passed Wyatt's open coffin without looking inside. Somehow, I made it through the entire speech without breaking down, my gaze fixed on the double doors at the back of the church.

When I was finished, I got down from the pulpit and returned to my seat, wishing for a drink or a smoke or, more than anything, a line of white lightning to dull the pain and make everything a little brighter. Instead, I bowed my head while the congregation prayed one last time to a god I don't believe in, and then I joined the other pallbearers as we carried my childhood best friend to the hearse waiting outside.

Solomon joined me in the parking lot once the hearse was on its way. Her mascara was running, and I saw no sign of her shoes. Historically, Solomon didn't really do funerals; now I remembered why. I pulled her into my arms as much for myself as her, and held on tightly while she mumbled something unintelligible into my jacket. Her hair smelled of honeysuckle, and I was acutely aware of the warmth of her body and the curves pressed against me.

Eventually, she extricated herself. She rubbed her eyes and sniffled wetly. "God, I hate funerals."

"Well, you certainly handle them well."

"I was fine until you got up there. I'm officially booking you for my final farewell."

"If there's any order at all in the universe, I won't be around for that day," I said. She was trying to be light, I knew, but I couldn't summon a smile at the thought.

She hesitated, studying me now. "It really was beautiful, you know. Are you okay?"

"You have to stop asking me that. I'll let you know if I'm not—or, more likely, you'll be able to tell before I can." I glanced at her bare feet. "Didn't you have shoes when this thing started?"

She swore, earning a sour glance from the few stragglers who hadn't left for the interment, and darted back into the church to retrieve her heels.

Solomon was just out of sight when I spotted Reverend Barnel again, ambling toward me. He wore a double-breasted blazer too small for his girth, and he was surrounded by three oversized white guys in equally ill-fitting suits. Danny was already headed to the cemetery with the rest of the family, which meant there was no reason for me to play the rational adult any longer. I bridged the distance between us in a few strides, my anger flaring as soon as Barnel opened his fat mouth to speak.

I had no interest in listening.

Instead, I tried to plow through his entourage, ready to beat the sanctimonious snot out of him—regardless of his age. A guy built like a Frigidaire—Brother Jimmy, Barnel's son—pulled me back. Before I could get away, one of his buddies delivered an uppercut that would have knocked me on my ass if Jimmy hadn't been holding me up. My leg, still throbbing from the snake attack the night before, buckled beneath me.

"Settle down, boys," Barnel said.

His voice was the clear, rich tenor of a lifetime orator. He squinted at me over his glasses while Jimmy continued to hold my arms.

"Daniel," he said. "Daniel Diggins, isn't it? I never forget one of my boys, son. I hear you had an unfortunate encounter last night with some of my babies. Them snakes do get testy 'round nonbelievers."

I stopped struggling, and Barnel gave his son a nod. Jimmy let me go. It was all I needed. I might not be able to justify pummeling the old man himself, but there was no love lost between Jimmy and me—he was a worthy substitute. I wheeled on him and managed one solid blow to the jaw before his friend attacked. He caught me in the nose, hard, and I tasted blood and saw stars.

Buddy Holloway emerged from the church and shouted something I didn't catch, then grabbed me and held fast to my arms, pulling me back. The world had gone red, images I was powerless to stop rushing over me in fast-moving waves:

Wyatt on that first day we'd met, smoking a cigarette out behind Barnel's Redemption Hall; racing bikes and drinking beer and the sound of his laughter on hot summer nights. And then, the sight of him that same summer, strapped down while Barnel brandished a blazing hot steel cross. The sound of his screams, flesh sizzling when the reverend pressed the metal into his chest…

I fought harder, the reverend watching with a smug, holier-than-thou smile.

"Calm down, doggonit," Buddy said "Get him out of here!" he shouted to the reverend's men, who did their best to shepherd Barnel away.

"Now keep your shorts on," Barnel said smoothly. He met my eye. "That rage has to burn itself out sometime, son, or you're lookin' at an eternity in the fire."

"You think I don't know who did this?" I finally managed, my voice choked. Barnel didn't move, his eyes as hard as stones. "I don't know why, or how, but I know this all comes back to you. Wyatt's death; those snakes last night. And when I figure it out, you're going down. People will see you for the monster I always knew you were."

Barnel took a step closer to me, his yellow, cracked teeth bared in what could have been a smile or a snarl. He smelled like tobacco and sweat. "I'm havin' a service tonight, son. We're gonna save ourselves some souls, put the Holy Spirit back in this demon town. Your friend Wyatt strayed, and the Lord smote him—just as the Lord's gonna do anybody who don't see fit to cleanse themselves but quick. You watch yourself, boy, or it just might be your broken body folks are mournin' next."

"Is that a threat?" I asked.

He smiled more widely. "It's no such thing, brother. That there's just a promise. I hope to see you tonight, Daniel. I plan on savin' your soul before the end's upon us. And that end's comin' sooner than you might expect."

"That's enough, Reverend," Buddy said. "Why don't you go on now, see if you can't find somebody else to save."

"I reckon that's a fine idea," Barnel agreed. "Always a pleasure seein' you, Deputy."

He tipped his hat, and he and his goons made their exit.

When he was gone, Buddy handed me a handkerchief for my nose, now bleeding all over my shirt and tie.

"Sometimes I don't know what gets into you," he said. "You know Barnel ain't worth the energy. Nice to know you haven't changed none in five years, though." He looked at Solomon, who'd returned with her shoes at some point in the excitement. "You think you can get him cleaned up and cooled down?"

She nodded with no enthusiasm. "Yeah, of course. Thanks. I'll handle it."

The rest of the crowd left. I sat down on the front steps, Buddy's hanky pressed to my nose. Solomon shook her head.

"You're hopeless, you know that?" She sat down beside me. "I was gone two minutes—what the hell happened?"

I didn't answer. Her arm was warm against mine, but the rest of the world had gone cold.

"Can I ask you a question?" she asked finally, after the

silence had closed in around us. "And you give me a straight answer?"

I had a feeling I knew where she was headed, but I nodded anyway.

"That scar on your chest—the one you won't talk about? The one in exactly the same spot, exactly the same size, as Wyatt's scar... Did Barnel do that?"

She studied me as I thought about the question, waiting for the bleeding to stop and the throbbing in my nose and fist and chest to ease.

"My old man was desperate when he sent me down here," I said, finally. "I mean—obviously. How often does a mainstream Episcopal minister turn to backwoods Pentecostals for help?"

"It does seem a little out of character for Daddy Diggs," she noted.

"You didn't see him that year after my brother died," I said. "He read about Barnel, and I guess he figured, 'What the hell? What else are you gonna do when you're raising Cain?'"

"You didn't kill your brother," she said impatiently. "You skipped school and took him swimming when you were twelve. It's not like you knifed him, for Christ's sake. It was an accident, Diggs."

"My father doesn't believe in accidents."

"Yeah, well your father has his head up his ass. No offense." Her hand slid over mine, our fingers entwined. I fought the urge to pull back, the contact too much just then. I could feel her watching me. I didn't meet her eye as I continued.

"Be that as it may, he packed me up and sent me to Reverend Barnel's church camp. And the rest is history."

"Really crappy history," she said. "Part of it including a brand on your chest. Clearly, there's more to the story than that."

This is why sharing things with Solomon is a pain in the ass: she's not happy unless she's got all the gruesome facts. I shrugged. "The whole thing is hard to explain unless you're actually there to witness it. You'll see tonight. I don't want to ruin the full effect."

"We're really going to that? You think Barnel's just gonna welcome you back into the fold after your meltdown?"

"He will," I said. "I'm the one who got away—the one who never bought into all his bullshit. Trust me, he wants me back."

"Okay." She took a breath, considering all this. "So, we go to the revival tonight. And you don't try to kill anyone. That's a deal breaker for me, FYI. But in the meantime, we're supposed to be at the cemetery laying your oldest, dearest friend to rest, and you look like you came out on the wrong side in the UFC."

"I know. I'm a genius."

"You are. But luckily, you have me." She stood, pulled me to my feet, and we walked back to the car in silence. She got her suitcase from the trunk and riffled through while I stared out at the horizon. When she returned to my side, she had a blue button-up shirt in hand.

"Here."

I made no move to take it. "Is that Juarez's?"

If it was possible, she looked even more miserable about the situation than I was. "I spent the weekend in DC before I came out here—it got mixed up with my stuff. I'm sorry. Unless you want to wear one of my tank tops, this is all I have."

"No. That's fine." I took off my jacket, unbuttoned my shirt roughly, and pulled on her boyfriend's Oxford. "It's a little tight," I said. "You know what they say about a man with a small shirt."

She took my bloody clothes and tossed them into the

backseat. "Spare me. I'll try to date someone closer to your size next time."

"Good," I said with a nod. "See that you do."

7
DANNY

DANNY THOUGHT HE'D SUFFOCATE in the church. There were so many people—he'd never realized just how big his family was. It turned out family was the least of it, though, because then there was Barnel and his people out there hollering lies, and his daddy there in the casket, and Ida crying, and Mama trying to hold on even though her whole world might as well be over. He sat there beside Rick, both of 'em quiet, and he just kept repeating to himself: *Keep it together. It's almost over.*

But when it was over, it only got worse. Danny watched the preacher close the lid on his daddy's coffin, and it hit him like a running tackle in the end zone—just took his knees out from under him and knocked the breath right out of his lungs:

He was really gone.

Danny rode to the cemetery with the family, and he stayed with them while they lowered the coffin into the ground. He kept it together when his Mama wrapped her arms around him and held on, whispered in his ear, "You had your differences, but your daddy was so proud of you."

He just kept hanging on.

Finally, back at the house, he told Rick he was going out. "I've gotta practice. The band needs me."

Rick frowned. "Can't you give it a rest just one day? Mama doesn't want you takin' off—you should be here to look after things."

"I thought that's what you was here for," Danny said. "Trust me, they won't even know I'm gone."

"That's bull and you know it," he said, his back up now. Rick was a little smaller than Danny, but he was in better shape thanks to tennis and runnin' and whatever else kept him busy while Danny was out causing trouble. Back in the day, Danny could usually be sure he'd win in a fight. Now, that wasn't so likely. Win or lose didn't matter just then, though; Danny didn't have any interest in fighting.

Diggs showed up from around the corner, looking hangdog and tired. Danny had missed it when he went after Jesup Barnel, but it looked like Diggs got the worst of it: his nose was swollen and his lip was split, his right eye turning purple. Danny wished he'd been there to see it.

"Let him go," Diggs told Rick.

Rick turned on him, pissed. "But Mama said—"

"I'll smooth things over with Mae," Diggs said. "Just take it easy, Rick. Why don't you go take a breather yourself? It'll do you some good."

He walked off before Rick could make anymore fuss. Danny followed along behind as Diggs led him out the back door, into the backyard, and out behind the shed where Danny used to sneak smokes when he was still a kid.

"How're you doing?" Diggs asked.

Danny shook his head. He felt tears start, and it took everything in him to push them back down. Diggs stepped back a little, looking sad and sorry. He touched Danny's shoulder.

"You're gonna be okay," he said. "It sucks right now, but it'll get better."

"You sound like one of them commercials they're always playing at school. 'It gets better.'" He wiped his eyes and let out a long sigh. "Shit. I need a joint."

Diggs laughed dryly. "Tell me about it."

"You really think it's okay if I take off a while?"

"Yeah," Diggs nodded. "You've put in your time. Go. Don't do anything stupid: no drinking and driving; no smoking and driving. I'll tell your mom I said it was okay. She can take it out on me if it's not."

"I won't be late," Danny promised.

"If you end up doing too much or you need anything, call me," Diggs added. "Doesn't matter when, I'll come get you. No questions asked, no explanations needed. Got it?"

"Got it."

Diggs pulled him into a hug before he could get away, the older man hanging on tight. Danny choked on a sob he hadn't even known was in there. They stayed that way just a few seconds, a weight the size of a pickup settled on Danny's chest. When he pulled away, Diggs' eyes were wet, too. Danny swiped an arm across his eyes.

"Be good, Danny," Diggs said.

"Yes, sir," he said.

And then, he got moving before Diggs changed his mind and made him stay. Because right now, there was no way in hell he could do that and hold it together a second longer.

Danny's pickup was parked at the head of the road, a good two miles' walk away; Mama had said they needed to leave space for everybody else to park. He loosened his tie and took off his suitcoat, wishing he'd thought to change before he left. Still, he had some stuff in the truck that would be all right for now. It's not like he was looking to get in any trouble. All he wanted was some space. Sweats and a ripe t-shirt would do just fine for that. He picked up his pace to a jog, grateful for the fresh air and the quiet.

About a quarter of a mile from the truck, he heard something behind him—like a cough, maybe, but not a cough. Like somebody clearing their throat. He turned, fast, a shiver riding straight up his spine. This time, he knew Rick and Ida weren't there, because Diggs wouldn't've let them follow. Casey was working... He should be alone.

"Hey—anybody out there?" he called. He spun on his heel, searching the trees for a sign that someone was there. Not a soul.

He turned his back and set out for the truck again, but he couldn't shake that feeling that he wasn't alone. It was late afternoon, the shadows reaching far out from the trees. Everything was still. He rubbed his palms on his pants and started running again, wanting only to get to his truck and the weed waiting in his glove box.

By the time he got there, he was convinced he'd just been hearing things. He got out his keys, glancing around to make sure nobody saw him.

Stick to the main roads, he heard his daddy say. It was so clear, the old man might as well have been right beside him. Danny fought the urge to look around for him. *And wait till you get where you're goin' before you spark up. Your mama doesn't need you to get in a wreck now, of all things.*

"I know that, old man," he said out loud. He felt like a fool. Or like he'd gone crazy, standing here in the quiet talking to his daddy—a man he'd seen put in the ground not two hours ago.

He paused at the driver's side door, frowning. His truck was an '04 Toyota Tacoma—the single cab, not the double. It was big enough to haul his mower when he was doing yard work over the summers, and all his band gear the rest of the time. The truck had been beat to hell before he got it, but since then Danny'd treated that thing like it was his very own, overgrown, chrome-plated baby. He'd inventoried every scratch, every bump and dent and ding.

Which meant there was no question that what he was seeing now was brand new. Just above the door handle, keyed deep into his cherry red paint, something that made his overheated blood run ice cold:

An upside-down cross, maybe six inches long.

Get in the truck, his daddy said. Except he didn't say that, because he was dead. Still, Danny got in the truck. *Lock the doors.* Danny did. *Now go on back to the house and talk to Diggs. Show him what they done to the truck.*

Danny sat there in the driver's seat for a second, torn. He reached for the radio. Closed his eyes, his hands gripped tight around the steering wheel. His chest burned. Guns 'n Roses' "November Rain" came on. Danny put the truck in gear.

He pulled out, paused for a second by the long dirt road leading back to the house, and then shook his head.

He turned the music up louder, and drove away.

8
SOLOMON

BETWEEN WATCHING DIGGS try to hold it together at Wyatt's funeral, the street brawl after the funeral, and then being trapped in the Durham house with two dozen Christian conservatives for several hours, I'd had it by the time Diggs finally came to save me at nine o'clock that night. I was in the middle of a debate over climate change with Buddy Holloway and three other guys whose names I hadn't caught when Diggs appeared at my elbow. I was winning that debate, for the record.

"We should go," Diggs said.

"Your Yankee girlfriend's tryin' to school the locals," Buddy said. However flawed his opinion of global warming might be, I liked him: he had nice eyes, a strong laugh, and he had the southern gentleman thing down pat. Which, I'll admit, I've always been a sucker for.

Diggs didn't bother correcting him on our romantic status, for which I was grateful. Honestly, it was more trouble than it was worth. "Well, if anybody could set you hillbillies straight, she'd be the one," he said. "But we need to get going."

"Oh, listen to this boy," Buddy said, shaking his head. "Hillbilly my eye, you dang hippie. Where y'all off to, then?"

"Just taking a ride," Diggs said.

"Not out to Miller's Field, I hope," Buddy said. He watched for Diggs' reaction. "Not with Reverend Barnel's tent meetin' set to go up at ten sharp. Seeing as how you already had one run-in with him today, you might oughta steer clear awhile."

"I'll take that under advisement," Diggs said.

Buddy frowned, but he didn't say anything more until Diggs was already headed out the door. Then, he pushed his business card into my hand. He nodded toward our mutual friend, now burning a path toward the car.

"You call me if he steps in anything, you hear? He's as much family as Wyatt was, and he can't see straight where that preacher's concerned. I don't care what time it is. Just pick up the phone and I'll be there."

"Thanks," I said sincerely. "I may take you up on that."

"You do that, darlin'. I'll be right here if you need me."

●

The tent meeting was held in a muddy field on the side of a long dirt road. We were flanked by cows on one side and a dank, muddy pond on the other, which Diggs told me Barnel baptized people in when the occasion arose. It didn't look that sanitary, but I was guessing that wasn't a priority.

I'd just assumed Barnel was one of those fringe extremists with a dozen misguided souls who'd follow him to the ends of the earth, but when we got there the place was packed. Cars lined both sides of the road all the way in, with more parked in the field. Old folks and young folks and Bible-toting babies all made their way up the hillside to Barnel's giant white tent. I was surprised at the teen contingent: at least two dozen freshly scrubbed college guys in jackets and ties, standing off to the side with their feet planted shoulder width apart, hands clasped behind their backs like career military men instead of frat boys who couldn't even buy their own beer.

There were a few people like Diggs and me, just there to check out the spectacle, but I got the sense we were in the minority.

Barnel's tent was a deluxe—I didn't even know you could get a tent that big. It was powered by a generator situated behind the stage. Speakers bigger than Barnel himself flanked the makeshift platform, and aisle upon aisle of folding metal chairs filled the space. It was a cold, damp evening, but the masses in the tent generated enough heat to more than make up for that. There was a table with refreshments: breads and cakes and cookies, soda and juice, a couple of industrial-sized tubs of potato salad. Apparently, Barnel was big on carb loading. I put a dollar in the jar of a little girl with a dress buttoned from her throat to her ankles, and helped myself to a cup of chocolate pudding and a spoon.

Diggs gave me the hairy eyeball.

"What? It's chocolate."

He just shook his head at me, like I was a lost cause. Which I may have been, but I didn't care. If there was ever a situation that merited chocolate, this was definitely it.

By the time we found a seat, the reverend's opening act had already started: a kid named Toby and his parents, playing guitar and singing hymns. I gathered from the reaction of the crowd that the family was a headliner around these parts, but they didn't do a lot for me. Within two minutes of a countrified version of "Go Tell It On the Mountain," I was ready to stab little Toby in the eye with my plastic spoon. All around us, hands went up in the air, people whispering prayers or shouting "Hallelujah" over the music.

Everyone got to their feet when Toby and his kin started up with a medley of country hymns I didn't recognize from my own church-going days. I set my empty cup under my chair and stood with Diggs. A wall of bodies closed in on all sides, the smell of sweat and Avon perfume obliterating the last remnants of my chocolate high.

I fought to maintain my good humor. The music faded to white noise. My breath came harder, locked in my chest as people pushed ever-closer, their energy like a dentist's drill tunneling into the base of my spine. I had an unexpected flashback to the Payson Church—the religious community where I spent the first ten years of my life. I was sitting in the converted hay barn that served as the Payson chapel while the preacher gave his sermon. Suddenly, I was right there, with Isaac Payson in front of me and my father's hand tight in mine. A woman was crying.

Past and present merged. I couldn't move. Couldn't breathe. Another image replaced the one I'd just seen—this one of my father on his knees in front of the congregation. He was shirtless, stripes of blood flowing down his back. A woman was holding me back as I fought to get to him.

"Erin!" Diggs whispered to me. I jolted back to the present, sweat rolling down my forehead. "We can sit," he said when he had my attention. Most of the rest of the crowd were already in their chairs. Diggs and I stood alone. I nodded, shaken, trying to pull myself back to the present.

As soon as Barnel took the stage, the energy changed. The crowd fell silent. A chill raced up my spine when he raised his hands to the sky.

"The time has come, my friends. I know you're here tonight for hope. You're waitin' on me to tell you that there's still time for you to save your kin, to change your ways, to do all the things you been promisin' the Lord you'd do all these years. But tonight I don't have a message of hope. If you ain't with us now, friends, you gotta get with the Lord this second. Now. There's no more waitin' on Him to come…"

Barnel mopped his sweating brow with the back of his arm. His face was flushed. A baby cried in the back, but otherwise the tent was quiet. Barnel grabbed his mic and took a couple of steps toward the congregation, leaving his pulpit.

"Jesus Christ himself spoke to me this week, brothers and sisters. Clear as day. Clear as I'm talkin' to you here and now. And he told me that I am the bringer of light. That's right—you heard me. He said, 'Jesup T. Barnel, it's up to you now. You gotta get this ball rollin'.'"

I looked at Diggs, who just shook his head like the whole scene was beyond nuts. His composure made me feel marginally better; the rest of the crowd was freaking the crap out of me.

"The clock is tickin', brothers and sisters. Forty-eight hours: that's all you got. At midnight this very night—just thirty minutes from right now—a series of events will start up to bring you to your very knees, right here in Justice. I don't know what they'll be, but I know it's my job to see us through as best I can. Which is why after tonight, the Lord has told me it's time for me to leave y'all for a little while." There was a collective gasp from the crowd. A woman started crying.

"Don't y'all worry none, though. We're gonna be reunited on them golden shores. And my soldiers are right here. They know their place—I've passed the Lord's message on to them, and they know what they've gotta do. And you know what you've gotta do."

Based on the way everyone seemed to be holding their breath at once, I was guessing I wasn't the only one who wasn't totally clear on that, actually.

"You've gotta repent," Barnel finally clarified. "You've gotta hole up, protect your loved ones, and get down on your knees and pray to almighty God. Those standin' with me know what's what: they know who's not worthy. Orders have been given from on high, and there will be those in this town—those among you this very night—who will be taken. And forty-eight hours from now, the final cleansing will be done. And those still standing will be taken to the Kingdom of the Lord, to live with Him for all eternity. Let me hear you say, 'Amen.'"

A chorus of "amen"s rose up around us. Diggs looked at me, then back at the man on the pulpit. Barnel raised his hands, and everyone fell silent once more.

"Are you on the right side, brothers and sisters? When He passes judgment, will you be found wantin'… Or will you set at his right hand?"

People were starting to freak out. It's all well and good to know that Armageddon's headed your way at some unappointed date in the near or distant future. It's something else entirely when a crazy old preacher with a branding iron tells you the end times are kicking off at midnight, so you best be ready.

"I think we should get out of here," Diggs whispered to me. "I'm not getting a great vibe."

Didn't have to tell me twice. The "amen"s and "hallelujah"s reached a crescendo as Diggs and I made for the exit, doing our best not to attract undue attention. As it was, we were almost home free when Barnel called after us.

"You run, Daniel Diggins—you know which side you done landed on. You run as far as you can, but you can't outrun the Lord. He's comin' for you."

Diggs turned back around to face the preacher. Their eyes held, and I wondered for the eighteenth time since arriving in Kentucky just exactly what in hell had happened between them. An old woman in an ankle-length green dress started singing "I'll Fly Away." Others joined in.

Diggs took a step toward Barnel.

Before he could get any farther, a sound like the cracking of a whip shattered the night. Someone screamed. Barnel's eyes widened. A starburst of blood blossomed on his left shoulder as he fell to his knees. The big guy who'd been guarding him earlier—Brother Jimmy—dove in front of him just as a second shot rang out, hitting the younger man squarely in the chest.

There was more screaming, even as the old woman who'd first begun resumed her song. People fled in all directions, their screams echoing through the night. Still, the old woman sang. Another woman joined in. Diggs grabbed my arm and pulled me out of the way before we were both trampled. My heart slammed against my ribcage.

Once we were outside, I saw a red pickup that had been parked behind the tent tear across the field, spitting mud from under the tires as the driver raced for the open road. The rain came down in sheets. A couple of teenage girls in the requisite neck-to-ankle dresses ran past us. Diggs called after them.

"Did you see who did it?" he asked.

They were both crying, eyes wide, when they turned to answer. "No way to tell—crowd was too big, and everybody up and panicked soon as the reverend went down. The devil hisself could've been in there, you wouldn't see him."

•

Within half an hour of the shooting, the cops descended—flashing lights, screaming sirens. A cold rain continued to fall, the sound of the faithful few still singing hymns clear in the distance. I could tell Diggs was torn as to whether we should stay or go, but ultimately I think curiosity won out. We walked back up to the tent as Sheriff Jennings himself arrived with Deputy Buddy on his heels.

A pudgy guy in glasses knelt by Brother Jimmy's lifeless body—the coroner, I assumed. A paramedic tended to Barnel's shoulder while he prayed with a slew of his followers. Buddy Holloway strung up crime-scene tape and pushed everyone—including Reverend Barnel—back to the other side of the tent with the order that we were all to stay put until we'd left our names and contact numbers. Diggs and I chose a couple of folding chairs in the back, and waited.

Before the sheriff could begin questioning anyone, Barnel called him over. They had a whispered confab, and then I watched as the reverend shuffled off into the night with the rest of his entourage, without so much as a backward glance.

I thought of Barnel's proclamation earlier about not being around for a while. It seemed to me that, if we really were facing the end times, it might be a good idea to keep tabs on him more closely than the sheriff seemed inclined.

With Reverend Barnel now out of the way, Sheriff Jennings turned his attention to the crowd.

For some reason, when Diggs had described the sheriff the night before, I'd pictured someone...older. And smaller. Someone vaguely inept, soft around the middle, with a poorly fitted uniform and not much going on upstairs. Barney Fife with a sheriff's star. Instead, Harvey Jennings was Diggs' age, and he was the closest thing I'd ever seen to a real-life Marlboro Man—minus the Stetson hat. His uniform was pressed, his hat perfectly centered, his boots shined, his jaw square. He had a full-on Burt Reynolds moustache, and stood about six foot two. If there was anything soft about him, I sure as hell wasn't seeing it.

"Now," Jennings began, addressing the crowd. "I

want y'all to try and stay calm. A tragedy's happened here tonight—we all know that. But you can rest easy knowing I won't stop till I find the evildoers that targeted the reverend and took Brother Jimmy from us."

I looked at Diggs, who stayed focused on Jennings, tensed and waiting.

"I got some more deputies on their way here," Jennings continued, "and they're gonna ask you what you seen. I just want everybody to think good and hard on that. If there was a vehicle of any kind drivin' away from the scene—a truck, maybe?"

He waited, leaving the question open.

"What the hell's he doing?" I whispered to Diggs, as one of the teenage girls we'd seen earlier piped up.

"There was a red truck!" she said.

"A Tacoma," a man shouted. At a nod from Jennings, Buddy wrote it down.

Diggs tensed beside me. "Why don't you just tell us what you want to hear, Harvey?" he asked. "You give us a description, we can just smile and nod."

Jennings strode toward us too fast, his eyes boring through Diggs. "You got something you wanna say to me, Diggins?"

Diggs didn't move, gazing up at Jennings with a slow, cold smile. "I heard you found Jesus, Harvey," he said. "I'll be sure and tell Sarah the next time I talk to her."

Jennings went full-on puce. Buddy grabbed his arm. "We got something," he said to the sheriff, lowering his voice—though not enough that I couldn't make out that they'd found the murder weapon, discarded out in the field. Jennings returned to us before he and Buddy left for whatever their next move was.

"You seen your nephew here tonight?" Jennings asked.

"No," Diggs said shortly.

"I heard tell y'all fought with the reverend today. Out to Wyatt's funeral."

"Danny didn't have anything to do with that," Diggs said. "That was all me."

"That boy's got a temper," Jennings said. "Everybody in town knows it. More than one person heard him threaten the reverend today. I got a mind to go on out there myself right now and see what he's been up to tonight."

Diggs stood. He was a good two inches shorter than Jennings, but he was broader, and based on what I'd glimpsed when he'd taken his shirt off this afternoon, he hadn't been idle these past six months: he had muscles on his muscles, his chest and arms more defined than I'd ever seen. It seemed I wasn't the only one preparing for battle while we'd been apart. Bottom line? I wouldn't bet against him if it came down to a fight between him and Jennings.

"Mae buried her husband today," Diggs said. "Half the vehicles on the road here are red trucks—you go out there tonight without reasonable cause and I'll make it my life's work to pry that badge out of your cold dead hand."

A vein throbbed in Jennings' forehead. "A great man was gunned down like a dog tonight. I don't care who they buried today—if Danny had somethin' to do with this, I'm taking that boy down. You just stay out of my way and let me do my job."

"I might if you had the first clue how to do it—"

Buddy called the sheriff again, abruptly ending the pissing contest between him and Diggs. When Jennings was gone, Diggs sat back down. His body was humming, anger coming off him in waves.

I shook my head. "I never thought I'd be the one telling you this, but your interpersonal skills could use some work."

"Bite me."

"I rest my case."

●

When we got to the car, Diggs blasted the heat and pointed us back toward the Durham homestead. He hadn't spoken since we'd left Jennings at the tent.

"You don't think Danny had anything to do with this, do you?" I finally asked, breaking the silence.

"Of course not. Jennings was just trying to piss me off—he knew that would do the trick. Every idiot and their brother has a red truck around here. Trust me, that's the last thing I'm worried about right now."

I let it go. There was still a long line of cars parked along the side of the road, barely visible in the darkness. In the rearview, I saw one of them pull out just seconds after we had. It U-turned after us and was soon no more than a car length behind.

As we passed by the flashing lights, I checked behind us again. My heart sank like a stone. The same dark blue sedan I'd spotted on the way to the funeral was back.

Diggs caught my reaction, glancing behind us at the same time.

I thought once more of the scenes I'd flashed back to when we were in the tent: baptisms and prayer meetings, my father on his knees, women crying, a child screaming… All of it part of the Payson Church and the mystery of my own past. My theory had been that the Paysons were innocent victims, murdered for reasons I still didn't understand by a nameless man in a hooded cloak who visited my darkest dreams on a nightly basis—a man I'd hoped to see the last of when I told him I'd stop asking questions if he would just let Diggs live.

I'd known then that it was too easy. He'd be back.

"Do you think it's him?" I asked.

Diggs didn't answer, but I had no doubt he knew exactly who I was talking about. I waited for him to hit the accelerator—to keep moving, as fast and as far as we could go.

"I don't know," he said.

"I think you're a liar," I said. "He's the one who's been following us since we got here, and you know it. With you and me here together, he thinks I'm digging into my father's past again…"

I hated the weakness in my voice—that little shred of panic I couldn't shake. My entire life, I'd been fearless, willing to take on anyone, anything, for the truth. For the sake of the almighty story. That had changed last summer, with Diggs by my side while we ran for our lives. I felt the same cold dread that had all but paralyzed me for the first two months out of the hospital after our escape.

"It might not be him," Diggs said. He'd never sounded less convincing.

He drove for another two minutes before he glanced at me, muttered "Screw it" under his breath, and slowed down. The car behind us got closer.

"What the hell are you doing?"

His eyes were steady on the road. "If it's him, I'm not running. And neither are you. I'm done." He hit the brake, hard, and jerked the wheel to the left.

Whoever was following barely avoided hitting us.

Diggs got out and slammed the door, striding toward our pursuer. If I hadn't been so pissed, I would have been terrified. As it was, though, Diggs seemed to have annoyed the fear right out of me. I bolted from the car and ran after him.

A man stood outside the driver's side when we got there,

waiting for us. He wore blue jeans and a yellow rain slicker. His hood was up, but rain still tracked down his thin face. I recognized him immediately—the same man who had chased me on a burning island when I was ten years old. The same man who had saved Diggs' and my life the summer before. The man who threatened to murder Diggs, if I ever asked another question about my father's past.

The man from my nightmares.

He smiled when he saw me. We stood close enough that I could see details I'd never noticed before: blue eyes; laugh lines; a scar above his left eyebrow. He didn't look like a man who'd killed men, women, and children in droves over the years.

"We meet again, Ms. Solomon," he said pleasantly.

"What are you doing here?" I asked. "This thing with Barnel—"

"Is quite a spectacle, isn't it?" he said. "But I'm more interested in the reunion between you and Mr. Diggins at the moment. Heartwarming, you two together again. I also wanted to remind you of our terms, lest you've forgotten."

"You didn't need to do that," I said. My mouth had gone dry. "I haven't told anyone what happened last summer. I gave up looking for my father. Trust me, I remember the terms."

"Do you?" he asked, looking directly at Diggs. "Because I feel as though I was very fair. Very clear. There won't be another pass like the one I gave you in Black Falls. We can't allow that."

"We haven't done anything," I insisted, fighting a surge of temper. "I haven't even seen him in six months, for Christ's sake. And when the funeral's over, we'll go our separate ways again. He's not a threat. Neither of us is."

The man looked at me. For a second, it seemed there was genuine sadness in his eyes. "I do hope that's true."

We were still in the road, in the rain, in the middle of the night. The hooded man surveyed the scene before he turned his attention back to me.

"I should be going. But if you don't mind a friendly word of advice: This isn't a good place to be right now. Jesup Barnel had some...unusual ideas about the world. He's set some things in motion that won't be good for this town. Or anyone in it."

He started to walk away. I've never been one to run for a fight, but this one time, I was okay with letting him go. Backing off. Anything to avoid a repeat of the horror show Diggs and I had barely survived the summer before.

Diggs wasn't as amenable, unfortunately.

The hooded man managed maybe three steps before Diggs caught hold of his arm.

"You think you hold all the cards right now," he said, "but that won't always be true. This isn't over."

The man stared at him coolly, his eyes locked on the spot on his arm where Diggs' hand rested. And then, in a fast-forward blur usually reserved for superheroes or sparkly vampires, the man took Diggs' wrist and twisted, forcing him to his knees.

"I hope you're wrong about that," the man said. He stood above Diggs, his eyes suddenly dark. "I truly do."

He let Diggs go without another word, got into his car, backed up, and drove away.

I was too pissed to speak when we got back in the car. Diggs glanced at me.

"You should call Juarez and see if he can use his resources to get some info on that blue sedan. I've got the plate number."

"Isn't that the exact opposite of what we're supposed to be doing?" I asked. My voice was tight, but it was nothing compared with the way my body felt. "Maybe you didn't get what he was telling us."

"No," Diggs said, his own voice just as tight. "I was the one on my knees, remember? Trust me, I got it. How much have you told Juarez about what went down last summer?"

I stared out the window. I was caught back in the woods of Maine again—standing at the lip of a cave while Diggs lay down below, bleeding, a lunatic standing over him with a very big knife.

"I never told him anything," I said. "They'll go after him if I do. You already know everything—the best I could do for you was walk away. The best I can do for anyone else is keep my mouth shut."

"Sounds like you've got it all worked out, then," Diggs said. There was no mistaking the bitterness in his tone. I chose to ignore it.

He glanced at me periodically during the rest of the drive, his forehead furrowed with concern or frustration or outright anger. I paid very little attention, too busy checking behind us for some sign that my worst nightmare was about to come true.

It was two a.m. by the time we got back to the Durhams' that night. Contrary to Sheriff Jennings' threat, there was no sign that the cops had been there. According to Barnel's prophecy, Armageddon should be in full swing by this time, but so far things looked pretty peaceful. The porch light was on, the rest of the house dark. Einstein and his pack of hounds greeted us with a few half-hearted woofs, but thankfully no lights came on inside. Diggs followed me into the house. It was quiet. Hard to believe upwards of thirty people had been crammed in the place just a few hours before for Wyatt's wake.

I went upstairs to my attic hideaway with Einstein by my side, anxious for some space and a little time to think. Diggs retired to his room—I assumed for the night. When I got to my door, however, he was back. This time, he had his duffel bag with him.

"What are you doing?"

"I don't want to wake the boys up," Diggs said. "And I need to talk to you."

"Isn't that what we've been doing for the past twenty-four hours?"

He made a face at me and pushed the door open, nudging me inside. Once we were in, I sat on the end of the bed, on the alert once more. The room was small—barely big enough for the double bed and a bureau. Diggs paced the three feet or so of space half a dozen times before I snapped.

"Diggs, seriously? Spit it out, or get the hell out so we can both get some sleep."

Abruptly, he set his bag on the bed, unzipped it, and pulled out a file. He tossed it on the bed beside me.

"What's this?" I asked.

"You don't run," he said shortly. I picked up the file, completely confused.

"What?"

"You don't run. You never run. You fight. You get answers, or you die trying. You don't just sit back and let some nameless monster take over your life."

I opened the file. My hands were shaking. "What did you do?" I asked hoarsely. I already knew, though. I knew exactly what he'd done.

There in front of me, keen eyes staring up, was a sketch of the hooded man. The angel of death. My nightmare, come to life. And beneath it, in bold letters, was a name.

9
DIGGS

THE ATTIC BEDROOM where Solomon was staying used to belong to Ashley, when we were still kids. I remembered sneaking in there one summer night when I was staying with Wyatt, sure she'd secretly been up waiting for me to come along. It hadn't worked out that way, though: She'd screamed bloody murder, and Wyatt's father sent me packing early that summer. It would have saved everyone a lot of heartache if I'd just seen the writing on the wall that night.

The room seemed smaller now. My heart was pounding and my palms were sweating, and the bedroom ceiling was so damn low I could barely stand up straight. My leg hurt like hell, as did my jaw. I had a headache, too, but none of that held a candle to the beating my ego had taken in the past twenty-four hours.

Solomon looked at the sketch I'd handed her, then back at me.

"What did you do, damn it?" she asked a second time.

I swallowed hard and wet my lips, nodding toward the file. "His name is Mitch Cameron. I had a friend of mine do a composite sketch based on my description, then I put his face through every database I could think of until something came back."

She closed the file. When she looked at me, her eyes were burning. I've been on the receiving end of Solomon's wrath more than once—the truth is, it's kind of a turn on. But not this time. Anger is one thing, fear another entirely. And Solomon was positively terrified.

"Where the hell do you get the right?" she hissed at me. "I asked you—"

"No," I said. My voice was raw. "You told me—late one night when you could barely breathe, a month after Cameron held the gun to my head, you called and told me not to look into it. You never asked. You never talked to me about any of this shit. And by then it was too late, anyway— I'd already started."

She ran her hand through her hair, turning her back to me. "And now, he knows," she whispered. She shook her head. "That's why he's here—he knows you've been looking."

"I don't think so. I covered my tracks," I said. "The very model of the modern paranoiac. I swept for bugs, used burner phones, tapped only my most trusted sources. He's here because we're together, just like he said—that's it. He would've just killed me otherwise. He's just making sure we stay scared."

She laughed. The sound was a hollow echo of the one I knew. "Well, mission accomplished. Goddammit, Diggs." She wheeled on me. "Why couldn't you just leave it alone?"

"Because this isn't you," I said. "You can't let this bastard break you like this. Your father's out there. A killer is out there, and they've waged a friggin' war. And you're letting them get away with it."

She looked me in the eye, her chin tipped up, her jaw hard. She pushed me lightly in the stomach, her anger mounting again. "You're the one who begged me—the one who tried to drive us in the opposite direction of all the trouble back in Maine, all the while telling me it was all too dangerous. We sat in that cave and you ran me up one side and down the other for being so selfish. You said I needed to back off, and I did. So why now—"

"Because I won't lose you over this," I shouted. The words felt like they'd been wrenched from somewhere deep; somewhere I was powerless to cap. Solomon looked at me with those brilliant green eyes, and I could smell her shampoo and the cinnamon on her breath and the fear that rolled off her in waves. "If you don't want me, that's one thing," I said. It was too late to go back now. "I'll handle it. I'll let it go. Wish you and Juarez the best. But I'm not saying goodbye with the lame friggin' excuse that you're being noble; that you have to walk away to save my life."

"So this is your ego?" she asked, incredulous. "You're gonna get us all killed because of your goddamn male pride? Juarez and I talked about this. He agrees—it's time for me to let this go."

"Juarez doesn't remember the first thirteen years of his life. And he's fine with it. I don't care how much time you spend with the guy, kid, you're never gonna be that zen."

She pushed me again, harder this time. For the first time, fury outweighed the fear in her eyes. "Fuck you."

"Nice comeback."

"Juarez is a good guy," she said. She advanced on me, pushing me toward the wall. "He's nice, and he's stable, and he's not tortured by every freaking mistake he ever made. He—"

My blood was boiling, and I knew she was just getting warmed up. There were things I could say, arguments I could make, but words had never seemed so pointless before. And so I grabbed her—one hand at her side, the other at the back of her neck—and pulled her to me. My mouth crashed down on hers. She fought me for a second, no more, before she fisted her hands in the front of my shirt, her body moving against mine.

I pushed her back against the wall, my tongue pressing past her lips, and for three miraculous seconds, she gave as good as she got: her teeth nipping at my lower lip, her hips pressed to mine. And then, she came to herself. Her hands flattened on my chest and she pushed me away so hard I stumbled. Her eyes were wide. We stood there, silent, our breathing ragged, for another quarter of a second before her hand came up. I caught her just before her palm made contact with my cheek.

"No hitting," I said. "It's bad form."

She lowered her hand. Pushed me one more time, hard, and grabbed her bag. "Drop it, Diggs," she said again. "All of it. Get on with your life. But do it without me."

She left.

●

Solomon slept in the car that night. Because I was feeling spiteful, I let her—something Jack Juarez sure as hell never would have done. In the morning, I brought her a cup of coffee. It was cold outside, a dismal gray dawn just breaking on the horizon. Solomon was cocooned in her sleeping bag in the backseat with Einstein, wearing half her wardrobe and a purple ski cap. She hid her head when I opened the driver's side door and got in.

"Go away," she said. Her voice had that whiskey rasp to it that I love about Solomon in the morning.

"Good news: we've kept the Four Horsemen at bay another day. And I brought you coffee."

"I don't care." She burrowed more deeply into the sleeping bag. "I'm not speaking to you."

"Because of Mitch Cameron, or because of the kiss? Or because you liked the kiss?"

She sat up. Einstein scrambled out of her arms. She opened the door and let him out, then closed it again and pulled the sleeping bag up around her. I looked at her in the rearview mirror, blinking in the harsh light of day.

"We're not talking about the kiss, all right? The kiss didn't happen. I'm with Juarez—you know that. I'm sorry, but that's just the way it is."

"Well, it's hard to argue with that logic. Let's just pretend it's not there and maybe it'll go away. I don't know why I didn't think of that before."

"You spent the first fifteen years we knew each other pretending it wasn't there, you asshole," she said, the fire back in her eyes. "You should be pretty good at it by now."

Touché. "All right, fine. I didn't kiss you last night. You didn't kiss me back. What about Mitch Cameron? Are we pretending he doesn't exist, either?"

She rubbed her forehead. I'd seen Solomon exhausted before, after days of not sleeping and emotional turmoil and serial killers…but I'd never seen her this bone weary before. "I don't know. That was the plan."

"Come on, Solomon. Were you really planning on going through life calling him 'the hooded man'? 'The guy in the cloak'? He has a name. A past."

She took the coffee from me. "Let's just drop it for right now, okay? Put a pin in it." It was clear she'd spent the better part of the night coming up with that. "Can we focus on one mystery at a time? I'd still like to figure out what the hell happened to Wyatt—and what Jesup Barnel had to do with it. Or is that no longer a priority?"

"It is. But I'm not giving up on Cameron," I said. "Whatever happens between you and me, someone still needs to bring him down."

"Diggs." I turned to face her. She studied me for a few seconds, the pain in her eyes palpable. Her voice quieted. "Do you know how much blood I've got on my hands? Matt Perkins; Joe and Rebecca Ashmont... Max Richards. Will Rainier. And I still don't know how much the fire on Payson Isle had to do with my father... But clearly this guy—Cameron—wiping the Payson congregation out had something to do with my dad."

"None of that's because of you," I said. "You didn't pull the trigger, for Christ's sake."

"But if I'd gotten the cops involved sooner, or I hadn't pushed so hard, or I'd warned someone..." she said. She shook her head stubbornly. "I'm not asking for absolution here. I'm telling you: I'm done. I won't watch him kill you, knowing I could have done something. I won't lose you."

You already have was on the tip of my tongue, but I held back. Instead, I took a deep breath and nodded.

"All right. We put a pin in it—for now. And we move onto Wyatt, and Jesup Barnel."

"Thank you."

It wasn't hard to make the transition from one case to the other: I'd been thinking about Wyatt and Barnel all night. When I wasn't thinking about Solomon, of course.

"Do you think Barnel did it?" she asked me. "Do you think he's the one who killed Wyatt?"

Before I could answer, Mae came flying out of the house with Rick on her heels. She headed for the car as soon as she realized I was inside, and I rolled down the window.

"Have you seen Danny?" she demanded.

"What do you mean?" I asked.

"Danny," she repeated. "He didn't come home last night."

I got out of the car. Solomon followed suit. "He buried

his father yesterday, Mae," I said. "I'm sure he's just taking a break. Trying to get some perspective." Or, more likely, he was just too stoned to move.

Mae looked at Rick.

"That's what I told her," the kid said. He was the polar opposite of Danny: buttoned up and put together, his blond hair cut short, his smile straight and pearly white.

"You know how he gets," Rick continued. "He said he didn't wanna go back to school yet. Maybe he's just takin' the day."

"He could be out with friends," Solomon suggested. "Or a girl, maybe?"

"Sure," Rick said easily. "Could be." I noticed that he wasn't looking at Mae, which told me he probably had a better idea than he was letting on as to where Danny had gone. I wasn't ready to call in the National Guard, regardless. I'd been a teenage boy, after all—one not unlike Danny. A kid like that… Things get to be too much, sometimes you just need some space.

"What about George's place?" I asked. "Have you dropped in there? It could be he's just bonding with the old man."

"George left town last night," Mae said. "He went on up to the mountains. Said he just needed some time."

"Now?" I said in surprise. "It seems like that could have waited a few days…"

"You know him," she said. "He puts on a good show, but he's takin' this pretty hard. Just needs to get his feet back under him is all. Anyway, I dropped by his place this morning to feed the rabbits. Danny wasn't there." A tinge of hysteria crept into her voice.

"Rick, why don't you go in and get yourself some breakfast?" I said. "Give your mom and me a chance to talk. Everything'll be fine, though. Danny will show up in no time, and you'll be laughing about this by supper. You'll see."

Rick looked at his mother. She nodded. He went inside wordlessly, leaving Solomon and me alone with Mae. Before I could reassure her, Mae looked at me with wide eyes, her hands clenched.

"There's something else," she said in a whisper. Mae's usually the coolest person in the room. Today, she looked ready to climb out of her skin.

"What?" I asked.

She wet her lips, her eyes sliding from mine. "Buddy told me about Wyatt's cross—what got done to him, how they turned it upside down and all. He said he saw it before, too, back when Marty Reynolds got killed in '02. He said maybe that's why they took Wyatt." I wasn't making the connection between this and Danny. Her tears overflowed, spilling down her cheeks. "Diggs, Danny's got the mark."

My stomach turned. "What are you talking about?"

"Reverend Barnel's cross. Danny has it."

Rage came before the fear—white hot and boiling over, catching me completely off guard. I fought to control it. Solomon touched my arm before I could speak. I held my tongue.

"When did he get it?" Solomon asked.

"Two summers ago," Mae said. "He was acting up: partying, drinking." She looked at me, eyes pleading. "I know what that night with Reverend Barnel was for you— Wyatt told me what the reverend did. How bad it got. It was different for Wy, though; it put him on the right path. Set him straight. We figured maybe it was just what Danny needed."

I walked away, afraid I'd explode if I didn't.

I thought of that night more than twenty-five years ago: The feel of leather straps cutting into my wrists and ankles, strapped in before a crowd that just sat there, watching me writhe. Strangers' hands on me. Bright lights. Sweat dripping from Barnel's face onto my naked chest. *Repent, Daniel. Beg the Lord's forgiveness for spilling your brother's blood. Turn your back on the devil. It's the only way to get back to the light.*

Solomon pulled me back to the present, her hand once more on my arm. Mae was nowhere in sight.

"You're freaking out," she said. You can't get anything past Solomon.

"You don't think I have reason to?"

"Are you kidding? I think anyone who tries to straighten out their kid by sending him to a guy like Barnel is batshit crazy. Haven't any of these people heard of Outward Bound? Jesus. But the horse is kind of out of the gate now… It's done. And maybe you've forgotten this, but someone was out taking potshots at the reverend last night."

"Danny didn't have anything to do with that," I said.

She didn't look convinced. "Why don't we just focus on finding him first, then we can get the rest figured out."

"I still say he's probably just off somewhere, blowing off some steam."

"Could be," she agreed.

"But you don't think so."

She looked at me. "Do you? Really?"

I shook my head slowly. "I hope so. But I wouldn't bet the farm on it."

10
SOLOMON

SINCE IT WAS A SCHOOL DAY, it was easier than it might have been otherwise to do a blanket survey of Danny's friends to see if anyone knew where he could be. Mae went over to the school and met with a couple of teachers, who in turn spoke with the students. The last time anyone had seen Danny was at the local Dairy Queen the night before. No one had heard anything from him since then. Or, if they had, they weren't volunteering that information.

The pall already over the Durham house was getting darker by the second; I wasn't sure how much more Mae could take. I didn't even want to think about what would happen to her—to all of them—if Danny met the same fate his father had.

At just past noon that day, Einstein and I went up to my room only to find Diggs sitting on the bed with the *Justice Daily News* and his laptop. My neck was stiff and my back ached and my ass hurt. Once you pass thirty, apparently sleeping in a car has the same effect on the body as being run over by one. Diggs eyeballed me as I sat down at the edge of the bed.

"You okay?" he asked.

"No, as a matter of fact. I think my spine's dislocated, thanks to you."

"I didn't make you sleep in the car. You could've come in anytime."

"That kind of would have killed my point, don't you think? Anyway, I thought we weren't supposed to be sharing a room. What happened to bunking with the boys?"

"It smells like a locker room in there. And Rick's depressing the hell out of me. All that kid does is read the Bible and stare out the window. It's creepy." He scooted over to one side of the bed, nodding to the other. "Just sleep—I'll be quiet. And I promise not to grope you unnecessarily while you're out, if that's what you're worried about."

I didn't have the energy to argue. Instead, I lay down on the bed beside him, kicked off my shoes, and stared at the ceiling. "What are you doing?" I asked.

"I pulled up some files I had, from researching Barnel a few years ago. Looking into his revival."

My eyes drifted shut. "And?"

"I've got two thousand, three hundred and eighty-six names. Boys he branded during his sideshow."

I sat up. "Are you kidding?"

"He'd been doing this since the '60s, an average of maybe one a week—more during the summer camp sessions, less in the winters. You do the math."

"I don't understand," I said. "How the hell did this guy get away with this for so long? I mean, it's not like he was just dunking people in the lake or laying hands…he *branded* them. That's assault. That's…" I looked at Diggs helplessly, completely baffled. "I'm not nuts here. Why didn't anyone shut him down?"

"This is a different world. His victims were all underage. All brought in by their parents. Around here, God's number one. Parents are second in line. You don't question either of them. Or at least you didn't when I was a kid."

"So, not once did someone try to press charges? Report him to the Feds? We were at his tent meeting last night—anyone could have come in. If the cops saw him…"

He shook his head. "Did you see anything last night that he could have been arrested for? The snake handling and the exorcisms and anything else remotely hinky were always done behind closed doors. Anyone in attendance was vetted first. In 1982, a kid named Wally Majors went to the police and the FBI investigated. Everyone clammed up. No one would testify. Six months later, the kid killed himself."

None of this was totally outside my sphere of experience, of course. I thought again of what I'd flashed back to during Barnel's revival the night before. Was whatever the Paysons had done on Payson Isle really so different from Barnel strapping kids down and branding them?

"What about you?" I asked. "You never went to the cops?"

He laughed with the same kind of cool distance he always assumed when I asked him something personal. "It was more a matter of pride at the time. No one wanted to be the pussy who couldn't take Barnel's treatment. Later, of course, the only evidence I actually had of what happened…" he faded out, though I knew where he was leading: The cross, ultimately transformed into the messy burn that he'd always refused to talk about just below his collarbone.

"How did you get rid of it?" I asked. "Barnel's cross, I mean."

"Divine intervention," he said with an awkward, cloaked smile. And that was the end of that conversation.

Rather than press him, I looked over Diggs' shoulder at Barnel's endless list of victims. The names were color coded in red, blue, green, and orange, and listed alphabetically.

"What do the colors mean?"

"Effects after the fact," Diggs said. "Blue is no discernible effect. Green is mental illness. Orange is a criminal record."

I spied Wyatt's name in red. Guess I didn't need to ask what that one meant. I scanned the list. Maybe half the names were blue, the bulk of the rest evenly divided between green and orange, with a lot fewer red scattered in among them. "How long have you been working on this?"

"A few years," he said. "I started while I was living here. I kept it quiet, though."

"Ashley wouldn't have approved?"

"Ashley didn't approve of much."

That stopped me, if only momentarily. "Why marry her, then?"

"Oh, you know…" he said with a vague wave of his hand.

"Actually, I don't, or I wouldn't have asked." My temper was rising again. It has a tendency to do that around Diggs. "We dance around this shit all the time. I'm tired of it. What did George mean the other day when he said you married Ashley because of me?"

His eyes darkened. "Sol—" he began, about to put me off again.

"You know, Juarez may not remember the first thirteen years of his life, but I still know more about his past than I do about yours, and you've been my best friend for seventeen years. Everything's this deep dark mystery with you: the women you married, the scars you carry…hell, you won't even tell me why you're a vegetarian. I mean, Jesus, Diggs. Were you a cow in a past life?"

He frowned. It felt like there was a war waging in his head: what to say, what to hold back. "You know more about me than anyone," he said. "You know that."

"I know the things I was there to see firsthand. No more, no less."

"Since when have you been all about sharing your deepest darkest, anyway? I mean, Jesus, Solomon. Have you joined a knitting circle, too? If you were looking for someone to help you get in touch with your feminine side, you've obviously picked the right guy."

"At least Juarez treats me like something other than his faithful sidekick," I bit out. My cheeks burned. I looked away, wishing I'd never brought it up. I focused on Einstein, my head ducked down, fingers moving through his fur. Somehow, it felt like I was the one who'd revealed something—which is the reason I don't usually do this emotional crap in the first place.

"I don't think of you as a sidekick," Diggs finally said. His voice was even. Serious. I met his eye. Okay, maybe he didn't think of me as a sidekick. It would have been a very different movie if Butch Cassidy looked at Sundance the way Diggs was looking at me just then.

I rolled my eyes, aware that my cheeks were now officially burning just a shade cooler than the sun. "I just think you should open up once in a while," I mumbled. Before he could respond, I took the laptop from him and focused every ounce of my energy on the screen.

"All right…you wanna share, huh?" he asked. He lay back on the bed, arms behind his head, and started reading the paper. His voice had lightened considerably. "I could tell you about my first time. Now there's sixty seconds worth remembering." I shot him a glare. He grinned. "Of course, I remember *your* first time a lot better."

"I hate you."

"Who can blame you? Now, let's see… I was thirteen. She was seventeen. Jessica Montgomery…"

He stopped. When he didn't continue, I looked at him curiously. He was totally transfixed by a page-one story on Wyatt.

"What's up?"

"'Local veterinarian Dr. Wyatt Durham disappeared from Jackson Burkett's farm early in March,'" Diggs read.

"So?"

He sat up and took the laptop from me. "They've been calling him Roger this whole time—that's why I didn't recognize the name." He scanned through the list and came up triumphant, jabbing his finger at the screen. I read the name he'd indicated.

Burkett, Jackson R.

"You think that's Roger Burkett?" I asked. "It could just be coincidence."

"I doubt it." He got up and grabbed his jacket.

"Wait," I said. "Where are you going now?"

"The Burkett farm. It's not like Sheriff Jennings is gonna keep us in the loop, and I'm sure the state cops haven't put this together."

I sat up and retrieved my shoes.

"You don't have to come with me. I'm fine," he said.

"You want me to send you out there alone? No offense, but your track record since we got to Justice isn't that great."

"I know you're trying to turn over a new leaf," he said with a smirk. I hate that smirk. "If this is too much action for you…"

I slugged him in the arm. "Don't push it, Diggins."

He pulled his jacket on, smirk still in place. "Yes, ma'am. And I can tell you all about Jessie Montgomery on the way."

"I can't wait."

●

There was actually a part of me—primarily in the lower intestine region—that was a little hesitant about heading to the Burkett farm with Diggs. I tried to appease my intestines by giving Mae the details of where we were headed and when we should be back, thus ideally minimizing the chances that we'd be butchered along the way. Or, if we were, at least we'd be found quickly.

I started rethinking my perspective about the time we left the outskirts of town for what appeared to be *Deliverance* territory, following a dirt road cut through a wall of trees in full bloom. I'd always lumped Kentucky in with the South, but the birches, maples, and oaks along the road were closer to the Maine woods than anything you'd find down on the bayou. It was still gray outside, a miserable drizzling rain falling. With the forest closing in, Diggs and my banter gave way to silence. Einstein stuck his head out the window, breathing in the fresh air. At least one of us was having a good time.

"You okay?" Diggs asked when we'd been on the Burkett road for a good five minutes. There were no cars in either direction—which could be a very good thing or a very bad thing, depending on your perspective.

"Yeah," I said. I kept an eye on the road behind us, searching for some sign that the hooded man—aka Cameron—might be back there. I checked my cell phone. Miraculously, there was still a strong signal. "I'm fine."

"You don't look fine. You look tense."

I eyeballed him for a second, noting the way his hands gripped the steering wheel. His nose was swollen and his eye was purple. "You don't look that hot yourself. Considering what happened the last time we were alone in the woods together, I think 'fine' would be asking a little much, don't you? How about we just celebrate the fact that I'm not fetal in the backseat, and run with that."

"Fair enough."

Eventually, we reached the end of the road—literally. About fifty yards back from the driveway, obscured by an overgrown field, was a ramshackle white house that may have been nice at one point a long, long time ago. Now, the paint was chipped, a couple of shutters were hanging loose, and one of the upstairs windows had been broken out. Plastic was taped over it, but I couldn't imagine it did much to keep out the draft. Or the beasties.

"Well, this isn't creepy at all," I said.

"Buddy said they found some tire tracks in the driveway," Diggs said. "And Wyatt's medical bag was still on the ground where he'd left it."

He stopped the car and turned off the engine. "So, we check the house first."

"Sounds reasonable."

"You want me to go alone?"

"Give me a break. Let's do this."

"Suit yourself." He reached across me to the glove box, opened it, and rooted around for a minute before he came out with a gun. A big gun, too—much closer to a cannon than a pea-shooter.

"What the hell's that?"

"It's a Glock." He checked the clip, slammed it back into place, and tucked it into the back of his jeans. Like it was the most natural thing in the world. Teeth brushed? Check. Clean underwear? Check. Fully loaded grenade launcher in my back pocket? Check, and check.

"Well, yeah. Do you know how to use it?"

"Yep." He got out without waiting for any follow-up questions. I scrambled out, snapped the leash onto Einstein's collar, and followed Diggs toward the house. I didn't want to be a dweeb, but up to this point in our lives, Diggs and I had navigated some pretty hairy situations without resorting to capping anyone's ass.

"You really think we need that thing?" I asked when I'd caught up with him, halfway to the house.

"I don't know," he said. "But I'd rather not need it and have it, than not have it and die."

When he put it like that…

Still, I was fairly sure the whole 'If we're all armed, no one gets hurt' argument had proven fatally flawed more than once.

We reached the front door. The cement step up was split down the center and the house had drifted about a foot from it over the years. Diggs had to lean forward to knock. I started to say something more about the whole gun thing, but he stopped me with a look.

"I'm not going down without a fight again," he said. Any trace of fun was gone from his eyes. "If someone comes after you—us—I'll damned well be ready this time."

I held up my hands in surrender. "All right, fine. Whatever. Just know that if you inadvertently shoot me, I'm gonna be pissed. And if you hurt my dog, all bets are off."

"I'll keep that in mind."

Diggs knocked again. Einstein whined at the door, pawing at the bottom. There was no answer, and I didn't hear anyone screaming from the bowels of the basement or anything. I took that as a sign from the universe that we should move on.

"Buddy said the barn's across the field there," I said. "Maybe that's where they are."

"Could be," Diggs agreed. "Up for a walk?"

We set out. Once we got past the house, an actual cleared path appeared within a few yards. Most of the land was fenced out this way—good, solid fencing that stretched all the way around, with no gaps that I could see. We followed the fence line over a couple of rolling fields, the grass surprisingly trim considering the condition of the house.

"Goats," Diggs reminded me when I said something. "Grass doesn't grow too long with them around."

I looked around for any sign of these alleged goats. Beyond the fencing and the close-cut grass, however, I saw nothing. Einstein gave the ground a perfunctory sniff, but even he didn't seem convinced there was anything to be found. The place was eerily quiet, interrupted by the occasional birdsong, a car engine off in the distance. Otherwise, I heard nothing. When we finally cleared the last hill, a bright red barn came into view. Diggs knelt beside a thick tire track deep in the soft earth.

"ATV," he said. "Looks like it was carrying a heavy load."

I wasn't sure whether it was my own imagination, too much TV, or recent experience that made the statement sound so foreboding.

The double doors leading into the barn were open, and the barn itself was pristine. Shelves of stainless steel buckets lined one wall, while two barrels of sweet-smelling grain sat nearby. Molasses, I suspected. Bales of hay tinged with green were stacked neatly in the corner.

"Alfalfa," Diggs said. He shook his head. "It's pricey— not the kind of thing people usually feed around here. They might not have known what they were doing, but they put some money into this venture."

All the stalls were mucked out, not so much as a stray goat pellet to be found. "Where are the goats?" I asked, going for the most obvious question first.

"No clue," Diggs said. We walked to the other side of the barn, where another double door opened up on the other side. Diggs scratched his head. "Nothing," he said. "I don't see a trace of anyone—goat or human."

"When did Buddy say they were out here last?"

"Thursday. The day after they found Wyatt."

"That was a week ago. It looks like maybe they split. No cars, no goats, no sign of anyone at the house." Roger Burkett was one of Reverend Barnel's conquests. That had to mean something. I don't believe in coincidences in general, but I especially don't believe in them where crazy branding preachers are concerned.

We headed back to the house, still searching the horizon for any sign of man or beast. I thought of Barnel's proclamation of an impending Armageddon. I had to admit, it did kind of feel like we were in one of those sci-fi movies where a mutant apocalypse has taken place while no one's looking. Any second now, I expected a pack of freakish southern zombies to appear on the hillside, arms outstretched, ready to save our souls and eat our brains.

"Maybe we should call Buddy," I suggested when we were almost back to the house.

"I'll call him when we've checked the place out," Diggs said. He didn't even slow down. Suddenly, I had a pretty good idea what he'd been dealing with from me over the past year. What a pain in the ass.

"What if there's someone in there?" I asked when we reached the front door.

He knocked on the door. "If there's someone there, they'll answer. And if they don't…"

I was familiar with the logic, having made the same argument myself upon occasion: *If they don't answer, we should bust in and make sure everything's all right.*

No one came to the door. Einstein whined and pawed at it, his nose pressed to the crack. Diggs started to knock again. His knuckles had barely grazed the wood when I thought I heard something coming from inside.

A whimper.

My skin crawled and my heart dropped toward my navel. Einstein nosed at the door, whining all the louder. "Did you hear that?" I asked.

Diggs shook his head. He tried the door, but it was just as locked now as it had been when we'd first shown up on the scene. I put my ear to the wood while he went around to the side, looking for a way in.

"Hello?" I called inside.

Nothing. Einstein was frantic now, scratching at the door with a steady, low whine. Two seconds passed. Then three. And then, again...

A whimper.

It was unmistakable this time—someone was in there.

I stepped back and jogged over to Diggs, who stood beneath a window that was open just a crack.

"There's something in there," I said.

"What do you mean, some*thing*?" he asked.

"I don't know. It could be a person, or it could be an animal. It's probably not a mutant southern zombie, but I make no promises."

He gave me a look, lip twitching to keep from smiling, then retrieved a plastic milk crate lying in the grass. He set it beneath the window and stepped up, pushing the window up farther before he pulled himself into the house. Since I'd seen this movie before and I was fairly sure it ended with someone decorating their cave with our skins, I took that opportunity to call Buddy Holloway. It went to voicemail just as Diggs' feet disappeared through the open window.

"Hi," I said to Buddy's voicemail. "This is Erin Solomon—Diggs' friend. Listen, I just wanted to let you know you might want to check out the Burkett place again. Soon. This afternoon would be great." I hesitated. "Please."

I hung up. So, that didn't actually incriminate us or say anything about the fact that we were currently breaking into a locked house. But hopefully the deputy would get the picture.

Diggs stuck his head out the window. "Hey—are you coming or what?"

I tied a very unhappy Einstein to the nearest tree,

promised I'd be back soon, and stepped up on the milk crate. Diggs took my hand and pulled me up.

That cannon he was hauling around was looking pretty good about now.

Once through the window, I found myself in an old bathroom in serious need of updating. I wasn't expecting much based on the *Hoarders'* exterior, but the room was surprisingly clean... and very monochromatic. Mint green fixtures—toilet, bathtub, and pedestal sink—were the perfect complement to the mint green tile walls and the faded, mint green towels.

"Pretty," I said.

Diggs nodded. "Green living at its best."

I groaned.

He pushed the door open, landing us in a dimly lit, wood-floored corridor. Whoever had been there last had left without turning off the heat: it was like a steam bath in there. I tried the light switch, and a naked bulb flickered in a wrought iron sconce on the wall.

The hallway was narrow, with a bizarre pineapple-print wallpaper and not a stitch of art work on the walls. A swinging door brought us to the kitchen.

I stopped moving.

"Do you smell that?" Diggs asked.

I definitely did: the smell of something rotting, strong enough to make me gag. I pulled my shirt up over my nose.

"You wanna keep going?" he asked.

"Hello?" I called out in lieu of an answer.

This time, the response was immediate and unmistakable: A whimper that grew to a full-blown whine when I called out again. I didn't bother to answer Diggs' question, instead plowing on toward a narrow stairwell at the back of the kitchen where the stench was strongest and the whining loudest.

The stairs were partially rotted, the ceiling was low, and the walls were narrow. I thought suddenly of negotiating the tunnels with Diggs last summer, and my newly regained courage wavered. It was even hotter here than the rest of the house, the air wet and as heavy as a blanket. I focused on taking shallow breaths through my mouth, and kept going.

At the top of the stairs, there was a small, windowless room that had clearly been used for storage. I shined my flashlight across stacks of boxes, dishes, and books. A dingy curtain cordoned off a section at the back.

"Anybody here?" I asked. The whining was coming from behind the curtain. I glanced back at Diggs. The smell was nearly unbearable now. "You're still with me, right?"

"Barely," he said grimly.

I took a step forward. Then another. The curtain moved. My heart was already thumping like a rabbit's, but that movement kicked it up another notch. I took a breath, mentally steeled myself for unspeakable horror, and pushed the curtain aside.

11
DIGGS

ROGER BURKETT WAS SEATED with his back against the wall, naked from the waist up. His eyes were open, both arms outstretched and his wrists fastened with twine to eye bolts screwed into the wall. His throat was slit from one end to the other. I stared at the insignia over his heart, excised and re-stitched: an inverted cross.

The combination of buzzing flies, heat, and the smell of putrefying flesh was overwhelming, to say the least. Solomon seemed unfazed. She moved forward, ignoring the dead body before us in favor of the live one beside it: a medium-sized golden retriever, its fur matted with blood. The dog lay beside Burkett with its head on the dead man's lap.

Solomon knelt beside the dog, talking softly.

"You should wait until we can get a vet here," I said.

I might as well have been talking to the dead guy.

She sat down and reached for the dog—palm up, fingers outstretched. Solomon's one of those women who's never actually still; I've slept with her, and even in her sleep she moves more than your average, fully conscious American. The exception is when she's around anyone sick or injured—

animal or human. It's like she becomes another person. Her mother always wanted her to be a doctor, something Sol adamantly insists she was never interested in pursuing. I've always thought she would be good at it, though.

The dog stretched its muzzle toward her, still whining softly.

"She's hurt," Solomon said. She scooched a little closer. The dog didn't shy away. "There's a gash behind her ear."

"Sol—" I tried again.

She ignored me, gently brushing her hand over the dog's head. It came back sticky with blood. "We need to get her out of here," she said. She removed the dog's collar, decorated with penguins and dark with blood, and put it in her back pocket.

"And the dead guy?" I asked.

She barely glanced at him. "The cops are on their way. It's not like he's going anywhere."

Once she was up, Solomon tried sweet talking the dog out of the room first, with no success. Then, she looked at me.

"What?" I asked.

"Maybe if we put her on a blanket, we could carry her down."

We made a couple of clumsy attempts. By that time, I figured if the poor dog hadn't bitten us yet, she probably wasn't going to. I hefted her into my arms. She whined when I started walking away from Roger, struggling against me the farther I got.

"Easy, girl," I said. She laid her muzzle on my arm and closed her eyes, still whining as I made my way down the steep stairwell. Sirens were headed toward us by the time we got outside, and I could barely feel the dog's heartbeat.

Einstein had slipped his collar by the time we got outside, and was waiting anxiously for both of us. He totally ignored Solomon and headed straight for me instead, bumping up against me as I lay the retriever on the grass.

"Will you get him out of here?" I said to Solomon. I like the dog, don't get me wrong, but there's a limit to how much canine bonding a man can take.

Before she could grab him, Stein lay down facing the retriever, his muzzle on his paws, and whimpered. She opened her eyes. Stein thumped his tail. The retriever thumped her tail. He licked her head, then settled in for what I was guessing was the long haul.

Buddy Holloway arrived on the scene a few minutes later, siren wailing. Solomon and I sat cross-legged on the ground, the retriever lying on her side next to us, panting while Einstein looked on anxiously.

Buddy pulled up, took one look at the dog's blood-matted fur, and I think was tempted to turn around and run back home.

"The body's on the second floor," I said.

"We found the dog in there with him," Solomon said. "I'm not sure how long she'd been there."

Buddy crouched beside the dog, gently ruffling its ears. Einstein growled until Solomon shushed him.

"Hey, Gracie girl," Buddy said. He shook his head. "She hurt bad?"

"I'm not sure," Solomon said. "There's a nasty gash behind her left ear. And she's dehydrated. Pretty freaked out. Her name's Grace, you said?"

"Yup," the deputy confirmed. "She was just a pup when they moved back here. About the only thing Roger cared two figs about was this dog."

"Apparently it was mutual," I said. "It took some doing to get her to leave."

"She may have tried to protect him, too," Solomon said. "It looks like her gums are cut up, which means she could have bitten whoever killed him. You could swab for DNA… I read about that working before, on another case."

Buddy looked at me. I shrugged. "She doesn't know about the way things work in this part of the world, I guess," he said.

"You don't have DNA in Kentucky?" Solomon asked.

"We don't have a lot of resources for *testin'* DNA," Buddy corrected her. "We can get it done, it just might take a while. In the meantime, I'll get her on over to the vet. We'll see what we can do for her."

I heard more sirens in the distance, which could only mean one thing. Sure enough, thirty seconds later Sheriff Jennings and two other cruisers pulled into the Burkett's driveway. It wasn't going to be a good afternoon.

Buddy Holloway might be convinced Harvey Jennings had turned his life around, but as far as I could tell the sheriff was exactly the same egomaniacal, abusive prick he'd always been. Einstein was already none too happy that Buddy was trying to abscond with his new girlfriend, but he went ballistic when Jennings showed up on the scene. Grace started whining as soon as Jennings got out of his cruiser, and Solomon had to physically drag Stein away while Buddy put the retriever in his own car so he could get her to the vet.

Once the dog situation was resolved, Jennings approached Solomon and me while the other cops started dealing with the crime scene. In the light of day, I noticed circles under the sheriff's eyes that I'd missed the night before, and an intensity that seemed to burn brighter thanks to the fatigue.

"Word is, Danny Durham never come home last night," he said to me.

"He was out partying," I said without missing a beat.

"You know kids. He just buried his father—he needed to blow off some steam."

"Boggles my mind how you can have one brother grow up so good, and one that just seems like he sprung up right out of the devil's seed," Jennings said. "But I guess you know something about that, don't you, Diggs? That brother of yours that died 'cause of your carelessness and lies—the way Wyatt told it, your daddy made it plain he thought he'd laid the wrong boy in the ground that day. Guess that explains a few things about you, don't it."

Solomon clenched her fists, clearly preparing to cold cock the bastard.

"What do you need from us, Jennings?" I asked. "We've got places to be."

"You say Danny was out," Jennings said. "Where was he? Who was he with?"

"I know the way you operate," I said. "I'm not answering anything without a lawyer. And you're sure as hell not getting Danny in a room without one."

"That's pretty much exactly what I expected," Jennings said. "Somebody's gonna catch up to that boy, one way or the other. No way you can protect him this time. So if you don't have nothin' to add, why don't you two just get on home. Let us do our jobs."

"Are you sure?" Solomon asked. "We were in the middle of the crime scene. I don't want to tell you how to do your job, but shouldn't someone fingerprint us? Compare our shoe treads with others in the room?"

"Sounds like a whole lotta work to me," Jennings said with a sigh. "You didn't kill Roger, am I right?"

"Sure," she agreed. "You're right: we didn't kill him. But wouldn't it be easier to go through the crime scene if you can rule out a couple sets of prints straight off the bat?"

"You know what kind of man Roger Burkett was?" Jennings asked her.

"Not a great one, from what I've heard," she said.

"That about sums it up: 'Not a great one,' " Jennings said. "He lied and cheated and stole. Chased skirts and beat on his girl and was just about the laziest S-O-B I ever laid eyes on. The Lord's siftin' through—that's all this is."

"I'm pretty sure it wasn't God who tied that guy up, slit his throat, and carved his chest to pieces," Solomon said. She advanced on the sheriff, her temper up. "Did you see him?"

"I haven't had the pleasure yet," Jennings said. "But I got a good idea what I'll find." I touched Solomon's arm, trying to get her to back off. Jennings looked past her, though, fixing his attention on me. With the burning eyes and the mouth pressed into a firm line, he didn't look even close to sane.

"You two was both there last night when Reverend Barnel gave his sermon," he said. "You might oughta think about what he had to say. We're not twelve hours into those last forty-eight he said we had in this world, and the sinner's are already fallin'. They's gonna be a lot more before the end of the day. You can mark my words on that."

"And on that note," I said, holding more firmly to Solomon's arm. "Maybe we should just be on our way."

"Maybe you should," Jennings agreed.

We went back to the car. I pulled out without waiting for Solomon to buckle up. Einstein careened across the backseat as I did a one-eighty in the driveway and sped out.

"That guy is certifiably nuts," Solomon said. "How is he sheriff?"

"He talks a good game, believe it or not," I said. "And he used to hide his crazy a little better than he is now. He's fooled a lot of people along the way." I thought of Sarah—Jennings' wife. Funny, gorgeous…and out-and-out terrified, by the time I helped her get out of town.

We were halfway down the road, still talking about

Harvey Jennings' psychotic tendencies, when a black tank of an SUV with federal plates appeared in our path. I looked at Solomon.

"Did you call your boyfriend?"

"No," she said. "I mean—I've talked to him. But I didn't tell him anything that was going on."

There wasn't enough room for us to pass, but based on the way the SUV was keeping to the center of the narrow road, I assumed that wasn't their intention, anyway. I backed up until I was back in front of the Burkett farmhouse.

The cops were in the middle of packing Burkett into the coroner's van. Everything came to a halt when the SUV pulled up, and a good looking woman with dark eyes, dark skin, and a well-tailored suit hugging curves that would bring any thinking man to his knees, stepped out of the driver's side. I looked at Solomon. She shrugged.

"Don't ask me—I've never seen her before in my life."

We got out of the car. Two men got out of the back of the SUV before the front passenger door opened and Jack Juarez himself stepped out. Solomon held up her hands at my raised eyebrow.

"I swear—I didn't call him."

The lady agent approached Sheriff Jennings. They spoke quietly while Juarez joined us.

"Hey, baby," he said to Solomon. "Fancy meeting you here."

"What are you doing here?" she asked. I noted with a petty twinge of satisfaction, that she didn't look that thrilled to see him. Juarez seemed to notice the same thing.

"I was in a briefing this morning," he said. "Someone mentioned that a Domestic Terrorism team was headed to Kentucky to investigate some recent activity. Naturally, my first thought was, 'Kentucky's a big state. What are the chances this has anything to do with my girlfriend?'"

"How long did that thought last?" I asked.

"Not that long," he conceded. "I managed to convince Agent Blaze to bring me along, since I've worked with the unit before." He lowered his voice, glancing back at the agent before he returned his attention to Solomon and me. "I didn't expect it to be a problem, though, since I didn't think you were directly involved."

"I'm not directly involved," Solomon said. Juarez looked at her doubtfully. "I'm not," she insisted. "Diggs is."

Agent Blaze joined us before we could continue the conversation. Sheriff Jennings clearly hadn't been happy about whatever she'd said to him, because he and his men took their toys and went home, tearing out of the driveway without a word to any of us. Blaze didn't seem fazed. Juarez made introductions, and she eyed Solomon and me speculatively.

"There's been a lot of activity here in the past week," she said. "I'll be working with the local and state police, but I'd love to get your perspective on things."

"Sure," I agreed. "But right now my main concern is my nephew—that's why we're here. He hasn't been seen since sometime last night."

"You have reason to believe he might be involved with recent events?" She watched me closely. Something in her eyes made me think she knew a hell of a lot more than I did about what was going on in Justice.

"Not involved," Solomon said. "But possibly a target. Apart from the shootings last night, the victims—"

"Had been part of a ritual Barnel performed illegally in his church," Blaze finished for her. "As were you, Mr. Diggins, I believe?"

I hesitated. Juarez looked at her in surprise. Maybe he hadn't known Solomon and I were involved in this, but Blaze sure as hell had. "That's right," I said. "But I'm not worried about myself right now. My nephew's the one in danger."

"That's noble of you," she said. "But it's too early for you to make that determination—and not really your place to do so, besides." She looked at Juarez for a second, as though trying to decide whether or not she should keep talking.

"They're all right," Juarez said. Blaze didn't look so sure of that, however. I may be on her radar, but she wasn't ready to take me into her confidence just yet. She and Juarez slunk off for a whispered rendezvous, one or both of them gesturing toward Solomon and me periodically.

"I don't like this," I said to Solomon under my breath.

"And you think I do?" she said. "What the hell's going on around here? Wyatt's dead, somebody takes a potshot at your lunatic preacher friend while he's babbling about the end of the world, we've got another body... And now we've got the Feds in the mix."

"Based on the way they're talking, I'd say we've barely scratched the surface here so far," I said.

I didn't care for the way Juarez was eyeing me, either. For a man who'd allegedly given his girlfriend his blessing to traipse around the countryside with me, he didn't seem so keen on the two of us whispering together now. He and Blaze broke from their huddle. Solomon took a couple of steps away from me.

"This is a sensitive subject," Blaze said as she approached. "It doesn't get printed in any papers. It doesn't get broadast on YouTube or written up in your blog or tweeted to your BFFs. The only reason I'm telling you anything is because Juarez here has suggested that you might be of use in the investigation. But you keep your mouths shut. Everything I'm telling you—*everything*—is off the record."

"And after the danger's passed?" Solomon said. I was glad to see that, despite everything, she was still thinking of the story. Blaze looked less pleased.

"Assuming we're all still breathing, we'll revisit the topic then. Do we have a deal?" Blaze said.

Solomon and I both nodded. Blaze began.

"Barnel performed rituals on roughly twenty-four hundred boys over the course of his career. In the past fifty years, three that we know of have now been found with the same inverted cross your friend Wyatt Durham had. Given that very low percentage, I don't believe now is the time for those carrying that mark to panic. At the moment, we're more concerned about some of Barnel's other activities."

"You mean this business about the end of the world?" I said.

"You know the man. How much influence does he have over his congregation?"

"He's convinced parents to brand their children in the name of God. I'd say that's a fair amount of influence," I said.

"And how large is the congregation?"

"I don't know," I said, thinking. "I stopped following his activity a while ago, but it's not huge. At the tent revival last night there were, what, maybe a hundred people?" I asked Solomon.

"Around that," she agreed.

"I'm still not convinced my nephew's not in trouble, though," I said.

"How old is he?" Blaze asked.

"Seventeen."

"Well, there you go," Blaze said. "Seventeen-year-old boys are unpredictable—I have a teenage daughter, and I'm tempted to plant a tracker on her half the time. I'm sure he'll turn up. In the meantime, we're more concerned with finding Reverend Barnel."

"What do you mean, finding him? You lost him?" Solomon asked.

"He went underground after the shooting."

"Do you think that whole Armageddon business he was spouting last night is something to worry about?" I asked.

The agent considered the question before she answered. "We're here to assess the threat. It's never wise to dismiss something like this outright, but I highly doubt a man like Reverend Barnel or his followers are organized enough to pose a significant threat to national security."

"That's super for the country," I said. "But it doesn't offer much reassurance of my nephew's safety right now. If you don't mind, I'll keep looking for him."

"Of course," she agreed. "But I'd appreciate it if you'd let us know if you find anything you think might be pertinent to our investigation. And I'd love any input you might have on Barnel's whereabouts." She paused, her eyes intent on mine. "I understand the two of you have a history. Your perspective could be helpful."

"I guess it's safe to assume that if you're looking for advice from a civilian, you're expecting rough seas ahead?" I asked.

She looked at the Burkett farmhouse, then back at me, and frowned. "Honestly? I'm not sure what to expect right now."

12
SOLOMON

JUAREZ'S SUPER-AGENT BOSS told him it would be all right to stick with Diggs and me and ask a couple of questions about Danny while she went into town to set up Command Central. There was a brief debate about who would sit where in the car, before I took the backseat with Einstein—who was happy enough to see me, but wasn't crazy about sharing his space. Diggs took the wheel, with Juarez riding shotgun. I expected things to be awkward between the three of us, but the fact that the country seemed to be under attack by a bunch of rogue rednecks bent on forcing the end days went a long way toward diffusing that.

Our first destination was the Durham house: Diggs wanted to check in and, ideally, get a better sense of where Danny might have gone since we'd seen the kid last. He went in first when we got there, giving me a minute with Juarez. Jack pulled me closer when he was sure we were alone, with a bemused smile.

"I can't leave you alone for a minute," he said. I stood on my toes and leaned up to kiss him. He met me halfway, his lips soft on mine.

"This one wasn't my fault."

"No," he agreed. "Probably not. But still… You do seem to attract more trouble than any woman I've ever known." He tucked a strand of hair behind my ear, studying me. "Are you all right? You look a little tired."

For a split second, I thought of the night before. Most notably, I thought of the kiss between Diggs and me the night before—the kiss to end all kisses, the one that jarred my front teeth and melted my under-things and had me tossing and turning in the back of the rental car all night long. I pushed that thought far, far to the back of my brain, and shook my head.

"Just didn't sleep that well last night," I said. It wasn't a lie, exactly. It felt a lot like one, though. "And there's a lot going on."

"True," he agreed. "We should get in there. If Diggs' nephew really is missing, time is an important factor. And Allie will want us back at the station soon."

"Allie?"

"Agent Blaze." Right. He hesitated, still studying me. "Are you sure you're okay? I know I'm working, but I can make time if you need to talk…"

I had a choice here: I could tell him what had happened between Diggs and me the night before, thus ensuring the bromance between Diggs and Juarez was effectively ended, or I could keep my mouth shut. Chalk Diggs and my exchange up to the heat of the moment, and vow that it wouldn't happen again.

I chose the latter.

"I'm okay," I said. "I'll feel better if we can get Diggs' nephew back home safely, though."

I got the feeling he didn't completely believe me, but he nodded all the same. "Then let's get in there, and we'll see what we can do."

Things hadn't gotten better at the Durhams' in our absence. Mae was frantic. Ida was crying. Angus—Ashley's kid—was screaming bloody murder. Rick had either shotgunned a bottle of Nyquil or he was entering some kind of fugue state. The second we got through the door, Ashley started yelling at Diggs—something to the effect that this was all his fault because he told Danny it was okay to leave, when Mae had expressly told the kid to stay. I had no idea if this was true or not, but based on Diggs' expression, she wasn't completely off base.

Clearly, it wasn't Diggs' best day.

Finally, at the height of the insanity, Juarez put two fingers in his mouth and whistled so shrilly that the whole house went silent.

Impressive.

"I know this is a tense time," Juarez said, calm as you please. "But arguing and casting blame doesn't help things. What we need to do right now is talk to any friends who may have seen Danny and establish a timeline for his last-known whereabouts. So, I'm going to ask everyone to take a deep breath, and recognize that sticking together and supporting one another is the best way to get through the next twenty-four hours."

Everyone went quiet. Juarez met Mae's eye and waved her over. "Is there somewhere we can speak privately?"

She nodded wearily, and led Juarez, Diggs, and me to the now-unoccupied sitting room. As soon as we were alone, she looked at Diggs.

"Is what Ashley said true?" she asked. "She said Rick told her what you did. Danny wasn't supposed to leave the house; you told him to go on ahead. That's right?"

Diggs nodded without hesitation. He's never slow to take the blame for anything—hell, at this point I expect he's found a way to claim credit for global warming and the national debt. Suddenly, I had a much clearer understanding of what had been going on in his head all morning:

Guilt, of the slow-killing, soul-numbing variety.

"Yeah," he said. "I'm sorry, Mae. I didn't see the harm in it—I saw what the kid was going through. It just seemed like if he could get a little space, it might do him some good."

Her eyes filled with tears, but there was a hardness I hadn't seen before. She turned her back on Diggs without another word, and looked to Juarez.

"What do you need to know?"

"Did Danny have any interactions with Reverend Barnel beyond the… uh, ceremony he went through?"

"No—Danny never cared much for the reverend. And after he got the cross, well… He had even less use for him then."

"And when was that?" Juarez asked.

"He'd just turned fifteen."

Juarez nodded. For someone who didn't think Danny was in any real danger, he played the part of the concerned Fed awfully well.

"I know you've called most of his friends at this point," he asked. "Is there anyone you haven't spoken with? Someone he's more likely to have visited than others?"

"I already talked to the teachers at school and all his friends while I was there," Mae said. "Nobody's seen him."

Rick peered into the room, knocking hesitantly on the doorsill.

"What is it, honey?" Mae said. "We're in the middle of somethin' right now."

"I know," he said. "That's why I'm here. I think maybe I know where Danny could've been last night."

"Come in," Juarez said. "Sit down."

Rick sat stiffly on the couch beside his mother. Diggs

might not have much use for him, but I really felt for the kid. He kept his eyes on the ground, looking miserable.

"What do you mean, you know where he could've been?" Mae asked. "Why didn't you tell me before?"

"Danny didn't want you and daddy to know," Rick said. "You told him to quit the band—"

"He *did* quit the band," Mae said.

Rick shook his head slowly, eyes still on the ground. "Nah, he didn't. He just told you he did. He's been sneakin' out most nights to practice—"

"And you never said somethin'?" Mae demanded.

Juarez held up his hand. "If you don't mind, maybe we can just focus on the story for now. The fact that your son is coming forward now is what's important. Who else is in this band?"

"This girl—Casey," Rick answered. "Her and Danny are real tight. She plays bass. They practice in her garage."

"And you think that's where he went last night," Juarez said.

"Yes, sir. But even if he was taking the day today, he should'a called by now. I figured I could just ask Casey, but she wasn't at school today neither. I didn't think too much about it—she misses a lot, you know? Was barely there at all this fall, missed a whole month back at the start of the year."

"Do you know where Casey lives?" Diggs asked.

"Yes, sir," Rick said. "Just on over to the other side of town, at the Shadyside Trailer Park. I would've gone over there myself after school, but Mama picked us up straight after last bell."

"That's all right," Juarez assured him. "Right now it's better if you stay with your family. Let us handle this."

As we were leaving, Rick grabbed Diggs' arm. "I'm sorry I told Aunt Ash," he said. "I didn't know she was gonna twist it all around—I was just tryin' to explain that Danny hadn't been trying to do anything wrong. That you said it'd be okay."

"Don't worry about it," Diggs said. "It's on me, not you. Now, you hang back here and hold down the fort. We'll have Danny back before you know it."

I hoped he was right.

●

When we got to Danny's friend's place, Casey was just pulling out of her driveway in a cherry red pickup with mud on the tires and the undercarriage. As trucks go, it bore more than a passing resemblance to the one I'd seen speeding out of Miller's Field after the shooting the night before. Diggs skidded to the side to block her path, and jumped out before he'd said a word to us. Two little kids peered from a window inside the trailer as Juarez and I strode after Diggs.

"Hey," he said, rapping on the girl's window. "We need to talk to you."

Panic flashed in her eyes. Understandable, since Diggs looked like your garden variety thug after his beat-down at the hands of Big Jimmy Barnel.

"It's all right," I said. I glared at Diggs. "You're not in trouble—we just have a couple questions about Danny."

"This is his truck," Diggs said to me. Which explained the psychotic turn he'd just taken.

The truck was still running, the window up. I thought for a second the girl might make a run for it. Instead, she nodded.

"He's in trouble, ain't he? Somethin' happened?"

"Just get out of the truck, please," Juarez said in his best FBI voice. "We can talk inside."

She turned off the truck and got out. It was only as she

was opening the door that I noticed the inverted cross carved into the paint.

"Y'all wait out here," Casey agreed after a little more back and forth in the front yard. "I'll open up the garage, and we can talk there. But I can't stay long—I got work, so whatever you've gotta ask me, you best make it quick. I can't lose this job."

She was cute—auburn hair, striking eyes. She was too skinny to be considered a babe by any self-respecting teenage boy's standards, but I expected she'd outgrow that before long. When she did, Casey Clinton would be a knockout.

For now, though, life didn't look like it was treating her that well. Once we were closer, I noticed a bruise on her right cheek that she'd done her best to hide with concealer. She walked carefully, too, like any unnecessary movement meant serious pain. I exchanged a look with Diggs, and could tell he'd noticed the same thing. I couldn't get a read on whether Juarez had picked up on it.

The ankle biters I'd seen in the window had emerged from the house while we were talking. The older of the two was maybe eight, the younger no more than four. Casey quickly herded them back inside.

Five minutes later, the garage door rose. Casey reappeared behind it and waved us in. Diggs whistled softly at the setup: a full drum set, a few guitars on stands, a couple of horns in their cases, a synthesizer, and a computer.

"Wow," Diggs said. "Nice."

"We all pooled our money for the building," Casey said. "I knew somebody who was sellin' it cheap. And we always put money aside for equipment when we get gigs."

"You play out, then?" Diggs asked.

"Sure," she said. "Not much around here—we're not really Justice style, you know? But we been getting a few paying gigs a month around Louisville and Lexington. Danny just got us one down in Nashville, and Rick got us a gig over to the college where he works."

Now that Diggs had put her a little more at ease, he nodded back toward the driveway. "That truck out there…"

"Is Danny's," she finished for him. "He left it here last night. I thought he just went off with some girl, and he'd be back for the truck when they was done. But he left it in my daddy's spot—that ain't like him. He knows I catch hell when anybody does that."

Bruises explained, then.

"Did you have a girl in mind when you figured he'd gone off with someone?" I asked.

"Could'a been anybody, knowin' Danny. He's not real particular, you know? But…"

"But…?" Juarez prompted.

She looked at Diggs again. "You're Diggs, huh? He's got a picture of you—but you're a little younger in it. Not quite so beat up."

"It hasn't been a great couple of days," Diggs said. Juarez looked frustrated at the apparent aimlessness of the interview, but he held off and let Diggs take lead. "You were about to say something before. About the girl Danny might have gone off with, maybe?"

She hesitated, gnawing at her bottom lip.

"If you saw something…" I prompted.

"I didn't see nothin'," she said quickly. "I was at work."

"But your brother or sister saw something," Juarez guessed.

Casey frowned. "I can't have you upsettin' them—Willa's scared of guys, and Dougie's got no love for suits. I can't make 'em talk if they don't want to."

"We just need a few minutes," Diggs said. "Please. This could literally be life or death for Danny. Just let Erin here go in and talk to them."

I looked at him in surprise. "Me? Why me?"

"You're not a man, and you're not in a suit," he said. "And kids love you."

"No," I corrected him. "Kids love *you*. Dogs love me. Kids spit up on me. Or they cry. Usually, they do both."

Casey actually smiled for the first time since we'd arrived. "I can't guarantee they won't cry, but they're pretty much past the spittin' up phase."

The Clinton trailer was spotless—a hell of a lot cleaner than my place, that was for sure. The kids were parked on the couch watching TV when we came inside. Casey looked at me with a defiant edge to her eyes.

"I know it ain't much," she said. "But we get by all right."

"Clearly," I said. "You obviously take good care of them."

"We do okay." She turned to the kids. "Dougie, turn off the idiot box and get in here. I got somebody wants to talk to you."

A minute later, two pairs of eyes peered in from the other room. Casey waved them in. I sat at the kitchen table. A box of generic Cheerios was out, alongside two dirty bowls and an empty carton of juice. Casey put everything away while the kids sat down.

"This is Erin. She's just got a couple questions. I want y'all to tell her whatever you can."

"You from the State again?" the boy asked me with a frown. "'Cause we're doing just fine."

"She's not from the State," Casey cut in quickly. "She's here about Danny."

"I was wondering if you noticed anything strange last night?" I asked, diving in.

The kids stared at me. The youngest, Willa—a little tow-headed girl with thickly lashed blue eyes—plunged her thumb in her mouth and blinked at me, swinging her feet under the table. Super. I was questioning Cindy Lou Who.

"We're afraid Danny might be in some trouble," I continued, undeterred. "If you remember hearing anything, or seeing anyone, it could help him a lot."

They looked at Casey. She nodded. "Go on—y'all won't get in trouble. Just say what you saw."

"Danny was in the garage," Dougie said after another second's hesitation. "I went out and he showed me a couple chords—I know I was s'posed to be in bed," he added, looking at Casey. "I couldn't sleep a lick, though."

Casey didn't look pleased, but she waved him on.

"Me and Danny got to talking," he continued, "but then we heard somebody comin'. I figured it was either you or daddy, but either way it didn't mean nothin' good. So Danny told me to get in the cubby—where we keep the drums?" Casey nodded her understanding. "We figured if it was you, Danny'd just smooth it over before you knew I was there. And if it was daddy…"

"You'd just hide till he got in and passed out," Casey guessed.

"Yeah," the boy agreed. "But it weren't neither of you. It was some girl."

"Did you recognize her?" I asked.

"I didn't get a look at her," he said slowly, like I was a moron. "I was hiding, remember?"

"Did you recognize her voice?" Casey asked.

"Nah, but it was low—like she was being all slinky like they do on TV. She got Danny to go on outside with her. I figured he'd only be gone a minute. But then I heard him start up the truck, and he never come back. I went on back to bed, and I didn't wake up again till you got home and daddy took—"

Casey stopped him with a killing glare. It was all right: I got the picture.

"Can we back up for a minute? You said you heard him take the truck... but it was in your father's spot when he got back from work," I said to Casey.

"He must've brought it back after wherever it was he went," Casey said. "After that's anybody's guess. All I know is, I got back at one o'clock, Danny's truck was in the driveway, Danny was nowhere in sight, and my daddy was fit to be tied."

I turned my attention back to the little boy. "And you say you heard a girl with a low voice talk to Danny, and he took off with her. Is that it? Did Danny say anything to you?"

"Oh, yeah," he said, his eyes lighting up. "He said he was pretty sure somebody was following him."

"You couldn't have started with that?" Casey demanded. "Why didn't you tell me?"

"I just remembered," he said defensively. "He said he just got a feeling. And somebody carved up on his truck."

"The cross," I said. "Do you have any idea who might have done something like that?" I asked Casey.

She shook her head, but I noticed she avoided my eye this time. "Danny's the kind of guy everybody likes, you know? Especially the girls—but even the guys don't mind him so much. "

I'd gotten good information from her, but there was still something she was holding back. I pulled a business card from my bag. "Well, if any of you think of anything else, just give me a call, okay?"

At the door, just before we rejoined the guys, I stopped and looked around the house.

"Is it just you and your dad and the kids?" I asked.

"My mama died in a car wreck a couple years back. But we do okay."

"I'm sure you do. But if you need anything while I'm in

town… I mean, you know. To talk or…" I trailed off, not even sure what I was offering. However awkward I may have felt about it, Casey nodded with an unexpectedly shy smile.

"I'll do that. And could you call when you find out about Danny? He's a pain in the butt sometimes, but he plays a mean guitar." A flicker of vulnerability touched her pretty eyes. "It'd be hard to replace him, you know?"

I agreed to keep her in the loop, and we parted ways.

●

When we got to the police station, Agent Blaze had already commandeered a tiny conference room in the back of the building to serve as headquarters. In addition to Diggs and me, there were only the four agents—including Juarez—plus Sheriff Jennings, Deputy Buddy, and a couple of other local cops, everyone gathered around a cheap-looking conference table with a pitcher of water and paper cups in the center. Somehow, Blaze still managed to lend a sort of dramatic, official flair to the whole scene. She pulled Juarez aside as soon as we were there so they could debrief each other, and I think I did a damned good job of ignoring the way her hand lingered on his arm when she led him outside. Or the fact that she was friggin' gorgeous.

Stupid super agents.

Diggs and I took our seats, and before long Agent Allie took her rightful place at the head of the table. Behind her, there was one of those nifty new computers with the giant screen where you can just slide things around and make them bigger with the touch of a finger. Much cooler than writing on the wall, which is what Diggs and I always did in our meetings. Blaze cleared her throat, and all eyes turned to her.

"Our primary focus continues to be locating Reverend Jesup Barnel," she began. She touched a photo in the corner of the screen, dragging it to the center and enlarging it: Reverend Barnel, in all his glory. "Our last confirmed sighting of Barnel was last night at approximately twenty-three hundred, when he fled the scene after his son, James Barnel, was killed."

"You make it sound like he was runnin'," Jennings interrupted. "The man was bleeding, and just watched his boy get gunned down. I asked him what I needed to ask, and then I sent him on home."

"Another example of fine police work from the Justice brain trust," Diggs murmured to me.

Diggs doesn't murmur nearly as quietly as he thinks he does.

Jennings' eyes flashed, but Blaze shut him down with a look and plowed on.

"Marx, Jameson," she said to the other two Feebs, "you'll go with Sheriff Jennings to the Barnel compound. Initial reports have indicated the entire camp has cleared out. We'll need confirmation, and I'd like you to do a sweep for any information on Barnel's plans."

Marx and Jameson, a nondescript, fair-haired pair wearing standard-issue FBI suits, nodded.

"Has anyone spoken with Jenny Burkett?" Diggs asked. Agent Blaze looked at him blankly. "The wife of the other victim—Roger Burkett. Burkett was alone at his place when we found him, just him and his dog. The wife and the goats were nowhere to be found. She's the last person to see both Wyatt Durham and her husband alive, as far as we know. There's no sign of her?"

"She dropped the goats off to Evie Raddick's place day after Wyatt died," Sheriff Jennings volunteered. "Then she said she was leaving town."

"And you didn't think to stop her?" Diggs asked. "She plays a key role in two homicides."

"Don't raise your voice to me," Jennings said. "Jenny Burkett didn't have anything to do with this. I told her to get out of here while the gettin' was good."

"Brilliant move," Diggs said.

"We all know who done this," Jennings said. "Danny Durham—"

"Sheriff Jennings, if you don't mind," Blaze said coolly. "I'll handle this. We are currently looking for Jenny Burkett, but so far we haven't been able to track her down," she said to Diggs. "Trust me, we recognize the importance of questioning her."

"Thank you," Diggs said.

"And now, if I may continue," the agent said. She brought up a second picture. I sat up in my seat, feeling Diggs tense beside me.

"We've received information indicating that this boy is now a person of interest in the Barnel shooting," she began.

"He didn't have anything to do with it," Diggs said.

"The hell he didn't," Jennings said. He stood. "A crime was committed last night—two good men were shot in cold blood, and y'all have been treating it like the reverend's the criminal here. It ain't right."

"Sit down, Sheriff Jennings," Blaze said.

"Yeah, Harvey. Sit down," Diggs said, cold as ice.

"You keep your mouth shut, boy," Jennings said. The table separated them, but he looked ready to leap across it. I eyed the gun in his holster uneasily. "I got fifty people who'll swear they saw Danny Durham's truck tearing away from the tent meetin' last night right after those shots were fired. You know as well as I do the kid's got a temper. Everybody at his daddy's funeral heard him threaten the reverend."

"Because the son of a bitch was preaching the end times

while he was trying to bury his father, you idiot!" Diggs said, on his feet now.

"Enough!" Blaze shouted, her voice sharp enough to draw blood. "Sit the hell down, or I'll toss both of you in a cell and you can sort it out on your own."

They faced off for a second more before both men sat. Blaze took a moment, her eyes on both of them, before she continued.

"As I was saying... Danny Durham is currently wanted for questioning in the matter of the Barnel shooting. He was last seen at approximately twenty-two hundred hours, here." She pulled up a map of Justice, with a red X over Casey Clinton's house. Another red X marked Miller's Field, where Barnel's tent meeting had taken place. "A truck matching Danny's make and model was seen leaving the Barnel shooting at twenty-three hundred hours. We recovered that truck this morning, and it's currently being analyzed for evidence. An inverted cross like the one on the previous murder victims—Marty Reynolds, Wyatt Durham, and now Roger Burkett—was found carved on that truck."

She doled out assignments and dismissed everyone but Diggs, Juarez, and me. Once we were alone, she shut down the computer, sat, and looked at us.

"Ms. Solomon, I'd like you to ride with Agent Juarez today. We have some members of Barnel's church that I want to interview, and it may help to have your perspective on the responses." In other words, I was being benched. "And Mr. Diggins." She looked at Diggs with an arched eyebrow. His jaw hardened. Diggs really hates being called Mr. Diggins. "You'll come with me. I'd like to go back to the Durham house and speak with Danny's mother, see if there's anything more we can get there."

Diggs frowned. "She's already been questioned—Juarez just talked to her. Trust me, no one there knows anything else."

"They may not realize they have information," Blaze said "This is now a key part of our investigation, whether you like it or not. Since you have a relationship with the family, Mrs. Durham may be more likely to open up to you, which is the only reason I'd like you along with me."

"Right," Diggs said shortly. "You're the boss."

"Yes," she said. "I am."

Once that was resolved, we went to our separate corners: Diggs with Agent Blaze, while I followed on Juarez's heels. There was no mistaking Diggs' annoyance when he left the station.

I didn't blame him. I wasn't all that crazy about being relegated to the sidelines myself.

13

DIGGS

SPECIAL AGENT IN CHARGE BLAZE had big, wet brown eyes and that delicately browned skin that always brings to mind hot nights in the tropics. Her dark hair was tied back, but I could tell it would be wild when it was loose—thick and curly and impossible to tame. The kind of hair that drives me nuts in the right situation. This definitely was not that situation.

We were on the road fifteen minutes before Blaze spoke. "Brooding won't help, you know."

"I'm not brooding."

"All right—sulking, then." She reached over me to the glove box, one hand on the steering wheel, and retrieved a pack of cigarettes. "You smoke?"

"I quit."

"Mind if I smoke?" She asked it as she lit up, clearly not really asking at all. "So, you were married to the first victim's sister?" she asked after she'd breathed in deep. I took a reflexive sympathy breath and fought the urge to ask for one from her pack.

"Wyatt would be the second victim, wouldn't he?" I

asked. "I mean, if we're looking at Marty Reynolds as the first vic, back in '02."

She conceded the point with a nod. "All right, then—you were married to the *second* victim's sister."

"Yes."

"How long?"

She obviously already had that information, since I assumed she had a complete dossier on me somewhere. I let it slide.

"Three years."

"And you were close to the rest of the Durham family in that time?"

"Yeah."

She frowned. "How close?"

I thought back to nights on the front porch with George; holidays with the whole family gathered around the table; kids racing up the stairs and out the door and underfoot; Pop Warner with the boys...

"Close," I said shortly. "I coached the boys' football team. We had Sunday dinners together. Wyatt would crash on our couch when Mae was pissed; I'd crash on theirs when Ashley was pissed."

"I bet you spent a lot more time on their couch."

"True." I scratched my chin and tried for a normal breath and an even tone. "Why the questions? What's this have to do with anything?"

She glanced at me, then back at the road. "I'm trying to figure out how well you knew the victim. Did you stay in touch after the divorce?"

"Not at first," I admitted. It was oddly comforting knowing I didn't have to fill in the blanks for her—she had the files. No doubt she knew about my addiction and my brother's death and my time with Jesup Barnel. I chose not to think of all the other sordid details she might have gathered about my life.

"Once I got sober," I continued, "I made amends to the family. Wyatt and I started talking again after that."

Blaze put out her cigarette when it was only halfway gone, and I directed her to the road leading to Wyatt's place.

"Is there something you're not telling me about Wyatt?" I asked. "Something that would explain why he was killed?"

She pulled up in front of the house, put the car in park, and cut the engine. "Let's just ask a few questions here first," she said. "Nothing's been confirmed yet."

"Confirmed about what?"

She considered whether or not to tell me whatever it was she clearly knew. Ultimately, she decided against it, shaking her head. The frustration I'd been feeling since I got back to town swelled. "Let me get some more facts," she said. "Then I'll tell you everything I've heard."

I would have argued the point, but she was already gone.

Rick gave me a look like I'd drowned his puppy when we got to the door. He called for Mae.

"I don't know what else I can tell you," Mae said to Blaze, who nodded.

"Often in these situations, the family knows much more than they realize," the agent said. "If we're going to find your son and get to the bottom of your husband's death, this is a necessary step. I'm just here to jog your memory."

Right. Mae led us to the kitchen. She poured coffee and set a plate of chocolate chip cookies in the center of the table. Blaze scowled at them like they were a mortal enemy, choosing the smallest from the bunch. Solomon had eaten at least ten in a sitting the night before. Mae sat.

"What can I tell you?"

Blaze didn't hesitate. "What kind of relationship did your husband have with Jesup Barnel?"

"He was a believer," Mae said. She didn't look at me. I

remembered a night on George's porch with Wyatt, after I'd published my first piece on Barnel. *You oughta be more careful with that man, Diggs. I don't trust Jesup Barnel as far as Mae could throw him. There's somethin' not right about him.*

Had things really changed that much since I left Justice five years ago?

"He knew the reverend had some ideas not everybody took to," Mae continued, "but he'd also seen firsthand the good the reverend could do."

"Was he active in the church?"

This time, Mae paused. "He had been. Not so much these last few months, though."

"Why not? What changed?" Blaze asked.

"He just got busy. And the reverend stopped doing regular services, only did his tent meetings every so often. We always went to the Justice Baptist church, anyway—that got to be enough." Something in her eyes told me that wasn't the whole story. Blaze picked up on it, too.

"How did Reverend Barnel feel about that?"

Mae didn't say anything, worrying at a spot on the tablecloth. Blaze looked at me.

"Mae," I said as gently as I could. "I know I'm not your favorite person right now, but if we're gonna find Danny, we need you to be straight with us."

She lifted her eyes to mine. "I don't know what happened. Reverend Barnel and Wyatt had a fallin' out, though—he said something to me once, about how Wyatt had crossed a line. Gone against the Lord."

"What was your husband's relationship with Sally Woodruff?" Blaze asked, with no preamble. I looked at her sharply. Mae tensed. I hadn't heard Sally Woodruff's name in years. And I'd *never* heard it in conjunction with Wyatt Durham before.

"That lady who gives the abortions out on the town line?"

Mae asked. "I'm not sure what you're askin'. We don't go near that place. Don't have nothin' to do with that woman."

"All right, thank you. Can you tell me a little more about your history with Jesup Barnel?" Blaze asked, switching subjects yet again.

"I grew up in Reverend Barnel's church," she said. "That's where me and Wyatt met. Wyatt wasn't his biggest fan back then, of course…"

I stood while Mae was still mid-sentence. "Listen, if you don't mind I'm just gonna step outside for some fresh air, stretch my legs. You mind?"

Blaze studied me for a long minute, eyes narrowed. For a second, I thought she would say no. Finally, she shook her head. "Don't be gone long—I want to get back on the road shortly."

"Of course," I agreed.

●

I meandered aimlessly for about three minutes, then changed direction the moment I was out of sight of the house. There was no way in hell I'd spend the day trailing Blaze when I had leads of my own to follow. If Mae didn't have the answers we were looking for, I had a feeling I knew where to find them.

Half an hour later, I was standing in line beside Casey Clinton at the local Dairy Queen—Casey's idea, not mine. It was eight-thirty on a Thursday night, which meant our wait wasn't long: a couple of acne-ridden teenage boys got Blizzards and headed for the other side of the restaurant, and we were up. When it was our turn, a slim teenage girl with dyed black hair, camo pants, and an Iggy Pop t-shirt two sizes too small took our order. Her right eyebrow was pierced, and she wore those trendy thick-framed glasses everyone likes so much. In Justice, Kentucky, she might as well have been wearing aluminum foil and a beanie.

"Hey, Case," she greeted Casey, then looked at me. "Who's your friend?"

"Danny's uncle," Casey explained. "Diggs, this is Sophie. Sophie knows pretty much anything that goes on in this town long before it hits the web."

"I'm at the hub of the rumor mill in this hell-hole," Sophie said. She had no discernible accent. "So this is Diggs, huh? I guess that explains Danny's weird surfing obsession... and how he got so good looking."

"We're not actually related by blood," I said. I tried for a rakish-but-completely-uninterested grin—something it pays to have in your repertoire when precocious high school girls are in the vicinity. "But thanks. Can I get a large Coke and a..." I looked at Casey.

"The usual," she said to Sophie, who nodded and promptly pulled two large cups from the stack beside her. "Listen," Casey continued. "I heard Danny stopped in here last night. We been trying to reach him, but he's not answering his cell."

"Yeah," Sophie said. "Sure—I already told Creepy Jennings. Word is, Danny's the one who freaked out and tried to cap the preacher. Is that true?"

Casey bristled, but I intervened before something started. "We don't know what happened last night. That's why we need to find him. Did he say anything to you?"

"Not really. He got here around eight. Got a dish of soft-serve and ate it over there." She nodded to a booth in the back. "He said he was headed over to your place. I guess this means you guys won't be playing next week?"

Casey hesitated. "I'm not sure. It depends on what happens with Danny."

"Well, if you're not playing, I'm not going," Sophie continued with a practiced eye roll. "The rest of the bands they're having are a bunch of losers. I heard if you don't make it they're bringing in Jake Six. If I wanted to listen to a bunch of drunk douche bags sing Toby Keith all night, I'd just come to work."

"I'll let you know," Casey promised. "And can you give me a call if Danny comes back here? Let him know we're looking for him."

"Will do."

She handed Casey an Oreo Blizzard and grinned at me when she slid my Coke across the counter. "Y'all come back now," she said with an exaggerated drawl and a wink.

Casey and I took a booth on the other side of the restaurant, well out of hearing range of the kids who'd come in earlier. She apologized for her friend, then got right down to business.

"So, what'd you want to talk to me about? How can I help?"

"How well did you know Wyatt Durham?" I asked.

She faltered. "Danny's daddy? I—I didn't, really. I mean… We talked a couple times. He gave me rides home every so often."

It wasn't the truth, but I'd expected that. For now, I just wanted to see her reaction when I mentioned his name.

"There were two other victims the police think were killed by the same people who killed Wyatt," I said. "They were bad guys—into drugs, beating up their wives, that kind of thing. But I know for a fact Wyatt wasn't that kind of man. So, I'm just wondering why anyone would lump him in with those losers."

She looked out the window, stirring her Blizzard into a melted mess. She was pretty, in an understated, trying-to-get-through-life-unnoticed kind of way—a wallflower in high school who'd likely go far, if she ever got out of this town and made it to college. I figured that was a big if, knowing even half of what she was facing right now.

"I don't know what to tell you," she said. "I know Danny, not his old man."

"Casey, please," I said. I took the damn ice cream from her, forcing her eyes to mine. "I think Danny's in a lot of trouble here. I don't think he ran away, I think someone took him. And if they did, we need to find him. Fast."

She bit her lip. I thought I was in, but then the veil fell. She shook her head, glancing at the crowd of teenagers getting louder by the minute behind us.

"Sorry. I don't know what you're talkin' about. I didn't know his daddy."

"Okay," I said. Rule number one when dealing with a reluctant source: Don't get pissed off. Bullying only works in rare cases, and it sure as hell wouldn't be effective here. "Let's forget Wyatt for a minute, then. What about Danny? I know he smokes a little dope... Anything else that could have made someone mad enough to take him?"

She looked relieved, which threw me. She'd talk about Danny, but not his father?

"Danny's harmless," she said. I pushed the Blizzard back toward her, feeling like an idiot for having taken it in the first place. "He smokes bud and plays guitar and sleeps with a lot of girls. That's about as bad as it gets."

"And Danny never talked to you about his old man? About problems they might be having?"

"They didn't get along too good," she said carefully. "But I always knew that was Danny's fault—like, he can be kind of a pain, you know what I mean? And Dr. Durham just seemed like he was always tryin' to do what was best. Danny's mama was more the problem, you ask me."

I didn't say anything, waiting for her to continue on her own.

"Dr. Durham couldn't ever say nothin' to her about any of it, but I know he didn't mind the band so much. Mrs. Durham was the one always tryin' to get Danny to give it up and go play at the dang church instead. Till one day she just up and had a fit, and made Danny quit."

"And you talked to Wy—Dr. Durham about this?" I asked, treading as cautiously as possible.

She lowered her eyes, returning her attention to her now-melted ice cream. "I told you, I didn't know Dr. Durham. It's just a feeling I got."

Right. While I was still trying to figure out my next approach, the Ford Focus Solomon and I had rented pulled in and slid into the space beside the Chevy Impala I'd borrowed from Mae when I ditched Agent Blaze. I watched Solomon get out of the driver's seat, then waited to see if she had reinforcements with her. No one else got out, though. She came in, waved to Casey and me as casually as you please, then went to the front and ordered herself a turtle sundae. Only then did she come over, sliding into the seat beside me with her dessert.

"Fancy meeting you here," she said. There was a spark to her eye that suggested she was more amused than annoyed by my exploits. I took that as an encouraging sign. She slid the sundae toward me.

"What are the chances?" I agreed.

"Hey, funny story." She turned in the seat so she could look me in the eye. "You know Agent Blaze? That super-hot, super-scary agent you were hanging out with this afternoon? She just got back. Turns out she got *three* flat tires while she was out at the Durham place. All at once. Crazy, right?"

"That is crazy," I agreed.

"That's not even the weirdest part," she said. She was on

a roll now, so I let her run with it. "She said you excused yourself to stretch your legs, and then…poof, you just vanished. You and Mae's old Chevy, gone. Apparently, she didn't even find a note."

I took another bite of her sundae. Casey raised her eyebrows at both of us.

"I should probably get going," the girl said.

"Don't let me interrupt," Solomon said. "If you guys were talking…"

I shook my head. Whatever happened between Casey and Wyatt Durham, there was no way in hell she was talking to me about it. "I think we're done. I'll give you a call if I hear anything, okay?" I said to Casey. "And if you think of anything, or you need anything at all, you know how to reach either of us. Right?"

She nodded, but I doubted I would hear from her. "I will. Y'all sure you don't need anything else from me?"

"No, we're good," Solomon said, too sweetly. "But we'll definitely call you if we hear anything else."

Casey went back up to the front to have a confab with Sophie, and Solomon moved over to the other side of the booth. Not before she'd cuffed me soundly in the back of the head, however.

"Ow! Don't try and tell me you were surprised when you heard I ditched G.I. Jane," I said. "You know me better than that."

"It's the principle of the thing," she said. "What'd you find out from the kid?"

"Not a damn thing," I said. "Danny smokes a lot of weed and I get the feeling he's dipped his wick in some unsavory places, but I don't see why that should get him kidnapped or killed. And Wyatt…"

I paused. She raised her eyebrows, a spoonful of ice cream halfway to her mouth. "Wyatt what?"

"I'm not sure. Casey knows something she's not telling me, though. Blaze hinted that there was something we didn't know about him…I have this feeling it might have something to do with Casey."

"Like an affair?"

I shook my head. "No. I can't imagine it—Wyatt wasn't that guy. And even if he *was* that guy, if he was going to have an affair, he sure as hell wouldn't have one with a fifteen-year-old girl."

"It does seem like a stretch. So…?" she prompted.

"So, I'm thinking of alternate theories," I said. I had an idea, but I wanted to give it a little time. Ask a few questions before I spoke out of turn. "How'd you manage to duck out on the masked avenger?" I asked, switching gears.

"The masked avenger, hmm? I think Juarez would like that, actually. We went over and interviewed a couple of weird old brothers who live together—they're big fans of Barnel."

"The Reese brothers?" I asked.

She nodded. "Yeah. They didn't have much to say, really. You know they have at least a dozen cats, all of them with little bells on their collars? It wasn't like a hoarding thing, though. More like… you know, everything was a little too clean, and the cats were secretly in control. It was like a horror movie. A horror movie with bells."

She was babbling, which meant however cool she might be playing it, she'd been worried when Blaze showed up at the station without me. I helped myself to more of her ice cream and let her babble.

"That's rough," I said.

"Tell me about it," she agreed. "Anyway, Blaze was just coming off a murderous rage when we got back there. You might want to wear a cup when you see her next, incidentally. And somehow, her not being happy with *you* turned into her not being happy with *me*. I decided it might be smart to make myself scarce."

"Good move."

"That was my thought." She fell silent, watching me while I pushed caramel around in her sundae. "What are you thinking?" she asked.

Landing the ball solidly in my court. I was just preparing to deflect the question when I read the look in her eyes and realized deflection was exactly what she expected. I thought of our conversation the day before. *Everything's this deep, dark mystery with you.* I wet my lips.

"I think Wyatt helped Casey get an abortion," I said.

Her eyebrows went up, eyes widening. "You just let me ramble about the cat brothers for five minutes when that's what you're sitting on? Thanks a lot. What makes you think that?"

"Timeline," I said. "Mae said Barnel cut Wyatt off about six months ago, telling him he'd crossed a line he could never uncross. Danny said Casey missed the first month of school, which would have been around the same time... And Mae mentioned the whole thing about Wyatt going to talk to Casey's father right about then."

"You really think he'd do that?"

I'd been going over that in my head. I had a hard time imagining it—Wyatt and I were long-time friends, but our views on sex and marriage and everything in between couldn't have been more different. I glanced up front while I was thinking it over.

Casey and Sophie were still talking, though it looked like their friendly chat wasn't quite so friendly now. Sophie said something and Casey looked back toward me, her cheeks coloring when she realized I was watching them. She leaned in and said something more to Sophie, clearly pissed, and Sophie grabbed her arm as Casey started to leave. Solomon followed my gaze.

"Looks like a cat fight's about to break out," she noted.

I stood just as Casey pulled her arm free, turned on her heel, and started for the door. She stopped halfway there, as though she'd spotted someone outside. When she turned toward me, all the color had drained from her face. I looked out the window, toward whatever it was she'd seen. The hair on the back of my neck stood on end. Everything slowed to that endless impotent crawl of nightmares.

"Diggs?" Solomon said.

"Get down," I said, my voice tight. Solomon just stared at me, forehead furrowed.

"What?"

"Now!"

The glass in the restaurant's front door exploded an instant later as a tan minivan tore through the front of the restaurant and came to a stop in the middle of the dining room. Screams filled the air. I dove for Solomon, pulling her from the booth to the floor, and covered her body with my own. There was a split second lapse in which everything went quiet, and I heard something small and metallic hit the floor. It rolled toward us.

"Stay down," I whispered in her ear, bracing myself.

The world hung suspended for a tenth of a second before the first explosion rocked the building. The force pulled me up off the ground for an instant, but I kept my body curled around Solomon and held on. Two more blasts went off around us before the van itself exploded.

I waited ten seconds, then fifteen, for something more to happen. The smoke alarm wailed; kids screamed. I still had my head down, my face pressed into Erin's neck while she lay pinned beneath me, but I could feel the heat and hear flames surrounding us.

"Diggs?" Solomon whispered to me. My ears were ringing, her voice coming to me from far away.

I lay there, frozen for an instant, before I recovered enough to speak. "I'm okay," I said. I lifted my head and took stock of the situation before I let her up. The kitchen was ablaze, the rest of the restaurant filling with smoke. I stayed low, noting gashes on Solomon's forehead and arm when she sat up.

"Are you okay?" I shouted over the noise.

She nodded. Her eyes were already huge, but they widened even further when she looked at me. Her gaze lingered on my shoulder.

"I'm okay," I repeated.

She shook her head. "You have a shard of glass above your shoulder blade." She pulled out her cell phone and handed it to me. "Call for help, okay? Don't take the glass out. Get whoever you can and get the hell out of here."

She scrambled away, toward the worst of the injured. I dialed 911 even though I was sure by this time the whole town had been alerted, and hung up when the dispatcher assured me that, yes, there was definitely someone on the way.

Casey was kneeling beside Sophie, her eyes wide with shock, her face bloodied. The other girl lay twisted, unmoving on the floor. I crouched low and began to move as Solomon checked Sophie for a pulse.

The minivan was engulfed in flames by now, the driver unrecognizable. Solomon ran to me and shouted over the noise.

"We need to get people out—if the gas tank blows…"

She didn't need to complete that thought. I began with the little kids that had come in with their parents, their mother's screams on a par with their own. The father lay on the floor, unconscious, his forehead bloodied. I picked up the bigger of the two kids, a boy maybe five years old.

"We need to get outside," I said to the woman. The left

side of her face was burned, but not badly. The kids seemed relatively unscathed. She stared at me blankly, then shifted her focus back to her husband.

"I'll come back for him," I said quickly. "You need to think about your kids right now—please."

I shepherded her and the kids outside to the parking lot, where emergency vehicles were already pulling in, then started back in for Solomon. A fireman stopped me, decked out in full gear. The back of the building was consumed with flames, every window in the place now broken.

"We've got this—you hang back, let somebody check you out."

He motioned to a paramedic to come get me. I was about to dodge them and force my way back in when Solomon came out with Casey's arm draped over her shoulder, half-dragging the girl to safety. I'd expected to find World War III in the parking lot, but apart from a couple of broken windshields, the damage was confined to the DQ. Solomon left Casey with the medics, then returned to my side.

"Come with me, okay?" she said. She took my hand and led me toward one of three ambulances. The medic looked at me, then back at the bodies still being pulled from the building. He was young—maybe twenty-one. Clearly out of his element.

"I'm a certified EMT," Solomon lied. At least I thought she was lying. She was just lying very, very well. "I can help you guys. You've got at least twenty injured in there; are you set up to handle that?" He shook his head, still looking dazed. "That's what I figured. I can help triage. Are these your only rigs?"

"Paducah's sending more," he said. "But they're an hour away."

"Okay. Is there any kind of air evac unit coming?"

The man who appeared to be in charge—a paunchy guy

with a handlebar moustache—came over. "You'll need to set down, ma'am," he said to Solomon. "Somebody'll get to you two as soon as they can."

"I'm fine," she said impatiently. "You've got a guy in his forties in there with a head injury, and I wasn't getting any breath sounds on his right side. Probable neumothorax. And there are at least five people still trapped in the kitchen. I can help with victims once you get them out here."

He looked torn for a split second before he nodded. "Yeah, okay." He pointed to the second ambulance, which appeared abandoned. "Go on over there, just assess as people come out. Don't do anything, you hear me? Just red tag the worst cases so we can get 'em out of here."

"Got it," she agreed. She led me to the second ambulance and made me sit on the back end while she snapped on latex gloves and checked me out. "I see you didn't listen to me about pulling out the glass. You're lucky you didn't bleed out before you got out of there."

"It didn't hit anything; it was just in my shoulder."

"Actually, it could've hit a few things," she said grimly. "And knowing I was right wouldn't have been that much comfort if you died." She took a pair of scissors and cut my t-shirt down the back, carefully peeling it away from the wound.

"You'll need stitches," she continued. "Are you up to date on your tetanus?"

"Yeah," I said "Got a booster last summer, remember?"

"Right." She put a compress to the wound, then took my left hand and guided it back to my shoulder. "Just hold it there, okay? Firm pressure, and stay still. When Juarez gets here, he can give you a ride to the hospital."

"Yes, ma'am."

A firefighter carried a teenage girl away from the building, heading toward us. I watched from the sidelines as Solomon worked with another paramedic, setting the girl up with oxygen and checking her vitals. The fire had spread to the front of the building by now, and the parking lot looked like a scene from some war-torn country: people of all ages milling around, clearly in shock, their clothing torn and faces bloodied.

One of the teenagers who'd been sitting behind us stood off to one side. The right side of his body had gotten the worst of the blast, his clothes and body burned, a deep gash down his right cheek. No one seemed to notice him, and Solomon was busy with three of the workers who'd just been pulled from the kitchen.

I jogged over to the boy. He spun toward me in confusion.

"Have you seen Reggie?" he asked. "I…" he trailed off, eyes welling. He was probably Danny's age, maybe a little younger.

"It's all right," I said. "I'm just gonna take you over to get some help, okay?"

He backed away when I tried to touch him, his voice tinged with hysteria. "Nah—my friend Reggie's still in there. He's got a piece of glass… They just left him in there. Somebody needs to help him. Please."

"What's he look like?" I asked.

"Red hair. He's got a pierced lip. And a tattoo."

"Just hang here a second, okay?"

I stopped one of the firefighters as he walked past, lowering my voice. "Did you see a red headed kid in there—pierced lip. Tattoo?"

"Reggie Bloom," the firefighter said grimly. "He's gone. Piece of glass severed his carotid. Bled out before we even got here."

The world blurred. Smoke made the air hazy, clouds roiling overhead. My stomach burned. I jogged back to the boy.

"I told them to look for him," I lied, figuring it was better than sending him into a tailspin while he was clearly in shock. "Everyone's doing what they can. What's your name?"

He wiped his eyes. His hand came away bloody and he stared at it in confusion.

"I'm Diggs," I said when he didn't answer. I still wasn't touching him, but I'd managed to herd him toward safety.

"Mike," he said absently. "I'm Mike."

"Good to meet you, Mike. Listen, I'm gonna bring you over to get checked out, okay? Let's let these guys do their jobs."

He let me lead him to Solomon. Just before we got there, he stopped and stared at me, eyes uncomprehending.

"Why'd he do it?" he asked. He shook his head. "I don't understand why anybody'd do a thing like this. I know he didn't like us, but why'd anybody go and do this?"

"He?" I asked. Solomon approached. I held up my hand to get her to hang on a minute more. "You saw who did this? You could tell who was driving the van?"

"Yeah," he said. "He was right outside the door. Casey saw him. We all knew who it was. He coached Little League—we'd been in that van a hundred times."

Solomon tried to lead the kid to a waiting gurney. I held her off one more second. "Who are you talking about, Mike? Who was driving the van?"

"Sheriff Jennings," he said. "He was coming straight for us."

14
SOLOMON

THERE'S A REASON I didn't become a doctor. Actually, there are several reasons—the main one being that, by not becoming a doctor, it was guaranteed that I would piss off my mother—possibly for life. The other reason, however, is one I would never, ever admit to aloud:

I always hated seeing people in pain.

Not because I'm secretly some saint in love with the human race or something. Please.

I just hate the chaos of it all. The lack of control. The loss of dignity. The screaming and the snot and the tears.

If it were just blood and guts, I'd be fine.

But it's not.

Strangely enough, my mother—the least empathetic person on the planet—seems to thrive amidst the screaming and the snot and the tears. Of course, she was never Miss Sunshine about it, but in New England that doesn't actually matter so much. Mainers are a pragmatic lot; we'll take competence over kindness any day. If my mother practiced in Kentucky, she'd probably be burned in effigy within the week.

Despite the screaming and snot and tears, however, about two months after the nightmare in Black Falls last summer, I enrolled in a basic course on first aid. And while I was recuperating and dealing with shitty surgeries and generally trying to pick up the pieces of my life after a year that had included a miscarriage, a divorce, multiple attempts on my life, and saying goodbye to the best friend I'd ever had, I kind of…found medicine again. After that basic first aid course, I took another, less basic course. Which led me to a harrowing eight-day Wilderness First Responder course, followed by my first ride-alongs with Portland Emergency Services.

I told almost no one—not Juarez, and certainly not my mother. I did tell my mother's partner, Dr. Maya Pearce, since I needed a reference and Maya seemed as good as anyone for that. I swore her to secrecy, though. I'd wondered more than once what Diggs would say about this unexpected development, but, of course, I wasn't talking to him anymore. And so, this odd new piece of my life became sort of my dirty little secret.

Until now.

Late that night in Kentucky, while doctors were still trying to sort through the casualties and nurses waded through the bleeding masses at Paducah General Hospital, I found a plastic chair and sat alone with my head tipped back against the wall. I was bruised and gashed and stitched in two places. Covered in other people's blood. My hand throbbed.

I felt movement beside me. Juarez sat next to me and draped his arm around my shoulders. I tensed, strung tight. I opened my eyes when he pressed a kiss to my temple.

"Hey," he said. He looked tired. I still hadn't seen Special Agent Blaze since the explosion, but I figured when I did we were all goners. She'd melt us with her poison-dart, über-military death-ray eyes. I snickered at the thought.

Juarez looked at me like I was nuts.

"I'm a little punchy," I said. "Sorry."

"You were incredible, you know," he said. He rubbed my knee. Usually, Juarez has a soothing effect on me, but his touch wasn't doing much just then. There was no part of me that didn't ache. Someone should make a PSA about getting caught in a car bombing. Those fuckers hurt.

"Can I get you anything?" he asked. "Tea? Soup?"

I arched an eyebrow. Even that was painful. "Have you met me? When have I ever wanted tea? Or soup?"

It came out snippier than I meant it to. Juarez removed his hand from my knee. I put it back.

"Sorry," I said. "Apparently, tragedy makes me bitchy... er. I'll get myself something in a minute. What about you? You okay?"

"You mean aside from the fact that my girlfriend and a restaurant full of innocent civilians just got blown up by a guy who was supposed to be on our side, and not one of us saw it coming?"

Right. Dumb question.

"Sheriff Jennings never really seemed like he was on our side as far as I could see," I said. "And, realistically, who thinks a guy like Harvey Jennings is gonna snap and drive his minivan through the local Dairy Queen? If you'd told me he would grab a semi-automatic and mow down the local chapter of the Sierra Club, I wouldn't be surprised... But this was a shocker."

"Well, it's my job to anticipate these things," he said.

We sat there in a mutually miserable silence until he squeezed my hand and stood. "I'm going to speak with the doctors one more time, then we should go." He hesitated. "If you'd like to stay with me at the hotel, there's room. Unless you wanted to go back to the Durhams' with Diggs."

I thought of sleeping in the car the night before. My whispered screaming match with Diggs. The Kiss. The feel of his body sheltering mine when the world exploded around us.

If I didn't have a headache before, I sure as hell had one now. "No," I said. "I'll stay with you. Thanks."

He left. Five minutes later, I was half asleep when someone pressed something warm into my hand. I opened one eye as Diggs sat down.

"You brought me coffee?"

"Only half-strength—I figure eventually you'll want to sleep. And here." He set a Hershey bar on my leg.

"Coffee and chocolate," I said. I looked at him. "Did you hear what Juarez tried to give me?"

"Rookie mistake. He's just trying to take care of you."

"I don't need someone to take care of me."

He harrumphed, but wisely let it go. We sat there in silence for a long time, arms touching, sipping our coffee. I closed my eyes again. Bloody faces swam through the darkness. Kids screaming. The smell of burning flesh. I thought of the look on Sophie's face—the terror she must have felt in those instants before she died.

"So, you're doing this now," Diggs said.

The bloody faces vanished. "Doing what?" I asked.

"Fixing people up," he said. "Don't tell me all that was just your mother's lessons from fifteen years ago kicking in. You knew what you were doing."

"I may have taken some courses over the winter."

When I opened my eyes again, Diggs was grinning at me. "What?" I asked.

"Nothing," he said. "I just love it when you surprise me."

"Glad I could oblige." I started to lean back again, but something about the way Diggs was looking at me stopped me. Like he was getting ready to dive from an airplane and he didn't have a lot of faith in his parachute. "You have something else you wanted to say?"

He thought about it for only a second more before he spoke. "My brother was a vegetarian," he said.

It took me a second to figure out what he was talking about. Then it came to me: our fight back at the house the day before. *Everything's this deep dark mystery with you.* I looked at him. He looked back at me. No flinching. No deflection. Despite that, there was no doubt how hard it was for him to share this piece of himself with me.

"He had been since he was six," he continued. "I told him where burgers came from, and that was it. The kid was crazy about animals."

"So, you stopped eating meat."

"I haven't had so much as a fish stick since the day he died." He got quiet and looked down, rubbing his palms on his jeans. "You know me better than anyone, Sol. You always have."

We sat there a second more before he stood. He lay his hand lightly on my head. "You should talk to Juarez. Let him be nice to you. Who knows—you might actually like it."

He walked away.

I sat there with my coffee and my chocolate and my bruises. I could still feel the weight and the warmth of his hand.

15
DANNY

DANNY SAT ON THE COOL GROUND with zip ties cutting into his wrists. He didn't know what time it was. He'd been fuzzy about details when he first woke up, but they were getting clearer now. Behind him was a cement wall. A big, thick steel door was the only way in or out. Above the door, angry red numbers below a bare red light bulb counted down:

24:09:52

He'd been watching those numbers so long he thought he'd lose his head. When he first woke up, they'd been at 38:42:20. He'd memorized that number. Couldn't get it out of his mind now.

His body ached. His mouth tasted like he'd swallowed a wool blanket.

Just like he'd been doing since he woke up, he thought back to the night before. Tried to remember what happened. He remembered talking to Dougie over to Casey's house. Playing guitar. Smokin' up.

He remembered somebody calling to him from outside. A lady's voice. Familiar, but none of the girls he knew. Saying sweet things that made him leave the garage like he was a puppet on a string. I *been watchin' you, Danny Durham,* she'd said in a low, whispery kind of way that made him ache in a way he never had before.

He'd taken his stuff—his backpack and his cell phone and his keys. Gone out into the dark night.

It all went black from there.

And he woke up here.

His backpack was gone. So was his cell phone, and his smokes.

"Hello?" he called out again. He'd been calling out since he got here. Nobody ever answered, though. His voice echoed in the small room.

Quite a pickle you got yourself into, boy, his daddy said. He sat down on the floor across from Danny, stiff 'cause his daddy never sat on the floor. He was wearing jeans and that flannel Rick and Danny got him for his last birthday—not the ugly brown suit they buried him in.

Tears needled behind Danny's eyelids. "Quit hauntin' me, old man."

You really wanna be alone in this place?

Danny shook his head. Fear knotted up his insides.

Nah, his daddy said. *I didn't think so.*

Somewhere above him, Danny heard music—he'd been hearing music for a while, actually. Not too bad, either: mostly classic rock, but a little of that indie stuff Diggs always sent him. Sometimes, he heard footsteps off in the distance. He wondered what would happen if he made a racket—a big one. Took off his shoes and threw them at the door. Screamed bloody murder.

"You think they'll kill me like they done you?" he asked his daddy.

His daddy just looked at him. *I don't reckon they brought you here for a game of checkers, son.*

PART II
THE FINAL
COUNTDOWN

16
SOLOMON

24:00:00

AT EXACTLY MIDNIGHT, someone blew up the power station that generated electricity for Justice and its outlying areas. Juarez got the call, and I watched a shadow fall over his face. He hid it well, but the fear in his eyes in that split second before he regained control spoke volumes. Juarez isn't the kind of guy who scares easily.

"They've called the National Guard in," he told Diggs and me. We were outside the hospital, standing in an ambulance bay far from prying ears. "They're talking about evacuating the town."

"Forget it," Diggs said. "Nobody will go with you. They don't like outsiders telling them what to do—and if they think there's a holy war coming, they're sure as hell not gonna want a bunch of Feds telling them they have to leave."

"That's what we assumed," Juarez said. "They've also taken out a cell tower, so communication is spotty. I'd like you two to stay back here until we can get you out of the area."

He said it like he was giving us a Christmas wish list: *A*

shiny red bike, a new sled for Jimmy, and for you two to stay the hell home. Not surprisingly, Diggs shook his head.

"You know I can't do that," he said. "Danny's missing. These people are family to me."

I didn't mention that Einstein was still with Mae, and there was no way I was sitting back and letting my dog get swept up in a zombie apocalypse. Einstein was occasionally a sore spot between Juarez and me.

Juarez held up his hand. "I know you won't stay. I said it was what I'd like—not what I thought would actually happen. Agent Blaze wants you both back at the station, anyway." He looked at Diggs. "You know the area, which could prove invaluable for us. That and your knowledge of Barnel and several of the key players in this plan mean Allie isn't anxious to see you go just yet. But it's my job to let you know the risks."

"We're fine," I said. "We'll go."

Diggs nodded, his decision already made.

We moved out.

22:48:01

About an hour into the drive, Diggs made me tune the radio to WKRO and his Buddy Crazy Jake came over the airwaves.

"If what our friend Reverend Barnel tells us is true," Crazy Jake said, "and we've got just a few hours left here on the planet, you know there's no place I'd rather be than right here, brothers and sisters. I've got a generator, a six pack, and a carton of smokes to carry me through, and to celebrate the end of the world as we know it, I'm spinnin' the full length, top twenty-four records of all time…"

I could all but feel Diggs perk up. "Damn. This'll be good," he said from the back seat.

"We just heard *Bridge Over Troubled Water*," Jake continued. Diggs groaned. "By the legendary Simon and Garfunkel, and now we're into an album that started as a rock opera but never quite—"

"*Who's Next*," Diggs said. Juarez looked back over his shoulder. I rolled my eyes when, sure enough, Jake listed the Who's sixth album as number twenty-three in his End of the World list. Diggs reached up front and turned down the volume.

"So, let's have it," he said. "Top twenty-four records of all time, you two. Don't think, just go."

Juarez started to speak. "Don't let him bait you," I said. "It's a trick. You start listing your favorite records of all time, and pretty soon you're in a lengthy debate over popular music and the decline of civilization and whether Frank Zappa could kick Tom Waits' ass in a fight."

"I resent that," Diggs said.

"But you don't deny it," I returned.

"Not completely."

I turned the music back up. We drove on. Shortly thereafter, Juarez stopped the SUV and a bright white light moved toward us. It was raining outside. I'd been lulled into a kind of trance state between the music, the rhythm of the windshield wipers, and my own exhaustion, but the white light brought me out of that. A man in fatigues and a rain poncho appeared, rifle at his side.

He stopped at Juarez's window and shined a MagLite inside.

"ID, please?" he asked. He lowered his light seconds before my retinas burst into flame.

Juarez handed over his badge. "Special Agent Jack Juarez. What's the status?"

The man grimaced. He was early forties, clean cut, military posture. "They took out another cell tower—

there's still some reception, but we may need to switch to sat coms before the night's out. Slippery bastards. Whoever they are, these sons of bitches are organized: they know the countryside a whole lot better than we do, and somehow or other they're having no trouble getting around us. We've got people covering every road in or out of town, but it's a lot of territory. Looks like it's more widespread than we thought, too—maybe the whole county."

"Thanks for all you're doing," Juarez said. He took his ID back. "Be careful—I don't have a good feeling about this."

"Agreed," the soldier said. "And you watch yourself, too."

The night was taking on a distinctly surreal quality.

"Can I ask you a question?" Diggs asked after we'd been on the road for a few minutes.

Juarez nodded. "Of course."

"How the hell is this happening? I mean… What about the Patriot Act? Wire tapping and satellite surveillance and all the rest—isn't that specifically to guard against something like this? Something this organized, shouldn't there have been some chatter?"

"We've been hearing some rumblings recently about something happening in this region," Juarez said. He didn't seem to take offense to the question. "Allie—Agent Blaze—has been following Barnel's activities for a while. But there's never been anything to suggest a plan of this magnitude. Someone new must have come on the scene, because we've watched all the old players. No one is sophisticated enough for something like this."

"But you don't have any idea who this someone might be?" I asked.

Juarez shook his head. "I welcome any suggestions."

I had none.

22:00:06

By two a.m., the rain was coming down in sheets and Crazy Jake was just kicking off *The Allman Brothers at Fillmore East*. Apparently, Jake wasn't a fan of anything recorded after 1975. The wind blew hard enough to take down branches and blow wayward woodland creatures hither and yon. Diggs, Juarez, and I were all wide awake now, bouncing between the police scanner and WKRO as Diggs directed us along deserted backroads.

When we were still about half an hour from our destination, I saw flames up ahead. Juarez slowed down. In a field to our right, someone had erected and torched a giant cross—upside down, of course. They were nothing if not consistent. Juarez called in his location and pulled over.

"You know whose house this is?" he asked Diggs.

"When I lived here, it belonged to a guy named Dickie Johnson." Clearly it wasn't the time for jokes, but still… "He cooked meth in there last I knew. Has half a dozen kids. Not exactly a pillar of society."

Juarez nodded, his hand already on the door handle. I grabbed his arm.

"What are you doing?"

"I need to go in and check on everyone. Evacuate the place. If that's a meth lab, a fire that close to the house could kill everyone in there."

"Shouldn't you wait for backup?" I had no idea when I'd become the voice of reason in this trio, but I wasn't loving it.

"I don't know when they'll get here. We've got people spread all over the county at this point. I'll be careful."

Diggs got out while Juarez and I were arguing. I followed.

"I'm not sitting here in the truck while you guys get blown up," I said. "Besides which, if there are a bunch of kids in there, you'll need help getting them out."

"Yeah," Diggs agreed. "Haven't you heard? Kids love Solomon."

I couldn't even summon a proper glare. Juarez took the lead, with Diggs close behind and me bringing up the rear.

The cross was burning only about ten feet from the house—which wasn't so much a house as a westward-leaning shack built on a hillside. The smell of gasoline fumes was strong in the air. A hound dog was chained outside, barking his head off at us. Beer cans and toys littered the yard. A garbage can had toppled over and animals had gotten into the bags, leaving soggy wads of trash drowning in the mud around us.

Juarez ordered us back behind a rusted-out car with no tires while he knocked on the door. I couldn't figure out why he didn't have his gun drawn, until I realized any spark from firing could send the whole place sky high. As realizations go, it wasn't a heartening one. I realized I wasn't breathing. Seconds later, he pushed the door open. Diggs crouched beside me in the rain. He didn't appear to be breathing, either. Finally, after I lost just under a decade of my life, Juarez reappeared at the door and waved us inside.

The shack smelled like a heady combination of backed-up sewer, chemicals, stale cigarette smoke, and beer. Dishes were stacked high in the sink. Three fly strips hung from the ceiling, the most recent victim still buzzing as it tried to free itself from the glue.

I stopped in front of the refrigerator. A picture from a Dora the Explorer coloring book was held in place with a magnet advertising towing services for a local garage. The picture was colored in with precision—not a single mark outside the lines. At the top, written in a child's hand, were the words:

To Daddy
Love Megan

I stared at the picture for a long time. My eyes burned. Juarez came over, took one look at the picture, and guided me away with his hand at my elbow.

"No one's here," he said.

"You think they were taken?"

"I don't know—but they're gone now. The fire crew should be along in five. I just checked in."

"What about the dog?"

He looked at me blankly.

"There's a dog outside, chained up. Is there somewhere we can take him?" I turned to Diggs.

"He's better off here right now than the pound," Diggs said. "We'll leave him some food and water. It looks like he's got shelter out there—we can check on him again tomorrow."

I tried to think of an alternative.

I couldn't.

We repeated the same procedure at another shack in the woods just down the road, with the same results: no one home, no indication whether the occupants had been hijacked or had taken off on their own.

The third time, Diggs spotted the cross first. "Shit," he said under his breath, just loud enough for us to hear.

Juarez pulled over. This place was different from the others, surrounded on all sides by sturdy steel fencing, topped by a line of barbed wire. We were deep in the woods, the house barely visible from the road.

"What is this?" Juarez asked.

"A clinic," Diggs said. He got out without elaborating. He didn't have to. In this area, I was guessing abortion clinics didn't exactly hang a neon sign out front.

The gate leading in was closed and locked, but the cross was burning on the other side—which meant clearly someone had gotten through.

"There's another way in around back," Diggs said over his shoulder, already on his way. Juarez got out his flashlight and we followed Diggs into the woods, traveling along the fence line.

It took twenty minutes, traveling through dense brush and half-obscured trails before he finally found what he was looking for. There was a gap maybe a foot wide, a creek running right through.

"The woman who runs the place is named Sally Woodruff," Diggs said. "She uses this when she doesn't want anyone to know she's gone."

I looked at him quizzically.

"She's not real popular around here—tends to get in trouble when she leaves the property, so she tries to fly under the radar."

Right.

The air was cool, rain falling a little less ferociously now. I followed the fellas through the creek to the other side, barely registering the ice water seeping into my sneakers.

Diggs didn't bother waiting for us once we were through, instead loping across the open yard toward a pretty, two-story brick house. Gardens that I suspected had been well tended were now in shambles, an arbor torn down, flowers trampled. A cherub that had obviously once topped the antique fountain at the head of those gardens had been knocked off. It lay in a pool of muddy standing water, one wing broken.

The cross continued to burn, the flames deep orange against the night sky.

The front door of the house stood open. We followed Diggs inside, and were greeted with chaos: furniture thrown, spray-painted epithets on the walls, more inverted crosses as far as the eye could see.

"She left," Diggs said. He sounded relieved.

"How can you be sure?" I asked.

"Sally has dogs—she rescues pit bulls. Has at least half a dozen of them. If they're not here, it's because she took them and ran before anyone got here."

He shook his head, running his hand through his hair. I tried to think of something comforting to say, but came up with nothing. It was five a.m. According to Barnel's timetable, we had nineteen hours left until "judgment." I wasn't sure any of us were prepared to deal with whatever his followers had in store for those nineteen hours.

18:46:02

We stopped at the Durhams' after Sally Woodruff's place. Morning was just breaking, gray and drizzling. It felt like the night had gone on for years. I lowered my visor and looked in the vanity mirror, watching as Diggs stared out the window, his forehead tipped against the glass. I tried to imagine the kind of sanctuary the Durhams must have represented for him—a teenage boy whose parents had both as much as told him he'd ruined their lives with one stupid, disastrous mistake.

Given his background, I could understand why it might be appealing for him to disappear here for those five years when he'd married Ashley. Try to start a new life as an official member of the Durham clan.

Juarez stopped the car and cleared his throat. Diggs looked up. I snapped my vanity mirror closed again.

"We'll just run in and check on them, and get our stuff," Diggs said.

"Go ahead," Juarez said, with a nod that included both of us. "I'll wait."

Einstein greeted me at the door with a kind of subdued, anxious enthusiasm—like he was well aware the world was falling apart around our ears, and he didn't appreciate being sidelined during all the action.

Mae was on the couch in the sitting room, surrounded by candles. Ida slept with her head in her mother's lap, her pale blonde hair hiding her face, while Mae thumbed through old photo albums. She put her finger to her lips when we came in.

"We just wanted to check on you," Diggs whispered. He looked so guilty you would have thought he'd personally engineered this whole plot himself. Mae nodded to the photos in her lap.

"I've been looking over some things," she whispered. "We had a lot of good times over the years, didn't we?"

Diggs nodded, mute. Mae put her hand over his and squeezed. "This wasn't your fault, darlin'," she said softly. At the words, Diggs swallowed convulsively. A good stiff breeze and I expected the whole room to dissolve into tears. "You don't listen to anything I said—you were lookin' out for my boy, the way you've always done. That's it."

He kissed the top of her head. "We'll get him back, Mae."

"I know," she said. Something about the hollow way she said it, though, made me think she didn't believe him. "I'm gonna pack up the kids and move on over to Ashley's as soon as everybody's up, at least till this is over. It's not good for them, me rattling around the house like this."

"What about Rick?" Diggs asked.

"Sleepin'," Mae said. "That boy can sleep through

anything. Always could. Danny was always restless, colicky, always after somethin'. Rick never seemed to need anything. Danny needed the world."

It felt like she wasn't even talking to us anymore, gazing at the photos of a life she'd lost in the blink of an eye. Diggs and I stood there awkwardly for a minute more before we said our goodbyes, and went upstairs together to pack the rest of our things.

18:00:02

The war room looked much more warrish when we got there at six o'clock that morning. For one thing, Blaze had moved from the tiny room in the back of the police station to a classroom at the local elementary school, now being powered by generators. The kids' desks had been moved out to make way for actual, grown up replacements. New computers and a dozen agents filled the space. In front of the chalkboard and a map of the U.S. was Blaze's nifty super-computer.

"Wait in the hall, please," she said to Diggs and me as soon as we crossed the threshold. She looked tired. And very pissed off.

We did as she ordered, seated in two of those god awful student desk/chair combo torture deals, beside a trophy case and a mural of dancing tigers. I had no idea why the tigers were dancing. Maybe they were excited about the end of the world.

Einstein took all of it in stride, seemingly just happy to be back under my feet again. A minute or two into our wait, however, he was up again, whining anxiously. Buddy Holloway came around the corner and Stein dashed after him like they were old friends, whimpering ecstatically. Another two seconds and it became clear that Buddy's appearance had nothing to do with my pup's warm reception.

Grace, the Burketts' golden retriever, appeared a few steps behind Buddy. Her tail was down and her head was bandaged. She looked miserable. Buddy waved to us; he didn't look all that happy himself. Einstein trotted over and gave Grace a perfunctory butt sniff before he very gently bumped against her side and licked her muzzle.

"Looks like you found a friend," Diggs said to Buddy.

The deputy scowled. "I didn't mean to, believe me. The dang vet closed his office, and nobody was around to take her. Otherwise they would'a taken her to the pound, and like as not she would'a been put down before the end of the day. My wife'll kill me, though. We've got a little one on the way and two dogs in the house already—I'll be sleepin' with 'em if I bring Gracie here home."

"I can watch her, if you want," I said, long before I really had a chance to think it over. Buddy looked like he'd kiss me.

"You sure? That'd sure be a load off my mind."

"What's one more? Though just for a few days," I qualified. "Assuming the world doesn't end at midnight, we'll need to find her a permanent home. One that's not mine."

"Sure thing," Buddy agreed. He eyed the war room. "How's everything goin' in there?"

"Not sure," Diggs said. "We haven't made it inside yet. What's the status on the DQ bombing? Any news?"

"Two dead. About twenty-plus injured. No damage beyond the Dairy Queen and…well, the sheriff's van, of course. Looks like he used a few homemade Malatov cocktails. Had some explosives inside his car, too." He shook his head. He looked as tired as I felt. "I still can't believe he's gone. And I sure can't believe the way he went."

Blaze opened the door then and greeted Buddy with

a perfunctory nod. "You mind giving me a few minutes, Deputy? Go on in and find a seat—I'll be in shortly to brief everyone."

"Yes, ma'am," he said quickly and stepped past her. I had a feeling Diggs wasn't getting off so easily.

Blaze nodded to our torture chairs. "Have a seat."

We sat. The dogs settled at our feet and Blaze walked down the hallway until she found a normal chair and carried it over. She set it facing Diggs.

"Are you all right?" she asked him.

"Yeah," he said. "Few stitches. Nothing major."

"That's good," she said. She looked at me.

"I'm fine," I said before she could ask.

"Excellent. I heard what you two did after the explosion— how you helped getting people to safety. Well done."

"Thanks," Diggs said. "It was mostly Solomon, though—"

"I'm not finished," Blaze said. Her eyes never left Diggs'. It was getting damned uncomfortable in that hallway.

"This worked out, in the sense that you're both alive, and you apparently were not the motive behind Jennings' attack. But, if you ever ditch me again, I will put that cute little ass of yours in jail faster than you can say 'prison bitch.'"

"I didn't—" Diggs began.

"Still not done," she said shortly. "Make no mistake, Mr. Diggins: I believe these people will come after you. It's not a question of if, it's a question of when. But I'm not just here to protect you; I'm here to stop a plot that as far as we know could kill dozens, if not hundreds.

"I know exactly what you and your little girlfriend here pulled on Agent Juarez in Canada over the summer. That will not happen here. When I tell you to do something, I want it done. And you two can roll your eyes and make snide comments all you want—I'm here to do a job. I'll do everything in my power to see that you and everyone here makes it through this. But if that doesn't happen, it sure as hell is not gonna be because you refused to follow basic instructions from me regarding this investigation."

And then, she took out a pair of handcuffs and slapped one around Diggs' wrist and one around his desk.

"This isn't baseball—there's no three strikes rule. Ditch me once, shame on me. Ditch me twice, your balls are in a vice. You're in protective custody from here on out."

She looked at me. I swallowed hard and tried not to look even remotely obstinate. "Agent Juarez assures me you'll do whatever he says regarding this investigation. So far, you've proven that to be true. See that it stays that way."

She got up, patted Diggs on the head like he was one of the pups at our feet, and walked away. I stared after her.

"Wow," I finally managed. I looked at Diggs. "Honestly? I think I'm a little turned on."

"I wish you two well," he said. He glared at his cuffs. "This really isn't going to work for me, though."

●

One of the new agents from Blaze's team—Agent Keith, an overly muscled little guy with an obvious Napoleon complex—came out a few minutes later, uncuffed Diggs, and led us back into the war room. Blaze's point had clearly been made.

Inside, Diggs and I took our seats in the back, the dogs once more at my feet. In addition to a dozen FBI agents, there were now half a dozen National Guardsmen and women lined up at attention in the back of the classroom. It made for a disconcerting meeting, to say the least.

"So, what do we know?" Blaze asked Agent Keith. He stood.

"Jesup Barnel was a preacher who began holding services at sixteen, back in 1962. He started the casting out of demons for which he was known, officially in 1967. However, there are indications that he may have begun as early as '63."

A video came up on the screen at the head of the class: A much younger Barnel, standing over a teenage boy strapped to a table. The boy was stripped to his tighty whities, surrounded by about twenty men, women, and children exhorting the Lord to rid him of his demons. Barnel's son— Brother Jimmy, the same guy who'd clocked Diggs after Wyatt's funeral—handed him a branding iron. The end was blazing orange. The kid screamed.

Blaze turned the video off.

"Barnel apparently fancied himself a filmmaker: his activities were well documented over the years. This is footage from one of Barnel's standard exorcisms, performed in 1986. Of more than two thousand such rituals, we've found video footage of more than half." I felt Diggs tense beside me. Blaze caught his eye, then looked away. I caught the significance of the look, though: they'd seen footage of Diggs. Or, if they hadn't watched, they at least had it there. Blaze continued, her focus back on the rest of the group.

"To date, four of Barnel's victims have now been executed and defaced by the removal of the preacher's ritual cross, and the subsequent reattachment of the skin upside down, resulting in an inverted cross. There are two possible meanings for this."

She shifted, bringing something up on the Smart Board. "An inverted cross is used widely in satanic ritual, and may be the killer's way of taking credit for the crime. The victim, in this case, would be viewed as a sacrifice."

"But you don't think this is Satanists," Diggs said.

"No," she agreed. "I've consulted with my colleagues, and we agree this is more likely rooted in Christian symbolism.

For those unfamiliar with Biblical scripture, there is a story in early Apocryphal works relating how Christ's apostle—Peter—requested that he be crucified upside down, as he didn't feel he was worthy to die in the same manner Christ had. From that point on, an inverted cross became known as the Cross of St. Peter, or the Latin Cross. In Catholicism and other Christian religions, it's become associated with humility and deference to Christ."

"So, these Latin crosses are to show the world that the victim isn't worthy of an actual, right-side-up cross," I said.

"That's our thought," Juarez agreed.

"And the upside-down crosses they're torching all over town?" I asked.

"Similar meaning," Blaze said. "A way for them to identify those unworthy during the judgment that Barnel has set in motion."

Diggs raised his hand. Blaze glared at him, but she gave him the floor. "You said four of Barnel's boys have been killed and marked with the Latin cross. The last I heard, though, there were only three: Marty Reynolds, Wyatt Durham, and Roger Burkett."

Juarez looked to Blaze, who nodded. "Last night," Juarez said, "we looked more deeply into town archives, and found something. In 1963, a nineteen-year-old college student named Billy Thomas took a bunch of kids hostage while they were on a field trip in the Justice Town Hall. He let most of the kids go. He kept three girls, however, saying they were possessed by demons. That night, he raped and killed all three girls."

"I remember that story," Diggs said. "What does that have to do with this? Billy left the town hall after he killed the girls, went back to school, and hanged himself."

Juarez rearranged a couple of images on the screen, enlarging one: Barnel's cross, excised and reattached—

though not nearly as neatly as those on Wyatt or Roger Burkett's chests. This one looked like it had been reattached with a staple gun.

Diggs turned away. I blanched, but held strong.

"According to the coroner's report at the time," Juarez continued, "this was self-inflicted by Billy."

I studied the gory handiwork. "There's no way it could have been," I said. "Any idiot would know that. And it must have been done shortly before he died—the blood hadn't even dried."

"That was our determination, as well," Blaze said.

"So, what does this have to do with what's happening now?" I asked. "You think the same person is behind all four deaths?"

"The date the girls were murdered and Billy Thomas allegedly killed himself," Blaze said, "was March 15, 1963."

"And the date Barnel gave for judgment is March 15, 2013," Diggs said. "Exactly fifty years later."

That statement hung in the air for a minute before Diggs spoke again.

"There was a rumor that Barnel put together some kind of a review board to follow the progress of the boys he cleansed," he said. "Supposedly in the mid-1960s. I could never substantiate that while I was here, though."

Blaze didn't look surprised, which made me think this wasn't the first time she'd heard of this.

"If there was something like that, do you have a sense who might be involved?" Blaze asked.

Diggs didn't hesitate. "Sheriff Jennings, of course. Ron and Walter Reese—I think Jack and Solomon already had the pleasure with those two. The mayor, possibly…" He hesitated. "I'm not sure who else."

"Is it possible that if we can either find Barnel or force him to stay in hiding, we could just wait this whole thing out?" I asked. "People may be panicked right now, but if they can just chill out till midnight passes and it doesn't start raining toads, shouldn't we be home free?"

"In theory," Blaze said. "But this is much larger in scope than we ever imagined. The sheriff's act was clearly one he'd been planning—it was very carefully orchestrated. Our chatter now indicates that Barnel and whoever he's working with have a series of similar scenarios planned for the hours leading up to midnight."

"And what about what happens at midnight?" I asked. "Do you have any clue what's in store?"

Blaze looked grim. Shook her head. "We don't know. We've tried to track down Barnel's followers, without a lot of success. Those we have tracked down insist they don't know anything about this. Everyone else has gone underground. Whatever they have in store, it will be bigger and bloodier than anything we've seen thus far."

Wonderful.

"So, is there a plan?" I asked. "Or are we just going to ride out the coming storm and hope for the best?"

"Our priority continues to be tracking down Jesup Barnel," she said. "As well as monitoring any likely targets over the next twenty-four hours. In the meantime, schools and local shops will be closed. A strict curfew is in effect beginning at eighteen hundred. Guards are stationed with orders to search every vehicle entering or leaving town."

"What about churches?" Diggs asked. "Because you better believe these people will be flocking to them right now."

"We won't keep residents from that," Blaze said, "because we can't. We will, however, be monitoring those services closely. If a pin drops within Justice town boundaries in the next twenty-four hours, we'll know about it."

"And where do you want us?" Agent Keith asked.

"We'll switch things up this time," Blaze said. She was looking right at Diggs and me. "Solomon, you'll ride with me. Mr. Diggins, Special Agent Juarez will have the pleasure of your company today. And I'd like to remind you that that means Agent Juarez's career is in your hands—if you pull something, it's his butt on the line."

Diggs grimaced, but he didn't argue. I pulled him aside before everyone saddled up. I'd seen him look better.

"In the past twenty-four hours, you've been bitten by a rattlesnake, beaten down, and blown up," I said.

"And your point?"

"My point is: let Jack do his job. Please. Work together, and you'll be two hundred and forty-five point six times more likely to get this done than if you freak out and take off on your own."

"I can't believe I'm getting this lecture from you."

"Trust me, I'm well aware of the irony. Just…be normal, okay? Don't be you."

"Ah, the message every mother tries to instill in her young."

"I'm not your mother. And I *will* kick your ass if you get yourself killed."

"Solomon!" Agent Blaze shouted. I jumped. Seriously, the woman would freak out a squadron of Marines. "Everyone'll get a few hours' rack time as soon as I can manage. For now, I need your ass in the truck."

"I have no idea what that means," I whispered to Diggs. "But I'm pretty sure it's a threat. I have to go." I hesitated. It occurred to me that with Armageddon a mere twenty hours away now, it might be a good time to say…something. The best I could manage was, "Be careful."

He nodded, holding my eye. "You, too."

17
DIGGS

THE TOWN SQUARE was deserted. Shop owners had boarded the windows at the hardware store and the Qwik E Mart. The town hall was locked up tight and the movie theater was abandoned, a couple of flyers washed up outside the ticket office. The only one still working was Jake Dooley, sitting behind a plate glass window at WKRO—home to one of the most schizophrenic programming mixes around: country, hip hop, gospel, bluegrass, top forty…and Jake.

Juarez and I walked down a dark corridor, turned a corner, and found the ON AIR sign lit above a glass door. Jake waved us in, adjusted a couple of sliders on his control board, and removed his headphones. We were into hour seven of Jake's twenty-four best records list, which was a genius way to go out as far as I was concerned. He'd blown over two hours on the complete *Muddy Waters Anthology*, which meant we were only up to number nineteen on the list: *The White Album*.

Jake wore John Lennon glasses, a baseball hat with a peace sign on it, and an Elvis t-shirt. He'd gained maybe twenty-five pounds since I'd seen him last. If that put him over a buck fifty on the scales, you could slap my ass and call me Lady Gaga. He got up and gave me a hug, shook Juarez's hand vigorously, and sat back down—the whole circuit completed in the space of maybe fifteen seconds. Good to know the end of the world hadn't slowed him down any.

"Seriously, Jake—*The White Album*? You think you could be a little more obvious?" I started out.

"Oh, I know it ain't edgy enough for the likes of you," he said. "I guess you'd rather I stick with records nobody never heard of. Sorry, boy, there's a reason somethin' gets to be a classic."

"Sure," I agreed. "Because unimaginative DJs the world over are too timid to spin anything new." Jake grinned at that, rolling his eyes. "How much you want to bet I can guess the rest of that list in two tries or under?" I asked.

"We don't actually have time for that," Juarez said. Jake looked disappointed. I was a little disappointed myself.

"All right, fine. Business it is," I said. "Listen, I know Barnel does a show here."

"Never misses a Sunday, the old bastard," Jake agreed. "One of the drawbacks of this kind of thing—can't turn 'em away so long as they come with a check."

"Have you noticed anything…off, about his message the past few weeks?" Juarez asked.

"You mean more than usual?" Jake asked. "Now that you mention it, I did. He's been real weird the last couple months—paranoid, you know? And actin' like the Lord's put this heavy burden on him. He's been talking more than usual about being called home, too—that's what he always calls it. I thought maybe he was sick, but when I asked he said the Lord showed him the future. Said the world was in for a wake-up call."

"Did he say anything specific about that wake-up call?" Juarez asked.

"Nah—but it's not like I listened too close. He seemed to think his days were numbered, but it was pretty clear he didn't think he was goin' down alone." He shook his head, uncharacteristically serious. "I wish to hell I'd paid closer attention—to tell the truth, it never even occurred to me he might talk the sheriff into somethin' like what he pulled last night, blowing that place up."

"So the whole thing was a surprise to you," Juarez said.

"A surprise only because you just don't think that kind of thing really happens," Jake said. "Not because I never thought he was capable. Everybody else might've loved him, but I always said Jesup Barnel was a creepy son of a bitch."

"You'll get no argument from me," I agreed. On the radio, George Harrison was just kicking into his mournful back-up vocals while Paul and the boys sang of gently weeping guitars. I looked around, trying to find some sign of the rest of Jake's list. "What about top five? You'll have Robert Johnson in there—you may be mainstream, but you've got taste. And I know *Astral Weeks* will be in one of those top slots."

Juarez shot me a look meant to shut me up. I took the cue. "Do you have any idea where Barnel and his followers might have gone?" I asked, getting back to the point.

"I know him and the sheriff were either out at Barnel's camp or they were out playin' with themselves over to the town hall. They got that ping pong table in the cellar, you know? They was always down there doing something or other. You checked the camp, I'm guessing?"

"Deserted," Juarez said. "We're trying to contact some of the more prominent members of his congregation now."

"The Reese boys?" Jake asked. I nodded.

"My guess is most everyone's gone underground," I said. "We're trying to figure out their next move, but it would be a lot easier if we could smoke out at least a few."

"There's a hell of a lot of places to hide in these hills—you know that," he said to me. He hesitated.

"What?" I prompted.

"A couple years back, Barnel started gettin' real antsy about the government nosin' around in his business. I didn't pay much attention—he was always paranoid, and it got old real fast listening to him. But I happened to walk in while he was talking to Ronnie Reese—you know those boys owned the woods out around Barnel's compound? I got the sense he was lookin' to extend his property lines."

"The woods are thick out there," I said. "It would be a good place to get lost."

"Barnel's a lazy S-O-B," Jake said. "Way I see it, he wouldn't go too far out of his way if he needed some privacy."

"That could be a good lead," I said. "Thanks. Anywhere else that comes to mind?"

"Not that I recall. Sorry. Hope I was at least a little help to you, though."

"You were, thank you," Juarez said. He paused. "Listen, we've got generators and we've set up a shelter at the local elementary school if you change your mind about staying here. You can stop by anytime. There's food and blankets, and it's somewhere to keep warm until this passes, anyway."

"And leave all this?" Jake asked. "Thanks but no thanks. I'll stay right here till the final bell's rung, if it's all the same to you."

Not a surprise. Juarez looked torn before he finally conceded. "Suit yourself. But you're always welcome."

"I'll remember that," Jake said. He shook my hand again, more solemnly this time. "Good to see you, Diggs. Nice to know you haven't changed too much since you been gone."

"Not in the ways that count," I said. "Number one's *Pet Sounds*, isn't it? I mean—it's the obvious choice. And then you'll have a little Zeppelin in there, some Dylan: *Blood on the Tracks*... Maybe *Blonde on Blonde*?"

Juarez grabbed my elbow and hauled me out the door.

From WKRO, our next stop was the police station. The lobby was empty—no secretary, no lights, no phones. We found Buddy in his office, stretched out on a too-small sofa with his hat over his eyes. He sat up and wiped the drool from the corners of his mouth at our entrance.

"Sorry you caught me like this," he said. "All-nighters ain't quite so easy as they once was, huh, Diggs?"

"You got that right," I said. "Listen, I know someone's already going through the sheriff's files, but we thought you might be able to answer a couple questions."

"Shoot," Buddy said.

Juarez pulled up a chair and sat, his elbows resting loosely on his knees as he leaned forward. "We've got two priorities right now: Finding Barnel's people, and figuring out what their ultimate target will be at midnight. If Jennings ever mentioned any place where he may have met with Barnel…"

"I've been thinkin' about that," Buddy said. "The only place I can think of where they'd be out of the way would be the reverend's camp—but we already sent folks out there to check it out. No luck."

"The man at the radio station mentioned something about Barnel extending the property lines at his compound. Do you know anything about that?"

The deputy shook his head. "Can't say I ever heard anything about it, but I'll look into it."

"What about targets?" I asked. "This isn't making a lot of sense to me. I would think the point of whatever they have planned at midnight is mass casualties, but with the warning they've given and the amount of damage they're doing leading up to it, everything's shut down. The Feds are keeping a close eye on the few gathering spots left—mostly churches."

"Don't seem like Barnel would want to take out the churches, though," Buddy said. "I expect the sheriff picked the Dairy Queen because that's where all the local kids in rougher crowds hung out—used to drive him crazy."

"And this is a dry county, so I'm assuming there are no bars," Juarez said.

"We used to have the Wilson Club," Buddy said. "You remember that place, Diggs…"

"Sure," I said. I remembered it all too well, as it happened. "It's an old factory they turned into a bar back in the '70s. There's a loophole in the law where private clubs can serve alcohol, so we'd all go there to raise hell."

"That sounds like a good bet," Juarez said.

"Except the reverend and Sheriff Jennings shut 'em down last year," Buddy said. "Now some rich fella from away owns the place. He keeps to himself, mostly." He shook his head. "Thanks to Reverend Barnel, there's not too many places left to cause trouble round here."

The deputy took off his hat and scratched his head. "You know, for a while there it seemed like Wyatt was gettin' along all right with the reverend. George was never much of a fan, but I think Wyatt made more of an effort 'cause Mae was so partial to Reverend Barnel. Whatever happened between 'em back this fall, though…"

Juarez looked at him expectantly.

"They cut all ties," I finished for him.

"More than that," Buddy said. "Seems to me around that time is when the sheriff went just a little more off-kilter than he'd been before."

"But you don't know what their falling out was about?" Juarez asked.

Buddy shook his head. "Wish I did. I'm not sure that anybody did, really, short of Wyatt, Reverend Barnel, and the sheriff. And…"

He looked at me guiltily. I knew exactly what was coming next.

"And…?" Juarez prompted.

"I could be wrong," Buddy said. "But it seems to me that the only other person Wyatt would tell that stuff—short of you, Diggs—would be his sister." He winced sympathetically. "Sorry. I don't know if she'll talk to you or not, but it seems to me Ashley's the surest one to know why all of a sudden the reverend just up and cut Wyatt out of his flock."

As soon as we were in the truck, Juarez looked at me. "You know where we need to go next, don't you?"

"Disneyland?"

He rolled his eyes. Juarez is funny, in that you think you have him pegged as this Latin creampuff until he gets tired of playing that role. Not a lot gets by the guy—something I'd learned while he was staying with me the year before. "Have you talked to your ex-wife at all since you got here?"

"In passing."

"So you think the deputy's wrong. You don't think she might have some idea what's going on?"

Actually, I thought Buddy was completely right: Ashley would have a better idea what was going on than anyone in Justice. Ashley isn't just some hillbilly I picked up after Sunday service when I was sixteen—between scholarships and summer jobs, she paid for a private high school back east out of her own pocket, graduated summa cum laude from Wharton, and knows money better than the Pope knows Rome.

"She's not real fond of me these days," I said. "Truth is, I'm a little afraid of her."

"Get over it," he said. "I'm not sitting by while this town implodes because you're too much of a pussy to talk to your ex."

I looked at him in surprise. "Pussy? Damn. You've been spending too much time with Solomon. All this time I thought you were a nice Catholic boy."

He started the truck, shaking his head. "Between the two of you, you've knocked a lot of the nice out of me." He continued before I could reply. "You knew about the falling out between Wyatt and Reverend Barnel."

"Yeah," I said.

"Yet you never mentioned anything. Why?" He put the truck in gear.

"I don't know," I said. "George and Wyatt and I disagreed on just about everything...except Jesup Barnel. It doesn't seem like George's feelings have changed any. According to Mae, though, Barnel and Wyatt developed some kind of friendship. I'm not clear on why that changed."

"Did you get a chance to talk to George Durham about any of that the other night? Before the rattlesnake attack, of course."

I wondered what Solomon had told him about that night. I assumed she hadn't mentioned the ride to the hospital...or the fact that I was in her arms during the bulk of it. At least, I was hoping she hadn't. Juarez was the calm and steady type, but I didn't think he was *that* calm and steady. I pushed aside any residual guilt I might have felt for kissing Solomon when I knew she was Jack's girl, and considered his question.

"I didn't really know anything was happening at that point," I said. "I mean, all we had then was Wyatt's murder. We weren't thinking about the end of the world yet. I know George was a little off that night, but I just assumed that was about losing Wyatt. And everyone was so busy reminiscing and chugging moonshine, we didn't really get into the nitty gritty of the investigation."

"You didn't mention anything about George Durham to Erin, then?" he asked. "You don't think she may have noticed something that you didn't?"

"I didn't talk to her about it, really. She'd had a little to drink that night. Between that and the incident with the pit viper, we didn't have much time to debrief."

He didn't say anything to that. Too late, I remembered that Solomon had told me at some point that she was supposed to call Juarez that night, but never got the chance. And now here I was, telling him she hadn't called because she was off getting wasted with me and my old cronies. I looked out the window, watching smoke rise from a distant fire on the horizon. I took a deep breath and let it out, nice and slow.

"I know you probably weren't crazy about her coming down here with me," I said. Juarez glanced at me. Shook his head.

"You're important to her. She needed to be here for you—it was as much for her as anything."

"Jesus, Jack. Are you applying for sainthood now?"

He laughed dryly, a trace of sadness in there. "I just want what's best for her." He paused. The silence stretched on. I'd almost given up on the conversation by the time he spoke again. "How are you, anyway? Since the summer?"

The million-dollar question. I shrugged. "You mean apart from quitting my job, dumping my girl, and running off to the beach for two months? Apparently Black Falls didn't slide off me quite as well as some people."

His jaw hardened as soon as the words were out. He glanced at me, then back at the road. His hands were tight on the wheel.

"If you think anything just slid off Erin after last summer, you don't know her as well as I thought."

"She's pulled herself together pretty well from where I'm standing. She looks better than I've seen her in a long time. She's working out, taking classes. She quit smoking. Dumped the whole quest for her father."

He didn't say anything for a long time. I watched the world go by, and didn't speak.

"She still has nightmares, you know," he said, after a while. I went still, waiting for him to tell me things I knew Solomon never would. "She wakes up in the night, calling your name. She barely left the house for two months after she was released from the hospital—though I don't know that firsthand, of course. I only know what her mother has told me. Erin wouldn't take my calls after we got back. The only way I eventually saw her was by showing up on her doorstep one day in December."

He paused, waiting for me to say something. I didn't have a clue what that might be, though. He continued.

"Did you know she lost the use of her hand after the second surgery?" he asked.

I shook my head silently. Something dark and heavy settled itself at the pit of my stomach.

"The doctors weren't sure she'd ever get it back. I thought Kat was going to murder someone until we knew that the third surgery had gone well. Erin refuses to talk about what happened in the woods that night—who killed Rainier and Max. What they did to her. What they did to you. She added a security system to the house. Asked me to teach her self-defense. And up until you left town, she called Maya nearly every day to get an update on how you were, and to make sure you were safe."

"She told you all that?"

He laughed humorlessly. "Of course not. I learned all that from paying attention. She doesn't talk to me. She talks to you." He didn't sound bitter—merely resigned. "As far as I can tell, you're the only one she's ever talked to."

"I hate to burst your bubble, but she's never talked all that much to me, either."

As soon as the words were out of my mouth, I knew

they were a lie. Solomon might not spend all day everyday telling me every little thought that crossed her mind, but I knew she confided in me more than anyone else. And I had a feeling that whatever she'd held back over the years was as much my fault as hers: no one wants to lay all their cards on the table when the other guy holds his hand as close to the chest as I tend to. Juarez shot me a look that suggested he was well aware that I was full of shit.

"Why are you telling me all this?" I asked. "Nothing's going on between us, Jack. Solomon's not the cheating kind, trust me."

"I know that," he said. "But you act as though she was unaffected by what happened in Black Falls. That's not fair to her. Trust me: whatever went on over those forty-eight hours changed things for her."

I hesitated a long while before I spoke again. Finally, I blew out a long exhale and stared out the window, carefully avoiding Juarez's gaze when I spoke again.

"I know she wasn't unaffected—I'm just pissed off that she's doing all right without me. That you two are together, and she's focused and sane and moving on with her life, when I feel like I've been walking a flaming tightrope over a sea of great whites for the past six months. I know what happened out there. There's no way anyone comes out of that unchanged."

I waited for him to ask me just what, exactly, *had* happened. I wasn't sure what I'd tell him. I thought of the warmth of Solomon's skin against mine in the shower; the sight of her on her knees with a belt looped around her neck, gasping for air; the words Rainier had said to me just before I lost it and nearly killed him with my bare hands. Juarez never asked, though. We drove the rest of the way in silence.

15:20:02

I thought when she first answered the door that Ashley would slam it in my face. She debated it for five seconds, clearly, before she turned around and walked away.

Juarez and I crossed the threshold.

When we'd been together, Ashley had a gassy boxer named Winnie who followed her everywhere. There was no sign of the dog now, though. The walls had been repainted and new furniture replaced what had been there before. With the power out and the day shadowed by clouds, it was dim inside. Not so dim that I couldn't tell the place was in a hell of a lot better shape than it had been when I was living there.

Crying came from the kitchen. Ashley looked over her shoulder at us. "I was in the middle of giving Angus his breakfast. Come on."

The kitchen had always been a good spot for us—maybe the only one in the house. Like the rest of the place, it had been completely refurbished since I left: new appliances, stylish backsplash, trendy paint job, the works.

"It looks great," I noted.

"Terry's good with his hands."

Terry: the new husband. "Where is he, anyway?" I asked.

She looked at me like I was trying to start something. I really wasn't. "He works out toward Paducah. He'll be back by six. He's committed to his job, but he won't let it keep him from us when it matters."

That may not have sounded like a jab at me, but I knew it was. She sat down in front of Angus, who was in his high chair with a cup of Cheerios, a waffle cut into tiny squares, and a plastic Sesame Street train.

"Sit," she commanded Juarez and me.

We sat.

"What do you want, Diggs?"

"I need to ask you about Wyatt," I said.

Her eyes flickered to me, then back to the kid. She was good at lying—I'd learned that over the years. I'd also learned her tells. "What about him?" she asked.

"I want to know why he was targeted for this. Why Barnel turned against him six months ago."

She popped a waffle square into Angus's mouth and pushed a strand of hair back behind her ear. Angus chewed amiably, blue eyes watching me.

"I don't know," Ashley said.

"You're lying," I said. Her eyes flashed. "The hair thing, Ash—remember? This is me. We know he was into something. Was he having an affair?"

"You've been gone way too long if you think something like that. There wasn't another woman on the planet for him but Mae. You know that."

I did. I was unaccountably relieved to know that hadn't changed, though.

"I'll tell you what I think, then. You can just tell me how close I am to the mark."

Angus picked up a yellow train car with Big Bird in the driver's seat and smashed it into his Cheerios. The cup went flying. Ashley righted it without so much as a grimace, moving the food safely out of reach.

"What do you think, then?" she asked me. There was no mistaking the challenge in her tone.

"I think Danny was in a band," I said. "His bass player—Casey Clinton—got knocked up. She couldn't go to her father, and she didn't know where else to turn. So, I think Danny took her to see Wyatt."

Ashley didn't argue. She didn't look at me, either, her attention focused on Angus.

"I think Wyatt probably started out with the usual spiel

on the subject," I continued. "She was young, sure, but she could always put the kid up for adoption. Life is precious. Et cetera, et cetera."

Her mouth tightened at my blasé treatment of a subject I knew she took very seriously.

Juarez took over. "I can understand your perspective," he said. "I was raised Catholic. I feel the same way that you do—trust me on that. But sometimes there are circumstances that can shift your perspective."

To my surprise, her eyes filled at that. She sighed wearily. "A year ago, Danny got a girl pregnant." She looked at Angus like she was afraid he might somehow understand the words. I took the toy train cars from him and crashed them into one another gently. He giggled, his attention successfully diverted. Ashley continued.

"Danny didn't tell anybody about it, of course. But the girl was new around here—didn't know much about anything, and I guess she panicked. She went to old lady McCintock—she's still doing those abortions out in her back shed, even though Sally Woodruff's threatened everything short of stringing the old bat up. So, Sophie ends up on the old lady's table, and she almost died—it was an awful mess. Danny's a pain in the butt sometimes, but he's got a good heart. It shook him up; he came to me later, and we talked. He said he would've kept the baby. Married the girl, even, the romantic little fool."

"Sophie… That's the same Sophie who was killed in the explosion the other day?"

"That's the one." Her eyes clouded. "I wasn't crazy about the girl myself, but she didn't deserve that."

"So, he must have been pretty upset when Casey came to him and told him the same thing happened to her," I said.

"I thought the boy was gonna have a stroke," Ashley said. "I never did figure out who the baby's daddy was, but

Danny was fit to be tied… I think he would've taken her to Sally himself, but she started to miscarry."

"So he brought her to Wyatt," I guessed.

"He didn't have time to do anything else—she was in bad shape. Wyatt called Sally, and she came to his office. They did the whole thing right there."

We sat there in silence. Ashley put another waffle square in Angus's mouth. Her hand was shaking. He spit it out, focused on her now.

"Afterward, Wyatt came to me," Ashley continued. "He was torn up—you know how he was. I can be reasonable about this stuff, but his heart was just too big. He wasn't sorry, though; I think that's what confused him more than anything else. After that, he went out to Sally's place, and he started helpin' out. Just doing some chores around the house, taking care of stuff that needed fixin'. All quiet as could be, of course, but you know there are no secrets in this town."

If I'd been there, I thought, Wyatt would have told me. We would most likely have done the whole thing together. Wyatt was like that: If he thought something was right, he'd make it happen. No matter the personal cost.

"Did Mae know?" I asked.

"No," Ashley said. "You know how she feels about this. I've got my opinions, but I can at least see both sides. With Mae, this is one of those sins you can't get around. It would've killed her."

"What about your father?" I asked. "Did anyone tell George?"

She paused. Her hands were still trembling. "Wyatt didn't want to, but somebody let him know—I always suspected Reverend Barnel was behind it. That maybe he told Daddy just to hurt him. He and Wyatt fought. Didn't talk for close to a month, before Daddy finally gave in. After that, they'd still play cards, have a drink or two at the end of the day, but I know Daddy didn't get over it."

And neither did Jesup Barnel, apparently.

"One more thing," I said before we left. Ashley actually smiled—a sad smile, the one I'd seen the most during our marriage.

"There always is, Diggs. What else?"

"Who else knew? I mean—knew for sure."

"Barnel, of course…"

"But how did Barnel find out?" I pressed. "Sally never would have said anything. And I can't imagine Danny or Casey would breathe a word about it."

"I never figured that out," she admitted. "Far as I know, the only people who knew were Wyatt, Danny, Casey, and me. Sorry. I wish I could be more help."

"No," I said. "This was good—thanks. I should have come to you from the start."

She laughed. Angus grinned, watching her like she was the center of the universe. "Well, I don't know how likely I would've been to talk to you if the world weren't ending."

"Right," I agreed. "Good point."

Juarez and I stood. "If they've already killed Wyatt and Sophie, we should make sure someone's watching Casey," Juarez said—something I'd just been thinking myself.

He excused himself to get on the horn with the hospital. I rested my hand on Angus's downy head.

"He's a beautiful boy, Ash," I said. "Terry's a lucky man. I always said you'd make a good mom."

"You did," she agreed. "I never thought I'd say this, but one of these days, you might even make an all right father."

"Let's not get ahead of ourselves," I said with a laugh. I shuffled my feet, and with some effort managed to hold her eye. "I'm sorry about that crack earlier—if I made it seem like I'm just dismissing what happened to Sophie and Casey.

You and I will never see eye to eye on the issue, but I don't take it lightly."

"I know that. Try as you might to make people think otherwise, there's not much you take lightly," she said. She took a breath and nodded toward the door. "And that's enough mending fences today. Now I need you to go out there and figure out what the hell is happening—and stop it—so this isn't all the time I get with my boy here."

"Yes, ma'am," I said. "Lay low today, okay? Keep the doors locked, and try to get that husband of yours back before curfew tonight. Mae mentioned she might be coming over with the kids later?"

"They should be here soon," Ashley agreed. Juarez returned, looking pained.

"What's up?" I asked.

"Casey's not in the hospital—someone claiming to be her father checked her out about an hour ago. And I talked to Blaze. They started looking out past the old property lines and found something at Barnel's camp. We need to get over there."

We said a hasty goodbye and were soon on our way. I was almost out the front door, leaving behind this strange house that had once been my home, when I heard Ashley call after me.

"Take it easy, all right, Diggs?" I looked back at her, standing in the living room we once shared. "You're not my favorite person, but I still like the world a little bit better with you in it."

"It's mutual, Ash," I said. "I'll be careful."

18
SOLOMON

15:05:00

IT WAS CLEAR FROM THE START that Agent Blaze and I would never be BFFs. My first clue was when she insisted we leave Grace and my "mangy sheepdog" at the hotel, because she had enough to worry about saving the town and keeping my ass out of trouble without adding a bunch of mutts to the mix. I would have argued that Einstein was neither mangy nor a sheepdog, but... Well, Blaze scared the living bejeezus out of me. And I could actually see her point—I'm not completely irrational all the time, contrary to popular belief. We settled the dogs at the hotel and I left them with extra biscuits and a stern warning not to raid the mini bar, then I got in the back of Blaze's SUV with another of the agents, and we set out.

By nine a.m., it felt like I'd been up for a month instead of just a couple of days. This is what happens when you start taking care of yourself—your tolerance goes straight to hell. We'd been driving aimlessly for hours, tracking down Barnel's followers and putting out fires—literally. We were doing just that when Buddy Holloway called saying he'd found something at the Barnel compound.

My adrenaline surged. We'd just gotten word that Casey Clinton and a couple of the other kids in the explosion had disappeared from the hospital. If Barnel's people were behind that, we assumed they'd taken their hostages into the woods somewhere. The energy among the other agents—including Agent Keith, sitting just a little too close beside me—had been flagging, but the news got everyone jazzed. Blaze pulled a U-turn in the middle of the road, and we headed off in the opposite direction to rendezvous with Buddy.

The Barnel compound was deep in the woods, the only path to get there a virtually impenetrable dirt road. From there, it was another half mile or so along a damp, well-traveled trail with National Guardsmen leading the march and Agent Keith and me bringing up the rear. The woods were cool and wet, new leaves on the trees and the fresh air sweet enough to taste. We reached a muddy clearing where half a dozen ramshackle one-room cabins were built close to one another, a well and a fire pit at the center. A wooden sign hanging above read, "Let Jesus Lead You Home."

I turned at a particularly nasty stench off to our left, and quickly switched direction once I realized the source: a pigpen, one sow and three piglets dead inside. Their throats were slit, flies buzzing over the open wounds.

Lovely.

A few yards farther down another path we found what I assumed was Barnel's version of a meeting house: a massive octagonal building with a sign reading "Redemption Hall" above the stately double doors. A soldier sat on the steps waiting for us—Private Abbott, I recalled from the briefing earlier. He was a redhead in camouflage with a buzzcut and an overbite who barely looked old enough to vote.

"We're set up inside," Abbott said.

He gestured for our crew to go on ahead, which we did. I followed Blaze up five wooden steps, then through the double doors.

The rest of the compound might seem like the set for some bizarre Appalachian reality show, but Barnel had pulled out all the stops for Redemption Hall. Bleachers all the way around passed for stadium seating, with a red-carpeted aisle leading to a round pulpit in the center with a podium, speakers, and a baptismal tank.

The *pièce de résistance* was an archaic-looking dentist's chair outfitted with straps to restrain Barnel's unlucky subjects. Behind that was a large wooden box that I didn't want anything to do with; the mesh windows and a padlock were the only thing that kept more of Barnel's fanged "babies" from escaping and having their way with the lot of us. I'd never been a fan of snakes, but Diggs' encounter the other night had really sealed that for me.

Juarez, Diggs, and Buddy Holloway were gathered around the podium with half a dozen soldiers and a couple of agents when we arrived. We joined them and got the rundown on what they'd found: an occupied cabin about a mile into the woods that had been spotted by helicopters. Soldiers had already been there and back, and so far hadn't come across any surveillance, security, or traps designed to keep people away.

"You didn't find anything at all?" Diggs asked skeptically.

"Maybe Barnel was counting on being well hidden enough not to worry about that kind of thing," Juarez said. He didn't sound convinced.

"I don't know what to tell you," Abbott said. "I can't give you the why—only what we've found. Or haven't, as the case may be. And these woods are clean."

"And the cabin?" Blaze asked.

"That's more of a problem," Abbott said. "It's a mile into the brush, due east. Infrared shows four armed subjects on the ground floor—we've had eyes on two. Both female." He looked uncomfortable.

"That's a problem?" Juarez asked.

"One's just a kid—not more than fifteen, maybe sixteen years old. The other one is maybe seventy."

"Barnel has a big extended family," Diggs said. "I wouldn't put it past him to use them out here. Could be his wife in there with the girl."

Blaze frowned, but made no comment. "Is there any sign of Barnel?"

"No, ma'am."

"Are there others in the building?"

"That's where the problem comes in," Abbott said. "There's a fortified cellar with ten that we've seen so far—kids mostly, and an elderly couple guarding them with rifles. Deputy Holloway helped us find a back way in, so we've actually been able to get inside to see what we're dealing with."

"Inside how?" I asked.

"Tunnels," Buddy said. "I took a gamble, figured the reverend would be paranoid enough to want a second way out."

"But no one was guarding that exit? You don't think that's a little weird?" Diggs asked.

"I won't look a gift horse in the mouth, but it does seem like if he went to the trouble of building this place, he would have put a little energy in protecting himself. We'll proceed with caution. Happy?" she asked Diggs.

"Yes. Thank you," Diggs agreed.

"Good. So, what did you find?" she asked Abbott.

The soldier took out a camera and started scrolling through the pictures, starting with the people on the ground floor they'd be squaring off against. The first was of a little old woman with her hair back in a bun, a hard stare in her dark eyes. It took me a minute before I recognized her as the one who'd started singing just about the time Barnel was shot in Miller's Field two nights ago.

Blaze flipped to the next picture, showing a teenage girl in the by-now-familiar ankle-length dress, her long blonde hair pulled back in a ponytail. She held a rifle in one hand. She looked vaguely familiar—I assumed also from the tent meeting. Diggs studied her for a minute.

"I think that's Jessie Barnel—one of the grandkids. He's got a whole posse of them. Smart girl; she made National Honor Society this year. She's the last one I would have expected to be involved."

I didn't ask how, exactly, Diggs knew that. If I stopped to question half the seemingly irrelevant facts Diggs has floating around in his noggin, we'd never get anything done. From there we moved onto the cellar, and the real problem we were up against.

The basement itself wasn't noteworthy, just a large room with a dirt floor, stone walls, and a low ceiling. A bare bulb hung from a wooden beam. There was a wooden table at the center with a plastic pitcher, a half-eaten plate of sandwiches, and a deck of UNO cards. Just as Abbott had said, an old couple stood guard, keeping track of the kids—eight of them.

"That's Ray Barnel and his wife, Etta," Diggs said. "Ray is the reverend's brother."

"So he really is keeping this in the family," Blaze said.

The next photo showed a couple of the kids seated at the table. Another photo showed four or five crowded in together on a double mattress. I stopped at sight of a little blonde girl with her thumb in her mouth, and a boy of seven or eight watching over her like it was his mission in life.

My stomach dropped. "That's Casey Clinton's brother and sister," I said. "What the hell are they doing in there?"

Blaze raised her hand to hold me off, suddenly tense. "That's not my biggest concern right now." She looked at

Abbott. "What the hell is that?"

I had to squint to see what she was pointing to: a small bundle of cylindrical tubes, barely visible beside the wooden stairs leading out. Abbott frowned and flipped to the next picture—a close-up of the same bundle.

"Dynamite," he said. "The whole place is rigged with it. That's why we didn't just move in and take the kids out. I'm guessing they have the detonator up top, but we weren't able to find it or determine whether we're looking at a timer or a remote trigger. There's no sign of a blasting cap."

"Son of a bitch," Blaze said, flipping back through the pictures. "Those are homemade. That's why they didn't bother with security: when you have that many explosives, you don't need somebody watching the place. We make a single wrong move and that entire house comes down on those kids."

"If we take our time, we can get everyone out," Juarez said. "We just can't lose our heads. I know we're on a deadline, but if we rush this, no one's coming out alive."

"There's a problem with that," Abbott said.

"What?" Blaze snapped.

"That," he said. He indicated the pitcher I'd noticed beside the sandwiches in one of the photos. Next to it was a vial, so small that it was barely visible.

"What are we looking at?" I asked.

"Cyanide," Blaze said softly. The word alone sent a chill through me. "They're gonna poison them. Before they ever set off any explosives, they'll just tell the kids to drink up. Everyone goes to sleep…"

"And no one wakes up," Juarez finished grimly.

●

Once we knew what we were facing, Blaze got everyone motivated and we headed into the forest together. The second the woods closed in this time, I felt the same sense of panic that had all but buried me just after Black Falls. I'd been avoiding the woods for a while, but obviously there wasn't much choice now.

Blaze and Juarez and the rest of the team were up ahead, absorbed in the mission. I took a breath, but the air went down wrong and my heart sped up while my chest got tighter. I kept my head down and put one foot in front of the other. Sometimes, that's the best you can hope for.

The soldiers hadn't been kidding when they'd said Barnel's cabin was well hidden. If I'd been on my own, I think I would have tripped over the damned thing before I saw it: a small wooden cabin with a front porch and boarded windows, almost completely buried in the undergrowth. By the time we got there, I was lightheaded from all the fresh air not getting to my lungs. The others circled up while I stood on the sidelines, waiting for some direction. I didn't even know what the hell I was doing out there; Diggs knew the area and he knew Barnel, so he could clearly add something to the mix.

Other than mind-numbing terror, I wasn't sure what I brought to the table.

They set Diggs and me and a couple of agents up out of the way with a video feed of the cellar, and Blaze ordered us to keep still. I sat on a fallen tree and didn't speak. On the little screen in front of us, I could see half a dozen of the kids now gathered around the table playing UNO. Casey's brother and sister had joined in. The pitcher stood between them, the vial still full beside it.

The air smelled damp and clean, the byproduct of a rainy spring. It occurred to me that the paths were wet enough that you wouldn't hear someone coming from behind. I thought of Will Rainier's hand twisted in my hair, a knife blade across my cheek and his mouth at my ear. *Every time I catch you, I get a little more. That's the game.* So far, breathing wasn't getting any easier.

"So… David Bowie? Cake? Prince, for sure," Diggs said quietly as he sat down beside me. I jumped, my heart hammering. He leaned in a little, voice low and light, his hand falling to the small of my back. "Keep breathing, Sol. It's just another jungle, kid."

My heart slowed. I gave myself a minute before I responded. "Prince what?" I asked. To my relief, I didn't sound nearly as shaky as I felt.

"Your top twenty-four," he said.

Of course. "I told you—I'm not playing that game with you."

"Why not? I won't judge."

I scoffed. I felt my breathing slowly shift. "Sure you won't."

"Don't you want to know my top twenty-four?" he whispered, close to my ear.

"I already know them." He gave me a look that suggested I was full of shit, which I chose to ignore. "What? You don't think I've been paying attention all these years? Twenty bucks says I can name every one of them," I said. "In order."

"If you do me, does that mean I get to do you?" he asked.

I rolled my eyes. Before I could respond, Blaze took her place in a little clearing in front of the house. I held up my hand to Diggs. "Hang on. I think the games are about to begin."

From our vantage, safely out of the line of fire, I could just see Blaze take another step forward with megaphone in hand. The second she was in the open, someone got a shot off from inside the house, kicking up the dirt a couple of yards from Blaze's feet. She backed up, holding up a hand to keep anyone from firing back.

"My name is Special Agent Allie Blaze," she said once she was safely under cover again. "I'm with the Federal Bureau of Investigation. I'd like to end this before anyone gets hurt—is there someone in there I could speak with?"

On our subterranean camera, a couple of the kids looked up anxiously at the sound of the gunshot. Willa Clinton, Casey's little sister, started to cry. The old couple gathered everyone together around the table. I eyed the vial beside the pitcher.

After an eternity and a half, the muzzle of a shotgun appeared in the front doorway of the cabin. The teenage girl we'd seen in the photo emerged, the gun raised to her chest, sights trained on Blaze.

"We don't have any quarrel with you," she said. Her voice was strained, her arms shaking under the weight of the gun she held. "So please just get on out of here."

I'd expected some backwoods Daisy Mae spouting scripture, but this girl was anything but. She had braces and a patch of acne on her forehead, and the fear in her eyes was palpable.

"I'm sorry," Blaze said, "but I can't go yet—not until everyone in there gets out safely and I'm able to locate Reverend Barnel. That's my only job here. Can you tell me your name?"

The girl hesitated. It looked like she'd been crying. "Jessie," she said after a second, confirming what Diggs had said. "Jessie Barnel. Nobody's getting out of here, though— you may as well just forget it. My granddaddy saw to that... He's goin' back to the beginning, he said. Back to where it all went wrong. Granddaddy got word from on high. He's to start there. We'll be goin' home with the Lord by sundown, Miss."

Her voice trembled.

"You can call me Allie," Blaze said. She made the transition from drill sergeant to den mother seamlessly. "Jessie, no one has to go home with the Lord today, all right? Nobody has to go anywhere but right back where they belong. We can put today behind us. I just need you to put that gun down, sweetheart."

On the video screen, Willa was still crying. The old man sat down at the table with her on his knee, bouncing her gently. Dougie Clinton looked ready to strangle him. Then, I watched with my stomach in a knot as the old woman picked up the vial of cyanide and pulled the pitcher toward her. The agent beside us had his walkie talkie in hand. He spoke into it quietly.

"Keith, what's your status? There's activity below."

Blaze must have had an earpiece in, because her shoulders tensed at the words. She lifted the megaphone again.

"Jessie, I know you have children in there. Those kids' families are looking for them; they just want them to come home safely. Now, I know your grandfather is a good man."

To my surprise, a tear rolled down Jessie's cheek, a flicker of something in her eyes. Anger, I thought—and not necessarily directed at us. Blaze didn't miss it.

"As good a man as he is, the position he's put you in here isn't fair. You're a smart girl—I did a little checking, and it turns out you're at the top of your class. You don't belong here, Jessie."

The old woman on the video dumped the vial into the pitcher. She stirred it, her face chillingly impassive, and then began pouring the liquid into a dozen paper cups.

"We have to move," the agent said into his walkie talkie. He said it quietly enough, but there was no mistaking his urgency. Jessie's head came up, like she was listening to someone inside the house. Her hands tensed around the gun.

"Whoever's in the woods out back best leave here," Jessie said. She shifted, eyes taking on a wild quality that wasn't reassuring. "My granny isn't happy about this. We can't have you folks back there."

"Jessie—" Blaze began. A shot erupted from the house, this time in the back. A second later, "Agent down!" crackled over the walkie talkie. Jessie jumped, her gun going off in the process. Another shot came from the back of the house. Most of the kids were crying on the video screen by now. Those who weren't just looked terrified. The old couple began handing out paper cups, moving with unnerving efficiency.

Someone fired back from the woods. This time Jessie took aim, her rifle pointed directly at Blaze.

"Y'all need to go!" the girl said. "You got no idea what you're doing."

"Jessie, please—let us get you out of there. Set down your gun, and let us take care of your family. You shouldn't have to face something like this." Blaze took a step into the clearing, both hands in the air. The girl's arms were shaking so much now that I didn't know how she held the damned gun up. Dougie Clinton and four other kids in the cellar picked up their paper cups. I wasn't breathing. No one was, as far as I could see. Diggs sat rigid beside me, his hand clasped tightly in mine. I didn't even remember taking hold of it.

"Dammit," he whispered under his breath. "Why the hell isn't anyone doing anything?"

"We have agents right now who can move in there and take care of this, Jessie," Blaze said. "I have a daughter your age, honey—this isn't the kind of thing I'd ever want her to go through. I know your granddaddy feels the same."

Jessie shook her head furiously, tears spilling down her cheeks. "Then you don't know my granddaddy," she half-whispered. Her eyes hardened. My hand tightened around

Diggs', and I think everyone there knew what was coming next:

She fired the gun.

It hit Blaze square in the chest, knocking her backward. The girl chambered a second bullet. Before she could take aim, a shot sounded from the woods. The girl fell to her knees, still holding tight to the rifle, blood spreading in a neat circle at the upper left of her dress. Her eyes went wide.

More shots erupted from the cabin, from the deep bass of a shotgun to the steady rat-a-tat of automatic weapons in the back. Juarez bolted from the woods, moving fast and low. He reached Blaze and she got to her feet, still gasping from the impact of buckshot on Kevlar, and the two retreated back to the trees.

"Hold your fire!" Blaze shouted hoarsely to her team.

Meanwhile, Diggs and I watched as the video picture jumped, like someone had jarred the camera. Two boys of no more than five drank down the liquid in their paper cups, one of them crying. Dougie looked at his but didn't touch it. I watched as, in the chaos, he quietly took Willa's from her and put it back on the table. Good boy.

The forest was alive with gunfire now, all of it coming from inside the cabin as agents and National Guard alike took cover. I couldn't remember the last time I'd taken a full breath. Another little girl drank from her cup, even as the first two boys sank to the floor as though suddenly too tired to stand.

Jessie sat on the front porch, her back against the door, blood soaking the front of her dress now. She still clung to the rifle. She'd gone very, very pale.

And then, down below, I watched on the video feed as the old woman suddenly looked up, eyes wide. The picture jostled again. The kids' faces turned up in the same direction. Someone had entered the room.

The woman clutched something by her side that I hadn't seen before—something dark and metallic.

"The detonator," Diggs whispered next to me. I wasn't sure if he was talking to me or himself. I could barely hear him over the rushing in my ears.

I heard a single shot from inside the house, and a second later the old lady dropped. The metal box fell to the floor. I waited for the world to explode.

It didn't.

The old man grabbed the pitcher on the table and I watched as he drank down whatever was left. The kids looked on, crying in stark terror as three agents in full SWAT garb—one of them Juarez—appeared on screen.

Juarez went up the stairs, rifle up, while the others focused on evacuating the kids. Time ground to a halt. There was another series of shots fired inside the cabin, and then possibly the longest silence I've ever endured. If I could have summoned enough focus to pray, I'm pretty sure I would have in that moment. As it was, all I could do was sit there and wait, as though in suspended animation, for someone to tell us what the hell had happened.

Finally, Juarez's voice came on over the radio. "House is secure. We need medics in here now!"

The front door opened and Juarez emerged. He took the rifle from Jessie's hand gently. She closed her eyes, tears still falling, and surrendered.

Diggs and I dove into the fray as soon as we were cleared to do so, me joining a team of medics who'd just swarmed in while Diggs went around to the back to help round up whatever kids were still mobile. A broad-shouldered Hispanic woman nodded me over to a clearing not far from the trees where the injured were being moved.

"You're Solomon?" she asked.

I nodded.

"I'm Stacy. Blaze said you're cleared to lend a hand. You up for that?"

"Yeah, of course," I agreed. My hands were shaking and I was pretty sure I was about to puke on someone's shoes, but it didn't look like anyone else was volunteering for the job.

Juarez came over carrying one of the two boys I'd seen drink the poison. I was on the job and thoroughly focused, but I still managed to brush my hand over Juarez's as he lay the boy on the ground in front of us. Another of the agents had the other boy, and another couple of EMTs went to work on him while Stacy and I looked for signs of life in our patient.

"His name's Tom. The other boy's Greg," Juarez said. He hovered over us, forehead furrowed.

"You know what they gave him?" Stacy asked.

"Cyanide," Juarez said promptly. I fought an overwhelming urge to panic, ordering myself back to that quiet, steady place my mother taught me to rely on as a teenager. "What can I do?" Juarez asked.

"Go help the other agents," Stacy said. "We've got this."

As soon as he was gone, Stacy shook the little boy gently. "Tom, can you hear me?" There was no response.

Close up, he seemed impossibly small, with curly black hair and dark skin. The other boy started to seize, and I realized at a glance that the two must be brothers. The other team tried to stabilize him. Stacy snapped her fingers at me.

"Hey—focus. *This* is our patient."

I nodded. It wasn't easy, though: our patient had a pulse. Our patient was breathing. We gave him a dose of amyl nitrite and set up an IV of sodium nitrite as soon as he was stable. Meanwhile, the other boy wasn't moving. The paramedics stopped chest compressions after what seemed an eternity.

"Greg Hernandez, age approximately six years," one of the EMTs said. "Time of death, 11:52 a.m. March 15, 2013."

I sat back on my heels and surveyed the rest of the scene, trying to get my bearings. Diggs stood at the edge of the woods holding Willa Clinton, Doug beside them. They were laughing, Willa's arms so tight around Diggs' neck I didn't know how he could breathe.

Jessie Barnel was already being carried out—they'd either sedated her or she'd lost consciousness, but she was still alive. Of the six members of Barnel's crew inside the house, she was the only survivor.

We prepped Tom for air evac, and then Stacy shook my hand. "We've got this. Thanks—we'll let you know how he does."

I nodded.

Beside me, the other little boy lay alone, a blanket pulled over his small body. For a second or two I just stood there, swaying, sure I would be sick. Across the way, Juarez knelt beside Blaze, their heads bent in conversation. She still sat propped against a tree, but he offered her his hand and she got to her feet.

Limping and rung out, we left the Barnel compound.

19
DANNY

12:06:02

DANNY WAS ASLEEP, DREAMING OF HOME, when the door opened and someone shined what felt like a floodlight into the room. He blinked in the glare.

"We're going for a little walk," a woman said. The same woman who'd talked to him outside Casey's garage—that soft, silky voice was unforgettable.

"Who are you?" he demanded.

She lowered the light and stalked into the room. Danny recognized her from around town, but he didn't know that he'd ever talked to her before that night at Casey's.

Jenny Burkett knelt beside him and picked up a black hood she'd tossed in. She was pretty—not Justice pretty, either. She was Hollywood hot, with blonde hair, great curves, and a soft, full mouth. She brushed against him, looking like she knew just what he was thinking. She moved in closer, till her mouth was at his ear.

"Ready for an adventure, Danny?" she asked, her voice husky and rich. She took a black hood and started to put it over his head. He shied away.

"You're gonna kill me anyway, ain't you?" he asked. "What does it matter if I can see or not? At least have the guts to look me in the eye when you pull the trigger."

"Relax," she said. "Nobody's pulling any triggers just now. The reverend just wants to have a little chat." He kept fighting her, scooting backward until his back was against the wall. His daddy taught him never to fight a woman, but it seemed like this might be an exception to that rule. He kicked out, catching her in the shin.

She swore, and everything soothing or soft about her just fell away. She dropped to her knees beside him, grabbed a hunk of hair at the back of his head, and pulled hard.

"Don't fight me, little boy," Jenny hissed. She kept a good grip on his hair, forcing his head back. Then, she pulled a gun from the back of her jeans and pointed it just under his chin. She put her mouth to his ear. "It's not a safe game. Trust me."

She pulled the hood over his head and pulled him up.

There were footsteps outside—heavy, loud steps, like some giant was headed into the room. Danny tried to stay calm, but his breath wasn't coming right and the inside of the hood smelled like old wool and sweat.

"You ready?" a man's voice he didn't recognize asked. Like Jenny, he didn't sound like he was from around here.

"Watch him," he heard Jenny say. "The little bastard's a fighter."

They grabbed him by both arms and led him outside the room. Once they were past the doorway, he could see a change in the light outside, even through the hood. They walked along a dirt floor, then stopped and somebody opened a door.

"Step up," Jenny said.

Even with the order, Danny tripped on the first step. They kept climbing until they reached another door.

Somewhere distant and just above them now, he could hear Dylan playing: "Temporary Like Achilles"—one of those deep tracks Diggs introduced him to. He'd always liked that song.

"Where are you taking me?" he asked. The man had a tight hold on his arm, like he was afraid Danny might make a run for it. He might, too, if he had any idea where in hell he was.

"The reverend wants you to make your peace," the man said.

"I don't want to make my peace," Danny said. "All I want is to get the hell out of here. I don't—"

They walked a little longer, their feet echoing like they were on concrete in a closed space now, and then went down a few steps. Another door opened. A blast of warm air hit him, and he smelled sweat and sickness and a kind of darkness he couldn't put a name to. For the first time since he'd been taken, Danny felt a jolt of fear so pure it just about knocked his breath loose.

"Keep moving," the man said, jerking him forward.

"Where are we?" Danny asked.

They guided him to a chair and made him sit, then took their hands off him. The door opened and closed again; Danny sensed they'd gone.

Someone took the hood off his head.

He blinked in the sudden harsh glare, lights pointed directly into his face. When he looked past them, he spotted Reverend Barnel. The reverend wore his usual suit, his right arm in a sling. He didn't look right, though—like maybe he was on something. His face was red, sweat running down his cheeks. He moved a music stand close to Danny, a piece of paper set on it.

"I'm sorry it has to end this way, boy," Barnel said. "The Lord works in mysterious ways—this isn't the path I would've chosen, but it got chose for me. I tried to turn around the evildoers that come to me. I really did."

The reverend's eyes were black, and his hands were shaking. Danny realized that the sweat and sickness he'd smelled was coming from Barnel himself.

Once his eyes had adjusted, Danny tried to figure out where he was. A boiler room of some kind, pipes and controls and steam all around. He could just barely hear the music over the sound of the big old furnace. A video camera was set up a couple feet in front of him, just to the side of the lights. When Danny didn't look at the paper Barnel had set out, the reverend pushed the music stand a little closer.

"What is this?" Danny asked, staring at the words.

"You done what's on that paper—don't try and deny it. I led you to the Lord, but that's as far as I could get you. It ain't my fault you turned your back. Now, I need you to read that. Folks need to know. They got to understand."

"Understand what?" Danny asked. He felt sick.

"Why the Lord's pushin' me to end this," the reverend said. He mopped the sweat off his forehead with a damp handkerchief. "Read it," he said again. "Read it right to the camera."

Danny shook his head. His eyes filled with tears. He couldn't stop them from falling, no matter how hard he tried. "I won't read this," he whispered.

"You will," the reverend said. "And maybe, if I believe you're sorry for what you done, you won't end up like your daddy did."

Danny wet his lips. Cleared his throat. A tear rolled down his cheek.

"God is good," he began, reading the reverend's words.

●

Once he'd read everything the reverend told him to, Barnel put the hood back over Danny's head and the others came back in. Jenny and the man Danny didn't know led him out like he was a damned dog, but he didn't complain—he was too happy to be out of that boiler room. He heard music again: something older this time. Chuck Berry, he was pretty sure. It had a good beat, and he thought somewhere in the back of his head that somebody out there—wherever they were—had good taste.

"Can't you shut that off?" the man asked.

"Not now we can't," Jenny said. "You know that. But we'll shut 'em down later—don't worry your pretty head."

The man grunted. Danny didn't think it sounded like he cared much for Jenny.

They hauled him along, not talking anymore. Finally, after they'd gone back down the stairs and concrete gave way to dirt floor again, he heard a door open. People were talking inside the room. He made out two voices, then three. Jenny pushed him and he stumbled in the doorway. Somebody said his name.

Jenny kept the hood on him while she tightened up the zip tie around his wrists. It hurt now, the plastic cutting into his skin until he knew he was bleeding. He just stood there. He heard another voice, then another. It should be a good thing that he wasn't alone anymore, but all it did was make him more nervous. What the hell was the reverend playing at?

Once he was secure, Jenny took off his hood just before she slipped out the door. He'd thought there would only be two or three people in there, but instead he counted half a dozen—all ages, everybody looking ragged and scared. They all sat with their hands tied behind them, backs against the wall.

"Fine mess you got us into," a girl's voice said. It took

him a minute before his eyes adjusted and he realized who it was. He fought the urge to break down and cry like a baby.

Casey sat in the far corner, almost totally out of the light. A couple of sketchy-looking druggies Danny knew from around town sat on either side of her. Danny shuffled over and plopped down beside her, almost sitting on one of the guy's laps to get him out of the way.

"Hey!" the junkie said. "Back off."

"You back off," Danny said. "I'm sittin' here." He was a little bigger than the junkie, and even though Danny wasn't much of a fighter, he knew he could hold his own. He stared the guy down until he slithered out of the way a couple feet.

Once that was settled, he took a second to get a look at Casey. She didn't look good—there was a burn on her face, and some cuts and scrapes and bandages. Her eyes had shadows the size of bruises under them. When he looked at her, he thought for a second she was about to cry.

"You okay?" he asked, quiet so nobody else would hear them.

She nodded, then took a second to pull herself together before she finally managed to get a word out.

"We're gonna miss our gig," she whispered, her voice hoarse.

He couldn't help it—he laughed out loud. She smiled at him, that smile that always made him feel like things might actually work out for the best in the end after all.

"You get your confession done for the reverend?" she asked.

"Yeah," Danny said. "You had to do that, too?"

"We all did," Casey said, nodding toward the others. Danny met eyes with the junkie he'd just pushed out of the way. The man nodded, serious and slack and shaking.

"He's got somethin' planned for us," the man said. "And whatever it is, it ain't good."

"I kind of figured that about the time they knocked me out and tied me up," Danny said.

"I'm Biggie," the junkie said. "I'd shake hands, but I'm a little tied up right now." Danny smiled at the joke. "What's your name, kid?"

"Danny Durham," he said. Biggie nodded, then looked at Casey. "No offense, but you're not looking so good. You was one of the ones in that explosion, right?"

"Explosion?" Danny looked at Casey. She wouldn't look back at him. "What's he talking about?"

"The Dairy Queen—Sheriff Jennings went psycho," Biggie said, "and blew the whole damn place up."

Panic ran through Danny in a sharp, sickening wave. He looked at Casey with the question in his eyes. "Sophie?" he asked. The word came out choked.

"I'm sorry," she whispered to him.

He felt dizzy. He couldn't get worked up about things right now, he knew, but for a second all he could do was sit there, feeling sick and lost and hopeless. He looked at Casey, studying all those cuts and scratches and burns with new understanding.

He knew he ought to be more sorry about Sophie, with her grin and her pierced eyebrow and that way she had of saying his name when they were together... But all he could think was, *Thank you, God*. The world wasn't a good place without Sophie, but he'd make it through.

He didn't even want to think about the world without Casey.

Danny looked at her, and her eyes held onto his in a way he couldn't remember them ever doing before.

"I'm getting us out of this, Case," he said. He sounded a lot more confident about that than he felt.

Casey was the kind of girl with an answer for everything. Today, she didn't say a word. They'd never been too touchy-feely, but she didn't complain when he scooted a little closer. She just leaned against his arm, her head on his shoulder, seeming smaller than he remembered Casey being in the real world.

He started thinking up a plan.

20
SOLOMON

11:50:08

IT WAS JUST AFTER NOON WHEN DIGGS, JUAREZ, AND I got to the Justice Sunshine Resort—a surprisingly nice place considering it cost next to nothing and was in… well, Justice, Kentucky. Blaze had given us until three o'clock to get some sleep and try to regroup, since we'd been running on pure adrenaline for as long as I could remember. With the electricity still out, the hotel was dark and felt every bit as creepy as you'd expect a hotel in a nowhere town on the brink of oblivion to feel. I lugged my suitcase along shadowy corridors with Diggs behind me and Juarez leading the way.

There were guards posted at the hotel entrance, rifles at the ready, while agents and soldiers and cops who'd flown in to fight the forces of evil milled around in the hallways. Diggs got a room on the second floor, and we parted ways at the stairwell after an awkward, "See you later." Juarez and I retired to our room alone.

Our new safe haven came complete with kitchenette, sitting area, and bedroom. When we got there, Grace and Einstein were curled up on the couch in the living room together like an old married couple. I was secretly relieved when Stein at least had the decency to get up and feign enthusiasm when I walked through the door, his butt wiggling happily. Grace lifted her head and whined, tail thumping, but didn't move.

I went in the bathroom, pulled off my clothes, and got in the shower. Without electricity, there was no hot water. I didn't care. I rested my forehead against the tile wall and let the cold water wash over me until every thought in my head was frozen out. When I emerged, shivering, I went straight to the bedroom and collapsed on the bed. Juarez came in and lay down beside me, stripped to his jockey shorts.

I thought of Diggs, in a room somewhere above us. I thought of the small, lifeless boy under the blanket; of what it would be like for his brother to wake up alone. I thought of Jessie Barnel's tears, and the blood soaking her ankle-length dress.

I really wanted to stop thinking.

"You tired?" I asked Juarez without moving.

He grunted. He really isn't the grunting type. I opened my eyes and rolled over.

"What are you thinking?" I asked. Juarez is the first man I ever met who actually answers honestly—or appears to—when I ask that question.

"I'm thinking you're cold," he said. He ran his hand over my shoulder and along my back. I shivered for an entirely different reason. "Jesus, Erin, you're freezing."

"I'm all right." He pulled the blanket up around us both and put his arms around me. He didn't tell me what he'd been thinking, though. "It was a rough day for you," I said. "Lots of heroics."

"Not that heroic," he said. "A lot of people died today."

And he was the one who pulled the trigger on more than one of them, I reminded myself. I propped myself up and tried to smooth the lines from his forehead. He looked at me with dark, sad eyes—as though something heartbreaking was happening. I just hadn't caught onto what that was, exactly.

"You did what needed to be done," I said. "That's a hard thing to take on."

"Sometimes it is," he agreed, still quiet. "And we're still not any closer to finding Barnel or figuring out what's in store for tonight."

"Maybe Jessie will talk," I said.

"If she wakes up in time. At least we got to the kids before it was too late, though," he conceded. "And probably put a pretty good dent in their explosives supply."

"You think?" I asked.

"They had enough stored down there to blow up half the forest. I can't imagine there'd be much left after that."

"See," I said. "Not bad for a day's work."

I laid my head down on his arm. He rolled over to face me, eyes still serious. He smelled like sweat and gunfire. There was a streak of someone else's blood on his arm that he must have missed when he was cleaning up. He ran a hand through my hair, toying with the strands. I moved in and kissed his neck, then his chin, before I finally found his mouth. I thought of the fires we'd put out in the night. Of the picture of Dora the Explorer on the refrigerator in a meth lab; the chained hound dog and the broken cherub.

Before the kiss could go anywhere, Juarez pulled back. He kissed my nose, looking conflicted about whatever was going on in his head. Then he sat up and nodded toward the bathroom.

"I'm gonna grab a shower, then I just want to check in with Allie," he said. "Try and get some sleep, okay?"

I nodded and watched him walk away.

Sleep was elusive from there. After Jack left to go find

Blaze, I went out in search of some kind of sustenance, even though I knew the vending machines wouldn't be working. There had to be something out there, though.

Somehow in my travels, I found myself on the second floor. Private Abbott was stationed by the stairs, seated with a rifle across his lap and his head back against the wall.

"Hey," I said. "Don't they ever let you people sleep?"

He smiled. "You're the ones that've been on for days. I just got here last night—I figure I got a good forty-eight hours before I start achin' too much."

"Oh, to be young again," I said. Then, I just stood there awkwardly for a minute, wishing I'd never come up here. I assumed everyone knew I was dating Juarez, so I really shouldn't be sneaking into some other guy's room during nap time.

"Diggs is in 206," Abbott said. "Just down the hall there."

"Oh," I said.

"Agent Juarez said you might be up," he explained. "He said it was fine for you to go on in, if you wanted."

Of course he did.

"That's all right," I said. "He's probably sleeping."

"He was just out here a couple minutes ago, actually. I doubt he'd go under so fast. He looked strung pretty tight." Abbott was unnervingly helpful.

"Ah. Well, I guess if I'm already up here, I should at least check in."

"Whatever you think's best," Abbott said.

It was idiotic for me to stand in the hallway freaking out about it, so I cut it short and went to Diggs' door. Then, I walked *past* his door. Twice. I finally stopped just outside with my hand hovering an inch from the wood.

It opened before my knuckles ever hit.

"What the hell are you doing?" Diggs asked. "Don't you know you're not supposed to lurk outside people's doors in the middle of an apocalypse? You'll freak someone out."

"Sorry. I'm rusty on the etiquette."

I waved at Abbott to signal all was copasetic, then went into Diggs' room without being invited.

Where Juarez and I had a whole little suite all to ourselves, Diggs' had just bed and bath. His clothes were draped over a chair in the corner. He went back to the bed and lay down on top of the covers, his arm over his eyes, his right hand resting on his stomach. He wore shorts. Very little else. There was no doubt about it: Diggs had been hitting the gym since our adventures over the summer.

My mouth may have gone a little dry.

"I've got condoms in my suitcase if that's what you're looking for," he said without looking at me. "Juarez didn't come prepared?"

"Funny."

He removed his arm from his eyes, but otherwise remained still. "Where's your better half?"

"Shower and a confab with Blaze. I couldn't sleep, so I thought I'd check on you. Make sure you're okay."

He sat up. The way he looked at me suggested he knew my story was bullshit. I waited for him to call me on it. He didn't.

"I should be asking you that," he said. "It hasn't been an easy twenty-four hours—you've been playing Florence Nightingale with a vengeance since you got here."

"Tell me about it," I said.

He sat up and nodded to the bed. "Sit." I sat.

"Juarez thinks most of the explosives Barnel had were in the cabin," I said.

"Yeah?" he said. There was a hint of doubt in the word.

"You don't think so?"

He shrugged. "If Barnel is the one orchestrating this whole thing, it's possible."

"But you don't think he is," I said.

"Not really, no."

"I don't suppose you have any ideas who the puppet master might be."

He shook his head, which was a little surprising. Diggs is rarely short on theories.

"Do you think Danny's the one who took out Brother Jimmy and tried to kill Barnel?"

"Nope," he said without hesitation. "If he'd done it, he wouldn't have run. He's a hothead—not the kind who thinks about something like that enough beforehand to get away with it."

I didn't question it. For one thing, I knew Diggs well enough to recognize that debating the issue would be futile. Of course, I've never minded futile debate with the man when I've had good reason. I had a feeling he was right about this, though: the whole shooting at the tent meeting had been so bizarre that I just couldn't see Danny being the one behind it. If he was, why would he just leave his truck at Casey's? And why would he go to Casey's in the first place, hang out shooting the shit with her little brother, then all of a sudden hear some kind of Siren song and take off to kill Barnel?

We fell silent. For the first time, I noticed a folder on Diggs' bedside table. I tensed. Diggs followed my eye.

"That's the file on Cameron?" I asked.

"Also known as 'the hooded man'? That's the one," he said. He was amiable enough about it, but I could tell he was watching me for a reaction. He took the folder from the table, set it on his lap, and began flipping pages, casual as you please. "He's former military, you know," he said. He kept his eye on the page. "Born and raised in Lynn, Indiana."

"Where my father's from," I said. Theories started forming in my head before I could remind myself I wasn't pursuing this thing anymore.

"And Max Richards," Diggs reminded me. "Cameron grew up a couple blocks from both of them."

"Do you think he has anything to do with what's happening here?" I asked. The question had been bothering me for some time now.

"I don't know," he said. "I still have no clue what his motivations are. Who he works for. It could be that he really is just here checking up on you—making sure you're following orders like a good little soldier."

"Which I'm trying to do."

"I know that," he said. He set the folder between us, open. Cameron's face stared up at me.

"This is exactly what he warned us not to do," I said. "You may not care what happens to you, but I do. So far, Kat and my father have been able to keep me alive thanks to whatever it is they know, but you know Cameron won't hesitate to take you out."

"I know that, too," he said.

"Then why are you pushing this?" I asked, my temper rising.

"Because you aren't. And that's not you."

"It could be me," I said. "People change. What the hell's wrong with that? I'm trying to evolve here."

"So evolve," he said, his voice rising. "I'm all for that—but don't have a friggin' lobotomy. You ask questions. Dig. Push so hard you almost make me nuts—that's what you *do*. It's what you've always done. It's what makes you one of the best reporters I've worked with. It's what makes you…you."

I picked up the damn file. Stared at Cameron's face. A barrage of images ran through my head: the Payson Church burning; my father on his knees, blood streaming down his back; Matt Perkins, dead; George Ashmont, dead; Rebecca Ashmont, Noel Hammond, Max Richards, Will Rainier…

All of them, dead. Diggs, hands bound, face bloodied, a gun at his temple.

It's not that I didn't want to know; trust me, I did. I wanted to know who Cameron was, where he came from, what kind of background had led him to my father. I wanted to know, once and for all, why Cameron had burned down the church on Payson Isle; if he knew where my father was, or if he was the reason my father was running in the first place.

Diggs watched me like he could see the hamster wheel spinning in my head.

I closed the folder and handed it back to him.

I don't think I've ever seen Diggs disappointed in me before. Certainly not to that extent. His eyes fell.

"I should go," I said. "Juarez will wonder where I am. He's already been weird since he got here."

"Maybe he's just tired of being with someone who's in love with another man."

It wasn't meant to be cruel—Diggs never means to be cruel. It still stung, though. There was a challenge to his eyes that told me he expected me to fight him on this one thing, at least. We'd get riled up, the heat would spark something…

Instead, I turned around on the bed calmly so I could face him, pulling my legs under me. I was very, very tired.

"Do you remember what happened the day you found out I was marrying Michael?" I asked.

He didn't look surprised at the question, despite the apparent lack of a segue. If he'd expected me to scream and shout, I definitely expected some kind of deflection from him. The flicker of regret in his eyes was impossible to miss when he nodded.

"Michael announced the engagement at that faculty thing we all went to at BU," I said.

"I told you I remember, Sol," he said. "And he only did

that because I was there. He was a forty-five-year-old, smooth talking, womanizing prick. You were twenty years younger, and you were gorgeous. And the friendship between you and me drove him nuts."

"I know," I said. I wasn't so sure about the gorgeous part, but the rest of the story certainly held up. "And as I recall, I apologized for that. Michael and I fought. I left the party; Michael stayed."

"To go home with his best friend's wife," Diggs pointed out. Correctly, as it happened. He closed his eyes. "Do we really have to relive that whole night?"

"I just want to make sure you remember the same things I do. Because the way George was talking the other night made it sound like *I* was the one who broke *your* heart. And that's not how I remember it."

"Fine," he said. He scratched his head and blew out a lungful of air. "Go ahead. Michael stayed at the party. You left."

"And at midnight, you showed up on my doorstep. Drunk. High as a kite. Any chance at all you remember what happened next?"

"I told you not to marry Michael."

"Because?"

"Because he'd gone home with his best friend's wife, and he was a womanizing prick who didn't deserve you."

"Exactly," I said. "And we kissed."

His eyes darkened. "If that's all you remember, your memory's even fuzzier than mine. We did a hell of a lot more than kiss that night, kid."

I felt my cheeks warm. "I was getting to that part, *kid*. We had sex."

"We had bone-melting, burn-the-house-down, once-in-a-lifetime sex," he said. Images from that night blew past me in a way I hadn't expected: my body pressed to his; the things he'd whispered and the way he'd whispered them. The heat of his mouth on my… everything. The way it had felt afterward, wrapped in his arms, like all the pieces of my life suddenly, out of the blue, fit.

He watched me like he knew exactly what I was thinking. My cheeks got warmer. I persevered.

"Remember what I told you, after?" I asked.

That regret flickered in his eyes again. "You told me you wouldn't marry him. If I was serious about you and me—if I wanted to give us a shot, you'd tell Michael it was over."

"And we fell asleep in each other's arms," I said. I was still surprisingly calm. Maybe I was having a breakdown. A very, very Zen breakdown. "And when I woke up in the morning…"

"I was gone," he said. He wet his lips. He wouldn't look me in the eye.

I stood up, too tired to fight anymore. "And the next thing I heard, you'd moved to Kentucky and married Ashley Durham."

"I know."

"So you don't get to act like this is all my fault, Diggs. Like I'm some stone-cold bitch when I'm not ready to jump back in bed with you just because—*right now*—you think it's what you want. I was protecting you last summer. I'm still protecting you. But also? There've been way too many times when I've thought we were about to ride off into the sunset together, only to wake up and find a note on the pillow and a fucking twenty-dollar-bill on the dresser."

He sat there, his eyes burning a hole through me. Regret and fatigue warred on his face, but behind that was that intensity I'd never trusted in the way he looked at me. Historically, whatever it was—love or lust or some combination of the two—had been too easily forgotten the moment I began to trust it might stay.

He nodded. I started for the door. I was almost there when he spoke again. I stood there, my hand on the doorknob, and didn't turn back.

"I know I'm not perfect, Sol," he said. "But you talk about evolving… What the hell do you think I've been doing for the past four years? There's something between us. I'm through running from it. Juarez is a good guy." I heard him get off the bed and start toward me, his voice low now. "He deserves better than being your security blanket because you're too scared to take a chance."

When he spoke again, he was directly behind me—his hand around mine on the doorknob, his body warm against me. His breath on my neck.

"Tell me I'm wrong, and I'll drop it. No harm, no foul." His mouth brushed against my ear with the words. My knees turned to mush.

"You're wrong," I said. I couldn't turn around, and I couldn't quite say it with a full voice, but at least I got the words out.

Diggs kept his hand on mine and turned the knob. Opened the door for me. "Liar," he said, low in my ear.

At that point, I should have turned around, looked him in the eye, and told him he was full of shit. Instead, I jabbed him in the stomach, hard, with my elbow—partly because he deserved it, and partly because any ability I might have had to come up with some kind of intelligent retort had flown out the window the second his lips hit my earlobe.

He let out a sort of *oof* and pulled back, but he was smiling when I looked back at him. It was an evil smile, too. No wonder half the people in Justice thought he was the antichrist.

"I'm going back to my room now. To sleep. With my boyfriend."

"You do that," he said, all cool and arrogant and

stupidly…hot. I walked away. He closed the door.

Private Abbott nodded his head in an impressively military fashion as I made for the stairs. I passed the vending machine again on the way back to my room. Still not working. Twenty candy bars mocked me from behind the glass.

Stupid apocalypse.

●

Juarez was in bed when I got back to the room. He rolled over when I slid in beside him, naked beneath the sheets. His hand found the hem of my t-shirt and pushed it up, his knuckles brushing against my stomach.

"Sorry—have you been back long?" I asked.

"A few minutes. It's all right. I knew you'd be along."

Usually, Jack is a pretty straightforward guy, but there was something cloaked, sad, about the way he looked at me now. I traced the line of his jaw, thinking of the nights we'd spent together over the past three months.

"Something's wrong," I said. "You're not happy." He kissed my fingertips, pulling me closer. His hand slid down my thigh and wrapped around my knee, draping my leg over his hip. I could feel him, naked, hard, pressed to me.

"I don't want to talk right now," he said.

I nodded. "Okay." I kissed the corner of his lips. His right hand was in my hair, his left burning trails of fire along my side, tracing the line of my breast through my t-shirt. "We don't have to talk now," I said.

He leaned in, taking my bottom lip between his teeth as his hand moved to the small of my back, holding me still. He drew back and watched my face, his dark eyes nearly black, as he pressed inside me—just barely, hardly moving.

My breath hitched and my eyes sank shut, heat coiled tight somewhere low in my belly.

Since we'd started dating, I'd learned some things about Jack Juarez: the way he liked his eggs (over easy); which part of the paper he read first (international headlines); how he took his coffee and which sweets he couldn't pass up and the few things in life that would make him postpone (but never skip) his morning run. I'd also learned that there were parts of Jack that he never quite unleashed—even when we were in bed together. I always got the feeling he was holding himself back, maintaining control at all cost.

Now, his fingers curled into my side. That tenuous control was slipping; I could see it in his eyes. Feel it in the way his body tensed beside me, nearly shaking with some kind of need he wouldn't give into.

I hitched my leg up higher, pulling him deeper. Leaned up and took his earlobe between my teeth.

"You don't have to be so careful with me," I whispered. I kissed his neck, dragging my teeth along his sweetly salted skin. "Take what you need, Jack."

His fingers twisted in my hair. Another second passed, taut and silent, before he gave in. His kiss was rough, nearly bruising, as he rolled me to my back and we began to move.

21
DIGGS

9:45:00

I WAS SURE I WOULDN'T SLEEP AFTER SOLOMON LEFT. I was wrong. I woke at quarter past two from a light coma, sore and still tired. My file on Mitch Cameron was still on the bed. I thought of Solomon again. There were things I could have said to her, pushing the issue of the two of us a little further: I'd changed. She'd changed. It was written in the stars. Maybe I was full of shit, but I actually believed some of that. But at the end of the day, it didn't change the fact that Jack Juarez was waiting for her—a good guy who would give her everything she deserved: less scars, less turmoil, less heartache.

Assuming we all survived, I should just go back to Costa Rica when this was all over. Surf and write and, maybe, meet someone else.

Put all this shit behind me.

I opened the file on Cameron and stared at his beady eyes. He was proof positive that Solomon truly had turned over a new leaf. Not once in the past few days had she asked to see the folder.

I was more disappointed by that than I cared to admit—it didn't say good things about me. I should be happy for her and her new life. A new life in which she was no longer a woman hell-bent on getting answers. Instead, she was some stranger who patched people up and listened to everything her boyfriend said. I thought of Juarez's words on the subject: *If you think anything just slid off Erin after last summer, you don't know her as well as I thought.*

I knew that—I did. I was beside her while Rainier tracked us like dogs, after all. I watched while he whispered God only knew what in her ear, touched her in ways he had no right, that belt looped around her neck the whole time. If Cameron hadn't killed the son of a bitch, I think I would have done the job with my bare hands once I'd gotten free.

Solomon and I had both known for a long time that the world is a scary place, but I don't think either of us ever had a clue just how dark it got until Black Falls.

Maybe it really was for the best that she was moving on from all that.

And maybe if I told myself that story enough times, I'd start to believe it.

I went into the bathroom and set my shiny new gun and my virtually useless cell phone on the counter, then turned on the shower. The water was cool, but I'd had worse. I stripped down and stood under the spray, letting the cold wash over me.

I thought of Solomon kneeling over the little boy who'd almost died today. That thought led me to Jessie Barnel's terror-filled eyes as she wielded a shotgun and defended a grandfather whom, I suspected, she didn't even like. Why? And what the hell was Barnel's endgame in this? What did he honestly expect to accomplish? Or did he really believe he was getting orders from on high, as Jessie had suggested. *He's goin' back to the beginning... Back to where it all went wrong.*

It seemed a safe assumption that Barnel wasn't going all the way back to Eden. It had to be something more personal than that. Billy Thomas seemed like a safe bet: the psychopath who'd raped and killed those three girls before allegedly killing himself and—according to legend—stapling the inverted cross on his own chest. It didn't seem presumptuous to assume that Billy hadn't, in fact, done that at all. Which meant someone else was behind the killing and the stapling.

Jesup Barnel wasn't a man to be trifled with—I'd learned that the hard way almost thirty years ago. As a young man just starting out on this path, what would he have done if one of the boys he'd supposedly purged of demons turned around and did the unthinkable?

I had no doubt that Barnel would exact revenge for that.

So, all I needed to do was figure out where Barnel considered the beginning to be, where Billy Thomas was concerned.

Before I could continue with that line of thought, I heard something in the other room—a shuffle, then a bang like something had fallen. My heart skipped in a way I'd become accustomed to since Black Falls, that breathless moment of blind panic before I got my wits back.

"Solomon?" I called out. "That you?"

I turned off the water and wrapped a towel around my waist. Reached for my Glock, waiting on the counter.

Except that it wasn't.

Neither was my cell phone.

I swallowed past the rush of distant thunder in my ears. "Juarez?" I called.

No answer. The bathroom door was ajar, just as I'd left it. I pulled on shorts without bothering to dry off, biding my time.

In the other room, I heard the door open and close softly.

I pushed the bathroom door open all the way.

The room was empty. Cameron's folder was still on the bed. My dirty clothes were on a chair in the corner, right where I'd left them.

My cell phone and gun were on the dresser now, though. I looked around the room. There was no one in sight. The sound of my racing heart in my ears reminded me that just because I couldn't see them didn't mean they were gone.

Still on the lookout for someone in hiding, I went to retrieve my gun and phone. There was no one, though. I saw no sign that anything had been taken, but it was obvious after a cursory look around that something had been left behind:

A Latin cross in red lipstick, on the full-length mirror mounted on the closet door.

My heart stuttered. I picked up the Glock, then reached for my phone and hit number 1 on speed dial, already on my way out of the room. I'd pulled open the door a quarter of an inch, no more, before someone kicked it the rest of the way and pushed me back inside. He was well over six feet tall, in black from head to foot, with broad shoulders and a hard, lean body. I whirled with my gun raised, but a second man—this one built like a fire plug, short and hard and barrel-chested—came at me from behind. He smelled like cheap aftershave and sweat, and when I moved to take a swing at his buddy he hurled himself at me, drilling me back against the wall. The big guy jammed a needle into my neck, deep, and I heard myself shout as my knees went out from under me.

The room swam.

"Repent," The Giant whispered to me. He smiled through his ski mask with gleaming white teeth.

I fought harder, trying to keep my head above water. My gun was empty—I pulled the trigger and it clicked. They laughed. Fire Plug took the gun away and dropped it to the floor. I still had my cell phone. All I had to do was hit Send.

The Giant took my phone before I ever got to the magic button, dropped it, and smashed it beneath his behemoth black boot. Then he pushed me down and followed me to the ground, where I swayed on hands and knees. I couldn't feel my body. Couldn't make sense of anything.

"Your time has come, Daniel," Fire Plug said. He knelt in front of me and looked me in the eye, still smiling. I thought of that summer at Barnel's camp, at twelve years old. Water gushing over my head. The smell of sackcloth over my mouth and nose while I tried to get free. The sizzle of my flesh and the rush of searing pain as the world went dark.

"Repent," Fire Plug said, echoing the Giant. His voice was a million miles away, like the buzz of ants underground.

"Fuck you," I said. I slammed my head down on the bridge of his nose, then used his body for leverage to stand, my hands curled around his meaty shoulders as I pulled myself back to my feet. I stumbled, slamming against the wall as I tried to reach the door. It was like I was made of liquid, a store of molecules with no way to contain them.

The Giant caught me and pulled me back before I could get away. He was pissed—his hold tighter now, Fire Plug's mask wet with blood. He wrapped his forearm around my neck and held on tight while I thrashed, gasping for air.

My legs went out from under me again.

Everything went bright white for an instant, and I thought of Solomon and of Danny and of Wyatt.

I closed my eyes, and fell.

22
SOLOMON

09:00:42

I WOKE AT THREE O'CLOCK, surprisingly refreshed considering I'd had an hour and a half of sleep in the past thirty-six. Juarez was already up and dressed.

"What did Blaze have to say when you met with her?" I asked from the bed.

He came in tying his tie and shook his head, both pups on his heels. Einstein hopped up on the bed. Grace sat politely on the floor and waited for an invite.

"She'll brief us when we meet up. We've got another few minutes. I figured I'd hold off as long as I could."

I sat up and rubbed my eyes, scanning the room for some sign of my underwear. Juarez found them under the bed and handed them to me with a sheepish grin.

"Looking for these?"

"As a matter of fact, I was," I said. He kissed me lightly, then went back to the bathroom to finish dressing.

"I already walked the dogs," he said, raising his voice to be heard from the next room. "I know you usually like to."

"No, that's good. Thanks. How long have you been up?"

"Half hour, maybe," he said. I got up and joined him. He stood in front of a full-length mirror mounted on the bathroom door, mangling his tie. I turned him toward me and pushed his hands away. I perfected the art of the Windsor knot with my father when I was a kid. Later, being married to a stodgy professor for six years kept me in practice.

Despite the domesticity of the scene, there was something off about Juarez again—a kind of coolness that was totally out of character for him. I started to call him on it, but there was a knock at the door. The dogs went nuts.

"I'll get it," he said. Which was good, since I was standing there in his t-shirt and nothing more. I took care of business while he went into the other room. When he came back, I was just pulling my jeans on.

"What is it now?" I asked over my shoulder. My hair was a catastrophe. "Locusts? Streets running with bile and viscera?" I turned when he didn't answer. "Jack?"

He didn't say anything.

"What happened?" My adrenaline had already kicked in, just at the look on his face.

"It's Diggs—" he started.

Those two words were all I needed. I ran from the room and up the stairs with Juarez and the dogs on my heels.

I stopped at the head of the hallway. The world slipped out of focus. Private Abbott sat in the exact spot where I'd left him, his head tipped back against the wall. The only difference was the blood spilled across his shirtfront and the way his throat gaped open. I walked past him, slower now, and only stopped when I reached Diggs' door.

The room was in shambles: a full-length mirror shattered, a dresser overturned. His clothes were still on the chair, Cameron's file on the bed.

"How did they get in here?" I demanded when Juarez caught up to me. Buddy Holloway and half the National

Guard were with him. "The place was supposed to be guarded—it's like a friggin' fortress here. How the hell did they get in?"

"There's another guard dead in the back," Juarez said. "They came through that way—we were already stretched thin because another fire was called in about an hour ago, but we had the place covered. They knew exactly what they were doing. Where our weak spots were, who was stationed where... The whole process of taking him was carried out with the precision of a military operation. We never thought they'd attempt something like this considering the police presence in the hotel."

"But they did," I said. "Because getting Diggs was worth the risk." My voice cracked. I thought of Diggs' words after Wyatt's funeral: *I'm the one who got away. The only one who never bought into any of this...* Of course Barnel would come for him.

Einstein whined and followed me into Diggs' room, sniffing at the glass on the floor. I pulled him back to keep him from getting cut. Grace stood in the doorway watching us, head and tail down. She wouldn't cross the threshold.

"Do we know how long ago they took him?" I asked.

"Forty-five minutes, maybe," Agent Keith said. I hadn't even realized he was there.

"We have people out there, though," I said. I was starting to feel unhinged. "Right? The National Guard is checking vehicles; there are eyes on every street corner. Someone must have seen something."

Juarez didn't say anything. No one said anything.

"What?" I finally demanded.

"A woman reported two men in black loading a blond male into a truck. He was unconscious," Juarez finally said.

"Well—that's good, then. When? Where did they go? Do we have someone following them?"

Juarez looked ready to punch something. Buddy shifted uncomfortably.

"It seems like maybe the call went to voicemail," the deputy said. "We don't have nobody answering phones right now… And with the electricity out and a cell tower down, communication's not what it usually is."

"Right," I said. "What with the end of the world and all. So, does anyone have anything at all? Any idea where they might have gone?"

No one spoke. Juarez looked at me uneasily, as did everyone else in the room. I started to say something more when he noticed the file on Diggs' bed and moved to pick it up. I grabbed it before he could.

"What is that?" he asked.

"Just a story he's—we're working on," I said. "It doesn't have anything to do with this."

"You're sure about that?"

I nodded. He didn't look convinced, but he didn't push it for the moment.

"So, what do we do next?" I asked. "Search houses? Bring in helicopters? Search and rescue?"

"Maybe you should get dressed," Juarez suggested gently. For the first time, I realized I was standing there in bare feet, blue jeans, and Juarez's t-shirt. "And then we can take it from there."

06:40:09

For the next three hours, nothing happened. I don't mean to say no one *did* anything: they searched vehicles; ransacked houses; went through Barnel's compound with a fine-tooth comb. Jessie Barnel was still unconscious. The kids who'd been rescued from the cellar didn't seem to know anything about anything, except some loons in black had taken them into the woods, locked them in a cellar, and then played UNO with them until all hell broke loose and people started dying.

We went back to Mae's house, but it was deserted. I peered in the windows, searching for some sign of life. There was none. George was still gone, his bunnies staring listlessly out at us. I opened the cage and put more pellets in, checking to make sure they had enough water.

The window was still broken out in George's shed. I thought of Diggs in my arms as we rode to the hospital our first night in Justice, his hand in mine.

"No one's here," Juarez said.

"I know."

"They're staying with Ashley. Do you want to talk to her?"

I really didn't. I had no idea what else to do, though. I was panicking, I knew—there were too many angles to the story, too many players, and only two possible outcomes:

We either stopped this from happening at midnight, or we didn't. Diggs lived, or he died. I took a deep breath.

"Whenever Diggs and I are working on a story that seems too big, we take a step back and try to deconstruct the whole thing."

"Sounds like a good approach," Juarez said. He sat on the front steps of George's cabin and patted a spot beside him. "Where do we start?"

I got out my pen and spiral notebook, something that never fails to amuse Juarez. He didn't look amused today, though. I sat beside him and stared at the blank page in front of me.

"Jessie said Reverend Barnel was going back to the beginning," I began, thinking of her words during the standoff.

"Yeah—Allie's on that, actually. They have a transcript of

the whole thing. We're assuming he was talking about Billy Thomas and the murders in 1963, since Billy was the first victim who turned up with the inverted cross, and everything Barnel's set up revolves around the fifty-year anniversary of his death."

"Billy took the girls while they were in city hall, right? And that would certainly be a public enough target—I mean, blowing up that place would be one hell of a statement, regardless of whether it's full or empty." I stopped. "Of course, now that Barnel's taking all these people, I guess it doesn't really matter whether the town's been evacuated. He's chosen the people he thinks should pay for their sins, and they're the ones who'll presumably die in this thing."

Jack lay his hand over mine, twisting our fingers together. "Are you all right?" he asked.

"Yeah. I'm fine. I just want to find him." I amended that at the look in his eye. "Them, I mean. Everyone."

He didn't say anything, but I knew he was watching me. I felt like I was under a microscope since Diggs had been taken; like Juarez was analyzing my every reaction, and I had no idea how to reassure him that I was still his when the only thing I could seem to think of was the feel of Diggs' body pressed to mine and his breath in my ear. The thousands of conversations we'd had over the years and the thousands more I'd always assumed we would have.

"So, what about city hall?" I prompted again.

"They're already on it. They've got bomb-sniffing dogs going through the place, but so far no one's found anything."

"Okay," I said. "What about where Billy was born? Or the place where Barnel branded him?"

"They're looking at all of it," Jack said with infinite patience. "They've got his file, baby. They're going over Jessie Barnel's transcript. They're looking through everything at the compound."

"What about the dynamite?" I asked. "I mean, people don't just give up that many explosives, right? Someone had to get them from somewhere."

"Everything was homemade—it's easier to get hold of that stuff than something like C4. Fertilizer, household cleaners, found items... There's no way to trace most of it."

"Well, that's great," I said. I pushed my notebook aside and stood. "I don't understand where the hell everyone's gone. It's not like this is a huge place—how are all these people just vanishing right under our noses? You'd think we were trying to find Bin Laden, for Christ's sake."

Jack picked up my notebook and pen and started writing.

"What are you doing?" I asked.

"You said you and Diggs deconstruct, right? We haven't really done that yet."

Right.

I nodded and forced some air into my lungs. This was just another puzzle, I reminded myself. I was good at puzzles.

"Okay, so...key players," I said.

"Jesup Barnel," Juarez said immediately. I nodded. He wrote it down.

"And whether or not Barnel had anything to do with their deaths, those first confirmed victims with the inverted crosses..."

"Billy Thomas, Marty Reynolds, Wyatt Durham, and Roger Burkett," Juarez said.

I thought about that for a minute. "What do we know about Marty Reynolds?" I asked.

"He was a bad guy who may or may not have killed his wife."

"But I still don't understand that," I said. "There are two thousand, three hundred and eighty-six guys on Barnel's list—and plenty of those guys have criminal records. Why Reynolds and no one else? Why no deaths from 1963 to

2002, then Reynolds gets axed and there's not another victim for eleven years?"

Juarez was looking at me strangely.

"What?" I asked.

"That's a very specific number," he said. "Twenty-three hundred and eighty-six. How did you know that?"

"Diggs' files," I said carelessly. "He's been keeping tabs on Barnel for years…" I stopped. I was an idiot.

"These files—they're on his computer?"

"They are," I agreed. "Back at the hotel."

Jack got on the horn to his people to tell them to grab Diggs' computer. When he hung up, he came back over while I stared at George's rabbits and tried to quell a growing sense of impending doom. He started to put his arms around me, but I shrugged away. There wasn't time to sit around and be comforted—not when Diggs was missing and the clock was running down.

"We should get back to HQ," I said. "I've got a couple of ideas I want to check out."

06:02:10

Command Central was buzzing when we got there: more troops, more equipment, more intensity. I walked down the school hallway to the dancing tiger on the wall and stood outside the war room for a minute, thinking of Diggs. He was still alive—I was sure of that. Barnel wanted us to know his victims, those sinners who'd strayed from his path to glory. He had something planned.

I just didn't know what it could be.

Something big, we all assumed. Something to rock Justice to its foundation. Something that took him back to the beginning; back when it all went wrong.

Blaze nodded me into the room, and I pushed those

thoughts aside for the moment. She looked exhausted. Clearly, that three-hour nap she'd given the troops hadn't extended to her.

There was a place of honor waiting for me at the front of the room. Jack nodded at me and I sat, feeling strangely out of place without Diggs beside me. I spotted his laptop on a desk off to the side, with a computer tech tapping away on it. I bristled, thinking of how much Diggs would hate that. Blaze followed my gaze.

"We're having a hard time getting in there," she said. "He has good security. So far we haven't been able to figure out his password."

I stood and went over. The computer tech was a woman, fifties to sixties, plump and blonde and efficient.

"I've got it."

"You know the password?" she asked.

"Yeah." She wasn't moving. "Just let me in there and I'll get you what you need."

"We'll need to scan the full hard drive," she said.

"Not without his permission, you won't."

"You're not authorized to work with our equipment."

Clearly, the woman had a death wish. "It's not your equipment, you—" Juarez intervened before I pulled her away from Diggs' computer by her bleached blonde hair.

"It's all right, Mandy," he said. "Let her take over."

Mandy got up, purposely bumping into me when she brushed past. Juarez grabbed my arm before I went after her.

"Let it go," he said under his breath.

Right. Instead of beating up the technology Nazi, I took her seat and got to work.

It only took two tries to get in. Juarez looked at me in surprise. I shrugged.

"Lucky guess."

Blaze came over and looked over my shoulder. I stopped

typing and turned around.

"I'll let you know when I find anything," I said.

"There may be files you're not familiar with that are relevant to this investigation."

I didn't budge. Diggs' entire world was on his computer—he didn't let anyone in there. Not even me. Certainly not Big Brother.

"Can you give us a second?" Juarez asked Blaze. She nodded and walked away. I didn't even look at him as he pulled up a chair beside me.

"We need to get in there, Erin," he said. "We have programs that will scan the files in a matter of minutes. It won't even be people looking at them."

"Not at first," I said. "But what about when the keywords you're looking for come up? Then, people will be going through everything here. And what happens when national security keywords that don't have anything to do with Barnel start popping up? His work is important too, Jack."

"Erin," he said seriously. He leaned forward in his chair and took my hands in his. There were maybe a dozen people in the room, and I realized that all of them were waiting for me. "This isn't negotiable. We'll be as sensitive as we can be, but I can't make any promises. You can oversee things if you like—let us know if there's a file that we think is pertinent but you know isn't. That's the best I can do."

I pulled my hands away and nodded. I got up abruptly, nearly knocking my chair over in the process. "Yeah, you're right. Go ahead."

Mandy came back over, just a trace of a smug smile on her lips when she reclaimed her chair. We had six hours to find Diggs—there wasn't time for me to get into it with her now. Jack put his hand on my shoulder while I stood by, arms crossed over my stomach, watching as they picked Diggs' life apart.

I excused myself after a few minutes and commandeered a computer, intent on doing a little investigating of my own.

I started with Marty Reynolds—the anomaly in all this. I knew why Billy Thomas was dead; I knew why Wyatt was dead. I wasn't completely clear on the reason for Roger Burkett's death, but the fact that it came on the heels of all this other violence suggested it had something to do with Barnel and Company's grand plan. But Marty Reynolds just seemed so random.

After I'd done some digging, though, I found I wasn't any clearer on motivation. He had a lengthy rap sheet: drugs, violence, everything we'd already found before. On a whim, I pulled up his wife—the woman he was suspected of killing. I found a photo of Glenda Reynolds online from an article in 2001 about the local Qwik E Mart, where Glenda worked as a cashier. She was surprisingly pretty: tall and slender, with long dark hair and striking eyes. Twenty-three at the time, she was younger than her husband by seventeen years.

I didn't find her maiden name until I pulled up the marriage announcement in the local paper, dated July 15, 1999. *Glenda Clifton to Marry Marty Reynolds Saturday, July 18.* Clifton didn't ring any bells for me, but I looked her up anyway. She'd been Junior Miss Kentucky Stars in '90, won blue ribbons in 4-H for horsemanship four years running, and made straight A's up until her junior year in high school. She dropped off the map in '92, no longer mentioned in any archived articles I could find online. If this were a real investigation with a manageable deadline involved, I'd head to the local library from there and look up hard copies of everything I could find.

Since the world was ending in six hours, however, I didn't really have that luxury.

Instead, I managed to find Glenda's birth certificate and Googled her parents.

Pay dirt.

Glenda's father was killed in a car accident in 1991. That year, I found an article on Jesup Barnel, with Glenda's mother pictured with a group of six others listed as new members of Barnel's church. Then, I looked for articles and images from Barnel's church youth group, since Glenda would be about the right age for that.

The fifth photo I pulled up told the story I'd been looking for:

Jesup Barnel stood with about fifteen teenagers, all of them looking appropriately pious. Glenda Reynolds had changed since her days as Miss Kentucky Stars. Now, she wore her hair shorter and her dress much longer. She stood beside Jesup Barnel, his arm around her shoulders in an unmistakably proprietary way. Glenda's own posture was tense, and you couldn't miss the way she tried to hold herself apart from the reverend.

I had no proof, but I was still willing to stake my reputation on it: Jesup Barnel had been sleeping with Glenda Reynolds, back when she was still Glenda Clifton. And Glenda, sixteen at the time, hadn't been happy about it.

I called Juarez and Blaze over and they listened to my theory. Blaze hedged as soon as I was finished.

"You may have a point in all this, but I'm not sure what it has to do with today. Even if Barnel was molesting this girl, and that had something to do with the reason Marty Reynolds was murdered... I don't know how that leads us to what he has in mind tonight. We can follow up on it later—right now, I need my people focused on more immediate leads."

"And what are those leads, exactly?" I asked. I was well

aware of the edge to my voice.

"We're looking at Billy Thomas's childhood home right now."

"What about Barnel's childhood home?" I asked. "For all we know, going back to the beginning means going back to Barnel's roots."

"We've got agents there now," Jack said. "Erin, you need to believe that we know what we're doing here."

"What about Diggs' files? Have you found anything?"

I followed Blaze back to the Tech Nazi's desk. The Nazi was immersed in her task of dissecting Diggs' personal life. She didn't look especially pleased to be interrupted. Or to have to admit, once again, that she might need my help.

"I've set aside a dozen folders here that look suspicious, but we haven't found a direct relationship to Jesup Barnel." She looked me up and down for a minute. "You're Solomon?"

"Yeah," I said. I pushed her out of the way and sat down. "Why?"

"No reason," she said. "You just take up an awful lot of space on his hard drive."

Juarez stood beside me, hovering just over my shoulder. He glanced at me, then back at the computer, doing his best to pretend none of this pertained to him. Or us.

"We've known each other a long time," I said. I refused to give her the satisfaction of trying to justify it beyond that.

"So I gathered," the woman said. She walked away.

"You really know how to get on people's good sides, you know that?" Juarez asked.

"I'm not going for Miss Congeniality here. I just want to find Diggs."

"Yeah," Juarez said. "I got that."

He left me to my work.

Of the dozen questionable files the Nazi had saved

to Diggs' desktop for easy reference, nine I identified immediately: stories Diggs had either finished or been working on over the past couple of years. Three others were encrypted, and apparently no one thus far had been able to break that encryption. One was labeled simply 'Hood,' but I knew it immediately: that would be Mitch Cameron, our hooded man. I couldn't identify the other two.

"You can try these two," I called over my shoulder. The Nazi returned, Juarez on her heels.

"You're sure about the others?" she asked.

"Positive," I said. "And I'm assuming you've already found the primary folder he had."

"Of course," she said, like I'd suggested something completely idiotic. "It's mostly names and newspaper clippings. He's very thorough."

"He's good at what he does," I said.

For just a second, I thought I saw a glimmer of humanity in her eyes. "We wouldn't be doing this if he wasn't."

23
DIGGS

WHEN I CAME TO, it was to a red glow and nausea and the cotton-throated feel of chemicals in my blood.

"Diggs?" someone whispered. I opened my eyes wider, searching for the source. The world came into focus and suddenly Danny was there, kneeling beside me.

"Where the hell are we?" I asked. I tried to sit up. I failed. My hands were bound behind my back, plastic ties cutting into my wrists.

"Give yourself a minute," Danny said. "It'll get better—you've just gotta adjust."

My synapses weren't firing right. I stayed where I was and counted down from ten, slowly, before I finally forced myself upright.

"If you're gonna puke, do it that way," Danny said. He nodded toward my right. My stomach rolled at the stench.

For the first time, I realized we weren't alone. I looked around, trying to focus on the details. About a dozen people were gathered in the small space. The dirt floor was damp and cool beneath me, but the rest of the room was suffocatingly warm. The entire scene was lit by a bare red bulb mounted above a very solid-looking steel door.

"Who else is here?" I asked.

"Casey," Danny said. "A friend of mine from this band—"

I nodded. "I know who she is."

"Right," Danny said. "Yeah, she told me you guys talked. And there's a couple kids from school." He lowered his voice. "And there are some other guys, too. It's not a good crew, Diggs."

He wasn't kidding. I counted at least three tweakers just going into withdrawal, another couple of burly guys with a look in their eye that intimated deep-seated anger and a tradition of violence. I thought of the shacks we'd come across the day before: crosses burning in the front yard, trash and debris inside. We'd already found the kids... Apparently, this was what had happened to the adults.

"So, I'm assuming you don't know where we are," I said. The nausea was fading, and with it that sense of panic. I was alive. So was Danny.

That was something.

"We don't know," Danny said. "They only bring us here while we're out of it. No idea how long it takes—we reckon we're not far out of town, though."

"Somebody's cellar, most likely," someone else said. A teenage boy with dirty gauze on one side of his face, a yellowish fluid seeping through the bandage. I recognized him immediately: the boy I'd spoken with about his friend just after the explosion Thursday night.

Danny shook his head. "You kiddin'? How many houses you know with underground rooms and halls and passages that go on forever? It's gotta be something else. Rick did this project about all the places in Justice with secret tunnels underneath them. This has to be one of those."

"How many people are here?" I asked.

"You make eleven," Danny said. "I was alone for a long time, then they brought a few folks in. They been throwin' 'em in pretty steady for the past few hours, though."

For the first time, I noticed a timer mounted beside the door, digital numbers counting backward.

"What's that?" I asked.

Danny didn't say anything for three seconds—I watched them tick by in fire engine red. Then:

"That's all the time we got," he said. "I don't know what happens when the numbers run out, but I get the feeling it won't be good. The reverend said we had to make our peace. Beg forgiveness."

I stared at the clock as the seconds counted down:

05:09:20, 05:09:19… Five hours till midnight, and whatever Barnel had promised came to pass.

I tried to get my head back in the game. Five hours wasn't a lot to work with, but it was something.

"What about sounds?" I asked.

"There was a boiler room—heard that pretty clear. Saw it, too. And there's music once you're outside this room."

That brought me out of my stupor. "What kind of music?"

"Good stuff, actually," he said, sounding surprised. "They were playin' *Blonde on Blonde*, I think, when Jenny Burkett come to get me. Then maybe Chuck Berry."

"So, nothing religious?"

"Nope. It's not coming from them—one of the guys got mad about it when he was takin' me."

I felt a sudden surge of hope. *Blonde on Blonde* would have made Jake's top twenty-four list without a doubt. As would Chuck Berry—probably *The Great Twenty-Eight*. Most of the area had no power, so what were the chances we were in someone's basement while they cranked WKRO?

Slim, at best. It was a good lead, I was sure of it. I just wasn't sure where it was leading.

The rest of what he'd said suddenly clicked. "Hang on—you said Jenny Burkett? She's here?"

I wasn't actually surprised to hear the name: from the start it had seemed like too much of a coincidence that Wyatt and Roger Burkett were last seen at Jenny Burkett's place. Add to that the fact that the sheriff made no effort to bring her in and it only made sense.

Danny lowered his eyes and nodded. "She's how come I'm here in the first place… I heard her whisperin' to me outside Casey's place. When you see her, you'll get it. You take one look at her, hear a little sweet nothin' from that pretty mouth, and you'll risk just about anything for a taste."

I let that go. I'd been seventeen before. If memory served, there weren't a lot of women on the planet for whom I wouldn't have risked anything if I thought the promise of sex—or anything close to it—was on the table.

"Do you know who else is behind this?" I asked. "Have you talked to Barnel?"

"We all talked to the preacher," the other teenage boy said. "You'll get your chance soon enough. Gotta make your confession. He don't mention anybody else, though. Just him and Jesus."

"Well—them and Jenny," Danny agreed.

"She's been draggin' us back and forth, doin' whatever Barnel wants," Danny continued. "There's a big guy, but I haven't seen his face. So far we make out one other guy besides Barnel, but we reckon there must be more."

"And you don't recognize any voices?"

"Nope, not so far. Seems like they know what they're doin', though. They know how to keep us in our place, keep everybody quiet."

Yet another sign of the organization Blaze had been

talking about earlier. There was no way in hell Jesup Barnel could pull this off on his own. I set aside the maddening question of who he was working with, and focused on more pressing issues.

"Have you looked for a way out?" I asked.

"No," Danny said with a practiced roll of the eyes. "We been sitting here playin' Tic Tac Toe, hopin' for a miracle."

"No need to get snippy," I said. "What'd you find?"

"Not much," he said. "There's just the one door leading in here. Floor's dirt. Walls are cement. I can't find no wires or pipes, so wherever we are, we're far enough out of the way that they don't put the electrical or the plumbing through here. We got the bare bulb and our countdown clock. Not much to work with."

I nodded. It wasn't much to work with at all.

24
SOLOMON

04:45:11

I STARTED TO PANIC at around seven o'clock that night. It wasn't that I was all that calm before then, of course... I was just much, much less calm by the time seven o'clock rolled around. Jessie Barnel still hadn't come to, which didn't bode well. We'd gone through city hall, the wreckage of Billy Thomas's old home, the old farmhouse where Reverend Barnel was raised, the church where he first started preaching, the church where Billy Thomas took his first communion. We had Feds and the National Guard and sniffing dogs and everything in between, scouring the entire county.

And still, we had nothing.

There was one more lead I'd been avoiding up to this point—partly because I knew the Feds had already been all over it. And partly because I really, really didn't want to go there.

I couldn't see my way clear of avoiding it any longer, though. I got up from my seat in front of the computer and found Blaze, standing beside a giant interactive map of the county. You could barely see the actual map for all the dots and dashes and highlighted lines covering it. She looked up when she saw me.

"You have anything?" she asked.

"No. But I have an idea." I hesitated. She raised an eyebrow, a look in her eye that suggested I'd do well to tell her that idea sooner rather than later. "You said you have video footage of Barnel's rituals—of him branding those boys in the church?"

"That's over a thousand hours of tape, Erin."

"I know that," I agreed. "I don't need to see all of it. Just four of the rituals: Marty Reynolds, Wyatt Durham, Roger Burkett…and Diggs."

"We've looked at them all. I don't know how helpful they'll be. And Diggs' tape… " She hesitated. "Well, let's just say it's not for the faint of heart."

So, I'd been right: she had watched the tape. "It doesn't matter. I'd still like to see them."

"I'll have someone get them for you."

They set me up with a VCR and an old TV in a cubicle in the corner. I set my pen and paper down. Put on giant headphones. Turned on the TV.

Marty Reynolds was thirteen when he was 'exorcised,' back in 1973. The A/V equipment was primitive back then: terrible sound, fuzzy picture. Reverend Barnel's hair hadn't gone grey yet, and he was carrying a few less pounds. Otherwise, he was pretty much the same lunatic I'd seen at Miller's Field the other night.

The service took place in Redemption Hall, at Barnel's compound—though in those days, Redemption Hall wasn't nearly as tricked out as what I'd seen the other day. There was a pulpit up front, rows and rows of folding chairs, and that same torturous dentist's chair I'd seen before, equipped with leather straps on both sides.

Marty was a big kid for his age. The ritual was hard to watch, but not extraordinary: it started with him being led in, stripped down to his boxers, and then strapped into the chair. Barnel asked him his sins. He didn't put up a fuss, copping to a few minor infractions and a recent theft within five minutes. He renounced Satan. Barnel branded him. Afterward, there was a hatred so deep in Marty's eyes when he looked at Barnel that I wondered how the preacher was still alive today. The crowd whooped and hollered and cheered. Barnel's lovely assistant—a gorilla-sized goon Barnel called Brother Hollis—unstrapped Marty and released him back into the wild.

Wyatt's ceremony was the same—the main difference being that he actually seemed genuinely remorseful for his sins. Those sins were hardly extraordinary: mostly lying and carousing and smoking cigarettes. Hardly worthy of the Barnel brand, in my estimation. By this time, it was 1984. Brother Hollis was gone, and a much younger Brother Jimmy—Barnel's boy—had taken his place.

Danny's was one of the more recent tapes, obviously, transitioning from video to digital. The ritual was still performed in Redemption Hall, with the Hall shown in the video looking much closer to the one I'd seen: stadium seating, red carpet, the works. The same dentist's chair was still set up in the middle of the action, but the video equipment and everything else had seen a major upgrade.

Mae, Wyatt, and Rick stood beside the reverend while the ceremony took place. Brother Jimmy led Danny in. The kid was a couple years younger in this, wearing only his boxer shorts, and he seemed a hell of a lot more calm than I expected. I waited for him to fight. He didn't. He didn't cry, either. He recited his sins and renounced the devil like he was reading a script. The reverend definitely wasn't happy with the lack of pizzazz, but there wasn't a lot he could do.

Then, I caught something just before Barnel lowered the brand to Danny's chest. I backed the tape up, and slowed it down.

Mae and Rick were completely rapt—mesmerized, even. Wyatt, on the other hand, looked like he was in that damn chair with his son. Just before the iron hit Danny's skin, I saw Wyatt mouth something to him. It didn't take long to put it together once I put the sound on: Wyatt was mouthing the words, just before Danny said them. Coaching him on how best to get through everything Barnel was putting him through.

Contrary to what Mae might have believed, I suspected Wyatt hadn't been so keen on Reverend Barnel after all.

That brought me to Diggs' tape. Watching it felt like a betrayal—it was the last thing he'd want me to see, I was sure of it. The last thing he'd want anyone to see. I couldn't think of another way, though.

I pushed the tape in.

He was so small.

Twelve—a short, skinny kid with a mop of blond curls and the attitude of someone a whole lot bigger.

Brother Jimmy brought him to the table. He'd already been stripped down to a pair of Bugs Bunny boxer shorts, and was fighting tooth and nail when Jimmy tried to strap him to the table. He bit Jimmy hard enough to draw blood, then kneed the reverend himself in the balls. Eventually, they had to call in reinforcements. After twenty minutes, they got him strapped to the table.

The reverend began to pray. Then he started in on Diggs. "Daniel, you need to learn that your actions have consequences. Your brother was taken from this life because of your careless disregard. His blood was spilled; and yet, you live. That rebellion you embrace so tight is Satan, havin' his way with your soul, son. Your brother died because you was too weak to turn your back on temptation. You need to beg for the Lord's forgiveness or you'll never be free of the devil. Are you sorry, son?"

A chorus of "Amen"s rose up from the audience. I clenched my hands so hard I left bleeding crescents in my palms.

"I'm sorry my brother's dead. But that doesn't have anything to do with the devil, and it sure as hell doesn't have anything to do with you," Diggs said. I smiled. Stubborn little bastard.

The preacher kept at him, trying to get him to "turn his back on Satan." Diggs joked and he fought and then, when it was clear he was too exhausted to do anything else, he went silent.

Barnel branded his chest.

Marty Reynolds had screamed bloody murder when Barnel did him. Even Wyatt and Danny had hollered good and loud. Diggs kept his mouth shut and his eyes straight ahead, his hatred so clear it was no wonder the reverend thought Beelzebub was pulling his strings. Afterward, Barnel sent everyone in the audience home, telling them he needed all his concentration on the demon child before him. Once they were gone, something else took hold in Barnel's eyes: something dark and manic. Something unhinged.

I turned the tape off and sat there for a second, nauseous. If there was a hell, I hoped Barnel ended up there with someone five times his size burning molten steel into his flesh for all eternity. I got up, got a glass of water, and returned to my cubicle. I turned the tape back on.

Diggs passed out about an hour in. Brother Jimmy brought him back around by dousing him with water. Then, he put a hood over his head, and doused him again.

I fast forwarded more of the same.

It went on like that for almost three hours.

Barnel never broke him. He never got him to renounce the devil; never got him to beg for forgiveness. By the time it was over, the reverend was sweating bullets and Diggs—twelve years old, maybe a hundred pounds soaking wet—was slipping in and out of consciousness, but he wouldn't give an inch. Finally, there was some kind of disturbance behind the camera, and it sounded like someone burst in. A minute later, a big man with dark hair and broad shoulders bulled his way past Brother Jimmy and tore the straps off Diggs' arms and legs. George Durham.

"Get away from him, you damn fool," George said, his voice raw with fury. Wyatt was on his heels. He started to pick Diggs up out of the chair, but Diggs pushed him away and got up on his own.

"Give me my fucking clothes," mini Diggs said hoarsely to Barnel.

"He needs to be cleansed," Barnel said to Wyatt.

"Save the party line, Jesup," George said. "My wife might buy it, but I don't hold no stock in a man who strips boys down and tortures 'em in the name of God. Now, give the boy his damn clothes and let's be done with this."

Barnel grabbed George by the elbow and pulled him aside. I got the feeling George Durham wasn't the kind of man accustomed to being manhandled: he jerked his arm away and wheeled on Barnel. The fear on the preacher's face was obvious. He stepped back enough to give George some room and lowered his voice until it was inaudible on the tape. I fiddled with the audio levels, trying to get some sense of what they were talking about.

I could only make out one thing through the entire whispered conversation, but it spoke volumes. Barnel said a name, and George's face went pale. I knew that name well:

Billy Thomas.

They fought a little longer before it seemed that the two men came to a stalemate. Finally, Barnel gave the nod and Jimmy brought Diggs his clothes. He was so weak he could barely stand, but he pulled on his pants and a Van Halen t-shirt, shot Barnel one more killing glare, and limped out alongside George and Wyatt Durham.

No wonder Diggs loved the Durhams. And hated Jesup Barnel.

I only had one question: What the hell did George Durham have to do with Billy Thomas?

25
DIGGS

03:30:16

JENNY BURKETT CAME AND GOT ME three and a half hours before the world was due to end, trailed by the ski-mask-wearing, gun-toting giant who'd taken me from the hotel. Jenny looked cool and collected, and Danny hadn't been kidding: she was definitely a looker. Heavily-lashed, wide brown eyes gazed out from a heart-shaped face, her full lips quirked up in a smile that was anything but pious. She came over holding a black hood that was clearly meant for me.

"Why bother with that?" I asked. "What's the point of secrecy if you're just gonna kill us anyway?"

"Who says we're killing you, slick? A few lucky guests may just walk out of this without a scratch. We'll see how it goes." Her smile was more predatory than I typically associated with Barnel's flock.

"So, the reverend's deciding who lives and who dies now?" I said. "Isn't that job supposed to go to the man upstairs, according to all the rhetoric?"

"You're just full of assumptions, aren't you." She knelt

beside me, leaning close enough that I could feel body heat and the press of her breasts against my arm. Her lips were close to my ear when she spoke again. "I never said the reverend was making any decisions."

That set me back. Before we could continue what was proving to be an illuminating conversation, the giant in black leveled a gun at my head.

"That's enough," he said. "Just put the damn hood on him so we can get moving."

I nodded. "Be my guest." I sounded a lot more cavalier than I felt. Once I was rendered fully blind, the Giant hauled me to my feet and led me out.

I'm not overly partial to hoods or blindfolds; Reverend Barnel ruined that particular fetish for me early on. Last summer, Will Rainier sealed it. My intestines knotted and the air left my lungs when the cloth fell over my face. I fought to stay calm, the smell of must and sweat in my nose, that claustrophobic blindness I remembered from my youth shutting out everything else.

I walked with Jenny on one side, her hand cool and delicately feminine on my left arm, while the Giant's sweaty mitt gripped the other. The floor of the first corridor was dirt, and the place smelled of cobwebs and old earth. They opened a creaking door and we walked up a flight of fifteen narrow stairs. Another, heavier-sounding door opened in front of us. It was warmer here, the floor concrete. I heard music that was either live or broadcast through a damn good sound system, coming from a floor above us. It was Stevie Wonder's "Higher Ground"—the original, not the Chili Peppers cover.

Halfway down the concrete corridor, "Higher Ground" ended and a chorus of trumpets began; that segued into the first strains of "Jesus Children of America." I felt another surge of excitement. "Jesus Children" is the track after

"Higher Ground" on *Innervisions*, Stevie Wonder's second album to go gold. There was no way it hadn't made it into Jake Dooley's top five records of all time.

Wherever we were, they were broadcasting WKRO. And there was a network of subterranean tunnels to which Jenny Burkett, Reverend Barnel, and all their foot soldiers had ready access. I didn't know where that led me, but it seemed like I was getting closer to some answers.

Jenny and her buddy led me down five steps and opened another door. A blast of hot air hit me like a sunburst. They hauled me over the threshold and inside the room. My heart was hammering—a sound that's deafening, incidentally, when you're locked in a pillowcase. I tried to orient myself, dizzy from the movement and more than a slight case of bone-crushing terror.

"He can sit," a voice behind me said. I whirled.

"That's all right. I'll stand, thanks."

A meaty hand locked onto my shoulder and tried to push me backward. I channeled my inner Jedi, tried to establish some sense of where I was in relation to my captors, and centered myself. I brought my knee up, fast, at the same time that I pushed myself forward. My knee connected with something soft; I heard an *oof* as the big guy hit the ground.

Of course, less than a second later I crumpled into a cool metal chair after the Giant retaliated with a ruthless rabbit punch to my left kidney. The whole thing had been an exercise in futility, but I felt better for at least having tried.

Jenny pulled the hood off my head.

I was in the same boiler room the others had described, a low-end digital video camera mounted on a tripod at eye level about five feet away. A couple of professional photography lamps were pointed in my direction, with a cheap white backdrop behind me. Barnel sat in a folding chair behind the camera equipment.

"Cecil B. Demille, I presume," I said.

"You never get tired of hearin' yourself talk, do you, Daniel?" Barnel said.

"That's rich coming from you. What do you want?"

"Same thing I've always wanted." He nodded toward the door, and Jenny and her fella stepped outside. I was alone with the master himself. "I just wanna save your soul, son."

"And I'll tell you the same thing I told you thirty years ago: keep your hands off me and my soul. I'm all set. Thanks for your concern."

He stood and produced a sheet of paper from his bag of tricks, then set it up carefully on a music stand just behind the video camera. My confession was two paragraphs long, written in 24-point Arial type. With the margins widened to half an inch on all sides, the writing covered the bulk of the page. I scanned the contents silently:

I, Daniel Jacob Diggins, am here to solemnly confess a lifetime of mortal sin.

I looked up. Despite the gravity of the situation, it was hard to keep a straight face. "Seriously?" I asked. "You expect me to say this shit?"

He paced the room, hands clasped behind his back. "You're gonna say every word of it, son."

"If torture didn't work on me when I was twelve, what makes you think anything you say will make an impression now?" I asked.

He stopped pacing and looked at me. There was a fever in his eyes—that religious fervor that had terrified me about him from the first time we met, now coupled with what I took to be chemically induced mania.

"You want that nephew of yours to walk out of here?" he asked. "And what about George? You want me to let George Durham, that father you never had, gather up his things and limp out of this buildin' intact? Because I got that power, son. You confess your ways, accept the Lord's punishment for the sins you done and the life you led, and maybe not everybody you love has to die."

I froze. "George isn't with us."

"He'll be in there when you get back, boy. The two of us had to have it out first—that man's almost as stubborn as you. But he saw the error of his ways by the end, just like you will."

"I thought the world was ending," I said. "If the planet's getting swallowed into hell in a few hours, how will my confession save anyone?"

For the first time, he hesitated. A flicker of uncertainty washed over his florid face. "The end of the world means different things to different people. You'll understand when all's said and done."

"Okay," I said. "So, I read this bullshit you've written for me, and you let George and Danny go. And then, what happens to the tape? Are you and your minions headed to Sundance when this is all over? Or does it just get added to your twisted archive?"

"People see it," he said, to my surprise—I thought he would have just put me off. "They watch, and they know who I was. What I done. The souls I saved before the Lord took me home."

It wasn't what I expected—not by a long shot. The biggest surprise, however, was the preacher's obvious exhaustion and the agony in his eyes. I could use that exhaustion.

"Fine," I said.

He looked at me in surprise. "What?"

I shrugged. "Screw it. You took the time to write it—I can take a couple minutes to read it. What the hell? It's not like I have anything better to do."

His eyes welled. He nodded, pulling the stand a few

inches closer so I could see more easily.

I looked into the camera and read his words—all of them nonsense, the gist of the message having to do with betraying God and embracing my inner demon for most of my life. When I came to the end, I looked up and noted that the preacher stood by with his hands folded, silently mouthing the words along with me. Tears rolled down his cheeks.

"Can I say one more thing?" I asked when Barnel shut off the camera. He looked at me suspiciously.

"What?"

"I'm assuming these are my last words," I said. My chest went unexpectedly tight at the thought. I pushed past that, maintaining eye contact. "If they are, I'd like to make my own peace, if I could."

He wrestled with the idea for a few seconds before he eventually nodded. "You gotta be quick about it, though," he said. "We ain't got much time for what needs doin'."

I didn't question that, as much as I wanted to. Instead, I waited until he'd turned on the camera, and began.

"Since this is apparently my last will and testament," I said, my eye on the little red button blinking at me. "I wanted to say one more thing." I hesitated for a second, working past the lump in my throat. It wasn't fair, what I was doing—if this was indeed all that would remain of me after the fact, it wasn't right to put Solomon through this. But if it were me in her place… As horrible a thought as that was, I knew I'd want those last words from her. I hung onto the memory of her eyes and went on.

"Erin," I said. I wet my lips. "I know I've made more mistakes in this life than most ten men. I stand by a lot of those mistakes. There are only two that I'd change. The first is that day I convinced a ten-year-old kid to follow me off a cliff. The second is the morning I walked out on you."

I took a long, deep breath. Barnel moved to turn off the camera. I shook my head and he stopped, waiting. I continued.

"I hope you get what you're looking for, kid. You're an amazing woman... even if your best record is *Original Soul*. You've made my life better in a thousand ways. I've always loved you, Sol. Even when it wasn't smart. Even when I had no right. I think I always will."

I stopped, trying to maintain control. Barnel turned off the camera. He looked very old, suddenly.

"Why are you doing this, Jesup?" I asked. "You've lost your family. Your congregation. Your friends. You clearly don't believe the world's really ending at midnight. So... why? You honestly believe this is what your god would want?"

He scrubbed his hand over his eyes. "The end may not be comin' tonight, but it's on its way. The Lord's been walkin' softly too many years. My time's up—and I ain't leavin' those I love for the hell that's to come. There's nothin' keepin' me here. Once I know I done my duty for Him, I'm taking my loved ones and we're gonna retire to those streets of gold."

"And you don't think any of this goes against those messages of peace and good will other followers of Christianity preach?"

His face darkened like a storm cloud had fallen. "There ain't room for mercy or coddlin' anymore. No room at all. The Brigade taught me that."

There was a light knock on the door. I thought about his words as Jenny came in without waiting for a response from Barnel. The storm cloud on his face darkened.

"We need to get moving, Reverend," Jenny said.

He glowered at her. "I ain't finished here—I told you I'd come for you when I'm good and ready. Your people might not think so, but I've still got the reins."

She ignored him and looked at me, a spark of interest touching those deadly brown eyes. Everything I thought I knew about what was happening had turned upside down.

"Don't get testy, Reverend," she said. "I just wanted to keep you in the loop."

She left. Barnel stared at the door for a second afterward, seething.

"Looks like they've got you on a pretty tight leash," I said. "Just who, exactly, are Jenny Burkett's people? What's this Brigade you just mentioned?"

He looked shaken for a moment. "It ain't none of your concern. You're gonna be long gone. Trust me, son. I'm doin' you a favor."

He took the video camera off the tripod and went to the door, refusing to answer anymore of my questions. "Everybody's got an agenda these days, boy," he said as he stood at the threshold, eyes on me. "I reckon the best you can hope is that you find somebody willin' to foot the bill for yours till you can bow out of the whole dang mess."

He pulled the door open viciously and left, slamming it behind him.

I was more confused than ever, except for one sobering thought: I was suddenly positive that Jesup Barnel's private battle in Justice, Kentucky, was just one front in a much larger war.

26
SOLOMON

02:45:46

SINCE NO ONE SEEMED TO HAVE ANY BETTER IDEAS,
I convinced Juarez to come out with me to talk to Ashley
Durham. Blaze agreed—which was proof positive to me that
they were out of leads. No way would she have sacrificed one
of her best agents if she thought there was somewhere better
he could be used.

The investigation was at a standstill.

On the way, I bounced my knee and looked out the
window and tried to ignore the minutes flying by.

"Did you have any dinner?" Juarez asked, after we'd been
riding in silence for some time. I had to think about it.

"I grabbed something for lunch. I'm all right."

"Lunch was nine hours ago. You should eat something."

"When we get back," I said. I ran my thumb over the scar
on my wrist, something that had become a nervous habit in
the past few months. Juarez reached across the console and
put his hand over mine. He has good hands: strong but soft,
warm and gentle.

"Worrying yourself sick won't help Diggs."

"You're right," I agreed. I leaned back in the seat. "Since I don't know what else to do, though, it seems to be my only option."

"Tell me about Ashley Durham," he said. We were on the main stretch in Justice. He took a left onto a back road that presumably led to Ashley's place, while I continued to stare out the window.

"What do you mean?" I asked. "I don't really know the woman."

"You've met her before, though," he said. I thought of George Durham's whole proclamation about me being the only reason Diggs married Ashley in the first place. I wondered if Ashley had ever heard that theory.

"She came to Boston with Diggs a few times while I was still married to Michael. We had a couple of dinner parties, that kind of thing."

"That doesn't seem like much of a reason for her to dislike you."

"Who said she dislikes me?"

"Diggs may have mentioned something."

Somehow I'd known he would. "It might have something to do with one of those trips," I conceded. "And the fact that two days into it, he holed up in my apartment for the night while he helped me with a story I was working on."

"It's nice to know I'm not the only one who's been relegated to third wheel while you two do…whatever it is you do."

Ouch. "You're the one who told me to come here," I reminded him darkly.

"I know that." He scrubbed his hand over his face. "And I think I was right—it's been important. And good for you to be out in the world again."

"Even if that world's ending?"

He laughed dryly. "I guess I could have done without

that part. I'm just saying that if Ashley truly isn't crazy about you, she may have a good reason for that."

"Point taken."

He slowed down in front of a pretty brick house with a landscaped front yard and flowers in window boxes outside all the windows. I could imagine Diggs living on Jupiter before I could imagine him living in a place like this.

I started to open the door before Jack had come to a complete stop, anxious to get on with things. He stopped me with a hand on my arm. "You don't need to go in there with guns blazing—wait just a second."

Once he'd finally parked the car, I hopped out and waited impatiently for him to join me. I knocked, Juarez beside me.

Ashley's husband answered. He was good looking in a not-terribly-interesting way: fine blond hair, receding hairline, eyes that weren't quite green but weren't…not green, either. He had a sleeping Angus in his arms, bouncing the toddler gently. He put his finger to his lips as he opened the door.

"Is Ashley here?" I whispered.

He nodded toward a swinging door that presumably led to the kitchen. To my surprise—and borderline dismay—Juarez told me he was gonna hang out with Terry and the kid, leaving me to deal with Diggs' ex.

"If I'm not out in ten, send reinforcements," I said under my breath.

"Got it."

I went into the kitchen alone.

Mae and Ashley were sitting at the kitchen table playing cards with Rick and Ida. At sight of me, Ashley put her cards down and looked at the kids coolly.

"Do you mind helping Uncle Terry with Angus?" she asked them. Ida hopped up without argument—one of the benefits of kids before they hit that angsty tween/teen stage. Rick didn't look nearly as happy about it, but he followed his little sister out of the room. I took Ida's spot at the table, facing off against Mae and Ashley.

"You heard about them taking Diggs?" I asked.

Ashley nodded.

"They still don't have any ideas where he might be?" Mae asked.

"No," I said. "Not yet. The prevailing theory is that they're taking all these people to a single location, though: Danny, Diggs, Casey Clinton, and whoever else they've hauled away."

"So, they think everybody's still alive," Ashley said.

I nodded. "I need to ask you about your father," I said to Ashley. "About his history with Jesup Barnel."

Mae looked confused. "George always hated the reverend." I ignored her, looking to Ashley. When she hedged, Mae piped up. "Didn't he?"

"They grew up together," Ashley said. "And when Barnel first started out, they were actually good friends."

"Did George ever say anything to you about Billy Thomas?" I asked.

"The boy that killed all those girls back in the '60s?" Mae asked. Ashley stayed quiet. I fixed her with a long look.

"Daddy never said anything," Ashley said. "But I remember the first time I ever heard that name. He and Mama had a fight—I think it was about the reverend, but I remember him saying something about him learning his lesson with Billy. That the reverend didn't have any special powers. I just remember because Mama got so angry."

"And he never mentioned the name again?" I asked.

"Not that I heard."

I took a minute to consider that before I continued, switching tacks. "Have you heard from George since he went up to the mountains?"

"He doesn't have a phone up there," Mae said. "No electric. He likes it that way."

I'd expected as much. "So you don't have any way of reaching him."

"We can contact the sheriff up there—he usually checks up on him," Ashley said.

"If I can get a satellite phone to you, would you call him?" I asked.

Ashley nodded. "Of course."

I wasn't sure where to go from there. So George had something to do with Billy Thomas; so he might even be one of Barnel's captives at this point. What good did that do me? I still wasn't any closer to figuring out where anyone was. I felt myself beginning to flag. We had less than three hours. Something had to give.

"Out at Barnel's compound, his granddaughter said something about going back to the beginning—where it all went wrong," I said. "Do you have any idea what that meant? We've turned the whole county inside out. It would have to be somewhere with some space, considering the number of people they're taking. But not so isolated that it wouldn't shake the town up if something happened."

Neither of them said anything. And then, Mae looked up suddenly. "The club," she said.

I shook my head. "What club?"

"The Wilson Club," she said. "It used to be this factory— years and years ago, there was a toy company run out o' here, and that was where they set up their operation. Half the town used to work there. I think the reverend might've even put in some time, back in high school. I know George did."

"I remember Diggs mentioning something about it," I said. "He said someone bought the place, though. That it's not a club anymore."

"Well, yeah," Mae agreed, looking hesitant. "But it's the only place I can think of where there'd be space like you're talking about. And I don't think that new owner's around much—he's from California somewhere, I think. Nobody could figure why he even bought the place."

I stood, a little flush of hope kicking my heart rate up. This could be it. "Thank you—I'll have them check it out. I really appreciate all your help."

"You think that's where they took everybody?" Mae asked. I had the sense she wasn't allowing herself to hope for the best right now. Too much had happened already. "You think you'll find Danny there?"

"I don't know. But it's a better chance than we had when I walked in here."

Before I could run out the door to act on this latest shot in the dark, Ashley stopped me with a hand on my arm.

"I know we haven't always seen eye to eye, but I'm glad you're looking for him. You're the only person I've ever met even half as relentless as Diggs is." The way she said 'relentless'—like it was some kind of fatal flaw—made it clear this wasn't necessarily a compliment. "If there's a way to survive this, I expect you two will find it."

"I'll do my best," I said with an awkward nod.

I assured them I had to get going since the clock was ticking, then scooted out before Ashley went completely nuts and tried to hug me or something. I nodded to Juarez as I breezed past him in the living room, making straight for the front door.

"Let's go," I said. "I think we've got a lead."

He didn't question me until we were back in the truck, then paused with the engine idling.

"So, what's this lead?" he asked.

"This old factory they turned into a club a few years ago…"

Juarez nodded. "The Wilson Club." He didn't say anything for a second. I turned to look at him when he put the truck back in park.

"What the hell are you doing?"

There was a world of regret in his eyes when he spoke again. "Erin, we've already been there. We took the place apart."

"You must have missed something," I said stubbornly. "I want to go there. Just let me look around." I touched his arm, holding his gaze. Desperation leaked from my pores. "Jack. I've got a feeling about this. Please."

I expected him to argue. He didn't. Instead, he put the truck back in gear, pulled out of the drive, and sped up the road.

We drove in silence until we reached a private road with a rusted metal gate across it, just off the beaten path. He pulled in.

"This is it?" I asked.

"This is it."

He got out, pushed the gate open, climbed back in the truck, and drove through. We continued on for another half mile before a hulking metal building came into view, rising out of the dense foliage like some monolithic monster. THE FACTORY was written in giant block letters across the front. I heard a car engine start, and a minute later a military Humvee drove over and blocked our path.

Juarez got out, hands raised, as two armed National Guardsmen greeted him. I recognized them both from our standoff at the Barnel compound. I hopped out of the truck and joined them.

"You mind if we take a look around?" Juarez asked them.

They both shook their heads. "We've been here a few hours now," the younger of the pair said. "No sign of any activity."

As soon as I heard the okay, I made for the entrance with flashlight in hand. I slid a giant metal door open, putting my shoulder into it to get the thing to budge. There was a whisper of hope in the back of my head: Maybe they really had missed something.

They hadn't.

The place was covered in dust and cobwebs, moonlight coming through a broken window high above.

A bar ran the length of one wall, industrial-looking metal stools in front. It was the kind of place you'd expect to find in LA; I couldn't imagine anyone in Justice, Kentucky, choosing to get their drink on here. Diggs would have loved it back in his drinking days, though—if only for the paradox.

I heard footsteps behind me, and turned to find Juarez headed my way. "You were right," I said. I shook my head, refusing to acknowledge the tears of disappointment welling in my eyes. "I thought maybe you'd missed something."

He lay his hand against my cheek, brushing a tear away with his thumb. "I'm sorry."

"We have to be missing something."

"Everyone's out there looking, Erin. We have two hours—the show's not over yet."

I realized that through all of this, never once had I heard Jack say, *We'll find him.* He'd said they were doing everything they could; that there was still time. But he hadn't lied to me, hadn't placated me with words of comfort that he knew might not prove true at the end of the day.

I pulled myself together, brushing the remaining tears from my eyes before I let them fall. Freaking out wouldn't do Diggs any good.

"Okay," I said, nodding. "So, it's not the Wilson Club. What's next, then?"

He took my hand and led me out, pausing to slide the

door shut behind him. I looked back over my shoulder, taking one last glimpse inside. The door was almost closed when the moonlight hit something on the wall high up—level with the second story windows. I held the door.

"Hang on—what's that?" I pointed up, pushing the door open again as I stood inside. Juarez followed my gaze, shining his light on the spot I indicated.

"I don't see anything," he said.

"It was the way the light played off it a second ago," I said. I paced, playing my light along the wall, trying to get the angle right. After half a dozen passes, I finally succeeded. I froze, keeping the light fixed where it was. My heartbeat thundered in my ears.

"Do you see?" I asked.

He nodded, suddenly serious.

A Latin cross.

Someone had gone to a lot of trouble to remove it, but it was obvious once I had the right spot.

"That has to be at least a few weeks old," I said. "They were here, Jack."

"But they're not here now."

"It's a lead," I said stubbornly. "I know it is—there's something about this place. It has to mean something."

"I'll send someone out to look into it."

"Look into who owns the place, too," I said. "They're not from around here—I think Mae said they were out in California. Whoever it is, I bet they're the ones working with Barnel."

"Maybe," Juarez agreed. He was still quiet. He shut the door again and I double-timed it back to the truck, Jack two steps behind. I took the wheel this time, tired of being the co-pilot, and revved the engine. As soon as he was in, he turned in his seat and looked at me seriously. I knew exactly what he was going to say. I didn't want to hear it.

"I'm not preparing myself for the worst," I said.

"How do you know that's what I was about to say?"

"Because you've got a very 'Prepare yourself for the worst' look in your eye. And I'm sorry, but I'm not gonna do it. He's out there somewhere, and he's not far away. So buckle your goddamn seatbelt, and let's go find him."

He smiled a little. "Yes, ma'am."

I may have laid a little rubber tearing out of the worn-down parking lot, but as far as I was concerned, it was totally justified.

PART III
THE IDES OF MARCH

27
DIGGS

JUST AS BARNEL HAD PROMISED, George Durham was waiting for me when Jenny threw me back into the room. He wasn't the only one who'd joined us, though—our crew of eleven had swelled to twenty seething, bound, terrified prisoners. The room barely held us all, and it had to be eighty degrees in there, the air humid and stale. A woman in the back wailed, the hysterical gasps of someone long past reason. Everyone else was coiled tight, the tension ratcheted so high that breathing was a chore and violence seemed inevitable.

As I waded through the bodies to get to George, Casey, and Danny, I spotted two of the tweakers I'd seen earlier crouched together in a corner, backs to the rest of us. The taller of the two—gangly, bearded, and shaking—cast a guilty look over his shoulder at my attention, then quickly looked away when we locked eyes.

George had a patch of blood on his shoulder. Even in the surreal glow of our red light, I could tell his color was bad.

"They got you?" I asked, nodding to his arm.

"Clipped me when I tried to get away," he said. As a kid, I'd always imagined George to be bulletproof. Another childhood fantasy shot to hell.

The wailing woman transitioned from cries to screams—jagged, ear-piercing shrieks that shredded any equanimity I might have been feeling toward the others in our group.

"Somebody shut her up!" a bearded, flannel-wearing guy shouted across the room. He was surrounded by two other men who may or may not have been his brothers.

"Why don't you shut up? How about a little compassion!" a woman shouted back. Flannel started to make a move, but one of the brothers held him back. The wailing woman quieted. I took a breath, knowing any peace we might have achieved would be short lived.

I scanned the room, studying the motley assemblage. George was the oldest among us, but otherwise Barnel's reach transcended socio-economic, cultural, and ethnic boundaries. Case in point: a small, sixtyish man in spectacles, undershirt, and tailored slacks stood to George's left. He caught me looking at him and attempted an awkward smile.

"Diggs," George said. "This is Dr. Munjoy. He's a professor over to Smithfield."

The surprise must have shown on my face. "How do you know Jesup Barnel?" I asked.

He shook his head. "I've never met the man," he said. He was mostly bald, with just a sparse bit of whitish blond hair ringing his pink scalp.

"But you know who he is," I said.

"Of course," he said. He had an accent—possibly British. Maybe South African. "I teach psychology at Smithfield. We're doing a research project at the moment; I've done a great deal of work in the fields of Christian fundamentalism and cultist behaviors."

"Ah," I said. "That would explain the reverend's interest in you, I guess."

He nodded. A couple of twenty-something women stood beside him—good looking, intellectual, and terrified. He introduced them as his graduate students.

"Do you have any idea what Barnel's got planned?" I asked George.

"Not a clue. I always knew Jesup was crazy as a bedbug, but I never pegged him for something like this."

"I'm not sure he's actually calling the shots on this one," I said, thinking again of Jenny Burkett.

The others looked at me with clear interest. Before I could elaborate, the wailing woman screamed again—so suddenly that nearly everyone in the room jumped. The difference was, this time she didn't stop screaming.

"Shut up!" Flannel shouted again.

I heard the woman who had come to her rescue before pleading for her to be quiet, but it fell on deaf ears. The screaming escalated until my ears rang and my head ached. Flannel lowered his shoulder and bulled one of his brothers out of the way so violently that he knocked a woman behind him to the ground.

I lowered my voice and addressed Danny and the others in our little clique. "Stay back against the wall, okay? Don't make eye contact. Don't engage with anyone. Just stay quiet and keep out of the way."

They all nodded readily—even George, which spoke to how bad off he actually was. George didn't take orders gladly from anyone.

I stepped into the fray, headed toward the worst of the trouble.

"We all need to calm down," I said, raising my voice to be heard above the growing noise. "The only shot we have of getting out of this alive is if we don't panic, and figure out a way to work together."

The woman who'd been knocked to the ground managed

to right herself, hands awkwardly behind her, and stood. She was painfully thin. Forty-ish. Small and frail looking.

I tried an encouraging smile at Flannel. "Just give me a second—maybe I can quiet her down?"

He nodded.

When I got closer to the source of the screams, I felt another shot of disappointment hit my bloodstream; we might be worse off than I'd thought. The wailing woman was hurt, crouched against the wall with her hands bound behind her back. The side of her head was bleeding—the result of her having beaten it repeatedly into the cement wall. She could have been anywhere from thirty to fifty, her dark hair pulled back from a gaunt face that I expected had been pretty once.

"What's your name?" I asked.

Her eyes were vacant when she looked at me. The woman who had come to her rescue before answered.

"Glenda," she said. "There's something not right about her—mental illness, clearly. Could be she needs meds."

The other woman had grey hair pulled back into a long braid, her familiar face the worn leather of someone who'd spent a lot of time outside. She smiled as soon as she saw me.

"Daniel Diggins. What in hell is Barnel doin', rounding up every sinner that ever crossed his path?"

Sally Woodruff. "I didn't think he'd gotten you," I said, thinking of Sally's clinic: the cross burning in the yard and the broken fountain and the decimated garden. "I went by the place, but the dogs were gone."

"They didn't burn the clinic down, then?" she asked. "Well, that's something, I guess. I got a couple threats. Then after they found Wyatt and that Dairy Queen blew, I figured maybe it was time to take a little vacation. I got the dogs off to the boarder and was on my way out of state when some gorillas in black 'jacked my car and brought me here."

"Any idea where 'here' is?" I asked.

She shook her head. "Hell if I know. They knocked me out… Next thing I know, I'm in a room with the dregs of Kentucky, and Jesup T. Barnel's telling me I best come clean about my sins."

Glenda the Screamer had settled down for the moment, her cries giving way to a low, incessant moaning while she rocked. I nodded toward her. "You know anything about her story?"

"She's got a Medical Alert bracelet, but all that's on there is her name—Glenda Clifton—along with a couple numbers, and NBD. Stands for Neurobiological Disease. She could have anything from Attention Deficit to schizophrenia."

"I'm no doctor, but I'm thinking we can rule out ADD as the problem here," I said.

"A safe assumption," Sally agreed. She looked around the room and lowered her voice. "You know, I worked with half the folks in here. Not bad people, but they're not exactly the type you wanna have to rely on when push comes to shove, you know what I mean? Most everybody here's comin' off something right now. Rapid detox ain't my choice in the best of situations."

"And this isn't the best of situations," I said.

"Not by a long shot." She studied me for a second, looking me up and down. "You look like you been through the ringer. Backwards."

"It's been a long week."

She fixed her intelligent brown eyes on me for a long while, a slow smile touching her lips. "How long you been clean, sweetheart?" she asked.

The last time I'd seen Sally, I was dropping Sarah Jennings off so we could sneak her out of state and onto her new life far, far from Justice, Kentucky. I was three sheets to the wind and looking for a fix at the time. I smiled back at her.

"Four long years," I said.

"Good for you." She grinned, shaking her head. "I always said you'd be one hell of a catch if you could just get your head out of your ass and dry out a little."

"Well... I dried out. I don't know about the rest of it."

Glenda the Screamer started up again. I crouched beside her. "We're going to try to get you out of here, Glenda," I said. "Can you try and stay calm for a little while? Just a little longer?"

Silent tears tracked down her face. She slid to the ground, blessedly quiet for the moment. I straightened and looked at Sally.

"If you can try and keep her quiet, that will help things as much as anything."

"I'll do my best. That mean you've got a plan?"

"Not in the traditional sense of the word," I said. "I welcome suggestions."

She nodded toward the tweakers in the corner. "You might want to check in with Biggie over there—the tall guy. He's a mess from the word go, but he's got a good heart. Has three kids I know of, all different mothers; another couple pregnancies I took care of. Hooked on everything under the sun. Couldn't hold down a job to save his life. *However*," she looked at me significantly and lowered her voice, "I do believe him and his buddy Riley are working on tunneling us out of here."

It took me a minute to figure out whether she was kidding. I shook my head. "We've got two hours. You couldn't have mentioned this sooner?"

"And interrupt our reunion?"

"Right. You mind doing a little introduction? I don't want to freak the guy out."

She told Glenda she'd be right back, then led me over to Biggie and Riley, both of them still up against the wall, their backs to the group. For the first time, I realized there was a significant difference between them and the rest of us:

Neither of them were bound.

Biggie jerked around when Sally said his name, his body hunched in on itself. I fought between empathy and disgust. My drug of choice was always cocaine: fast acting, fun, toxically addictive, and—comparatively speaking—free of physical symptoms once I finally got clean. I'd seen buddies try to kick meth or heroin; it was the major reason I'd never gone down those roads in the first place.

"Biggie, this here's an old friend of mine," Sally said. "I want you to let him help you, all right? He's good people."

She made hasty introductions and then left us to it since Glenda was starting up again. When she was gone, Biggie looked at me shyly.

"We was thinking maybe we'd tunnel out," he said. Beads of sweat rained down his face, his body shaking so hard his words came out in frenzied jerks. Beyond the physical manifestations of addiction and withdrawal, however, I saw a glimmer of intelligence from surprisingly soft blue eyes.

"How? The walls are cement…"

"The floor ain't, though," he said with a pained smile. He nodded toward their corner. "There's another room behind that wall. There's gotta be a way out there, right? Nobody makes a room that ain't got no doors."

"You have an idea what we should dig with?"

"Ground's soft—it don't take much. I been usin' my hands. Riley's got a spoon he found over there."

"I can't help noticing you guys aren't tied."

He smiled at that, producing a zip tie from his pocket. He fastened it around his wrists, pulling it tight with his teeth. A second later, I watched as he wriggled out of the tie again and it fell to the ground. When he showed me his hands with a flourish, there was blood dripping down his left thumb. I caught a glimpse of bone shining through, and my stomach turned.

He caught the look. "You ever come off meth?" he asked. I noticed that his teeth were jagged, several missing, when he smiled again.

"No—just coke," I said.

He laughed, still racked with tremors. "That ain't nothin'. You come off something like this and you know: this here," he nodded toward his hand, "is a relief, compared to the pain in my gut and in my head; the bugs crawling under my skin. A distraction. Now, have a look."

He nudged Riley, who stepped aside. Sure enough, they'd managed to make a dent in the dirt floor. Not a big dent—but if two tweakers in the throes of withdrawal could get this far in a couple of hours, we might actually stand a chance.

"I need to get out of these," I said, nodding over my shoulder to indicate my own hands. I had no idea whether we were being monitored in here, but it seemed likely since our captors had gone to the trouble of providing us some light. In all likelihood, Big Brother was watching. To compensate, I tried to make sure we were well concealed by the wall of bodies around us, and kept my voice low. "You mind giving me a hand?"

"You okay with a little pain? Shouldn't hurt too bad, but it might cut a little."

I lowered my voice further. "Do what you need to do."

He grinned. "Yes, sir. I reckon we got ourselves an escape plan."

28
SOLOMON

01:50:22

THE PARTY HAD GOTTEN EVEN BIGGER by the time Juarez and I got back to headquarters, with another batch from the National Guard and a few more spooks, everyone now gathered in the school gymnasium to accommodate the swelling numbers. So far, we'd learned that the creepy post-modern bar in the woods was listed as being owned by something called J. Enterprises, out of San Francisco. J. Enterprises, sadly, was a dummy corporation, and everyone was having a hell of a time figuring out how to connect a name with that dummy corporation.

Once we'd gotten that disheartening news, Blaze pulled Juarez and me aside.

"A package was left on the front steps at the police station," she said, her eyes steady on me. "Deputy Holloway just discovered it. It's a tape."

"What do you mean?" I asked. "What kind of tape?"

"It's from Barnel," she said. "In it, he makes very vague references to whatever he has in store at midnight. He also has messages from those he's holding hostage."

"Diggs is on the tape?" I asked.

"He is," Blaze confirmed. "I need you to take a look— we think he may have put some coded information in there for you."

I nodded blindly. She led me to the little A/V cubicle I'd been at before, and set me up with the digital tape. This time I wasn't alone, though: Blaze, Juarez, Agent Keith, the Technology Nazi, and another handful of agents stood by, watching alongside me.

The tape started with Barnel, talking about everything he was planning: the end of the world at midnight; holding everyone accountable for their sins; taking his family out with him. Your garden-variety psychotic ramblings, in other words.

"This is not suicide," he said, looking into the camera with sweat running down his face and an odd, glazed look to his eye. "This is a revolutionary act. We won't be held hostage by the devil and his minions no more."

He signed off. A whole parade of others were next: Casey, Danny, Wyatt Durham, along with a slew of faces I didn't recognize. Each read from a prepared statement held off camera, detailing their past indiscretions. Most everyone looked like they'd been through hell already—bruised, bloodied, out-and-out terrified. George Durham came on and I cursed softly, realizing I'd been right: he never made it to his mountain hideaway.

And then, Diggs appeared.

I pulled my legs up into the chair, all but curling into myself when he looked at the camera. He read the words with dead eyes and no inflection in his voice, using a steady monotone that sounded beyond wrong coming from him. He looked exhausted. The tape switched off; half a second later, it came back on. Diggs was still there. The dead eyes were gone suddenly, replaced with something raw and sad and so deeply personal that I wanted to shut it off until I was alone. I fought the urge and remained there, my attention riveted to the screen.

"Since this is apparently my last will and testament..." he began. I steeled myself against an onslaught of emotion, managing to hold it together until the end, when he looked into the camera with those sparkling blue eyes and smiled at me.

"You're an amazing woman... even if your best record is *Original Soul.* you've made my life better in a thousand ways. I've always loved you, Sol. Even when it wasn't smart. Even when I had no right. I think I always will."

No one said anything for a respectful few seconds after the tape ended, while I sat there trying to get a grip, fighting a losing battle against the tears tracking down my cheeks and a pain in my chest I knew wouldn't go away until I had Diggs back.

Finally, I cleared my throat. "*Original Soul,*" I said. "That's not my favorite record—I don't even know who recorded it. That's his clue."

It took us thirty seconds on Google to track down what he was trying to tell me:

Original Soul: the 2004 debut album by Grace Potter and the Nocturnals.

"Jenny Burkett," I said, as soon as I saw the band's name. I turned around in my seat, pulse racing, heart jumping, ready to lead the charge.

Juarez looked at me blankly. "How do you get there?"

"Grace Potter—Grace is the Burkett's dog," I said. "Roger's dead... Jenny disappeared. J. Enterprises is out of San Francisco. Mae told us early on that Roger brought Jenny out here from San Francisco. She's in on it. I'm sure of it."

Blaze gave the word and a dozen agents sprang into action.

I turned off the TV, still frozen on Diggs' face.

"You okay?" Juarez asked. We sat together, alone in the darkened room now.

I nodded. He waited for me to give him something—I could all but see him doing it. Waiting for me to break down, share my thoughts, give him something to hold onto to make it seem like we were even remotely in this together. I took a deep breath, and forced it out slowly.

"I kissed Diggs the other night," I said. I looked at him. He didn't even look surprised, a flicker of anger in his eyes the only trace of emotion I could see.

"I mean—technically, he kissed me," I continued awkwardly. "But there was a second when I kissed him back." I looked down, tracing the scar on my wrist. "I'm sorry. I didn't plan on it happening…"

"I know that," he said. He reached out and tucked a strand of hair behind my ear, his head tilted a little. There was something naked, soulful, about his dark eyes when they met mine. The anger was gone.

"I was fifteen when I met Lucia," he said. It wasn't what I'd expected—Lucia was Juarez's first wife. His only wife. I'd been curious about her, but had never asked. It seemed too personal, somehow. And what woman really wants to talk to her boyfriend about the lost love of his life?

"It was one of those instant connections that you read about sometimes, with her," he said. "We met, and…that was all. We dated, we fell in love, we married. So easy."

"I'm sorry," I said.

He smiled a little—that sad, dark smile he didn't really show the world. The one I was just getting to know. "I know. I am, too. She was killed, and it was like all the light went out of my life, for a long time. But we had something…

important. As though, when I was with her, all the planets were aligned. Everything was exactly as it should be."

"It's not like that with you and me," I said quietly. He shook his head.

"I didn't realize, when we first met," he said. "I should have—the two of you denied it enough. I should have understood then."

"Understood what?"

He smiled. Rolled his eyes. "That your planets were already aligned."

I opened my mouth to protest, but one look from him stopped me. What was the point arguing something I didn't even believe anymore?

"You saved my life this year," I said instead. I looked at my hand again, studying that angry white line. I wiped my eyes, which continued to leak copiously. "I mean—beyond the thing where you actually found Diggs and me and dragged us out of the woods last summer. I've really…" I stopped and wiped my eyes again. I was dangerously close to getting maudlin. "Well, hell." I did a little deep breathing since words were obviously failing me, and eventually gave up trying for grace and eloquence. Clearly they were beyond me. "You know, I think Blaze has a thing for you."

I don't know what I expected him to do with that revelation, but it wasn't laugh at me. That's exactly what he did, though. "You mean Allie?" he asked.

"Yeah, Allie," I said, indignant. "That's so hard to believe? I haven't seen a ring on her finger."

"That's because she's single," he said. "I'm not really her type, though."

"She doesn't like tall, gorgeous, sensitive guys? You sure seem like her type when you two are in your little huddles together."

He brushed the tears from my eyes and shook his head at

me, as though I were the most hopeless idiot on the planet. "I just mean, *you're* more Allie's type than I am," he clarified.

"Oh." I took a very long, very deep breath, then let it out very slowly. I sat back and looked at him. "So…this is it, huh?"

"I think so. You don't?"

I thought of Diggs again—hopeless Diggs, with his temper and his past and his passion and his ability to push every friggin' button I had. Then, I looked at Juarez: stable, sensitive, heroic. And gorgeous. I was an idiot.

I shook my head. "No, you're right."

He stood, leaned in, and kissed me on the cheek. Then, he pulled me to my feet. "We should go see if there have been any developments. It could be a good lead you've given us—Jenny Burkett and the California connection. We could be closing in on something."

"Do you mind if I go back to the hotel for a while, actually?"

"Now?"

"I want to look through Diggs' room again. Check on the dogs. Get a little breathing room. Just for a few minutes."

"Yeah, of course," he agreed. "I'll just let Allie know and we can go."

"No," I said. "Stay here. If you feel like I need an escort, get someone else—you're too valuable to be playing bodyguard right now."

He looked at me. "You're sure?"

"Positive."

He hesitated, his eyes dark with sympathy. "We'll find him, Erin," he said. It was the first time he'd said it since this whole thing began. I looked at the clock: 10:35. An hour and twenty-five minutes.

"Yeah," I said, with a slightly embittered laugh. "Because things always work out that well."

"Not always," he agreed. "But sometimes, they do."

01:05:42

Agent Keith took me back to the hotel while Juarez retreated to the war room with Blaze and the others. When I got to our room, I grabbed Einstein and Grace and then lingered for just a second, staring at the rumpled sheets. Jack's clothes hung neatly in the closet. There wasn't time to cry about it, but Diggs was wrong if he thought Jack Juarez was just an easy way for me to deal with life without him. It had definitely run deeper than that.

With that uncomfortable realization behind me, I took Stein and Grace up to Diggs' room to enact the only plan I'd been able to come up with thus far.

The glass from Diggs' broken mirror had been cleaned up, but otherwise his room was in the same condition it had been when I'd left: overturned bureau, dirty clothes, blood on the carpet…and no Diggs. I went in with Einstein and Grace, closed the door behind me, and went straight for the window. I already knew what I was there for—I'd known the moment Blaze had said a business called J. Enterprises owned that bar in the Kentucky woods.

J. just happened to be the initial my father had gone by as a kid, years and years ago. It also happened to be the initial carved into the chests of more than a dozen girls brutally hunted and murdered in northern Maine over the past forty years.

It was probably just coincidence that now a shell corporation with that very initial was tied to a rash of kidnappings, murders, and a potential mass murder-slash-suicide with the potential to rock the nation.

Probably. But, Mitch Cameron had been here when Diggs and I flew into Kentucky. He claimed it was to check up on me, but what if he had other business in the state? I thought of his words just before he shot Max Richards point blank last summer: *You've become a liability, Max. We warned you about this when you left the fold...*

I had no idea what "fold" he was talking about. And maybe I was just reeling with fatigue and hunger and the sting of just being dumped for a guy who would probably end up dead before the night was out, but this seemed like a lead to pursue. If my father and J. and Mitch Cameron and the Payson Church were somehow tied into J. Enterprises and the clusterfuck surrounding Jesup Barnel, I planned on getting to the bottom of that connection.

I took a roll of masking tape from my bag and went to the picture window along the far wall of the room. I looked at Einstein, now up on Diggs' bed beside Grace.

"Don't look at me that way," I said. I imagined Diggs' reaction to all this. He'd never let me hear the end of it. I didn't have a bat signal, though, and I was out of good ideas.

I tore off three pieces of masking tape and taped them into the shape of an awkward, block J on the inside of the window. Then, I took the MagLite I'd taken from Juarez's room and trained it on the tape, so anyone outside would be sure to see. If it worked for Scully, why shouldn't it work for me?

Grace hopped off the bed and trotted over to me, tail wagging.

"Don't start," I said. "If you'd told me when this whole thing started that your owner was the one behind it, we might not be in this mess."

Grace whined mournfully, which I took to mean she was sorry for dropping the ball. Or else she was hungry. Either way, I scratched her behind the ears and went to the bed with her.

"Come on. We give this ten minutes... Then I'll have to

come up with something else."

I had no idea what that something might be, but I wasn't about to tell her that.

I leaned back on Diggs' bed and picked up his file on Mitch Cameron. *So evolve—don't get a friggin' lobotomy*, he'd said earlier that day. I thought yet again of all the people who'd died so far in this quest to find the truth about my father. Diggs was right: I hadn't pulled the trigger. Still, he was crazy if he thought I could consider myself completely blameless in all the bloodshed of the past year.

Now, he might very well join their ranks.

And I had no idea why.

I opened the file and began reading.

It didn't tell me much, really: Mitch Cameron had been Special Forces until 1975, when—according to a very official-looking death certificate—he was killed just before the fall of Saigon. From what I could gather from the file, Diggs had worked with a friend of his to do a composite sketch based on his memory of Cameron the night we'd both nearly died last summer. From there, they must have done some kind of reverse-aging process, because the final result was a computer-generated printout eerily similar to the photo in a newspaper article on Cameron's death in '75.

Cameron was born in Lynn, Indiana, in 1950. Diggs had a map he'd marked of the town. Just as he'd said earlier, my father, Max Richards, and Mitch Cameron lived on the same block together.

I scratched Einstein's head. He sighed and rested his paw on my thigh while Grace kept a polite distance from us, her head on her paws and her eyes half closed.

To pass the time once I was finished with the file, I amused myself by going through Diggs' stuff. Which wrong. And he would hate me for it. And yet...I didn't care anymore. The way I figured it, if we actually found him at this stage of the game, he probably wouldn't waste his breath bitching about me poking around a little. It could be faulty logic, but I chose to run with it.

In the worn old duffel beside his bed, I found a flip portfolio of photos I hadn't seen before. A lot were shots from his travels over the years: Tokyo, Yemen, Fallujah, Capetown, Bangkok, Sydney… It's not like I've never left the country before, but I might as well be a shut-in when you compare my passport with his. After the travel pics, there was a shot that I'd seen framed in his father's office—the only one he had of Diggs as a kid. In it, Diggs was probably eight or nine. He stood beside an awkward-looking, pudgy boy with the same ash-blond hair and the same Diggins grin. Diggs' arm was draped over the boy's shoulder. His brother, Josh.

There were half a dozen shots of me over the years, from fifteen on up. One was from the only summer we actually dated. I was nineteen. We were on the lam at the time, running from a ritual killer and a bunch of drug dealers we were doing a story on together. I was in bed in the picture, a sheet pulled up to my chest, while the sun poured in the window of our seedy hotel hideaway. He'd taken it the morning after our first night together. Biblically speaking, I mean. We'd spent plenty of nights together non-biblically before that. And after.

He told me that night that it would change everything. *I don't want to just sweep this under the rug—I can't do that with you. I won't.*

He was right: nothing was quite the same for us after that. I'd never actually been with anyone before, biblically speaking. And you know how everyone always says the first time is the worst, and if women gauged sex by that fumbling first encounter they would probably never knock boots with anyone again?

Their first time definitely wasn't with Diggs.

Of course, it wasn't just the sex—it was the laughter and the moonlight, the urgency and the feel of his arms around me and the way he whispered my name, his forehead tipped to mine, the first time he pressed past that final barrier between us. People may have been trying to kill us just outside that sleazy hotel room, but I'd never felt safer in my life than I did in his arms. That night, my universe was knocked sideways. The man who'd been my best friend, my mentor, my confidante…

It sounds corny as hell, but I can't really help that. That night, Diggs became the love of my life.

And then, of course, Diggs and me being the stubborn jackasses that we are, spent the next thirteen years doing everything conceivable to push each other away.

I flipped past the picture and looked at my watch. Time was moving way too fast.

After the shots of me and every third-world country on the planet, there were a slew of photos of Wyatt and his family: baby pictures and candids and that prom shot of Rick and Danny that I'd noticed in the Durhams' parlor when we first got to Justice. I flipped through quickly, but then turned back when something caught my eye.

Before I could fix on exactly what that something was, both dogs catapulted themselves off the bed in a fit of frenzied barking so sudden I nearly jumped out of my skin and into next Tuesday.

There was a knock on the door.

I made both dogs settle down, then went to the door and pressed my ear to the wood. The peephole might have come in handy, but they're not that useful during power outages. Einstein growled from his spot on the bed.

"Hello?" I said.

"I'm assuming that sign is for me," Mitch Cameron said.

"Though I suppose I could be wrong."

I opened the door.

He was drenched, wearing a blue LL Bean raincoat that left pools of water on the floor. He looked around uneasily before he came in the room. There was a black leather briefcase in his left hand. Einstein was on his feet now, the fur on the back of his neck on end. His growl deepened. Grace stayed where she was, whining.

"Have you started a kennel?" Cameron asked. He kept his eyes on the dogs, his hand creeping toward what I suspected was a gun at his side.

"They're all right," I said. "As long as you don't come after me, they'll leave you alone." At least I hoped they would.

He nodded toward the window. "You need to take that tape off there. And move the damned light."

I didn't argue. Once the tape was gone, I turned back to him. He was still standing in the doorway, hand at his side. Grace had laid back down on the bed, but Einstein stood next to me, watching Cameron's every move.

"Diggs is missing," I said. "I didn't know what else to do. Since one of your favorite pastimes seems to be spying on us, I thought maybe you'd seen something. That you could tell me where he is." I decided to leave out the part where I suspected he might be in on it, at least for now.

"I'm not your partner," Cameron said. "We aren't in this together."

"You think I don't know that?" I asked, my voice rising. "You think I want to be playing out little *X-Files* fantasies with you when my—" I stopped, willing myself to calm down. "I told you: I didn't know what else to do."

"What makes you think I would help you? Your friend hasn't been sticking to our agreement as well as you have. It would be easier if he was simply out of the picture."

"I know that, Mr. Cameron."

I watched his face. He didn't look especially surprised at my use of his name. The smile that he offered chilled me to the bone. I took out the file Diggs had put together and handed it to him.

"You can take that. I won't let him go near any of it again. He'll drop it."

"Because you say so?"

"Yes," I said simply.

He didn't question that. Instead, he took the file without looking at it, opened his briefcase, and slid it inside. He snapped the briefcase closed again, straightened, and we stood there, staring each other down. Einstein sat at my feet, his body warm against my calf. The candles flickered and the clock ticked and Diggs' life hung in the balance.

"When we talked to you that first night, you said you didn't have anything to do with Jesup Barnel or anything that's happening in Justice right now."

"I didn't say that, actually," he said. "I told you I was more interested in you and your friend—which was true, at the time."

"But it's you and…whoever it is you represent, who are pulling the strings on this whole thing. Isn't it?"

He looked away, a flash of annoyance crossing his face. It was the first real reaction I'd seen from him, and it made him seem unexpectedly human.

"I've told you how many times now to leave this alone?" he asked.

"I *was* leaving it alone—you know that. We came here because someone killed Diggs' friend. That's it. Neither one of us had a clue that you had anything to do with this. You have to believe that."

He scratched his head. There were circles under his eyes that I hadn't noticed before. "I do believe that, actually," he said. "We have many interests at the moment—a number of projects around the globe. It seems to be one of those tragic tricks of fate that your friend Wyatt got caught in the mix on this one."

"So, you know what they have planned for midnight."

He nodded infinitesimally.

"And you know where they are." Another nod. A surge of anger burned through me. "You have to tell me how to find Diggs."

"Why?" he countered. "Why do I *have to* tell you anything?"

I took a step toward him, my voice rising. "Because none of this would have happened if not for your people—whoever the hell they are. Diggs is out there somewhere, and you know where. You saved us last summer. Since then, I've spent every second trying to make sure I never have to see you again. All I can see when I look at him now is that friggin' gun pointed at his head."

"Because I'm the enemy, Erin." His voice rose, his eyes suddenly dark. "I am not your guardian angel. Don't make the mistake of thinking otherwise. I am your worst nightmare—and they will have me prove it, at the first opportunity."

"I don't care!" I shouted. "I don't care what they'll do to me. I don't care who they are, I don't care who you are, I don't care what they have to do with my father or who burned down the Payson Church or why they're feeding Barnel's insanity by helping him with this whole apocalyptic nightmare. All I care about is finding Diggs. I don't give a rat's ass about the rest of it—I've already proven that once."

I advanced on him fast, my eye on the briefcase. I don't know what I thought I was going to do—Juarez taught me a couple of nifty moves if a second-rate thug jumped me in the street, but he sure as hell hadn't schooled me on how to lift a briefcase of deadly secrets from a world-class assassin.

Cameron picked up the case when I was still a couple of feet away. For a second, I thought I saw a flicker of sadness in his eyes. Regret, even.

"I can't help you, Erin. It isn't my place." He buttoned his trench coat and nodded toward the window, indicating the spot where my magic J had been. "Don't do that again—it was very stupid. They watch me, just as I watch you. A private meeting between you and me would not be received well. Particularly now."

"Right," I said numbly. "God forbid."

He got as far as the door before he looked back. There was no mistaking his inner conflict.

"Do you ever watch magicians?" he finally asked.

I shook my head, confused. "Like Houdini? Not really."

"Their secrets are all the same—there's no such thing as magic, of course. You've heard the phrase 'smoke and mirrors'?"

"Sure," I said. "It's all about misdirection: having the audience focus in one direction while the magician does his thing somewhere else."

"Precisely." I started to ask another question, but he shook his head. "That's all I can say. And trust me, it's far too much. I'm sorry about your friend… I've come to like him. The fact is, I've come to like both of you. That's not a good thing in my line of work." He stopped, torn. "Don't contact me again, Erin. I'm not an ally in this."

He slipped out the door without another word.

29
DIGGS

"ALL RIGHT, PROFESSOR. YOUR TURN," I said. I scooped another handful of dirt onto the pile and set back to the task. My arms ached and my wrists were bleeding—which would teach me to ask a tweaker just coming off his drug of choice to set me free. But I was making progress. The professor looked flummoxed.

"Top twenty-four…" he began.

"Records, Munjoy," I said. "Albums. The music that rocked your socks way back when."

"Probably some classical shit," Biggie said.

"Shut it, Nickelback," I said. "Let the man speak."

"I don't really listen to newer music," the professor said. "I'm partial to the groups I liked in high school."

"No shame in that," I said amiably, already mentally forming the list: Tony Bennett, Burt Bacharach, The Four Tops. We'd been playing this game for the past half hour while we tried to dig ourselves to freedom. So far, everyone had proven predictable in their tastes.

The rest of the group was more subdued now, focused

as they were on our imminent escape. Even Glenda had settled down to a quiet, rhythmic rocking, still crouched against the wall with her head down. I was working with Danny, Sally, and Biggie, whose buddy Riley's tremors were debilitating by now. We'd decided to limit everyone else's involvement in the actual digging, just in case someone was watching. Besides which, you can only have so many people digging one damned hole before efficiency is significantly compromised.

"Come on, Doc," I said again. "This isn't a hard question."

Actually, I'd been going back and forth on the question for nearly twenty-four hours now, but he didn't need to know that. Your top twenty-four records of all time isn't a list to take lightly.

Finally, the professor took a deep breath. "*Licensed to Ill,*" he began. I looked up. Biggie stopped digging. "Uh—that's the Beastie Boys," he clarified. "*Nothing's Shocking*—Jane's Addiction, of course. *Darklands*… The Jesus and Mary Chain. Though I do love *Psychocandy,*" he admitted in his proper British voice.

"Where the hell did you go to high school?" I interrupted.

"And when?" Biggie added.

He looked at me innocently. There was a twinkle in his eye that made me suspect I was being toyed with.

"I didn't say I was partial to the groups I liked when I was *going to* high school," he said. "Just when I was *there*. I used to teach; always found music to be a good way to reach my students. And their tastes just rubbed off on me, I suppose."

"I suppose," Biggie said, mimicking the professor's accent. "If that's your record collection, Doc, I reckon you can party with us anytime."

"Now that's a party I'd come to," I said.

"We make it out, and everybody here's invited," Biggie

said. "We'll do it up right."

Beside us, George swayed slightly. He leaned against the wall, his color worse now. I looked at Sally, crouched beside me.

"Will you take a look at him?" I asked.

"She's not comin' near me," George said. "I don't need no baby killers touchin' me."

"Well, that's intelligent," Sally said. She straightened, wiped her hands on her pants, and pushed George back against the wall.

The issue of who was bound and who wasn't had been a contentious one. We finally agreed that only a few of us should be loose—everyone had to be able to get back into the zip ties quickly when Jenny came back, and the more people expected to do that, the greater the chances that someone would screw up and we'd all be caught. We'd also been going back and forth on whether or not to simply take out Jenny and her man when they came calling next, but I had a strong feeling the only thing that would accomplish would be getting a slew of us killed a little sooner than midnight, while the rest of us were tied up so tightly there would be no hope of escape.

And it didn't hurt that the threat of violence wasn't quite so immediate when everyone was tied up, of course.

"You've lost a lot of blood," Sally said to George, unbuttoning and removing his shirt. "But it looks like the bullet just grazed you—it would be nice if we could clean the wound. How long ago'd this happen?"

He had to think about it. "Wednesday, I guess. Maybe Thursday. I was headed up to the cabin and got jumped. A car run me off the road, and a couple fellas pulled me out of the truck. They tried to put a needle in me, but I don't hold with none of that. I got a couple jabs in and took to the hills. Didn't get far before they took me down, though."

"You didn't see anyone's face?" I asked.

"Nope," he said. "Like I said—everybody's in black. But they knew what they were doin', for sure. Ow—dammit, woman, stop that." He pulled away from Sally, who was tying an awkward bandage using the shirtsleeve of his discarded flannel.

That left George in his undershirt. When I looked at him, my eye was drawn immediately to a too-familiar scar just under his collarbone. I'd never seen it before.

He caught me staring and scowled. "What the hell are you lookin' at, boy?"

I nodded to his chest. "That cross."

"What about it?"

"You got it from Barnel?"

"I know what you're thinkin', but it wasn't what it is now," he said, his voice rough. "He's got one, too. We come up together; went to school together. Took a vow, together. It was all voluntary—nobody was holding the other one down, forcing 'em into something they wasn't ready for."

"And Billy Thomas?" I asked. My voice didn't sound quite right. "Did he take that vow?"

Biggie continued digging, but the others were looking at George and me with great interest. George looked down. It took some time for him to tamp down his emotions.

"We vowed to follow the Lord. Accepted that brand over our hearts—it was a sign of our faith. Our devotion. Our willingness to endure hardship, to stay on the right path."

I wet my lips, fighting a wave of revulsion. "You killed him," I said.

Danny looked up sharply. George shook his head. "He turned his back—violated something holy. The things he did to those girls…" He looked at me, his eyes dark with conviction and despair. "You think a man like that deserves to live? A monster like Billy Thomas deserves hell."

"And you and Jesup Barnel sent him there," I said. I waited for George to deny it. He didn't.

Footsteps approaching cut the moment short. I pulled myself back together, quickly grabbed Biggie's zip tie and cinched it around his wrists, then did a half-assed job of binding myself again. We situated ourselves in front of our escape route just as Jenny opened the door. The Giant shined his light in. The crowd shrunk back.

Jenny looked at each of us, appraising us like we were cattle. Then, she began pointing at individuals among the ranks.

"Him, him—the junkie," she said, nodding to Biggie. She singled out the professor and both grad students, and then set her gaze on Casey. "And her," she said. Danny stepped in front of Casey and looked at me desperately, begging me to do something.

"She's hurt," I said. "Badly. Whatever you're doing, she'll only slow you down."

"We're not running a marathon, slick," Jenny said easily. "She'll be fine."

Casey struck me as the kind of girl who could hold her own in most situations, but the bombing and the circumstances had taken their toll. Danny didn't move, shaking his head.

"If she goes, I go," he said.

Jenny shrugged. "Fine. Come on."

I stepped between them, lowering my voice. "Hang on. I had a deal with Barnel… Just pick someone else, all right?"

"Sorry," she said. "But Barnel doesn't have the authority to make deals right now." She nodded to the Giant, and he grabbed Casey. Then, she pressed her gun to Danny's temple. "Come on, lover boy. You wanna play Romeo and Juliet, be my guest."

She stepped aside, nodding to the door. I watched as the

kids walked out, Jenny behind them, Casey so scared I could see her trembling from across the room. And there wasn't a damned thing I could do.

30
SOLOMON

0:40:35

SOMETHING CLICKED AS SOON AS CAMERON left my room. I grabbed Diggs' portfolio of photos and flipped back to the prom picture. One look was all it took to confirm what I should have recognized when this whole thing began: The Goth girl beside Danny in the photo was Sophie. Rick's date was the one I was interested in, though.

It was Jessie Barnel.

I found Agent Keith in the lobby and forced him to surrender his satellite phone, since cell towers were still down and reception minimal.

"It's a misdirect," I said as soon as Juarez picked up.

He didn't say anything for a second. "I need more than that," he said when I didn't elaborate. "What's a misdirect?"

"This whole thing. They're not in Justice. We have to go," I said to Keith.

"Go where?" Juarez asked.

"Not you—you meet me at Ashley's. We need to talk to Rick Durham. But I'm telling you: they're not here. If they were here, we would have found them by now. The reason they keep disappearing is because, somehow or other, they've found a way out of Justice."

It was still raining outside. I followed Keith out to the car, chafing at the thought of sitting idly in the passenger's seat while someone else took the wheel yet again.

"Erin—" Juarez started.

"I don't have time to explain, okay?" I said. "Just…start looking at other targets—ones that Jenny Burkett has ties to, rather than just Barnel. It won't be too far off, because it has to be within driving distance. Someone would have noticed if they were flying people out of here. Two or three hours away, max."

I heard him shout something to Blaze. Relieved that I wouldn't have to fight him on this, I said a quick goodbye and told Keith to put the pedal to the floor, half expecting a fight. Instead, Keith got a gleam in his eye, hopped in the driver's seat, and glanced at me.

"Buckle up."

I did. The thought crossed my mind, suddenly, that as much as Juarez might trust this guy, I didn't know a damned thing about him. And if Cameron's people were watching me, who was to say they didn't have someone on the inside? Or Barnel didn't have someone on the inside? In fact, that seemed likely—through this whole thing, it seemed like Barnel and his people were three steps ahead of us.

"How long have you been with the Bureau?" I asked, trying to sound casual as we squealed out of the parking lot.

"Twelve years," he said promptly.

"So you've been around the block, I guess."

"A few times." He glanced at me, then back at the road. "You have something you want to ask, Ms. Solomon?"

I hesitated. "How long have you known Agent Juarez?"

"About a decade."

Not the answer I'd expected, but I should have known Juarez wouldn't just send me off into the night with some stranger. I looked at my watch again. It didn't make me feel better about life. I decided to use the time to my advantage.

"So you knew his wife," I said.

He nodded. So far, he didn't seem all that surprised at my questions. "I did."

"Did he ever mention his…childhood to you?"

"You mean those missing thirteen years?" he asked promptly.

That was a surprise. I took a second, trying to figure out how to pose my next question. "But he's never really talked about looking into that, huh? It's just kind of an accepted fact?"

He glanced at me again, with a small smile. "Not everyone wears their obsessions on their sleeve," he said. "Doesn't mean they don't have them."

We fell silent after that, since I had no idea how to follow it up. While Keith continued hurtling us toward Ashley Durham's house, I rummaged in my bag for a notebook and pen. Keith eyed me warily.

"What are you doing?"

"I need to think," I said. "I think best when I write shit down." Instead of my notebook, however, I came up with a dog collar. I vaguely remembered stuffing it in my pocket when Diggs and I first found Roger Burkett, then tossing it in my bag when I was packing at the Durhams' place. That felt like a lifetime ago.

I pulled it out and started to set it aside in the possibly fruitless search to find a pen in the bottomless pit that is my purse. A dozen pudgy penguins trekked single-file across a winter snowscape on the frayed collar. I recalled a conversation I'd had with Diggs when we first hit Kentucky:

Why does a Kentucky college have a penguin for a mascot?

I snagged the sat phone and dialed Juarez again. Keith glanced at me. "You have something?"

"Yeah. I think I do."

Juarez picked up immediately. I spoke before he could say anything.

"I know where they are."

We pulled into Ashley's driveway and pounded on the front door until Ashley's husband appeared, his wispy hair standing straight up. His pajama top was unbuttoned and his glasses were askew.

"I need to talk to Rick," I said.

Ashley appeared behind him. She took one look at my face and apparently decided arguing would be futile. Before she could go rouse the kid, however, Rick appeared at the top of the stairs. He looked exhausted, and hardly the pious, put-together teen I'd met when Diggs and I first hit town.

"Your mother said you did a project about Smithfield College that got you in early. What was that on?"

He came down the stairs gnawing on his bottom lip, forehead furrowed. "I did a project all over the state, mapping out tunnels and passages for the Underground Railroad. Smithfield played a big part in gettin' slaves up north in those days."

"Did you ever tell Jessie Barnel about that? Maybe show her the project?"

He hesitated. "I took her out there," he said. "They gave me a key—said I could go wherever I liked, lookin' at some of those old places while I was mapping them out. I took Jessie."

"And there were passages no one knew about?"

"Yes, ma'am," he agreed. Slow realization dawned. "You think Jessie told the reverend about it? That maybe that's where they're holed up now?"

I nodded. "I think so."

He turned around at the bottom of the stairs and ran back up. "Hang on—let me grab my stuff. We gotta get out there."

00:30:45

"Smithfield," I said as soon as I got Juarez back on the line. "I'm sure of it, Jack. The whole thing's been a diversion, making us think whatever Barnel was planning would go down in Justice."

Juarez didn't say anything for another second—long enough for Keith to pull out of Ashley's driveway and back onto the highway.

"What makes you think that?"

I told him about the classes Mae had mentioned Jenny teaching at the college; about the secret tunnels and the connection between Rick Durham and Jessie Barnel.

"But what does he have against the school?" Juarez persisted, still not sold.

I asked Rick, who shook his head. "I dunno—it always seemed like he thought they was godly enough. They got a clinic there, and some of the students run a residential home for the mentally ill right on campus. He had a lot to do with that stuff."

"How many people are on campus right now?" Juarez asked. "What's security like?"

I put him on speaker and made him repeat the question. It was dark on the road—profoundly so, with no other vehicles, no streetlights, no houses lit up in any direction.

"There's no security there," Rick said. "It's a low-residency program. It used to be a full-time college, but they couldn't afford it no more. Now, they just run a few ten-day residencies every semester. They rent Kildeer Hall out for special events, concerts, that kind of thing."

I looked at the clock. It was eleven-thirty. "How long does it take to get there?" I asked Rick.

"Little over an hour, maybe," he said reluctantly. "A little less with no cars on the road."

Juarez still didn't say anything. "Jack," I pressed. "This is it. They're spreading you thin on this end—you said it yourself. You've got all units on call here in Justice to respond to whatever happens at midnight. Places outside Hickman County aren't even on your radar right now."

I thought I'd have to argue some more, but a second later I heard him call Blaze over. They conferred.

"Where are you now?" he asked me.

"About five minutes from you."

"Good. Rick—you have those plans you made for your project with you?"

"Yes, sir. If you can get me a computer, I reckon I've got everything you need."

00:30:29
DANNY

DANNY FIGURED he ought to be happy they weren't bothering with the hoods anymore. Instead, all he could think was what that meant. No more hoods: Jenny was leading them straight to death's door. They might as well be walking the plank. Casey leaned on him a little, but she stayed strong, not shedding so much as a tear.

"What do you reckon they'll tell Dougie and Willa?" she asked. "Once I'm gone, I mean?"

It was the first time she'd mentioned her kid brother and sister. Danny shook his head, a lump in his throat.

"They'll be all right," he said. "We're gonna get back to 'em."

She got quiet, trudging along beside him with her eyes straight ahead.

"You never said yours," he said to her as they topped a steep flight of stairs and then waited while Jenny unlocked the door.

"My what?" Casey asked.

"Top twenty-four," he said.

The door opened. They blinked in the glare of fluorescent lights. They were in a hallway with a cement floor and blank white walls. There was a red exit sign and metal double doors at one end, and a freight elevator like they had in the basement of his school. A janitor's closet door stood open. Jenny walked them past and down the long hallway, in the opposite direction of the exit sign. He saw a few stairs leading down to a door marked BOILER.

Jenny stopped at a stairwell at the end of the hall. Her friend in black opened the door, and she waved her gun at them.

"Go on," she encouraged. She'd been pretty easygoing up till now, but she was getting tense—he could hear it in her voice.

"C'mon, Case," he coaxed when he realized she still hadn't answered. "Your top twenty-four albums of all time."

She looked at him and kind of smiled. Her eyes were bright and her body was warm against his side, like maybe she had a fever.

"Top twenty-four," she said. Her voice was rough. In the distance, he could hear music again: Van Morrison... "Sweet Thing." He'd always liked the song, but it didn't much fit what he figured they were headed for.

"No Doubt—*Tragic Kingdom*. Janis, of course. *Cheap Thrills*—the cover art on that one's as good as the album. Fleetwood Mac. And don't give me that look," she said before he could say a word, bumping into him a little. "You just don't give nothin' a chance if it don't strike your fancy in the first minute. You settle in and listen to *Rumours* again with me—the whole album—and I'll change your mind."

He bumped back into her and nodded. "It's a date." He could feel his face burning when she met his eye and smiled.

"I'm gonna hold you to that, Durham," she said.

They reached the first floor. Jenny pushed the door open. The music was louder now, the place wired with a sweet sound system. They were in another hallway, but this one looked more like a building than a basement: linoleum floor, more cement walls, doors with numbers on them lining both sides.

"Smithfield," Casey said quietly. Danny nodded. They'd come here for a couple of gigs before—they were supposed to play here next week, as a matter of fact.

Jenny poked him in the back with her gun.

"Pick up the pace, kids. There's not a lot of time."

Danny tried to remember what he knew about the building. Besides the classrooms, there was an auditorium on one end, and he thought there might be offices above. He'd kind of dated a girl who went here. She told him Kildeer Hall was the best place to work because they wired in WKRO. *You just rock out all day and do your research. Nobody ever bugs you there.*

Jenny stopped them and looked at the Giant. "Take them," she said, nodding at the professor and the hot college girls he worked with. "I've got these guys."

The Giant nodded without an argument, and pulled the three Jenny had pointed out from the group. One of the girls started crying. Casey started to say something, but Danny shook his head. The Giant pushed his gun into the crying girl's back and shoved them on ahead. He stopped at a doorway, took a key from the professor, and unlocked it. Danny stood there, frozen, until Jenny pushed him to keep going.

They walked another few steps and he heard one of the girls scream. A gunshot went off. Casey flinched beside him. He wished he could hold her hand. Wished he could just run off somewhere. Two more gunshots went off.

They were at the door to the auditorium when the Giant came back, alone.

00:28:16
DIGGS

WE'D GOTTEN MAYBE THREE FEET DEEP with our tunnel when I heard the gunshots—three of them. Glenda screamed. I saw the horror on George's face, and shook my head.

"Don't give up yet," I said. "We don't know what that was. Or who."

He nodded. Beside me, Sally kept digging without a word.

By the time Jenny came in to get her next batch, we'd broken through to the room next door—not enough for anyone to actually make it through, but enough to give me hope that we'd get there. When we heard someone coming this time, George plopped down on top of the hole like a nesting hen while I tried not to look like I'd been digging an escape route for the past two hours.

It didn't matter, though: Jenny skipped right over George and me, picking Glenda, Riley, Sally, and three others. She smiled at me, and I was grateful for the dim lighting.

"I'll be back for you, slick. Just in case you start to feel neglected."

"Can't wait."

As soon as she was gone, I set back to work, shutting out the sound of Glenda's deafening screams as they led her away with the others.

00:25:40
DANNY

JENNY LED THEM to a bunch of seats on the right side of the auditorium. Danny and Casey sat together, both of them still tied. Biggie and a couple of the big flannel-wearing rednecks sat in front of them. Casey let her head drop onto Danny's shoulder like she was too tired to hold it up anymore. He knew how she felt.

The reverend was up front, a couple video cameras pointed at him from the center aisle of the auditorium. There were about seventy, maybe seventy-five others in the audience—all of 'em people Danny recognized from the reverend's church. Maybe a quarter of them were just little kids.

Another dozen guys were spread out all along the walls. They were all young, maybe a little older than Danny, with buzzcuts and camo pants with pressed white button-up shirts.

Every one of them carried a rifle.

"What in hell is goin' on here?" Casey whispered to me. He shook his head.

"Hell if I know."

Whatever it was, Danny wasn't loving their chances of

getting out.

A couple people fiddled with the video cameras, and one of them cued the reverend. He straightened out his tie and cleared his throat before he started up.

"Brothers and sisters," he said. "The devil is on our doorstep. There's no more time to waste. We can't wait another minute before we take that final leap of faith and walk into the arms of the Almighty. We been persecuted and mocked and belittled on this earth too long, friends. The government's men are on the way, prepared to take our children and say whatever lies they have to say to pull the wool over your eyes."

A couple of the ladies in the audience were crying. So were the kids. Danny felt sick. There was a table up front with five pitchers filled with purple liquid, a bunch of crackers on platters beside them.

Casey shifted beside him. He turned and looked at her. She tried to smile, but she couldn't quite make herself. Danny wished he could take her hand. Hold her. He tried to get that across with his eyes, while the reverend kept up babbling and everybody in the audience prayed and cried.

"You remember what Diggs said?" he asked, low in her ear. She nodded.

"Soon as midnight's close, duck down low. Stay down. Don't panic," she recited.

He nodded, even though he was already way past panicking.

"I'll do everything I can to get us out," he said to her. "But if we don't…" He trailed off.

"Me too," she said, her pretty eyes on his.

They just sat there after that, watching the clock wind down, arms touching. Casey's head stayed on his shoulder, even when the reverend told his people to stand up and get in line. A couple of the boys went to the tables and poured the grape juice into little paper cups.

"This is our final communion on this earth, brothers and sisters," the reverend said.

Danny swallowed hard, trying to fight back the fear. One way or another, they didn't have long.

00:15:22
DIGGS

THERE WERE ONLY FIVE OF US left in the room. I was breathing hard, covered in dirt and sweat, my fingernails bloody from digging.

But we'd done it.

"Go," George whispered to me as soon as we were sure I'd broken through. "We'll stall 'em as long as we can, but you need to get out of here. Try and find a way out. Get to Danny."

I nodded. The fact that I knew he was right didn't make it any easier to leave him. He looked pale and weak—nothing like the man I'd known; the man who'd saved me all those years ago. Whatever had happened with him and Barnel and Billy Thomas when they were still kids hardly mattered to me now. I hugged him quickly.

"I'm coming back for you," I said. "This isn't the way this ends."

"Just go, son," he said. "One way or another, I reckon I'll see you on the other side." He held onto me fiercely, his hand at the back of my neck, mouth at my ear. "I'm proud of you, boy," he whispered. "You're a good man. This ain't the way your story ends."

He released me. I wiped tears away with a muddy hand, and dove down the rabbit hole.

I emerged to find myself in almost total darkness—no ticking clock, no bare red bulb. A thin strip of light filtered in from beneath a door about ten feet from me. My pulse quickened. I stood, tread carefully across a packed dirt floor, and tried the knob.

It stuck for a minute, then gave way.

The door creaked as it opened, the sound deafening. I waited a second, then another, and pushed it open a little more.

The corridor—dirt floor, stone wall, wood beams overhead—was empty. I searched for a sign of a camera somewhere that might be capturing my movement, but I found nothing.

My hand was on the door, ready to free George and the others, when I heard footsteps on the stairs. Jenny's voice echoed down to me.

"We need to get them up there—then the bus is waiting. Everything's on schedule."

"You don't think it's a risk, us leaving our post before the clock's up?" the Giant asked.

"The alternative is going up in flames with Barnel's nuts," Jenny said. "You might be up for that. I'm not. We've done our jobs."

I searched desperately for a place to hide as the footsteps got closer. The only doors in the narrow space belonged to the rooms I'd just come from, and as far as I could tell, the only exit was the stairwell Jenny and the Giant were using.

I flattened myself back against the wall just behind the stairwell door. It opened, the knob narrowly missing me as Jenny stepped into the corridor. I waited for her to discover me, pulse pounding.

Just as she was getting ready to shut the door behind

her, subsequently finding and probably killing me, I heard George shout from inside our prison. Someone else followed, their voices raised until it sounded like they were about to kill one another in there. Jenny swore, and she and her comrade hurried over to intervene. Or watch the fight. The motive hardly mattered, as long as the end result was the same: they left the door open and the stairwell empty.

I raced up the stairs and opened the door into a bright white corridor with an exit sign on one end. I stayed low, scanning corners and doorways for guards.

There was no one.

My gaze lingered on the exit for only a second. If I left now, there was no way in hell I was getting back in to try and save anyone else. The best thing to do was figure out where I stood and locate Danny and the others. Then, when I made an escape, I could do so with everyone.

I found the stairwell leading up to the next level and took the steps at a run, just as I heard Jenny's footsteps pounding toward me on the stairs below. She shouted my name, and she didn't sound happy.

The hunt was on.

00:10:02
SOLOMON

THE CHOPPER RIDE TO SMITHFIELD only took half an hour. Unfortunately, we only *had* half an hour. Juarez called ahead and sent local cops and every other resource available to him out to the site, but so far we'd gotten no word back. I sat buckled in the back beside Rick, both of us on the edge of our seats.

"I didn't know she'd tell anybody about the place," Rick said, shouting over the noise of the engine and the whirring rotors. He looked miserable. "Jessie, I mean. I was just tryin' to impress her. Danny's good with girls—not me." He stopped, swallowing hard. "You think Jessie only went out with me 'cause of that project I did?"

I didn't say anything. That silence was all the confirmation he needed, though. He looked down, eyes filled with tears, and didn't speak again for the rest of the interminable flight.

Ten minutes from our destination, Juarez got a call. When he hung up and looked back at me, I knew my hunch had been right. And we still might be too late.

"They sent a couple of local cops out," Juarez said. "When they didn't report back, someone went to check on them. Both shot dead. It looks like Barnel has fortified himself inside Kildeer Hall. You know where that is?" he asked Rick.

Rick nodded.

"He's broadcasting a live feed from the college's closed circuit TV station," Juarez continued.

"Can you tap into it?" I asked immediately. Juarez shook his head.

"They're watching down there. Barnel has armed guards at all the exits. No one's getting in or out of the place. His entire congregation is in that auditorium."

"What about the others?" I asked. I wasn't sure I even wanted the answer. "Are they there, too? Danny? Casey?" I swallowed, trying not to sound like my heart was tied up in the name. "Diggs?"

Jack hedged. "We spotted Danny and Casey in the audience, along with more than a dozen others they'd taken."

"But not Diggs," I said.

"They could be keeping him somewhere else," he said. I nodded.

"Do you have a plan for getting in?" I asked.

He looked at Blaze. She looked at me. "We're still working that out. If the place is set to blow at midnight, though…"

I looked at the clock.

We had six minutes.

00:05:59
DANNY

DANNY SCOOTED BACK IN HIS SEAT to talk to Casey. The line of Barnel's worshippers was halfway through, everybody walking away with a cracker and their shot of grape juice—which was supposed to be wine for the blood of Christ, Danny knew. Instead, Danny'd bet his favorite guitar that it was poison. Everybody went back to their sets, still holding their communion cups.

He kept waiting for somebody to get him and Casey up and force them in line, but so far it hadn't happened. Maybe everybody else was supposed to get poisoned, but the reverend was gonna let the sinners die in the flames. Barnel kept talking at the camera, all about how there was a conspiracy of men going against God, and they were out to strip everybody of their freedoms. Take their kids. People were getting more and more worked up, but it was nothing compared with the reverend. Sweat poured off him. He'd taken off his jacket, and his shirt was soaked through.

"You think it's safe to break out yet?" Casey whispered to Danny.

He looked around. The second and third wave of sinners had been rounded up, taking up a good section of the right side of the auditorium. Everybody's hands were still tied, and they all looked sore and beat up. Diggs had already given them their instructions:

Wherever they take you, your best shot at escape is during the confusion of whatever they have planned at midnight. Don't drink anything they give you—spit it out if you have to. And just before midnight, get out of the zip ties the way we showed you. There are too many guys with guns for you to try and fight. Just wait. Stay low. Seek cover just before twelve o'clock.

They had four minutes to go.

Danny shook his head. "One more minute," he whispered back.

He gave the signal to the others to hold off, everybody staying calmer than he ever would have expected of such a bunch of deadbeats and dirtbags.

That was thanks to Diggs, he realized.

You keep cool and stay strong, Danny imagined his daddy saying to him. *You do that, and nobody can beat you down. You can do this, son.*

Danny swallowed hard. He stayed strong.

00:03:29
DIGGS

I SPOTTED THE FIRST EXPLOSIVES at about the same time I spotted the first guards, posted outside the double doors of an auditorium. I ducked into an unlocked room, my heart hammering, and crouched low while I worked on an alternate plan.

The first thing I noticed about the office was the smell. It wasn't a good one: human waste and the underlying, sweetly metallic scent of fresh blood. The office was dark, but light filtered in from a window in the upper half of the door. A wash of pale yellow illuminated a tidy, carpeted office with three desks and a coffeemaker. Two bodies lay slumped together in the corner.

In the corridor, I heard footsteps approaching. Doors opened and then slammed shut again. Jenny shouted to me with growing desperation, drawing closer by the second.

I ignored the bodies and sought a hiding place, opting for the desk in the furthest corner of the room. I bolted for it, nearly there when my foot caught on something warm and solid and I sprawled forward.

I got back up on my hands and knees, winded. Beside me, lying on his belly with his eyes vacant and the color gone from his face, was Dr. Munjoy. His arm was up, as though he'd died mid-crawl. His fist was clenched. Jenny's footsteps were just outside the door. I crawled past the professor and dove under the desk just as Jenny opened the door.

She flipped the light on. I sat with my knees up to my chin in the narrow space under the desk, my heart beating a rhythm I could feel to my toes. From the small space below the desk, I could see her shoes—boots, actually. Black leather with a low heel, laced to her knee. Perfect for the psychotic dominatrix in your life. She stayed at the door for a minute, surveying the scene.

"Jenny! If we're leaving, we gotta go now!" I heard the Giant say.

"I'll be right there," she said. The panic was gone from her voice. I thought she was leaving.

She wasn't.

Instead, I watched as she walked across the floor. She stepped over Munjoy's body without hesitation, walked around the desk, and pushed the chair out of the way. She leveled her gun directly at my head, her eyes bright.

"Hello there," she said softly. There was a grin on her full lips. "I thought I might find you here."

"Jenny!" the Giant called from the doorway. Jenny looked at me one more time, lowered her gun, and winked.

"See ya in hell, slick."

She turned on her heel and walked back to the door. Turned out the lights.

And locked the door behind her when she left.

00:02:16
DANNY

"NOW?" CASEY ASKED.

Danny nodded. He kicked the seat in front of him gently and Biggie turned around. They exchanged a quick smile. "Go," Danny mouthed to him.

"Good luck," Biggie mouthed back.

That set off a chain reaction as everybody got the cue.

Zip ties weren't hard to get out of, it turned out— especially if you weren't alone. Biggie showed everybody how you just used your thumbnail to shim the locking piece and slide your partner free. Then you returned the favor, and presto, no more plastic tearing into your wrists.

Danny maneuvered himself back-to Casey and they sat up enough to touch hands over the armrests. He went first, every passing second speeding by like a freight train.

Reverend Barnel had everybody in their seats praying. All the kids were crying by now, and it seemed to Danny that the reverend's plan wasn't as popular as he might have thought. Because as far as Danny could see, about half the congregation was talking about how maybe it wasn't their time after all, and couldn't they just get those fellas with the guns to step off and go about this another way?

"This is the path the Almighty has set for us," the reverend hollered.

"This is the path you set for us, you damn fool," Sally Woodruff hollered back. A few of the people in the congregation hollered back at her, but it didn't look like everybody thought Sally was so off the mark.

Danny couldn't get a grip on the plastic. In front of him, Biggie freed one of the rednecks, who turned in his seat to help him.

"Now, I want you all to take these cups representing the blood of the lamb," Reverend Barnel said.

Only about a quarter of the people did. Everybody in the place was crying and praying. Danny watched a couple of little boys hanging onto their mama, their faces red from wailing. The reverend stayed strong, ignoring everybody's complaints.

Danny's finger finally found the tiny hole locking the zip tie in place. He slid his thumbnail in. They had one minute.

"Drink it down, brothers and sisters," Reverend Barnel hollered. "Drink it down, and know that our pain has ended."

A man in the front row sobbed. About twenty people toward the front tipped their cups up, draining the blood of the lamb.

Casey's zip tie came loose. Another dozen people tried to get their kids to drink. A little girl threw hers on the ground and started screaming, her face pink like Ida's used to get when she was throwing a tantrum.

Casey's tie slid off her wrist.

She was free.

00:00:20
DIGGS

MY HANDS WERE SLICK with sweat and blood and shaking as bad as Biggie's by the time I got the door unlocked and let myself back out into the hallway.

It was deserted.

The music from WKRO had long since stopped. In its place, I could hear Barnel talking—shouting, actually, in his best fire-and-brimstone tenor. The source was obvious: It came from behind double doors with a plaque beside them reading KILDEER AUDITORIUM in bold letters. I could hear children crying and people wailing through the walls.

I looked at my watch:

Fifteen seconds.

I thought of Solomon. Of all the time I'd wasted that I wasn't getting back. There were a hundred places I wanted to take her, a thousand things I wanted to say. When she's pissed, Erin gets this fire in her eye that undoes me in ways I'm almost ashamed to admit to. I would have given anything and everything to see that fire again. I wanted to hear her laugh; watch her sleep...map every curve, every slope, every delicate detail of her body, until night gave way to morning and we slept tangled in one another, oblivious to the world.

And then I wanted to start all over again.

It didn't matter what I wanted, though: I'd officially gotten my last chance to screw things up.

The end was here.

00:00:04
SOLOMON

"NO ONE'S GOTTEN IN THERE AT ALL?" I asked Juarez. He looked grim. We were flying over Smithfield now. Below, I could see ambulances and flashing lights, fire trucks and cop cars. Rick hung onto his seat so hard his knuckles were white.

My eyes were dry. It felt like I was living in some kind of nightmare—like there was no way to move, nowhere to go. I watched as the clock struck midnight.

No one said anything.

Thirty seconds passed.

Forty-five.

Juarez held a rosary in his right hand. He looked up. "Maybe they didn't—"

And the world exploded.

The helicopter canted far to the left from the force of the blast, the pilot losing control for a second. Orange balls of flame burst into the air, debris falling in every direction. A second blast followed maybe five seconds later, rocking us again. Rick closed his eyes. Blaze swore softly, her eyes haunted in the way of those who have seen tragedy before, and know all too well what it means.

I kept my eyes on the ground, watching the chaos below. "How soon till we land?" I asked, my voice flat.

No one answered.

March 16
12:05 a.m.
DIGGS

THE HEAT WAS THE WORST PART. I remembered interviewing guys in a burn unit in Fallujah years ago, but I never really understood what they were telling me until the flames were raging just above my head and I could feel my shirt melting into my back. I crawled toward the auditorium, screams splitting the air over the roar of the fire.

The door was hot to the touch. I took my shirt off, wrapped it around my hands, and pushed.

Inside was the stuff of nightmares: images that will never leave me. Boy soldiers lay fallen beside their rifles, some of them already burning. All of them dead, as far as I could see. Children screamed. The auditorium was ablaze. I spotted Barnel seated on the floor of the stage, inert, the flames dancing closer. He sat with his back against the lectern, eyes half open.

He was smiling.

I crawled into the fray, searching for a sign of our group, but the smoke was thick and the noise was deafening. The flames were everywhere.

And then, I spotted a familiar face.

Three aisles away, George was crawling beside a little girl. I got to my feet, staying low, and ran to him. The left side of his face was burned, but not as badly as I might have expected. And he was alive.

"Danny says there's a way out behind the stage," he rasped. The little girl in his arms was silent, her eyes wide with shock.

"Where is he?" I shouted.

"I don't know," George said. He looked frail and terrifyingly mortal. I nodded to the girl.

"Get her out," I said. "I'll find Danny."

I watched him for only a second before I turned back.

I found Biggie with two little boys clinging for dear life to a burning chair, trying to get away from him. When he turned to look at me, it was clear why they were terrified. His face and body were black. Charred.

"Diggs! Help me." His voice wasn't even human. "They won't go. I can't get 'em to let go."

There was a madness to his eyes, borne of failure and pain and imminent death.

"It's all right," I said. "I've got them."

Biggie let them go. He smiled at me—another image I'll never escape. "It's gotta mean somethin', ain't it?" he asked me. "A lifetime screwin' up at every turn..." He lay down, just out of the aisle. "Save them boys, huh, Diggs? Don't let me down."

"I won't." When he made no move to go, I hesitated. "Come on, Biggie—it's not much farther. Get up, and we'll get you out of here."

He just laughed. "I ain't goin' nowhere. It's all done. Now, you get the hell out of here with them kids. Save somebody for me." The boys were screaming in terror now; there wasn't a choice. Not really. As I was leaving him, Biggie looked at me once more with that mad light shining in his eyes. "Pain, boy," he said. "It's all a distraction. Ain't nothin' to me."

He didn't get up again.

I urged the boys forward, making sure they stayed on their hands and knees. When we reached the bottom of the aisle, I prodded them to keep going onto the stage. Which was on fire, so not an entirely easy sell on my part. One of the boys began to cry. I picked him up and took the other by the hand. The stage curtains were ablaze, but I could see movement behind them. People. When the stage door out back was in sight—open, a clear black night shining through—I gave the boys a little push.

"Go on!" I said. "You'll be safe there. Somebody will get you."

They ran.

I remained there for a second on hands and knees, thinking of Solomon, and took a steady, burning breath.

I turned around and went back.

12:15 a.m.
SOLOMON

"WE CAN'T SEND ANYONE INTO THAT," a fireman told me. We were surrounded by emergency personnel and at least forty survivors with varying degrees of burns and injuries. George was among them, as well as more than a dozen kids.

Danny and Casey weren't. Neither was Diggs.

The building was engulfed in flames—they rose high into the sky, the smoke so thick it was all but impossible to breathe. I thought of Payson Isle and my father; of Mitch Cameron and Isaac Payson and Reverend Barnel.

But mostly, I thought of Diggs.

"Danny's still in there?" Rick asked. George was on a gurney with an oxygen mask over his mouth and nose. He nodded, eyes haunted. He pulled the mask away from his face.

"Diggs is looking for 'em," he rasped. My heart stuttered.

"He's still alive, then?" I asked.

George nodded again. I turned back to the fireman.

"There are still survivors in there," I insisted.

"It's too unstable. I'm sorry, ma'am, but they did a hell of a job wiring this thing. They must've misjudged something because they missed that one exit, but this thing won't stay up for long. The whole building could come down anytime."

"And what the hell are we supposed to do in the meantime—let them burn?"

He looked genuinely tortured. I didn't care. He shook his head. "I'll talk to my men; see what we can do. In the meantime, you might wanna say a prayer."

12:25 a.m.
DANNY

THEY DID EVERYTHING RIGHT: got themselves untied, found cover, stayed low.

It didn't matter, though, because Danny hadn't expected the pillar beside them to come down. It nailed him in the shoulder, sending him sprawling with pain like he'd never felt before. When he got up, Casey was underneath it, and she wasn't moving.

He tried hauling it up; tried pulling Casey out. She still didn't move, blood on her forehead and flames coming closer and screams from everybody around them filling his ears.

"C'mon, damn you," he hollered—or rasped, more like, tears streaming down his face. He couldn't tell if he was crying or it was just the smoke. He sat down beside Casey, trying to get out of the way of the stampeding people. He picked her hand up and set it on his lap, pushing the hair back from her face.

His lungs burned, screaming for clean air. He closed his eyes and leaned his back against the wall, waiting for the end. And then, a hand closed around his wrist.

Casey came to life, coughing. Gasping. He jumped up. The pillar was over her left leg, crushing it so Danny could barely stand to look. But she was alive—that was what mattered.

It took her only a second before she figured out what happened. She went white.

"You've gotta go," she said.

He shook his head. There was no doubt about it now: his tears definitely weren't just from the smoke. "I'm not leavin' you here."

"You're not gonna sit here and die with me," she said, like he was an idiot for even thinking it. Her voice was so calm. "Danny—you gotta go. You're gonna get your butt out of here, and you're gonna look after Willa and Dougie."

"I'm not leaving you alone," he insisted. The flames were all around them—he could smell bodies burning, the screams getting worse, people panicked and running in every direction. A man caught fire two rows down and Danny turned away, sick.

Casey reached out and put her hand on his cheek. "You got too much to do to die today, you hear me? Now you go. Leave me be. I don't feel nothin' anyway right now—it'll all be over and I'll be okay." She curled her hand a little around his neck, pulling him closer. He kissed her.

"Now get outta here," she whispered.

Danny hesitated.

He shook his head, got up, and attacked the pillar again. Teeth clenched, he hauled on the thing with all his might.

It budged half an inch, no more.

He tried again, thinking of his daddy. He'd be able to do this. If it was somebody Wyatt Durham loved under this pillar, he'd move heaven and earth to get 'em out.

He put his shoulder into it, grunting with the strain.

Suddenly, it felt lighter. Moved further. Danny opened his eyes and Diggs was beside him. They moved the pillar together, just enough so Danny could slide Casey out.

"I've got her," Diggs said. "Now you go on ahead. I'm right behind you." He started to argue, but Diggs wasn't having any of it. "Go, dammit!"

Danny turned and ran down the aisle toward the stage exit, keeping low to the ground the whole while.

The fire was worse on the stage—everything burning, the flames loud like some monster, something alive and hungry. The curtains had fallen, still burning on the ground, and flames licked at the ceiling and along the walls. He watched a woman and three kids make it through the door. Then, there was a massive screech, like the building itself was dying, and a beam came crashing down, sparks flying. The top of the door gave way.

Their only way out was gone.

12:30 a.m.
DIGGS

THE GOOD NEWS—if there was any—was that Casey had passed out, which meant she wasn't in pain. At least I was fairly sure she had passed out; the alternative being that I was killing myself carrying a dead girl to safety. I started down the aisle toward the exit, focused only on putting one foot in front of the other and trying to breathe the poisonous air choking into my lungs.

George was out. Danny was out. Solomon would be waiting.

I just had to get through the damn door.

It was a good plan, in theory—until Danny re-appeared a foot in front of me, his face burned and his clothes scorched.

"The exit's gone," he said. His voice was raw from the smoke. "But I know another way."

I didn't ask questions. Instead, I followed in silence as the kid led us up the aisle, into the belly of the building.

1:15 a.m.
SOLOMON

I WATCHED ANOTHER AMBULANCE tear away, while firefighters tried to control the blaze and the building continued to cave in on itself. The exit everyone had been coming from had long since vanished. Rick sat beside me, silent. More than forty-five minutes had passed since the last survivor had emerged from the wreckage.

I felt a hand on my shoulder. "Erin," Jack said. His voice was soft. I set my jaw, my eyes dry.

"He's alive," I said.

"They're trying to evacuate. They're worried about toxins."

"I'm not leaving." My lungs ached from the smoke; my eyes burned. Rick got up when Juarez told him to, and I sensed more than saw the two of them walking away.

I thought of Payson Church again, trying to push past the memories I had to whatever lay beneath: my father on his knees, Isaac Payson standing above him. *This is an act of revolution*, I remembered Isaac saying. *We are reinventing the word of God.* My father, head bowed. And then, later, the two of them arguing outside—I could see myself, suddenly, watching them from the safety of the bushes. *This was supposed to be our Utopia*, my father said. *But you're doing everything we swore we would never do.*

Mitch Cameron was behind this. His people—whoever they were—were at the root of this fire, and the death of Barnel and his followers. J. Enterprises. Max Richards had been part of it. My father had been part of it.

How many people had they killed, for reasons I couldn't begin to comprehend?

My chest tightened until there was no room left for air. The last of the ambulances pulled away. Juarez and Blaze stood on the sidelines, talking strategy.

Diggs didn't come out.

Finally, at 1:30, Jack came over again.

"Come on," he said. He put his arm around my shoulder. I didn't move.

"Wait."

I could barely get the word out. He stopped, caught by my tone. My pulse picked up. I tried to say something—anything—but I couldn't make another sound.

A figure appeared, a phoenix in tattered clothes, coming up over the hillside half a mile from the still-burning auditorium. I stood.

A second figured followed, this one carrying someone in his arms. The last remaining paramedics sprang into action. Emergency vehicles turned around and headed back. Another twenty people appeared on the hillside, silhouetted against the night sky, broken and limping and, miraculously, alive.

I ran to meet them.

1:30 a.m.
DIGGS

MY LEGS GAVE OUT as soon as I realized we were safe. Casey wasn't moving, but I could feel her heartbeat and at some point she'd roused enough to wrap her arms around my neck. I fell to my knees, just barely managing to keep from dropping her. My lungs were screaming—it was a kind of pain like I'd never experienced before, like I was breathing rusty razorblades. Danny turned and saw me fall. One of the other survivors in our group took my arm and helped me up. Sirens flashed. Ambulances and cruisers raced toward us. Someone took Casey from me.

I fell again.

This time, I stayed down. The ground was cool on my chest, my cheek, my legs. I closed my eyes.

I don't know how long I lay there before I felt a hand at the back of my shoulder, cool and familiar. Solomon rolled me over, and I stared at a smoke-filled sky and fiery green eyes.

"You're okay," she said. She sat down on the ground beside me and stroked my forehead.

"That depends on your definition of okay," I rasped.

"You're alive."

I nodded. Or attempted to. "Then, yeah. I'm okay."

She leaned down and kissed me, barely touching her lips to mine. I reached up and settled my hand at the soft slope of her neck, holding her there before she could get away.

"Don't go," I whispered.

She half-laughed, half-sobbed, brushing tears away. "I won't," she whispered back, her lips at my ear. "I'll stay as long as you will."

I smiled. I was still breathing razorblades, but it didn't seem as bad, somehow. "Then you're gonna be stuck with me for a while, kid," I said. I closed my eyes again. Somewhere beneath the ash and the smoke, I could smell Solomon's honeysuckle shampoo. I clung to that, letting it wash over me like a healing rain, until the night receded and sleep took me.

31
SOLOMON

"SO, NO SIGN OF JENNY BURKETT?" Diggs asked. Again. He'd been asking that a lot, actually.

His voice still sounded like sandpaper, but it was better than it had been. *He* was better than he had been. Despite everything that had happened, against all odds, etc. Doctors around Paducah General had taken to calling him Miracle Man—which he, of course, hated. But given the fact that he'd survived snake attacks, brawls, a kidnapping, and two bombings with minimal damage, Miracle Man seemed pretty apt. There were burns, of course, but compared with the dozens of others either dead or permanently disfigured, a few second-degree burns were nothing.

Juarez shifted in his seat in Diggs' hospital room, looking at Agent Blaze, George, and me before he returned his attention to Diggs. "We've been looking—sorry. There's no sign of her. She may have died in the fire."

"She didn't," Diggs said. "What about death toll? Do you have any numbers yet?"

"It was only three days ago," Blaze said. "It'll take some time. There's a lot to sift through."

"There were eighty-six survivors, though," Juarez pointed out. "Many of whom never would have made it without your help."

"Have you found out anymore about Glenda Clifton?" he asked, deftly changing the subject. So far, Diggs hadn't been keen to talk about his heroics, characteristically uninterested in taking any credit.

"Not yet," I told him. "Glenda was Marty Reynolds' wife," I explained to Blaze and Juarez. Diggs had asked about her before, and after comparing notes we had made the connection. "She was the one Marty supposedly murdered. According to records at the residential home, Barnel admitted her to the psych ward in 2002. She was diagnosed with schizo-effective disorder, and she'd been staying there ever since."

"So, who killed her husband?" Juarez asked. "And why?"

George cleared his throat. He had burns on the left side of his face that would never fully heal, but—like so many— he'd made it out. At the question, he and Diggs shared an odd look before George looked away.

"I think I can answer that one," the old man said. "Jesup told me during our little session together—when the cameras *weren't* rollin', of course—that Glenda called him one night, back in '02. Hysterical, screamin' about demons... He took her out of the house, 'cause she said she was afraid of her husband. Brought her out to live at the camp. Then, one night he gets another call from her. She was back at the house."

"And she'd killed her husband," I said.

George nodded.

"But what about the cross?" I asked. "Dressing Marty up in a new suit? All the weird ritual crap that was repeated on Wyatt?"

"I think that was all him," George said. "Including turnin' the cross upside down…" He studied his hands for a minute, looking unmistakably guilty.

Diggs had already told me the source of that guilt: George and Jesup Barnel had killed Billy Thomas together back in 1963. Barnel himself had removed the cross and stapled it back to Billy's chest, upside down. The fact that George had been there when all of this started, however, was weighing heavily on the old man. After much debate, I'd ultimately agreed with Diggs: we wouldn't tell the cops what we knew. George would live out the rest of his years a free man. I still wasn't completely sure it was the right thing to do, but I also knew I didn't have it in me to turn the old man in now.

I caught another look that passed between George and Diggs before he continued. "Jesup told me he believed Glenda when she said she saw the devil in her husband—that it was his duty to step in once he got there and found the man dead. So, he turned the cross so there'd be no mistakin' Marty Reynolds for a righteous man, dressed him up nice, and delivered him someplace where people would find him."

I went over the rest of the details in my head, trying to fill in the gaps. I knew Barnel had killed Wyatt because of his involvement with Sally Woodruff's abortion clinic, because Wyatt had said as much in the "confession" Barnel made him record before his death. It still didn't make a lot of sense to me, though.

"Why take Wyatt early?" I asked. "Why kill him before anyone else, more humanely than anyone else, and leave him on the side of the road in a nice suit instead of blowing him up with the rest of you?"

"I've been thinking about that," Diggs said. "The only

thing I can think is maybe he stumbled on something while he was out at the Burkett farm. Maybe Jenny said something, or…I don't know. Something. Barnel was obviously drugged to the gills when I talked to him. If Jenny suggested Wyatt needed to be taken out early because the devil was in him, Barnel wouldn't have argued with her."

"Okay, I'll buy that," I agreed. "It still doesn't explain why they dosed him with ketamine, dressed him up, and left him for us to find, when they just slit Roger's throat and left him chained in the attic."

"I think Jenny killed Roger," Diggs said. "There's no confession from him on those tapes… I think she just got tired of being married to the guy, and cute little psychopath that she is, decided it was time to sever ties. Permanently. She may have gotten someone else to do his cross or she may have done it herself, but I doubt it had anything to do with whether or not he was a righteous man. And Wyatt…" he stopped, at a loss.

"Jesup always liked Wyatt," George said. Everyone turned to look at him. He shrugged. "I think maybe it's that simple. Before everything got turned around and kids were gettin' poisoned and colleges blown up, I think he felt bad for what he'd done to a man that he knew, deep down, was good. And Wyatt was that. My son was a good man."

I looked at Diggs, watching his face change as he thought about that. He nodded.

"Yeah," he agreed. "That he was."

We sat there for a few seconds of silence. I was reminded yet again of all that had been lost in this, for reasons I still didn't understand. I finally had some names to hang on the conspiracy involving my father, whatever it might be: J. Enterprises; Max Richards; Mitch Cameron; Jenny

Burkett… The fact that I wasn't just running around after some nameless guy in a hood anymore was moderately comforting, but it didn't help me sleep any better when I thought of just how little value these people seemed to place on human life.

I rallied, intent on finding a few more answers before everyone scattered to their separate corners. "And the rest of the story?" I asked. "Who the hell killed Jimmy Barnel and shot the reverend at the tent meeting earlier this week?"

"Jenny Burkett," Diggs said. "She took Danny's truck right after she doped him, drove out to Miller's field, then took out Jimmy and winged the reverend."

"I don't suppose you have motive or evidence to support that theory," Blaze said dryly.

"Motive is easy: she was trying to stir the pot," Diggs said. "Fuel Jennings' and Barnel's paranoia by making it seem like there really were people out to get them."

"Ensuring that Jennings would go through with the bombing the next night," I said.

"And Barnel would be that much more convinced that the world was ending and he needed to get the hell out," Diggs said. "Thanks in large part to an endless supply of speed and barbiturates I suspect Jenny Burkett and her people supplied."

"All of which is supported by the final video he recorded before he took the stage in Kildeer auditorium," Juarez said. "Most of it is just a lot of paranoid ramblings about the end of the world and government mind control, but it seems clear that he genuinely believed he was working in everyone's best interest by taking out the hardcore sinners he couldn't save, and then bringing the rest of his flock home with him."

"That's all well and good," Blaze said, "but the bigger

question for me is who the hell was pulling the strings? Who is this J. Enterprises? What part did Jenny Burkett-Lanahan-whatever-her-name-is play in all of it? Did she actively pursue Roger Burkett while he was in San Francisco, with the intention of moving here? And if so, why would *anyone* put the time and money and energy into a plan like this in a nowhere town in Kentucky? I still don't understand the endgame here."

The doctor walked in then and cleared his throat as he approached Diggs, who was clearly starting to flag.

"And I think that's my cue to clear the room, folks," the doctor said. "No playin' twenty questions with my patient."

"Of course," Blaze agreed, standing. "We need to get on the road, anyway—my kid's been virtually on her own for a week now. God only knows what I'll have waiting for me when I get back." She shook Diggs' hand, then looked at us both solemnly. "No offense, but the next time the world's ending, I hope you two stay home."

"You'll get no argument from me," Diggs said.

Jack leaned in and hugged Diggs with a surprising absence of malice. It's not that I wanted them to duel over me or something, but a trace of tension between them might have been a little reassuring.

"We still on for July?" he asked Diggs.

"You bet," Diggs said. "I'll supply the lobster if you bring the fireworks."

This was news to me, but I said nothing. With the other goodbyes taken care of, I locked eyes with Juarez and felt a flash of panic. Decisions had been made and, logically speaking, I knew they were for the best. It didn't mean it was easy, though.

"I'll walk you out," I said.

Blaze and George excused themselves once we were in the sterile hallways of Paducah General, leaving Juarez and me alone.

"You still have some stuff at my place..." I began.

"You can box it up," he said. For the first time, a wash of sadness shined through. "Just mail it. I'm not sure if I'll be back in Maine before summer."

"Okay." A couple of nurses walked by—both of them clearly checking out Jack on their way past. I held on tight when he hugged me, focused on deep breaths and not becoming a puddle on the floor. "I'm going to miss you," I said into his neck.

He smiled when we parted, reaching out to cup my cheek in his hand. "You can call me if you need anything. Anytime—you know where I am."

"You, too," I agreed. I thought of Agent Keith's words: *Not everyone wears their obsessions on their sleeve.* I got serious, holding his gaze. "If you need someone to talk or listen or... whatever, I'm here. So's Diggs. I mean—I know it's not exactly what we had in mind when you and I first started dating, but you mean a lot to him. To both of us."

"It's mutual." He took a deep breath and glanced at his watch. Instead of leaving, however, he stayed for a second longer. He hesitated. "Stay safe, all right? I know you can take care of yourself, but it seems like you have more than the normal number of demons in your past. Promise me that if you and Diggs keep pursuing whatever it is you're pursuing that you won't tell me about—" I started to protest, but he held up his hand. "Just promise me, please? Promise that you'll call me if you need help. I can't guarantee that I can do anything, but I'd at least like the chance to try."

I nodded. "I promise." My ability to maintain any

semblance of control was slipping fast, so I stood on my toes and kissed his cheek quickly, then nodded toward the exit sign at the end of the hall. "You should probably get going. You don't want to keep Allie waiting."

"Right," he agreed.

We hugged one more time. He left. I stood outside Diggs' hospital door for a few minutes after that, thinking about everything that had happened and everything that would happen, most of which seemed completely beyond my control. I'd be lying if I said I had no mixed feelings about watching Juarez walk out of my life—even if I did have Diggs waiting for me. As much as I love the man, Diggs has never been the safest bet where my heart's concerned.

The doctor came out of Diggs' room then and smiled when he found me waiting there.

"He said to send you in, if you were still out here."

"It's all right if I stay a while?" I asked.

"You seem to have a way of getting him to settle down that my nurses haven't figured out yet," the man said. "Stay as long as you like."

Diggs' eyes were closed when I went back into the room. I took advantage of that rare moment of repose to study him—this man I couldn't seem to shake, no matter what fell across our path. He'd escaped the fire with second-degree burns on his back and first-degree burns to his hands. The bruises from his fight with Jimmy Barnel almost a week ago had faded, and three days of forced bedrest had done a lot to address the circles he'd had under his eyes when this whole thing began.

"Are you just gonna stand there staring, or are you coming in?" he asked without opening his eyes.

"I thought you were sleeping."

"Nope." He looked at me then, his blue eyes shining. There was a very faint trace of doubt in there, but no one but me would ever have noticed. "So...does this mean Juarez is on the road?"

"He is."

"And you're still here."

"I am," I said with a nod, trying for casual. "I mean—you're still burned and broken and concussed. It didn't seem right to just leave you in Kentucky."

"I appreciate that." He patted the side of his bed. "Come here."

I went over and sat gingerly on the edge.

"I'm not gonna break, Solomon. Get up here." He scooted over. I scooted over. We both lay back, his arm around my shoulders, my head on his chest. He smelled like burn ointment—surprisingly, not in a bad way.

"You all right?" he asked.

"I think so." I fell silent, thinking yet again about everything that had happened. "Mitch Cameron was behind this," I said quietly, after a long while. We hadn't discussed this yet, but he didn't seem surprised—at the revelation or the direction the conversation had taken.

"I thought as much," he said.

"And J. Enterprises..."

"...has to have something to do with your father," he finished for me.

I closed my eyes, listening to Diggs' heartbeat. "They've killed a hell of a lot of people."

"They have."

He rolled to his side so he could look at me. I studied him for a minute, running my finger along the slope of his nose, his cheekbones and jaw. I lingered at his lips, tracing the lines there. He kissed my fingertip, scraping his teeth along the pad with just a hint of devil in his eyes. We had yet to acknowledge the kiss-at-the-end-of-the-world thing, or what we planned to do about it. The feel of his lips on my skin made the question seem more pressing than it had.

"So," he finally prompted me. "What are you going to do?"

"About?"

"Are we still pretending Mitch Cameron doesn't exist?" He looked at me seriously. "Because if that's what you want to do, I'll do it. We'll pretend we never heard the name. Never saw his face."

"And all those people you watched die three days ago?" I asked. "Glenda Clifton and the professor and your druggie friend? The boy soldiers and all the other men, women, and children… Casey, who almost lost her leg? The families I knew from Payson Church? What do we do about them?"

His eyes held on mine, eyebrows up. "I don't know. This is your call, kid."

I bit my lip, considering that. "I can't drop it this time," I said. Even saying the words was terrifying. He leaned in and kissed me, light and fast.

"Okay," he said. "Then we've got work to do."

He nodded to the drawer in the nightstand by his bed. "Open that up and hand me the envelope inside there, would you?" Suddenly, he was all business. I almost got whiplash at the shift. "And grab my laptop."

He all but pushed me out of bed. Ah, the joys of dating a newspaper man.

"I thought you were supposed to be resting."

"I'll rest in a minute. First, I need to show you something."

I fetched the envelope and his laptop. He pulled a memory card from the envelope and fired up his computer. A jumble of meaningless numbers scrolled endlessly across the screen as soon as he put the card in.

"What is that?" I asked.

"It's encrypted."

"Well, yeah," I said. "I got that part. But where did you get it? What's the relevance to what we're doing here?"

"I'm not sure. But that professor I told you about? When I found his body, he was clutching this in his hand. When we were talking, he told me he studied Christian fundamentalism and cult behaviors. My focus at first was the fundamentalism, but what if that was a smokescreen? What if J. Enterprises—and whoever they represent—is more focused on the cult side of things?"

"The senator found murdered in Washington last spring—Jane Bellows," I said. "She did a lot of work around legislation regarding cults. And obviously my father and the Payson Church…"

He nodded. We were on the same page. "The professor and his grad students were the only ones at Kildeer who were shot. As though Jenny needed to make sure that, whatever else happened, those three didn't get out, and that the building went up in flames…"

"You think all this was over a professor in a third-rate college in Kentucky and his thesis on cults?"

He ran his hand through his hair. I caught just a hint of a tremor there and stood, taking the laptop from him.

"Okay," I said. "We're gonna talk about this later."

"Why? I'm fine."

"No. You're not fine—you got blown up. A lot." I took out the memory card, returned it to the envelope, and put the computer away. Diggs scooted back down in his bed. The fact that he didn't fight harder told me he really wasn't quite as unaffected by all this as he'd like me to believe.

"I'll go and let you sleep."

I caught a flicker of vulnerability on his face before he could hide it. I thought of the boy I'd seen on Barnel's tape, with the Bugs Bunny boxers and the will of steel; the kid who wouldn't be broken.

"Unless you'd rather I stay," I said.

"You can if you want," he said. God, he was a pain in the ass. "I mean… you know, if it'll make you feel better."

"It'll only make me feel better if you actually sleep."

He patted a spot beside him. "I will if you will."

I kicked off my shoes and returned to the bed. We lay down facing one another.

"So…" he said.

"So…" I said.

He rested his hand on my side, niftily finding the hem of my shirt with little to no effort. I quirked an eyebrow.

"I thought you were sleeping."

"I want to take you out." His fingers moved lightly along my bare skin. It wasn't doing a lot for my concentration.

"And I repeat: I thought you were sleeping."

"Not *now*," he clarified. "When we get home. It's been a long time since we've gone on a date."

I curled my hand around his roving digits and returned them to the outside of my clothes. "You know I just broke up with someone, right?"

I expected him to make a joke. Possibly disparage Juarez's manhood or something. Instead, he stayed serious, a line at the center of his forehead.

"I know that," he said. "If it makes you feel any better,

Juarez gave us his blessing. He even wished me luck; I think he might be under the impression that you're more woman than I can handle."

"And what do you think?"

He grinned. "I think I'm gonna have a lot of fun trying."

I fell silent again. I was completely on board with the fact that Jack and I weren't meant to be; really, by the end it couldn't have been clearer. But that didn't change the reality, which was that I still had a bunch of his shirts in my dresser and his spare toothbrush beside mine back home. Diggs may have made a habit of bed-hopping for the past twenty years, but that had never really been my M.O.

"Well, I'm glad you guys have it all figured out for me, then," I said. Diggs smiled, amused at my indignation. Somehow, his hand had made it back under my shirt. Tricky bastard.

"I told you: I just want to take you on a date." He leaned in and kissed me, very lightly, his hand migrating a little higher up my shirt. He nipped my lip before he moved back again. That devil spark was back in his eye. "I've decided to sweep you off your feet."

I laughed, though the look in his eye and the thing he was doing with his hand was really making me rethink my policy on bed-hopping.

"You have, huh? I don't know that I'm ready for that."

The spark faded, just a little, replaced with an intensity that Diggs rarely showed the world. "I've been half-assed about being in love with you for too long," he said, his eyes never leaving mine. I forgot how to swallow. "I plan on making up for that."

"Okay," I said. Or croaked, really. He looked infinitely amused, the intensity gone as suddenly as it had come.

"And that starts with a date," he said simply.

"All right," I said. His eyes drifted shut, but he was still smiling. I leaned up and kissed him, fast, then snuggled in with his arms around me.

Finally, an apocalypse with a happy ending.

EPILOGUE

THREE DAYS LATER, Diggs and I were ready to hit the road for Maine. The Durhams' yard was overflowing, as Mae seemed to have had some kind of epiphany when Danny survived Barnel's end times. She'd even invited Danny's band, including a wheelchair-bound Casey Clinton and Casey's brother and sister, Dougie and Willa. At the moment, the littlest Clintons were hanging out with Grace and Einstein: Einstein and Dougie chased each other around the yard while Willa sat beside Grace, gently brushing the dog's silky fur.

George Durham was smuggling out paper cups of rotgut whiskey, and Buddy Holloway—who in all likelihood would be crowned sheriff before long—was pretending not to notice. The rest of the Durhams were also in attendance: Rick and Ida, Ashley and Terry and the Nordic toddler, Angus. Sally Woodruff had threatened to make an appearance, but Diggs assured her that while Mae might have turned over a new leaf, there was no way in hell she was ready to embrace a godless abortion doctor. At least, not yet. Sally had been surprisingly gracious about that.

"You sure you had enough to eat?" Mae asked when Diggs announced that we were heading out.

I was so stuffed I'd never button my jeans again. Diggs looked at me. "We should probably pack another couple of cookies for the road."

I didn't argue.

Diggs went over to say goodbye to Rick and Danny, who hung out together on the sidelines with the band. It seemed even they had gotten closer since the whole end-of-the-world thing. The fact that Rick had nearly gotten everyone killed by falling for a Bible nerd with a crazy apocalyptic grandpa had apparently endeared him to Danny; he said it took his brother down a couple of pegs. It didn't hurt that Danny's recollection of Rick's project on the tunnels and catacombs beneath Kildeer Auditorium had saved everyone's lives, either.

"You guys can come visit us in Maine anytime," Diggs said. He seemed to be talking to the whole band. That was definitely their impression, anyway.

"Sure," Danny said. "We could do a tour of New England." His hand rested on Casey's shoulder.

Of everyone, Casey was the one I worried about the most—for the obvious reason that, according to doctors, she was in for months of physical therapy and potential surgery before she was back on her feet. Beyond that, though, there was a weariness about her that I hadn't seen when we first met. It was inevitable after what she'd been through, but I hoped that somehow she would make it through everything intact.

While Diggs was chatting with the boys, I pulled Casey aside and gave her my card again.

"If you need anything, this is how you can reach me. Even if it's just to talk. Or bitch about dating a music geek."

She laughed at that. I smiled, then got serious. "If you have any problems with the dog, or anything else… Medical stuff with your leg, even—you can call me. My mother and her partner are both surgeons. If you feel like you're not getting what you need down here, just pick up the phone."

"I will," she said with a nod. "Thank you."

I thought of everything she had stacked against her: an abusive father, no money, two kids depending on her, and now the physical issues she'd be facing with her leg. Then, I thought of Mitch Cameron again. Right now, Casey was relying on her father's crappy insurance to handle her medical bills. Which meant that added to all the other problems she had, she'd be fighting with insurance companies for at least the next year or so.

Whoever was in charge of J. Enterprises had seemingly limitless resources.

If no one else got it, Casey Clinton deserved a little justice in all this.

"I'll be in touch," I told her earnestly. She looked at me in surprise, clearly caught off guard at my intensity. "I don't want you to worry about things, all right? There'll be a lot coming at you, but you're not alone in this. People will be looking out for you."

"Uh…Okay."

Good job, Solomon: Freak out the girl in the wheelchair. Well played. Diggs looked at me, nodding toward the car.

"You ready to go?"

I nodded. Definitely ready to go. We hugged the rest of the crew and then Diggs slipped his hand in mine as we headed for the car.

With our goodbyes behind us, Einstein hopped into the backseat without too much coaxing, then promptly settled his fuzzy chin in the back window with his mournful brown eyes on Grace. The retriever had reclaimed her place beside Casey, with Dougie and Willa at her feet. Grace looked at Stein once, then reached out and tentatively licked Willa's face. The little girl giggled.

Diggs leaned in with his arm around my waist and his lips at my ear. "You really think Stein will make it without her?" he asked.

Grace lay down and offered her belly to the Clinton trio. "Honestly? I don't think he has much choice."

Einstein whimpered once, then circled in the backseat before he settled in for the ride. I was selfishly pleased I wouldn't have to share him with another woman, but I chose not to acknowledge such pettiness.

I took the wheel for a change this time out, since Diggs was still under the weather. Once we hit the main stretch headed for Maine, I checked the rearview. Diggs followed my gaze.

"See anything?" he asked.

"No. I don't really expect to, though," I said, thinking of Cameron's words to me. *I'm not an ally in all this.* Ally or not, I knew he was out there. And there was no doubt in my mind that we would be crossing paths again. "We'll need to be careful now, you know. No more charging into the fray. We know they're watching. Cameron already said he'll kill you if we don't stop."

"So, we'll be careful," Diggs said. He squeezed my hand. "We just won't back down this time."

I expected him to turn on the radio once we were on our way, if only for a final fix of Crazy Jake Dooley. Instead, he settled in with his feet on the dashboard and looked at me speculatively.

"All right," he said, serious as a heart attack. "You've put me off long enough. Let's have it."

"Let's have what?"

"Your top twenty-four, Solomon. From the top."

It was going to be a long ride home.

Looking for more Erin Solomon?

Turn the page for a free excerpt from
the next novel in the critically acclaimed series,

BEFORE THE AFTER.

PROLOGUE

FOOTSTEPS.

Behind her, somewhere close, Kat hears boots pounding on the frozen ground. Sharp, icy pellets of sleet sting her cheeks as she crouches in the brush, heart thundering.

They're coming for her—there's nowhere else to hide.

No way to protect herself anymore.

No way to protect any of them.

There's a ravine on the far side of the island; Kat remembers seeing it before. She runs for that, through groves of dying pine trees and over slick island trails, the ground blurring at her feet. Voices behind call to her, order her to stop, but she drives herself further. She has a bottle clutched in one hand, a knife in the other.

If she's going to die, it sure as hell won't be on their terms.

She thinks of Erin, suddenly: At Adam's funeral, her pale face blank, her hand clutched in Diggs'. Mother and daughter barely spoke that day... Like it was Kat's fault, somehow, that the Payson Church burned and Adam was weak and then, in the end, faked his own death and vanished without a word to his only daughter.

As if Kat could somehow change that reality, for either husband or child.

As if she could ever change a damn thing.

By the time she reaches the ravine, Kat can't hear anyone on the path behind her. Can't hear anything, really, beyond the pounding in her ears and the racing of her blood. The island is dark, the air cold and wet, but somehow in that mess she finds a path among rocks and the thin layer of slush now coating the ground. Head down, focused on every step, she makes it to the bottom.

And there, exactly as she'd feared, she finds them. Curled in close, silent and rotting and ended, they huddle together: Women and children she knew. A man she'd met years before.

"Kat! Come on out—you can't hide from this," the woman calls from somewhere close. "It's time to stop running."

Kat grinds her teeth and fights back fear and nausea and a marrow-deep weariness she's been denying too long.

She lays down among the others, her head down, holding tight to the bottle…

And she waits.

1

TWO MOSTLY EMPTY PLATES sat on the coffee table in my mother's house in Littlehope, Maine, set aside in favor of my laptop and a notebook filled with illegible notes. Tonight the house was unoccupied, since Kat and Maya—my mother and her girlfriend, respectively—were doing some kind of puffin-related project on an island up the coast. If puffins had been a passion of my mother's in the past, she'd never shared it with me. Now, however, she was braving a late-season snowstorm to catalogue the damn things. Which meant that for the past few days, I'd had the dubious pleasure of returning to my hometown to keep the home fires burning in Kat's absence.

Not that it was all bad, mind you.

At the moment, I was settled on the couch with Daniel Diggins, aka Diggs: rogue reporter, longtime best friend, and... Well, we were working on the third thing. He sat just behind me looking over my shoulder, his breath distractingly warm on my neck. My mutt, Einstein, lay on the floor with his chin on his paws, not remotely impressed with the seating arrangement.

"This makes no sense," I said, nodding toward the computer screen. "I've done everything I can think of, and

...g's working. What idiot decided to make encryption freaking effective?"

It had been two weeks since Diggs had nearly been barbecued in a barely averted apocalypse in western Kentucky. Since then, most of our spare time had been devoted to trying to decrypt a memory card he had literally pried from someone's cold, dead hand, just before the Smithfield College auditorium went up in flames.

So far, the whole decryption thing wasn't going that well.

Diggs rested his chin on my shoulder, his hand sliding up my side as he studied the screen.

"What did Jesse say?"

I tried to focus on the question, rather than the fact that Diggs' hand had come to rest just under my breast, his body distractingly warm behind me. With tremendous restraint, I removed said hand, set it back on his own leg, and scooted to the edge of the couch to retrieve my notes.

Jesse was a high school buddy of Diggs' who'd moved back to the area a few years before. Once just as much a degenerate as the rest of Diggs' old gang, now he was a semi-respectable family man… who happened to be a computer whiz consulting with the government on some of the most cutting-edge technologies in modern surveillance and national security.

"Honestly?" I said. "He said like three things I understood, followed by forty-five minutes when I just smiled and nodded and tried not to look like an idiot."

"I told you—you should have let me come."

"Because your manly brain would be able to sort through all that techno-babble, whereas my lesser, pea-sized woman's brain can barely handle anything more elaborate than a meatloaf recipe?"

"More or less," he agreed. He kissed my neck; I elbowed him in the stomach. "Ow. Jesus—it was a joke, woman.

First off, I would never trust you with a recipe of any meatloaf or otherwise. And secondly: the only reason might have been more effective is that I would have actually taken notes."

"I took notes," I said, picking up my battered notebook as proof.

Diggs took it from me, giving up on seduction for the moment. "The only thing I can even read here is 'Hackers' in capital letters and... I'll give you the benefit of the doubt and say that's a very bad rendering of the Washington Monument."

"It's the Eiffel Tower."

"That's what they all say."

He tossed the notebook back on the coffee table. "We could just bring the card to Jesse—that would be a hell of a lot easier than explaining some hypothetical code that he never gets to see."

"Are you nuts? He's got a wife and two gorgeous kids—no way am I dragging him into this thing. We've got enough blood on our hands as it is. No. There has to be a way to do this on our own."

He sighed. "Fine. You know, if I'd realized this was why you were inviting me, I might not have been so eager to come over."

Einstein hopped up from his spot at our feet and loped into the other room, ears and tail up. Since Stein is forever chasing beasties invisible to the human eye and ear, I ignored him.

"What did you think I was inviting you over for?" I kept my eyes on the screen, very determinedly ignoring Diggs' hand as it slid up my thigh.

"I know what I was hoping for. Your mom's not home... We have the place all to ourselves. I bet if we put our heads together, we could think of some way to pass the time."

What are we, fifteen?" I asked. "If I was planning on seducing you, I would have chosen something a little sexier than my mother's house and my best flannel pj's."

"Works for me." He lowered his head to that spot between my neck and shoulder that tends to obliterate all reason for me.

"We're grown ups, Diggs," I said. It came out a little more Marilyn Monroe than I'd intended. I took a breath. "If we wanted a house to ourselves, we could go to yours—or my place in Portland, for that matter—any time."

"And why haven't we done that, again?"

At the moment, that reason eluded me. Since getting back from Kentucky, Diggs and I had been in kind of a holding pattern, for very good reasons. He was still recovering from that whole nearly-being-blown-up thing, for one. Then there was the fact that I'd just broken up with someone else. And, finally, Diggs and I had made the mutual decision that we were going to venture into the treacherous world of dating slowly, with eyes wide open.

All of which was a lot easier to keep in mind during the light of day with a few miles between us, when Diggs' clever fingers weren't creeping up my inner thigh. He pulled me back toward him, his legs spread so I was cradled between them.

This time, I didn't push him away. "You should put the computer away. You work too hard," he whispered, his breath hot on my neck. His teeth scraped my earlobe before he began to work his way down.

I tried to suppress a low moan, but gave up when his hands got in on the act. He found the hem of my t-shirt, the feel of his callused palms on my cool skin ultimately my undoing. When he puts his mind to it, Diggs is one persuasive son of a bitch.

I twisted backward to meet him, my eyes sinking shut

when his lips met mine. Diggs lay back, pulling me o,
of him in a single, fluid move. His hands moved under m,
shirt, up my back, his usually bright blue eyes now dark with
desire.

Diggs is a powerful man: six feet tall, a lifelong athlete
who spent his youth playing hard and living fast. At forty,
he's slowed down a little, but there's still something slightly
dangerous about him—some reckless passion that takes my
breath away, forever keeps me guessing. I felt that power,
that passion, as his hands spanned my back and pulled me
closer.

"You said in Kentucky that you were going to sweep me
off my feet," I said breathlessly, my forehead tipped to his.

"I thought that's what I was doing." There was a trace
of the devil in his smile. When I rolled my eyes, he got
marginally more serious. "I'm sweeping you off your feet
when we go out this weekend. Tonight, we're working."

"I'm pretty sure there's only one profession where what
we're doing right now qualifies as work."

His hands shifted to my hips and he gave me a lazy,
seductive grin as he arched up, hard and hot against me.
My breath hitched. Rational thought faded to gray. "You're
right," he said. "We should probably stop."

Friggin' tease.

"Not so fast, slick." I leaned back down and kissed him
again, harder this time, my tongue moving against his before
we broke apart and he pushed my shirt up over my head.

That was about the time Einstein came tearing back
into the room, a growl rumbling in his throat. The growl
escalated to high-pitched barking as he bolted back into the
kitchen.

"Should we check that out?" Diggs asked unhappily. His
mouth was already moving with definite purpose along my
neck, down to my collarbone.

Mmm," I murmured, though more in response to the feel of his knuckles moving over the sheer fabric of my bra than in answer to his question. Einstein kept barking. I closed my eyes and pretended he didn't.

Diggs stopped working his magic. "I think we should check it out."

"That's a terrible idea," I said. I moved back, though, since there were worse things in the world than Diggs and I being interrupted before we got our groove on. We had experienced almost all those 'worse things' over the course of the past year; I wasn't taking any chances.

Diggs and I got up, his blond hair mussed and his torn jeans noticeably tighter. I wasn't feeling all that put together myself, but my annoyance gave way to anxiety the longer Stein kept up the racket.

"You have your gun?" Diggs asked.

"Just a second." I pulled my t-shirt back on, then went to an antique writer's desk against the far wall, unlocked it, and yanked the top drawer open so hard I nearly pulled it off its runners. Inside was the Ruger LCR Diggs had purchased for me, despite my protests.

When I had it loaded and in hand, Diggs nodded. "Good. Now, go on upstairs and call Chris. I'll grab Einstein and meet you there."

"I'm not calling the sheriff until I know there's actually something out there," I said. Diggs frowned. I ignored him and crept toward the kitchen, where Stein was still barking. His nails clicked on the linoleum as he paced beside a picture window looking out on my mother's backyard.

It was just past midnight on a Thursday night in April, but at the moment the only thing I could see outside was snow. Because this was Maine, and in Maine you can't actually count on spring until you're well into summer, at which point you wake up and realize you've been gypped out of the whole damn season yet again.

While the snow was annoying, however, I didn't consid... it life threatening.

Einstein and Diggs weren't so easily convinced. Stein... pushed past me and continued to stare outside, all fifty pounds of scruffy white fur and terrier tenacity coiled tight. He'd finally canned the barking and returned to a continual menacing growl. Diggs stood beside me at the window, his own gun in hand.

I was just about to tell him we were being idiots when a shadow moved along the perimeter outside my mother's garden shed, low to the ground and moving slowly. My heart rumbaed halfway up my throat. Einstein started barking again. I grabbed his collar and dragged him away from the window, back toward the living room.

I dimly registered the fact that Diggs had his phone out. "Get Einstein and go to the bedroom," he said again, in that this-isn't-a-debate voice he only seems driven to when I'm around.

"Only if you come with me," I said.

A garbage can clattered out back. Einstein tore away from me, headed straight back to the window. I heard glass shatter outside.

I didn't actually lose bladder control entirely, but we were on shaky ground for a few seconds.

Diggs was dialing the sheriff when the intruders finally stepped into the light and revealed themselves.

All three were fat, masked, and clearly looking for trouble.

"Diggs," I said. He was on the line with Sheriff Finnegan, so I had to repeat his name a couple of times before he came back to me. "Call him off," I said once he had. "We've got three masked bandits here, but I don't think they're armed."

He stared at me blankly, phone still in hand.

raccoons, Diggs," I said, feeling every inch the idiot I knew I was. My hands were shaking—not exactly what you're hoping for from someone locked and loaded. "I'm fine. Look: It's just a trio of varmints getting into the trash."

"We should get Chris out here anyway. Just in case."

"Just in case what? The coons start rioting? Diggs—come on."

He looked out the window as though to confirm my story, and nodded before he returned to the phone. "I think we've got it under control, Chris. Sorry to wake you."

After he'd hung up, he returned to my side. "You okay?" He looked shaken, all the light and humor I'd seen earlier gone.

"It was just raccoons, Diggs," I reminded him. "I think we'll all survive."

He didn't look so sure. He double checked to make sure the back door was locked, and turned off the outside light while I got Einstein back in hand.

"I won't feel safe until everyone behind whatever you've stumbled onto in the past year is behind bars. Or better yet, wiped off the planet."

Diggs is a reporter, not a warrior—those aren't the kind of declarations he makes lightly. I took his hand and pulled him back toward the living room.

"You want to catch these guys? Then stop distracting me, and help me figure out this fucking encryption."

An hour later, the house was still. Diggs snored softly on the couch while I sat on the floor in front of the coffee table, eyes burning, and stared at the computer screen.

During our consult, Diggs' pal Jesse had steered me toward a few decryption programs created by friends of his in the business. So far, I had tried almost all of them without success. Einstein lay with his head in my lap, fuzzy belly in the air, while I continued to torture myself.

This memory card was all we had—a card that may o.
may not hold the key to an alleged mass suicide nearly twenty-
five years ago; to the motivation and people behind the near-
apocalypse in Kentucky; to a serial killer who had nearly
claimed Diggs and me as victims last summer. Otherwise,
I had nothing to show for the past year of work—a year
that had almost killed Diggs and me multiple times over. A
year when I'd learned that my father's supposed suicide the
summer of 2000 was staged and he was alive... A year when
my whole life, in essence, had been turned upside down.

There had to be something on this card that could
explain why.

I rubbed my eyes, took a deep breath, and returned to
the computer. Diggs shifted behind me, his hand settling on
my shoulder.

"You should get some sleep," he mumbled. "Start fresh
tomorrow."

"I just want to try one more thing. You can go on home
if you want, though." Absently, I hit a couple of keys on the
computer, then gave the okay for the program to run.

"I can stay," Diggs said. "I'll sleep on the couch."

"You don't need to do that."

He sat up, stretched, and began massaging the knots
from my shoulders. "I know I don't. I'd feel better, though."

"So you can save me from anymore wildlife gone rogue?"

As if on cue, Einstein righted himself and sat up, ears
perked. Diggs and I both ignored him when he raced to the
kitchen this time.

"Maybe," Diggs said. "Or maybe—shit." His hands
stilled. "Erin."

I'd been focused on the incredible things Diggs was
doing to my tensed muscles, but at his tone I looked up.
"What?"

It's working."

For a split second, I wasn't sure what he meant. Then, I looked at the computer.

What had been a screen scrolling miles of meaningless symbols suddenly transformed, replaced by line after line of data—mostly alphanumeric entries, about twenty characters long. I still didn't know what they stood for, but they were at least legible.

"Do they mean anything to you?" Diggs asked, nodding toward the numbers.

I looked at the first entry: 40N85W30622105111115DM.

"Not really, but it looks a hell of a lot easier to break than what we were dealing with before."

Einstein raced back into the living room, barking furiously at Diggs and me.

"Tommy's down the well again," Diggs said. "I hate to break it to you, ace, but I think your dog needs sedation. Or intensive therapy."

"He's just oversensitive since Kentucky. Can you blame him? Stein—seriously, chill. We're all right." I returned my attention to the computer screen. "What do you think this means?" I asked Diggs.

Before he could answer, my cell phone rang. It was after one a.m. The number came up as Private Caller.

Nothing good comes from calls after midnight, in my experience.

One look at Diggs told me he was thinking the same thing. Einstein gave up on rallying the troops and raced back to the kitchen.

I answered the phone. "Hello?"

"Get out of the house."

If the words themselves hadn't scared the bejeezus out of me, the voice did the trick. Fear climbed my spine and rattled my heart.

"What? Who is this?"

"You know who it is. Damn it, Erin, get out of the house. Now."

Diggs looked at me curiously. "Mitch Cameron," I mouthed to him. He was on his feet in an instant, looking just as unnerved as I felt. For more than twenty years, Mitch Cameron had shown up in all the wrong places at the worst possible times in my life. I happened to know for a fact that he was a murderer several times over... And yet, more than once, he'd been Diggs' and my saving grace.

"What's happening?" I asked Cameron.

"I don't have time to explain," he said. "But you're in danger. The evidence your mother has been holding over my people was just destroyed—there's no more leverage. Jenny is coming for you."

"Where the hell are we supposed to go?" I demanded.

"I'll contact you; just don't go to the police. That's the first place Jenny will check—and they won't slow her down, if that's where you are. Lie low until you hear from me. I need to try and find your mother before they—" There was the distinctive pop of rapid gunfire on the other end of the line.

"Cameron?"

The phone went dead. Before I could even contemplate that, I heard glass shatter on the second floor. The house alarm blared as the lights went out. Fear seized me like a fist. There was no time to hesitate—no time to think.

"We have to get out of here," I said to Diggs. "Grab the laptop and your gun; I'll get Einstein."

He didn't ask questions, just closed the computer and shoved it into my backpack. Einstein cowered beside me, all bravado long gone.

"Through the garage," Diggs shouted over the alarm. He pulled me toward the door, Stein on my heels. Less than ten conds after we'd heard the glass break, we bolted through the side door into the attached garage, where I hoped like hell someone wasn't waiting for us to make exactly that move.

The garage was empty.

I shoved Einstein into the back of my Jetta, manhandled him into a doggy seatbelt I'd gotten for slightly less dramatic scenarios, and got in the front as I mashed my hand down on the garage door opener. Diggs jumped into the passenger's side and slammed the door.

Inside the house, there was a whoosh like all the air had been sucked from the building. I slammed my foot down on the accelerator without waiting for the garage door to come up all the way, bracing myself for the impact when the top of the car hit the bottom of the door. The sound of metal on metal screamed through the night. Einstein yelped, cowering behind us. I was barely clear of the garage door when an explosion rocked the house, propelling the Jetta into the street and almost into the neighbor's yard before I regained control. A second explosion followed. The windows of my mother's house blew out.

The second I was in control of the car again, I was blinded by the glare of high beams.

"Shit—Erin!" Diggs shouted.

"I see it, I see it." I put the car in gear and hit the gas, veering out of the way as a black SUV sped past, narrowly missing us. I could just make out a woman's face on the way by, her hair pulled back and pure murder in the set of her jaw. Jenny Burkett: The bitch who'd left Diggs for dead just before the final countdown in Kentucky.

"It's her," I said. "Cameron was right."

Diggs already had his phone out. "Head for the sheriff's station. We can regroup there—give them a description and let them handle this."

"Cameron said we can't go to the police," I said. "We need to hide until he calls back."

"And you're listening to him? You've had nightmares about the man since you were ten years old.... Now you think it's a good idea to start taking his advice?"

"Diggs, just—please. We need to get in touch with Kat. The puffin thing is through the college up in Bar Harbor—you should be able to reach someone if you contact them."

I sped down Littlehope's main stretch. Behind us, Kat's house was now a fireball in the rearview mirror. Littlehope's volunteer fire department was already mobilizing at their station on Main Street, but I didn't dare to stop. I knew from experience that Jenny and her people—whoever those people were—didn't give a rat's ass about collateral damage. They wouldn't blink at the idea of taking out all of Littlehope at this point, if it meant they could get rid of Diggs and me.

I drove past Diggs' father's church and Kat's medical clinic, Bennett's Bar and Lobster Shanty, the turnoff to Edie Woolrich's residential home.... The pavement was greasy on Route 97, the two-lane stretch of rutted, twisting road that leads from Littlehope to coastal Route 1. Diggs white-knuckled the car's Oh Shit handle while I clutched the steering wheel. He craned his neck to see behind us, looking for any sign of Jenny.

"What are you doing?" Diggs asked.

I eased off the accelerator. Made the conscious decision to avoid tapping the brake.

We were still ten miles from Route 1, with nothing to prevent Jenny from running us off the road into oblivion.

"At that speed? I'm thinking it's a pretty good bet."

"Can you tell if it's her?"

"Someone's coming up fast behind us," he said.

It didn't take long.

for any sign of Jenny.

"Just trust me," I ground out. The SUV got closer. And closer. Ahead of us, the road dipped and curved, a barely discernible turnoff just ahead on our right.

"Erin—" Diggs warned.

I didn't listen. At the last possible second, I turned the wheel hard to the right. The car slid, losing purchase on the slick pavement. I willed myself not to panic. Jenny sped past, continuing along 97. I was too focused on recovering from the slide to see whether she turned around to come at us again.

Einstein whimpered in the backseat while I prayed silently that we could stay upright. Time froze in a haze of fast-moving trees and the terrifying, weightless feeling of a car out of control.

Somehow, miraculously, I recovered from the skid. Another endless second or two later, we were back on the road. I took a fraction of a second to get my breath and my bearings. We were on Cross Road, a series of picturesque twists and turns that's beautiful in the light of day. By night at sixty miles an hour in a snowstorm, it's not nearly as idyllic.

I pressed my foot back down on the accelerator.

"She's back again," Diggs said, a few minutes later.

"Damn it."

"You're doing great. Just keep going—we'll make it."

"Have you reached the college?" I asked. "You have to keep trying them—we have to get to Kat."

"She's on Raven's Ledge, right? Out near Mount Desert?"

I checked the rearview, noting the high beams bearing down on us. "Yeah," I agreed. "I think she said there's a boat that goes out from Bar Harbor."

"Jamie Flint's business is out there. You want me to call her?"

Jamie Flint made her living training some of the best

search and rescue dogs in the country. Last summer, she and those rescue dogs were responsible for tracking down Diggs and me during our debacle with the serial killer in northern Maine. I hesitated.

"Sol?" Diggs pressed.

"I'm thinking." Behind us, those high beams were getting closer by the second.

"This isn't like bringing a civilian in on it," he insisted. "Jamie's good. She knows what she's doing, and she's got muscle behind her. We can't do this alone—if we've learned anything in the past year, it should be that."

Up ahead as we came around a hairpin curve, blue and red lights flashed on the side of the road. I saw the glow of the SUV's brake lights in my rearview, and slowed down myself. A pickup had turned over on the shoulder along one of those picturesque twists and turns we were currently navigating, the top of the cab smashed and the wheels still spinning.

I barely waited until we were clear of the emergency crew before I hit the accelerator again.

"Go ahead," I said to Diggs, after a long few seconds of thought. "Call Jamie. See if she can get us out to that island."

"There's another call I think we should make," Diggs said.

"I'm not calling Juarez."

"We need someone on our side here, Sol."

"Not him," I said evenly. "I told you: Call Jamie. I'm not calling my ex-boyfriend in the middle of the night to save our asses."

"Goddamn it, Erin—"

"No."

I knew he was frustrated, but at the moment I didn't much care. I stayed quiet, focused on the road ahead. Finally, he punched in Jamie's number. I kept driving.

I managed to get some distance from Jenny by rocketing along a series of side streets once we hit the town of Thomaston. She was back again by the time I turned onto Old County, a country road that serves as a less-traveled shortcut for locals determined to avoid Route 1 at the height of tourist season in midcoast Maine. Diggs snapped his phone shut.

"Jamie will meet us at the Bar Harbor ferry terminal," he said. "She'll have a boat and a crew."

"Just like that?"

"Just like that. She's apparently got some interests out on the island herself... If there's trouble, she wants to stop it before it gets out of hand."

I sped up along a twisting stretch of road where metal guardrails and cement walls hemmed us in. Rockland, Maine, is home to some of the deepest quarries in the world, thanks to a once-booming market for the limestone found there. The deepest of those quarries run along Old County Road— vast, watery graves where people have killed themselves and one another for decades. Diggs' brother had died in one such quarry, when they were just kids. Now, Diggs hung onto the dashboard with both hands as the guardrail loomed closer.

"Erin—"

"Just hang on," I said through clenched teeth.

We made it over the narrowest of bridges, along another stretch of open road, and then I hung another fast right with no warning. A stone wall loomed large at the corner, but I kept my head and managed to avoid it.

Behind us, Jenny wasn't so lucky. I heard a crash and the blare of a car horn. I didn't waste time celebrating.

"Nice driving," Diggs said beside me.

My stomach churned. "Thanks. This reporting thing's getting a little stale... I'm thinking NASCAR would make a nice second career."

He leaned back in his seat, exhaling slowly. "You're a natural. Just do me a favor and leave Stein and me in the stands, would you?"

To bring that point home, Einstein puked in the backseat.

I knew exactly how he felt.

On Main Street, Rockland, all the lights in town were out. The only vehicle in sight was a plow truck, yellow lights casting shadows on old brick buildings and trendy shop windows. We had lost Jenny, but I didn't plan on waiting for her to catch up to us again. Cameron still hadn't called back. Since it had sounded like high noon at the OK Corral when he hung up, I wasn't holding my breath until we heard from him again.

I took a left down a little side alley off the main drag, and stopped in a dark parking lot that stood empty except for a hulking green dumpster and a very well-used pickup truck. Einstein perked up, his tail wagging hesitantly now that we were back in familiar territory.

"I assume you have a plan," Diggs said.

We were in the employee parking lot behind the Loyal Biscuit, Einstein's favorite local hangout. I nodded toward the pickup beside the dumpster.

"That's Mel's truck," I said. "They use it for local deliveries… We can take that."

"Seriously? I don't think that's a great idea." Mel is one of the gang at the Biscuit: a pint-sized pirate who's run Diggs up and down more than once for some story or other he's reported over the years. She's cute as hell, tough as nails, and Maine to the core. Diggs is alternately turned on by her or terrified of her—though he'll only admit to the turned-on thing.

"Who would you rather face: a slightly-pissed-off Melody, or Jenny and her psychotic syndicate?"

Diggs frowned. "Hang on—let me think about that one."

"Suck it up, Diggins. Unless you have a better idea, this is our only option."

I scrawled a mostly illegible note in my notebook promising my firstborn if we wrecked the truck, and stuck it on the dashboard of my car. Meanwhile, Diggs took Einstein for a quick pee on the nearest brush pile. Mel's key was strategically placed in one of those magnetic Hide-A-Key deals under the wheel well. I snagged that, unlocked the pickup, and transferred our stuff. Five minutes later, Diggs, Einstein, and I were crowded into the cab of the pickup. This time, Diggs was behind the wheel.

"Just remember," I said as he pulled back onto Main Street, "it's your ass on the line if you break this thing."

Diggs grimaced, but he didn't ease up on the accelerator. He headed north while I prayed to some nameless deity that Kat was still out there somewhere. Preferably alive, with all of her limbs. If we could reach her safely, I swore to the heavens that I would change my ways: clean up my language, save the planet, help little old ladies cross the street.

Whatever it took, I just needed all of us to survive this.

More Erin Solomon Mysteries

In Between Days
Diggs & Solomon Shorts
1990 - 2000

Midnight Lullaby
Prequel to
The Erin Solomon Mysteries

The Payson Pentalogy
The Critically Acclaimed 5-Book Set
Readers Can't Put Down!

Book I: All the Blue-Eyed Angels
Book II: Sins of the Father
Book III: Southern Cross
Book IV: Before the After
Book V: The Book of J

And the First Novel in the Jamie Flint K-9 Search and Rescue Series

The Darkest Thread

ABOUT THE AUTHOR

Jen Blood is a freelance journalist and author of the bestselling Erin Solomon mystery series. She is also owner of Adian Editing, providing expert editing of plot-driven fiction for authors around the world. Jen holds an MFA in Creative Writing/Popular Fiction, with influences ranging from Emily Bronte to Joss Whedon and the whole spectrum in between. Today, Jen lives in Maine with her dog Killian, where the two are busy conquering snowbanks and penning the next Erin Solomon mystery.

Made in the USA
Monee, IL
05 June 2022

97505177R00226